PLAGUED

a novel by
Conway Titty

Book Cover + Illustrations by Eliza Alejandra Art
@satanssweetcupcake
https://beacons.ai/satancupcake

Paperback ISBN
979-8-9998381-0-0
979-8-9998381-2-4

eBook ISBN
979-8-9998381-1-7

First Edition: 2025

http://authorconway.com

For my beloved Stardusty...

Author's Note

Dearest Reader,

Hark and Heed, my curious soul! What you are about to read is not for the faint of heart nor dainty of constitution. What lies ahead is no merry tale; nay, within these pages lie truths as raw as an open-sore. Trigger warnings abound, like plague rats swarming a city you once called home. I present to you a list of official warnings that you may choose to ignore or allow to consume you entirely. Please take them seriously. Your peace of mind and mental health do matter more than my plot twists. If you seek comfort, I suggest a hot cup of tea, a squishy companion and closing this book immediately. But if you are bold (or blessedly stupid), then enter, friend. Proceed with caution, a sense of jest, and maybe a bite to eat. You have been warned.

Farewell,

Conway Titty

Trigger

Notices & Alerts

- Emotinal Abuse
- Physical Abuse
- Self-Harm
- Trauma
- Confrontation w/ Rapist/Abuser
- Anxiety + Panic Attacks
- Post Traumatic Stress Disorder
- Traumatic Events Nightmares
- Sexual Abuse + Harrassment
- Sexual Assault + Rape
- Death + Grief
- Murder
- Death of a Loved One
- Graphic/Gore Deaths
- Torture

- Sexual Predator
- Slut Shaming + Bullying
- Body Shaming
- Sexism + Misogyny
- Female Oppression
- Escalating Violence
- Extreme Violence
- Described Blood/Gore
- Graphic Violence
- Suffering
- Decapitation
- Body + Genitalia Mutilation
- Mass Death
- Body Horror
- Dismemberment

Warnings

Kinks & Fetishes

✦ Monsterfucking	✦ Explicit Sex Scenes
✦ Footjob + Foot Worship	✦ Blowjob + Handjobs
✦ Olfactophilia	✦ Multiple Orgasms
✦ Anal Sex, Fingering, Gaping	✦ Licking + Sucking
✦ Vaginal Sex, Fingering, Gaping	✦ Foreign Object Insertion
✦ Double Penetration	✦ Gagging
✦ Cunnilingus	✦ Urophilia + Watersports
✦ Facials	✦ Face Fucking
✦ Bathing + Washing	✦ Threesome + Multi- Partner
✦ Spit Play	✦ Drool/Drooling
✦ Fingers in Mouth + Other Things	✦ Body, Breast, Cock Worship
✦ Breath Play + Choking	✦ Nipple Play
✦ Edging	✦ Free Use
✦ Orgasm Denial + Orgasm Delay	✦ Peeping Tom Play
✦ Dirty Talk	✦ Cuddling
✦ Swallowing Fluids	✦ Masturbation
✦ Hair Pulling	✦ Begging
✦ Dominating Female	✦ Pet Names
✦ Submissive Female	✦ Size Kink
✦ Dominating Female	✦ BDSM + Aftercare
✦ Submissive Male	✦ Orgasm Control
✦ Sensation + Temperature Play	✦ Deep Throating
✦ Praise + Degradation	✦ Titty Fucking
✦ Cock Milking	✦ Massaging

PLAGUED

Chapter 1

Rosannah

Stars fill my vision, twinkling like distant fireflies against the velvety darkness of a night sky. My eyesight blurs, eclipses, as if the very fabric of this world is slipping away from me.

The rise and fall of my chest is shallow and laborious, as though each inhale is an onerous battle for oxygen. It's a surreal experience, and one thought dominates my mind: his calloused hands wrapping around my throat. This singular image is a vortex of horrifying beauty that leaves me breathless. Its intensity is a mixture of stark fear and inexplicable thrill. I allow him to squeeze harder as I continue towards the summit of my climax.

Incapable of holding my breath any longer, I release an extensive exhale, savoring the moment before taking a deep inhale to intensify the desire even further. I can see his expression as he enters me. His bushy black eyebrows arched in expressive delight, while his intense green eyes are closed. His lips part, sharing a hint of vulnerability as he secretly utters my name. The heat of my body increases. The tingling sensation between my thighs is potent. I let out another extended exhale, panting hard from holding back a devilish amount of desire.

As my fingers trace delicate, deliberate circles over my most sensitive spot, my skin vibrates with anticipation. A welcoming pulse of pleasure builds beneath my touch.

The thought of his fingers will undoubtedly take me to a realm of pure ecstasy. His arms, thick with muscle and bulging veins, speak of the countless hours spent lifting and hammering. Showcasing a physique that would make the Gods envious.

I want his bulky biceps to curl around my neck while he sits behind me. Teasing me endlessly and telling me just how fucking beautiful I am. He is a work of art, and how I would love to run my fingers through his hair as he is on top of me. Letting the soft strands slip through the spaces between my fingers. While his hair may not be very long, I can imagine the springy texture of his dark curls.

He has enormous feet, and you know what they say... *I can't help but wonder if his cock matches.*
I am certain it's perfect. The ideal complement to the perfect man. I ache for him so immensely that the mere thought of him being inside of me creates a phantom sensation.

The tension in my body has surged to its maximum, and I know I can't endure this any longer. I take one last inhale, filling my lungs, while my fingers move intentionally over my clit. A tender vibration spreads through my body, making my teeth chatter. My toes curl involuntarily as I respond to the rush of sensations swirling within.

My body begs for oxygen as I convulse into an orgasm. Euphoria crashes over me as I reach my limit, and my lungs cry out for release. I let out an exuberant exhale that echoes in the surrounding stillness.

With the taste of freedom drifting on my lips, I take slow, thick gasps, filling my lungs with fresh air, savoring every heightened sensation. My mind is empty, and I allow my body to descend from this high. I'm drenched in sweat. I pull my hand away from between my thighs. The secretion prize of a hard-earned afternoon masturbation session remains on my fingers.

As I sit up in bed, the dizziness subsides, and clarity returns. Disgust, defeat, and dread beset me as I catch my breath.

Why do I always fantasize about him?

Why? Why? WHY?

I know he is perfect physically, but he doesn't want me. There's no hope for me with him. Why do I even allow myself to be sexually charged by someone who is so disgustingly in love with another? And not just any "other," the vilest, most pretentious, rotten "other." Of everyone in this town, why does his heart have to long for Felicita Donati? She may possess a fair countenance and be most fitting for his matrimonial aspirations.

But why her?

I, for one, hope those two trip over their own smug smiles and tumble straight into the sea, never to be seen again. And if it doesn't happen soon, I shall start begging the universe for a well-placed storm myself! Then I wouldn't have to spare a single miserable thought for that dreadful shrew after my well-deserved *"me time."*

The bitter memory of her intrudes every time I think of him, leaving a foul taste in my mouth, and I loathe myself for it. Why can't I appreciate my fantasy without overthinking it afterwards? That's what a sexual fantasy is. A specifically crafted realm of my deepest, darkest, and most depraved desires. And yes, that distinctly includes certain circumstances I would never share with another living soul. Some thoughts are private and should remain so.

Just when I wanted to luxuriate in scandalous daydreams of stripping the man I long for bare; my conscience intervened. Prompting me to acknowledge my true feelings.

Unfortunately, those feelings remind me that when two people are meant to be wed, they're considered off-limits, and I, for one, would never intrude upon a couple unless explicitly invited by *said couple.*

Which, to be fair, has only happened once or twice—and they weren't my type—but that's neither here nor there! From now on, I need to close off that part of my mind the next time I bring my knight in shining armor, Fino Binachi, into my sexual air castle.

An orange glow bathes the window next to my bed, a sure sign that it's dusk and time to begin my day, or perhaps my night. As I shake off the remnants of my melancholic thoughts, I begin the familiar routine of getting ready for tonight's work.

After rolling out of bed, my bare feet hit the cool surface of the hardwood, sending a shiver up my spine. I stand tall, letting out a massive yawn and stretch. Reaching my arms overhead, I savor this beautiful autumn afternoon air that wafts through the open window.

The refreshing breeze pirouettes around me, brushing against my skin, invigorating my senses, and rousing me from my post-self-care state. It's not freezing, but it's enough to make my nipples stand at attention like little soldiers.

Approaching my window, the stunning ocean comes into view. The waves crash against the rugged shore and create swirling white foam that spirals into the air with every surge. This view fills my soul with tranquility every single day.

As I reluctantly pull myself away from this serene moment, my mind drifts to the looming responsibilities of work. Dread comes uninvited at the prospect of heading into another long night at the tavern.

I must confess, dealing with drunken fools and cleaning up their messes is more taxing than keeping a candle lit in a windstorm. They stumble about like babes, unable to find their own feet, and I swear no one has ever taught them the proper art of relieving themselves.

As for conversation, once they've had a few cups of ale or wine, it's as if they've forgotten how to form anything more than a grunt or a belch. I love a few of the regulars, mind you, but most patrons are as intolerable as a mule with a thorn in its hoof.

However, I understand I need to fulfill my responsibilities and be a productive member of society. And honestly, how is one supposed to find a partner if one does not venture into social environments?

As I reflect on my entire existence, I slip into my mossy green dress. The fabric sways gently with each movement. I lace up a simple pair of brown leather boots that complement the outfit perfectly and admire how the dress drapes over my shoulders. It creates an elegant but relaxed silhouette. While the lighter green corset straps keep me from spilling my breasts every time I reach for a glass.

The fabric falls gracefully, enhancing my figure without feeling constrictive. Moreover, I can't help but appreciate how well my bosoms are supported and showcased. They sit proudly upon my chest like two noble steeds ready for battle.

The mirror awaits me, a tall standing piece that invites me to address my unruly hair. I approach it, determined to transform my endlessly curly long mane into something more polished than the typical bedhead.

I run my fingers through my luscious dark locks, feeling their soft texture beneath my fingertips. Carefully, I part my hair, creating two small sections at the front that I begin to braid. The braids take shape, framing my face beautifully and adding an air of whimsy to my rather common attire.

To complete the outfit, I reach for a handful of tiny daisies. Their cheerful yellow centers shine bright against the dark backdrop of my hair. Gently, I tuck the flowers into the braids, creating a delightful hairstyle that reflects my mood. There is no need to pinch my cheeks because the earlier self-induced activity still flushes my skin.

I massage a blend of olive oil and beeswax onto my lips, creating a glossy sheen that enhances their natural color. Once my lips are moisturized, I follow up by applying a fragrant concoction of delicate lilies and sweet rose oil to my neck. Enveloping myself in an enchanting floral aroma that hopefully remains throughout the day. I say this with my fingers crossed because, knowing me, I'll probably end up spilling wine all over myself in the first ten minutes of tending to the bar.

I take one last glance at myself in the mirror, admiring the reflection that beams back at me with confidence. My curly hair, full of bounce and movement, catches the light just right, adding to my self-assurance. I give it one last playful toss to enhance the volume before reaching for my apron—the fabric still bearing the marks of last night's busy shift.

I step out the door, feeling the cool autumn wind brush against my skin as I descend the steps into the lively alley. The sounds of rowdy townsfolk and bustling vendors fill the air, creating an atmosphere of fieriness and anticipation of the night ahead.

My daily walk from my residence to work is always a vibrant adventure filled with new discoveries. Each day brings a different assortment of vendors showcasing their unique offerings, and I can never predict what delightful treasures I will encounter. Living in the bustling port city of Messina, I am fortunate to be surrounded by the constant flow of exotic spices, handcrafted wares, rich fabrics, and intriguing trinkets that arrive almost daily from distant lands.

As I make my way down the steep, weathered stone path toward the town square, the atmosphere comes alive with sounds and scents. The lively chatter of customers haggling with vendors blends with the sharp cawing of seagulls soaring overhead, always on the lookout for an easy meal. The sea's salty tang merges with the fishmongers' stalls, where freshly caught fish glistens

I navigate through the bustling marketplace and find myself captivated by the colorful displays of fruits and vegetables. Each stall, a riot of colors and textures, inviting me to explore further.

The sunset cresting above the horizon transforms the sky into a grand canvas painted in warm hues of orange, pink, and gold, casting a glow over the town. In these moments, amidst the beauty and vibrancy of my surroundings, I have an overwhelming gratitude for the life I get to live in this charming city.

Unfortunately, as I turn right through the busy town square, a large wooden sign that boldly proclaims "Lupo Tavern" draws my attention. Made of heavy evergreen oak, the sign hangs, proud and imposing. It sways and creaks in the breeze.

The tavern itself, with its massive, intricately carved wooden doors, looms ahead, firmly shut as if guarding the jolly energy within. Despite their closure, the raucous laughter and spirited chatter of rambunctious patrons spills out, creating an inviting hum that beckons a promising night filled with camaraderie and good cheer for anyone who passes.

However, I am not a high-spirited on-looker. Instead, I find myself surrounded by the lively chaos of a hectic tavern, filled with exasperating hierophants who seem eager to engage in flirtatious banter—both verbal jests and physical advances—directed at me. As they loudly chug their jugs of cheap wine and indulge in platters overflowing with an array of smoked meats and rich cheeses, the atmosphere grows increasingly wild.

Amidst the energetic laughter and clinking glasses, I am left to navigate the aftermath of their revelry. Constantly cleaning up spilled drinks, discarded food, and the remnants of their indulgent feasting. While I appreciate the generous tips from those customers who recognize my hard work and show their gratitude, it does little to alleviate the discomfort caused by the unwanted catcalling, intrusive remarks, and fondling that comes my way. It's a whirlwind of noise and mess;

but sometimes, I long for a moment of peace away from the fray.

As I emerge from the flashback of the nights prior, I stand before the imposing wooden doors. Their surface is rough yet polished from years of use. Just above where I placed my palm on the wood, a carved wolf gazes down at me. Its fierce expression, both commanding and protective.

I take a moment to gather my thoughts. Sucking in a heavy inhale to calm my nerves, I prepare for the night ahead. My heart races as I contemplate what lies beyond these doors. Expectation hangs in the air, filling me with a mix of apprehension and determination as I push open the doors. I whisper to myself, *"Hopefully, tonight won't be too bad..."*

Chapter 2

Rosannah

The heavy wooden doors swing open with a groan, revealing a welcoming main room filled with stimulating chatter. The musty air is heavy with the cloying sweetness of spilled ale and the acrid tang of sweat from the hard-working crowd. It's a stale and potent stench.

The iron lanterns on the walls cast long shadows across the room, illuminating scattered townsfolk in their work-worn clothes. They are engaged in animated conversations about their day. They trade stories about their crafts, share personal woes, and indulge in their favorite drinks to unwind after a long day's labor.

Amidst the throng of people, my eyes are drawn to Alessandra; tall, curvaceous, and in her mid-thirties, with striking blonde hair that flows down her shoulders. She's standing behind the bar; her purple dress is partially obscured by the dark wine stains she has accumulated during her long shift.

Despite the pandemonium, she flashes me a quick hello accompanied by a weary but polite smile. It's clear she's already feeling the weight of exhaustion creeping in. The bar remains full even during daylight hours, while the morning hours are a tad quieter. The tavern has a way of coming alive as soon as lunchtime rolls around. It morphs into an operating social hub of laughter and jubilating cheers.

Alessandra darts past me, arms laden with mugs and jugs. "Is it already evening time?" She exclaims, a note of disbelief coloring her voice. "The day has truly flown by! Could you grab a meat board for the table in the back right corner? I'm buried beneath tasks and toil!"

Her plea hangs as she rushes to serve another round, embodying the tireless spirit of the tavern that has become what seems like her second home.

No sooner had I crossed the threshold; I found myself amid the chaos. I hurry to grab the overflowing food platter and rush it to the correct table. Setting it down with a grin, I swiftly rush to the back to put on my apron and check the stock before heading behind the bar to take over for Alessandra.

"I've got this handled, Al. Why don't you take a moment to clean up and grab a bite? When busy, I know you forget to break your fast." I say to her in a caring and almost motherly tone.

"You sure love? I'll stay right here until the rush fades, if you need me?" She replies with a sense of

20

unwillingness.

"Trust me, I can bear it. And you know the rush never ebbs."

Alessandra smiles with relief as she heads to the stockroom to indulge in a well-deserved meal.

A swell of barked commands surge through the air as I gather my bearings and tend to the four older gentlemen sitting to the bar top's left. This lively group of farmers, my favorite regulars, reside on the town's outskirts. Their faces weathered by the sun. Their stories are as rich as the soil they till. They often stroll in a couple of times a week for card games, bringing with them the unmistakable scent of fresh earth and hay.

Their side of the room erupts in boisterous laughter, the sounds bouncing off the wooden walls as they gather around the scarred, eroded table. They delight in recounting exaggerated tales of mythical monsters and elusive sea creatures. Their eyes sparkle with mischief and nostalgia as they reminisce about their youthful adventures. Each story is more outlandish than the last, and I can't help but giggle at their enthusiasm. Their jovial presence brings light to my evenings, and I eagerly anticipate our interactions.

"Ciao, Miss Rosannah, sei bellissima stasera.[1]" The older farmer of the four coos endearingly towards me.

---

[1] Italian Translation: You are looking very beautiful.

"Caro[2], hush your sweet mouth." I shyly grin and blow him a coltish kiss before rushing off to another table.

I am lost in the rhythmic swish of the bar towel against the polished wood. The sharp scent of red wine curls through the room. I barely noticed him walk in— the man of my dreams. Fino Binachi.

He settles into his accustomed spot beside his friends at the large, round table that dominates the center of the room. Every time he and his group enter, a hush falls over the room. Their presence is a palpable, captivating force that draws everyone's attention.

While he jokes and banters with his friends, my mind is consumed by the fantasies that I have been pleasuring myself with for the past week. And now here he is. His eyes sparkle, and his hair perfectly in place, looking as dashing as ever. The telltale flush of embarrassment spreads across my cheeks. My knees buckle beneath me, prompting me to turn my back toward him. I desperately hope he doesn't notice the flurry of emotions on my face.

I struggle to compose myself, knowing full well that my only defense against this most vexing tempest of emotions is to sit here like a stone, blink occasionally, and hope no one notices the existential crisis happening in my soul.

Anticipating their thirst, I procure a carafe of wine and proceed to Fino's table. He is dressed in a striking dark orange V-neck shirt with an embroidered chestnut

---

[2] Italian for dear or darling.

brown trim around the collar. His light grey trousers, a stark contrast to the colored shirt; give him a most relaxed fit. Completing his outfit are heavy-duty dark grey leather boots, striking the perfect balance between practicality and rugged elegance. His ensemble, though simple, brings an undeniable charm that is hard to overlook.

Glancing down, I see a sturdy leather sling belt cinched around his waist. The leather is worn, hinting at years of use. The belt holds various iron tools, each meticulously arranged in a holster, that reflects his readiness for work. The tools vary in size and shape, hinting at both craftsmanship and expertise. They suggest that he is well-prepared for whatever tasks may come.

One thing true about Fino is that he has effortless charm. If he were to don a mere fishing net, the nearest prized fish would leap forth in admiration. His inherent masculinity exerts an interesting influence. The air around him carries an earthy scent—like rich firewood crackling in a cozy hearth, combined with the spicy, piquant aroma of black pepper.

His complexion exhibits a lovely honey-toned quality, subtly infused with olive undertones. Soot from the forge frequently stains his skin, and minuscule metal fragments cling to it, resembling glitter after a long day's labor as a blacksmith.

"Good evening, fine sirs, would any of you care for a hearty pour?" I hold up the ceramic jug filled with rich red wine and say nervously, trying not to make eye contact with Fino. They nod in unison, their gazes riveted on Fino, who deliberately avoids my gaze.

With a subtle movement of his wrist, he gestures towards his wine glass. A silent command for me to fill it. I pour the rich burgundy liquid into his glass first, savoring how it cascades with a satisfying sound, before moving on to the other glasses. Carefully, I place the heavy jug on the table after finishing the pours.

With a smile that betrays my desire to please, I ask, "May I fetch a platter for you lads to bite at, perchance?"

Fino's sharp reply cuts through the jovial atmosphere. "What are we, hares? The wine shall suffice!" He snaps, his tone laced with impatience.

He then rejoins his friends' lively conversation, waving me away with the indifference one might show to a bothersome insect. The convivial sounds of conversation resume, momentarily excluding me. Feeling agitated, I promptly retreat to the bar top.

And just like that, his statement destroys the carefully constructed atmosphere of affection I had cultivated.

He must've had a rough day at work, which is probably why he was so eager to grab his drink first. Or maybe not. Or maybe I'm just a gudgeon[3], hopelessly obsessed with a complete ass. 'Tis a riddle for the ages, and only time shall reveal the truth.

Wiping up sticky spills and stray crumbs from the serving board, I see Fino staring at me. Honestly, this situation is so convoluted and frustrating. I simply don't

---

[3] Medieval phrase meaning: "a gullible fool"

have the energy to waste on his manipulative antics. Making brief eye contact with Fino, I glance past him to see a familiar face step into the foyer.

A tall woman, easily a head taller than me, who has dark olive skin, rich like sunbaked earth. A thick yet graceful neck holds aloft her slender form. While her long legs extend to the sky like elegant pillars, promising boundless movement.

Her facial features include delicately hollowed cheeks, which accentuate her expressive, doll-like eyes, framed by full, dark eyebrows. The warm brown of her large, almond-shaped eyes, a color that perfectly complements her hair, is dramatically emphasized by the thick, dark, sweeping lashes, which enhance their allure.

A tiny beauty mark rests subtly on the right side of her rosebud lips. With her bangs swept back in a stylish clip, her striking features are unveiled for all to behold.

There was no mistaking those features, even from a distance. "GIA!" I yell from behind the tankard's perch.[4]

She waves enthusiastically and heads for a quieter corner spot at the back of the taproom. Gia is wearing a vibrant blue dress, the color as bright as a summer sky. Her outfit is thoughtfully accented with colorful embroidered flowers on the hem and collar.

Her fingers are adorned with delicate gold rings, their subtle shimmer complemented by two gold

---

[4] A medieval way to describe a bar top

necklaces—one bearing a pendant of Saint Rosalia, the patron saint of Palermo, a city Gia longs to see.

A black leather belt cinches her waist, highlighting her slim figure. While sleek black leather boots clad her long legs, completing her ensemble.

From the counter, I can see Gia working on some sketches. That girl's always busy making something or other. Gia's an incredible designer. She comes from a long line of seamstresses. She inherited the family shop from her Nona and Mamma. While their thinking was less innovative than Gia's, she acquired all her skills through their more traditional approaches.

Gia never goes anywhere without her trusty satchel—a charming patchwork creation stitched together from an eclectic mix of scrap fabrics. Both stylish and practical, it holds her sketchbook, an assortment of writing utensils, and, naturally, her emergency sewing kit—always ready for a quick fix when creativity (or calamity) strikes.

Gia's unstoppable; she handles everything with ease, and I truly admire her amazing ability to fix almost anything. Her talent leaves me in absolute awe. It's effortless, breathtaking, and far beyond anything I could ever hope to master.

Gianni Opizzi, my best friend for almost 15 years, has been a constant presence in my life since childhood. Our bond has only grown stronger over the years, evolving right alongside us—into even goofier, more unapologetic versions of ourselves. Gia adds a vibrant spark to my life, like a golden sunbeam piercing through a veil of tempestuous storm clouds. Each day, her creativity – a boundless wellspring of innovation – inspires me.

I've seen her artistic genius in action, turning a tangled heap of furs and pelts into a most wondrous ball gown fit for a queen. She is my heart-kin, and I am lucky to have her in my life.

I make a hasty cleanup so I can steal a moment to gossip with Gia. It also gives me a place to hide for a while after Fino shooed me away.

"Ciao! I'm glad you're here... I simply must tell you what Fino has done!" I blurt out upon taking the seat beside her.

"I will never understand why you trouble yourself with such vainglorious fools. Rosannah you are far above such company, and you know it," she states, eyes remaining fixed on her sketchbook.

"Aye, I know... but he is so devilishly comely that I am absolutely powerless to resist him."

She glares at me skeptically, her eyes rolling upwards. "Seriously?"

"Knock, knock, Rosannah! Anyone home? Let us return to reason! You don't *need* him; you just *want* him... deep inside you!" She bursts into laughter, as she clasps a hand over her mouth, muffling the sound into teasing snickers.

"GIA!" I call out, my voice caught between a sigh and a laugh.

I can't argue with her; she speaks the truth. My desire for Fino burns hot. Yet in my heart, I know he is not necessary. Sure, I crave him, but only for certain indulgences... and let's be honest, those are never going to happen.

"What are you working on?" I ask, my curiosity piqued as I lean in to examine the sketches spread across the table. Gia is completely engrossed in her artwork. Her pencil glides purposefully across the page.

"It's a floor-length dress made from leftover curtains." She explains, her eyes sparkling with enthusiasm. "It boasts a candelabra headpiece—something I first saw in a dream. The moment I woke, I couldn't shake the vision, so I grabbed a sketchpad and brought it to life."

Once again, Gia has managed to conjure up an eclectic masterpiece. "What will you call it?" I ask, genuinely impressed by her creativity and the unexpected materials she's using.

"Home Décor Couture!"

The name rolls off her tongue with effortless confidence. It fits like a dream, perfectly capturing the essence of her style.

"I just know that one day, I'll have the chance to showcase my designs in Palermo," she says, "and you know I'm heading there next week..." She pauses, glancing at me. "You should come with me! We can roam the city, scout out potential storefronts—imagine it, Ros! We've dreamed about this since we were eight. This is our moment to make it real!" She excitedly continues to ramble.

Gia and I came up with a rather ambitious plan. She'd design and sew unique clothing, and I'd sell wine and host tastings. And one could imagine the chaos of spilled wine on fine clothes by a few inebriated patrons. Despite the potential pitfalls, the idea has stayed with us throughout the years.

Honestly, it would be a refreshing change to leave Messina behind. I've spent my entire life in this town, and my world has always revolved around it. The farthest I've ventured is to the serene forest near Mascalia. I've always been happy with my life here, surrounded by the familiar sights and sounds, and never felt the need to journey far. Nonetheless, the very thought of venturing to distant lands, even those close by, and beholding the manifold wonders of life does bring great delight to my spirit.

This dream is a gateway to adventure, creativity, and the promise of a fresh start. Along the way, I may even discover something even greater—someone who genuinely loves me, just as I love them.

"I have to get back to work," I sigh at Gia. The weight of unfinished tasks presses down on me as I pick up the grimy rag and push my chair back with a groan.

She offers me kindness and continues to sketch her heart out. I don't know what fate would befall me if she were to vanish from my life. She is my solace and my joy, and I cherish her beyond all reckoning.

I return to the bar top, navigating through the sea of riotous, ale-soaked revelers. As their raucous laughter and boisterous shouts transform the tavern into a squall of merriment and mayhem. I am already visualizing the adventures in Palermo with Gia.

I imagine us wandering through the city's lively streets, discovering quaint cafes, and immersing ourselves in its rich history. Palermo, the very jewel of the Kingdom, must be a marvel to behold — its markets teeming with wares and voices alike. I can only dream of what splendor awaits us

My musings often lead me to consider my parents' perspective on such a life. I do miss them dearly and often find my thoughts dwelling upon their hopes and dreams, as though their spirits survive in the quiet corners of my heart.

Did they dream of exploring far-off places or pursuing grand adventures?

A pang of nostalgia pushes forth, as I yearn to know more about their dreams and the life they once envisioned. The notion of seeing them once more is both sweet and sorrowful, a wistful ache.

The night stretches on, slipping further into the late hours. I became so engrossed in my own labor that time slipped past unnoticed. Now the tavern stands near empty, with few scant patrons left. Most fall bottomless into their cups. Their laughter and words are only muddled ramblings. With a gentle hand and a knowing smile, I bid them to take their leave.

The tavern, which had been alive just moments before, now cloaked in an uncanny hush. Though, it is a welcome reprieve from the night's clamor and chaos. Sticky tables, spilled drinks, and crumbs on the floor are all that's left of tonight's merrymaking. Gathering the soiled mugs and jugs from the emptied tables, I stack them high in my arms and stride toward the back of the tavern, where the washing basin awaits. I finish this chore quickly, as there is much more to be done.

I grab a broom; its bristles sweep across the wooden floor, gathering up the night's detritus. As I sweep, the tranquility of the tavern settles around me, and I take a moment to appreciate the calm that envelopes the space I've come to know so well.

Lost in thought, I find myself daydreaming about Fino. I weave a vision of him in my mind. No longer the man he is, but one who bears the virtues I so dearly crave in a companion: kindness, passion, and a love unwavering and true.

I imagine him whisking me into his embrace, his words a tender confession that sets my soul to flight and makes my heart stir with a new life. Yet, with each romantic fantasy I create, a wave of vexation overtakes me. This is a cruel ache that I know all too well. These dreams are but fleeting phantoms, never to take root in the soil of reality. The more I wish for such a love, the more I despise my own longing.

For what use is yearning if it is beyond my grasp?

As my reflections return to the present, I realize I've been fixated on the same spot for far too long. One by one, I blow out the iron lanterns. Their flames flicker and die, plunging the room further into darkness.

With the back door securely locked, I open the large wooden front doors, letting in the night air. Before locking them, I take in the clean, calm space. It's quiet, and unnerving, but I wish it were like this all the time. How easy my work would be.

The walk home is bitterly cold. The wind bites at my exposed skin as the darkness envelops me like a heavy cloak. Above is an endless expanse of inky black. The only illumination comes from the bright full moon hanging low and luminous, surrounded by a canvas of sparkling stars that twinkle like diamonds scattered across the night sky.

With each step, my feet strike the cobblestones. The muted thump echoes in the stillness of the empty town square, a sound that blends with the gentle crash of waves on the shore.

As I walk, the rhythmic thud of my feet on the pavement becomes a meditative counterpoint to the loneliness in my heart. I can't help but think of companionship. I wonder what it would be like to arrive home, having someone eagerly waiting for me.

What would it be like to open my front door to see a husband reclining comfortably in bed, an inviting smile spreading across his face. The scent of his cologne and the balminess of the room would wrap around me like a blanket the moment I step over the threshold.

The image evolves, and I envision him there, naked under the bed cloth. The dim lantern light casting a peaceful aura. My thoughts, once gentle with nostalgia, now stray into bolder realms. Each fleeting vision kindles a fire that flickers with my restless, untamed curiosity. My wandering reflections shudder to a halt as my eyes fall upon a shadowed figure in the distance. It stands stark and still across from a lifeless body sprawled in the cold, quiet street.

The hazy glow of a nearby streetlamp bathes the scene in a ghostly light. It casts long, shifting shadows that twist and writhe about the lone figure, clad in the deepest black. It all but vanishes into the shadows. Their form a specter against the night.

Though their features remain hidden in darkness, I catch the outline of a peculiar beak-like mask veiling their face. Its eerie shape lends an ominous air to the already unsettling atmosphere.

I quickly glance behind me, then redirect my attention back to the man lying motionless on the cold ground. In that moment, the mysterious figure must have dissolved into the shadows. I am left disoriented and shaken in the sudden languor.

I hasten to the man's side; my initial assumption is that he's simply a sleeping drunk, lost to the night's excess. Who probably indulged too much at a nearby alehouse. Seeing this besotted man at this hour is typically unremarkable. Kneeling next to him, I smell the overpowering scent of alcohol, just as I suspected. But the more I observe him, the more that masked figure remains vividly in my mind. I convince myself that my fatigue from the long day is causing illusions, conjuring tricks that play in the shadows of the night.

Thoughts of the mysterious, beaked figure race through my mind as I hurry the rest of the way home. I am left shaken after that encounter as my nerves are filled with both concern and curiosity. With every step down my street, the inky shadows of the night seem to relentlessly chase me. Causing the hair on the back of my next to rise.

I ascend my stairs, each step grounding me as the night's events unfold in my mind. Relief washes over me as I reach my door. I kick off my boots, and a shiver takes hold as the cool wood touches my bare feet. I saunter toward my awaiting bed and let myself collapse into the welcoming embrace of the mattress. My head sinks into the pillows. Weariness settles over my body as my eyes flutter closed. The gentle interlude of slumber has arrived.

Chapter 3

Rosannah

My body thrashes against the sheets. A silent scream trapped in my throat as vivid visions of the man in the bird mask plague my mind.

Unrelenting nightmares of horrid memories begin to invade my sleep. Each visualization brings with it a massive heap of trepidation, conjuring past encounters with men that were marked by brutality and disdain. I am haunted by the echoes of physical, verbal, and emotional cruelty. Even in slumber, peace eludes me.

I am starkly reminded that none of these men ever loved me in truth. They did not care for the soul within me, nor the dreams I held close. They never cared about the person I was, nor the person I wanted to be. They only cared about what they could take from me.

My mind races, depicting a bleak, solitary future. The emptiness is an unsettling prospect that disrupts the cycle of torment in my dreams. This sudden onset of horrifying imagery sends me spiraling into a state of panic. Activating a survival response in a perilous attempt to escape my own mind. I am imprisoned in a hell of my own making, haunted by the wraiths of bygone days, with no clear path to liberation.

I awake drenched in sweat, the moisture trickling down my back and seeping into the sheets beneath me. My breath comes in quick, shallow gasps, and my heart races wildly, seemingly trying to escape the confines of my chest.

The sun's ascension is notably precocious this morning, contrary to its established daily schedule. Golden rays penetrate the curtains, illuminating my room with a bright, almost harsh light. Dust motes perform an elaborate dance, resulting in a shimmering effect that is like a host of tiny dawn sprites capering in the air.

Confusion overcomes me as I slowly sit up. I feel adrift, untethered, and lost. Surviving fragments of those terrible hallucinations continue to torment me, intensifying the stress in my gut. I rub the drowsiness from my eyes and draw a sharp lungful, seeking to calm my spirit and anchor myself once more to the waking world.

I peer around the familiar room at my belongings that remind me I'm home. Slowly, I start to understand where I am, and I regain my composure. Relief washes over me, a gentle wave reminding me I am safe within these walls, as the echoes of the nightmare finally fade.

A searing pain, like a thousand needles, erupts in my bare foot as it hits the cold, hard oak floor. I crumble back onto the bed. I clutch my heel, desperately rubbing the sore soles in search of allayment. The fatigue from carrying stacks of heavy dishes and moving wine barrels all day is finally catching up with me.

My feet feel as though they've endured a Swiftmen's journey. The tops are swollen and tender, while my heels feel as if they have been dragged through nails.

In this moment, I find myself longing for a partner with large, skillful hands. Someone to knead away the stubborn knots and alleviate the soreness that has settled deep within my tired muscles.

I can't even fathom how fucking exquisite that would be right now.

With muscles screaming in protest, I manage to stand. Releasing a few mild winces as I shift my weight. I stroll over to the window, fling it open, as the sea breeze carries the scent of salt and seaweed into the room. I close my eyes, inhaling the crisp, salty air, and am instantly transported to a world of relaxation.

The rich, mouthwatering aroma of freshly baked pastries, perhaps croissants or fruit tarts, wafts into the room, wrapping around me like a friendly hug. A hungry *"Mmmm"* escapes my lips as my rumbling stomach anticipates breaking my fast.

I should pick up a mornmeal for Gia and myself before heading to her shop. I'm sure Gia will appreciate it, as she always forgets to eat in the morning.

I hastily dress and exit my humble abode. Down the groaning wooden stairs I rush, then hurry across the narrow alleyway that leads to the bakery.

I push open the door, and a delightful wave of scents engulfs me. The display counter is a feast for the eyes. Overflowing with an array of golden loaves, delicate tarts, and charming littlesome cakes. Each one highlights the baker's years of expertise. My eyes are drawn to the glossy, jam-filled pastries.

After much deliberation, I settled on two delectable ones filled with blackberry jam. At the counter, a friendly baker greets me with a polite smile, waiting for payment. After settling my fee, I exit the bakery. The morning sun heats my face as I begin the short walk towards Gia's boutique.

I can see the charming garment shop just up ahead. Its maroon sign hangs proudly above the door, embellished with elegant golden letters that read "Opizzi Modiste."

The glass window displays three magnificently designed dresses. Each gown stands as proof of the love and craftsmanship woven into its very seams by Gia's mother.

She was a talented seamstress, who passed away two years ago, leaving a profound void in Gia's life. She was not just a blood relative, but a guiding light. Gia's family lives only in her memories. And like me, Gia suffered the loss of her father, who died in the war when we were still young.

Gianni and her mother were inseparable, a duo that radiated adoration and innovation. Her mother always

38

embraced our wild ambitions, treating them as treasures rather than wistful fantasies. She never made either of us feel peculiar about our aspirations; instead, she listened intently as we rambled on for hours about our hopes and dreams, encouraging us to chase them wholeheartedly.

She was truly a remarkable woman, possessing a remarkable ability to nurture talent and instill confidence. The skills she imparted to Gia were immeasurable. Every stitch tells a story, and it's clear that Gia, with her mother's teachings, is making both, her Nona & mother proud as she carries on their shared passion for fashion and artistry.

I step into the quaint little shop, and I catch a glimpse of Gia rushing out from behind the sketcher's rest. She flings her arms around me, pulling me into a heartfelt embrace. "Merry morn!", she exclaims, her voice ringing with joy.

"Look who woke with a song in their heart!" I tease, matching her energy.

Gia beams back at me, "I have news to share! I received a letter from Lady Francesca Colonna! She wants me to do a fitting in Palermo for her and create a resplendent gown for an upcoming courtly masque." Her words tumble out in a squeal of excitement.

Overcoming with happiness, Gia grabs my hands, and together we bounce up and down like younglings, as laughter spills from our lips. The shop, vibrant with silks and satins in every color imaginable, seems to come alive with our joy. After one last exuberant hop, we manage to regain our composure.

"Gia! That's extraordinary! I'm so proud of you!" I exclaim, my spirit swelling with admiration. I lean in and plant a kiss on her cheek, wrapping her in a tight, supportive hug, feeling the excitement of her dream coming to life.

She steps back from our embrace, her eyes wide with urgency. "This is yet another reason for you to join me, Ros. I must travel there next week, and I can't make that journey alone. I need you by my side."

She grasps my shoulders, giving me a gentle shake, her voice rising with desperation. "Please, please, pleeeeeaaassseee!" Her earnest plea echoes in the air, making it hard to resist her request.

I let out a heavy sigh. "Sure, but I need to talk to Alessandra first. I've never been away from the bar for more than a day, and I can't help but worry about how she'll manage without her star barmaid." I give Gia a wink as she happily hops and claps with joy.

"Oh, here, I brought you a mornmeal." I say cheerfully, passing her the warm pastry filled with sweet blackberry jam.

"I swear it, you are the very best!" She exclaims, a grin spreading across her face as she eagerly takes a big bite, crumbs escaping as she savors the flaky texture.

As we enjoy our treats together, I begin to share the unsettling details of my recent nightmares. I tell her about the chilling visions, and the mysterious masked figure that haunted my dreams last night.

"Wow, that's intense, Ros," she replies, her eyes widening in disbelief. "I'm sorry you had such a rough night. At least you made it home safely. That sounds extra ghastly." She pauses, chewing thoughtfully on another bite of her pastry.

"It was definitely harrowing." I say, my gaze drifting out to the front display window, focusing on the streets beyond, where townsfolk scurry about their day, unaware of the tumultuous strife in my mind.

"I think the most toilsome part about nightmares is accepting that they're just dreams. Yet the feelings of loneliness and the painful companionships I've experienced, are all too veritable." I admit, trailing off as I fall into a daze, lost in my own contemplation.

Gia notices my quietness and leans in closer; her eyes filled with empathy. "Fear not, all shall be well Ros." She reassures me, her voice steady and soothing. "We are going to be okay. All shall mend in time, as the fates so will it."

As she grabs my hand, there's a sense of comfort in her touch. I embrace the moment, returning her kindness with a weary simper, grateful for her unwavering support.

"Plus men are heathens anyway. All they want is to be wed, be fed, and be fucked." She remarks.

"I likewise want to be wed, fed, and fucked." I smirk back at her. She tosses a green velvet scarf at me, cackling with laughter.

We both let out joyful sighs of happiness, and Gia stands, brushing the crumbs away with a casual flick of her wrists. Her eyes dart to a chaotic heap of fabrics sprawled across the weaving parlor. With a deliberate stride, she approaches the pile and begins folding the

41

fabrics with methodical precision. She sorts them into neat sections by color—rich crimsons, sunlit yellows, and cool blues forming a vivid spectrum across the trestle.

As she works, her tone shifts, carrying a sultry undercurrent. "On a serious note," she begins with teasing candor, "I really could use some tumbling[5]" Gia's lips curl into a sly smile, her dark eyes glitter with mischief. "It's been ages. And to speak plain, I wouldn't mind being explored by a debonair man. Hells...," she pauses for effect, her grin widening, "maybe even two battle-hardened thanes. Letting them worship me like I'm a sacred divine deity."

Her words are as bold and unapologetic, as she reaches for a swath of white fabric. With theatrical flair, she drapes it over her body, adjusting it to mimic the flowing robes of ancient statuary. The cloth clings to her form, evoking the smooth, carved marble of the countless Saint-like statues.

"Behold!" She declares with mock grandeur, striking a pose that accentuates her silhouette. "A vision of hallowed perfection, adored by all."

Her voice echoes with playful drama, as she tosses her head back. Her laughter spills into the room, and I can't help but burst into jollity at the mirthful jester that she is.

"Yeah, it's been a while since I've had some *excitement* too." I lean toward Gia, letting the corner of my lips bow into a teasing smile. "Don't judge me, but I

---

[5] A common medieval term for having sex

wouldn't mind a visit from the mysterious man with the bird mask. There's something about the anonymity, the intrigue... It's intoxicating."

I pause, letting the thought simmer before adding, "Maybe I'd encourage him to keep the entire ensemble on—the mask, the leather gloves, the clothes covering every inch of his skin. There's something about the forbidden, the untouchable, that just makes the whole idea so... irresistible."

I drift into the vivid embrace of my fantasy. The room around me fading as my mind paints a tantalizing scene. The air seems to thicken, charged with the energy of my wandering notions. My pulse quickens as the imagery grows more daring. My lips part, as I lose myself in the allure of the moment.

Suddenly, Gia's voice cleaves through my ideal musings. "You wicked temptress!" She exclaims with mock accusation.

The creaking of the front door announces a customer, breaking the spell of the delightful moment Gia and I were sharing.

I hesitate, reluctant to part from our laughter. "I'll see you later, try not to miss me too much," I say, "I must go forth to battle the trials of the marketplace!"

With a final giggle and glance back at her, I whisper a goodbye, and exit through the creaking door, leaving the sincerity of our recent exchange behind.

I make my way towards the hectic harbor wharves.[6] I can't help but note the unusually large

---

[6] Common term for docks where ships load and unload

throng of buyers. The docks seem alive with energy today, possibly because a couple of new vessels have arrived.

Intrigued by the lively chatter and sounds of bartering, I explore the various merchant stalls lining the waterfront. Wandering through the maze of colorful booths, each overflowing with unique treasures, I stop at a silversmith's display. I am mesmerized by the gleam of a stunning silver necklace featuring a delicately crafted sparrow pendant. I approach the vendor and inquire about the price. After some friendly banter and a bit of haggling, we settle on a fair amount.

I reach into my pocket and pull out a handful of coins, my fingers brushing against the metal as I submit them to the saleswoman. With the necklace now clasped securely around my neck, the sparrow rests just below my collarbone.

Continuing my exploration, I find yet another stall, this one brimming with beauteous flowers. The fragrant air draws me to a florist overflowing with a bountiful array of fresh blooms. A cluster of Madonna lilies catches my eye—their white petals, unfurling gently. Each one like tiny works of nature's art. Bringing the lilies closer, I sniff their perfume, a heady sweetness that tickles my nose. Convincing enough, I decide to buy a bouquet.

I continue walking along the harbor promenade. Seagulls are loudly calling from above. Luckily for me, I spot an unoccupied bench just up ahead that appears to be waiting for me.

44

I run my fingers lightly along its rough, timeworn surface before settling down with a soft sigh. I place my delicate bouquet carefully to my right, its petals flutter in the wind.

My gaze shifts outward, drawn to the vast expanse of the ocean that stretches endlessly before me. The water sparkles like liquid sapphire under the morning sun, but it's the waterborne fleets that command my attention.

These towering vessels, their grandeur impossible to ignore, rest anchored in the gentle swells. Their enormous white sails are furled tightly, tucked away like sleeping giants. These mighty crafts creak smoothly with the rhythm of the waves, a low, groaning melody that speaks of voyages and stories untold.

At the prow of one vessel, a remarkably carved mermaid figurehead rises boldly. Her expression frozen in a gaze of serene defiance. Every curve of her form, every strand of her hair, is painstakingly rendered, as though the artisan had poured their soul into her creation. She bobs gracefully with the motion of the sea as if dancing to the ocean's timeless song.

I absolutely adore living here. Surrounded by the salty breeze and the harmonious sound of waves lapping against the quay. Though, the hope of escaping at any moment on one of these salt-kissed wanderers fills me with a purpose of adventure.

I can picture myself sailing into the effervescent sunset, leaving everything behind. My name fading into the deafness of the sea. It would be a chance for a

45

completely fresh start, an exhilarating escape from the mundane. As I take to the waves, I would let the wind catch my sails and the vast ocean steer my dreams, carrying me far away to uncharted horizons.

Ensnared within my daydream, I reach into my pocket and retrieve my book. The front cover, adorned with the title "Inferno by Dante Alighieri[7]," catches the sunlight as I open it. I flip through the delicate pages until I locate the passage where I last immersed myself in Dante's intricate narrative. I brace myself ready to plunge into the profound depths of the manuscript.

---

[7] Inferno is the first part of Italian writer Dante Alighieri's 14th-century narrative poem, The Divine Comedy. The Inferno describes the journey of a fictionalized version of Dante himself through Hell, guided by the ancient Roman poet Virgil. In the poem, Hell is depicted as nine concentric circles of torment located within the Earth.

Chapter 4

Rosannah

As the sun dips below the horizon, painting the sky in fiery oranges and pastel pinks, time slips away from me. My work at Lupo Tavern starts soon.

Although, nearly finished with my book, I reluctantly pause to mark my place. Annoyance and boredom rise to the surface. I sigh, shoving my belongings into my bag, as I trudge towards the hall of toils. It's not all wretched, I don't loathe my place of labor, but I just do not have the will to set forth and conquer today.

As I make my way, the air is thick with a medley of aromas, drifting from the nearby cookshops. Their savory scents winding through the streets like an unseen feast.

Walking past, the rhythmic kneading of the chef's hands against the counter, and the sight of perfectly

47

formed pasta, awakens treasured memories of my Nona. I can almost hear my Nona's voice, as her laughter socializes with the sound of rolling dough. I do miss her beyond what mere words may convey, and my heart aches in her absence.

Every Sunday, we would gather in her cookroom, flour dusting the wooden trestle, and our hands. She would share stories of her life, her youth, and the traditions passed down through the generations. Those days overflowed with love. Whether from crackling fires, love shared in laughter and embraces, or the abundance of richly flavored foods. My Nona was the very beating of my nature; a presence that time shall never replace.

With time to spare, I decide to treat myself to a quick meal. Pushing open the door to the cookshop, I am greeted by the comforting ambiance of dim lights and muted chatter. I settle into a cozy corner table and order "tria di vermicelli sardine."[8] It is humble, yet hearty and satisfying. Now pair it with a goblet of white wine, and it makes the perfect accompaniment.

When the steaming dish is placed before me, I can't help but admire the arrangement. I dive in, savoring each bite and relishing the explosion of flavors that leaped in a merry jig across my tongue. While it may not be identical to the pasta my Nona used to make, it brings a comforting familiarity.

---

[8]. This is a recipe from the 14th century, also known as Anonimo Fiorentino. The translation sounds like "pasta of vermicelli with sardines." It is made of durum wheat flour, eggs, water, and salt. It is usually paired with some kind of fish.

As I finish my meal, I push my empty plate aside and place some coins on the table for payment. I stand, say, thank you for the most toothsome fare, and step back out into the crisp autumn air, ready to face the night's long spell.

Arriving in front of Lupo Tavern, I let out a weary sigh. I cannot shake the sense of monotony that surrounds me. Each day appears like a fate's reflection of the last. A routine so ingrained that it is almost ritualistic. I do not mind the repetition itself, I just long for a kindred soul to share such moments with. To bridge the gap between the bustling tavern atmosphere and my quiet solitude. I crave the reassurance of knowing that, when my day finally ends, there will be someone waiting for me, ready to share laughter and stories instead of this lonesome silence.

Stepping into the habitual whirlwind of activity, I am greeted by a symphony of voices and merriment that hums like a lively melody throughout the drinking hall. I make my way to the scullery. Navigating through the rowdy crowd and finding a moment of swift solace before donning my well-worn, stained apron. Once an unblemished off-white, its fabric is now a canvas of splatters and smudges from the countless laborious rounds. I can't help but grimace at its current state.

I really need to wash it soon—it's reaching a level of grime that's becoming most unbearable.

Shuffling back into the main area, my feet echo against the stained floor. The sprightly drone of conversation fills the room, but my attention is

49

immediately drawn to the doorway. There he is again— Fino. His steadfast stride is unmistakable, but this time, a wretched knot takes hold of my belly, twisting in ill favor, as I see he's not alone. Clinging to his arm is none other than *her... Felicita Donati.*

With swanlike elegance, her slender neck rises, framing her angular features and leading down to a thin torso with small breasts. Her waist is hardly defined, yet her form is well-framed by ample birthing hips, lending her a most beguiling silhouette.

Her skin, a mellow golden hue, carries a radiant quality that seems to glow in the firelight. Her light brown hair, smooth and straight, falls just below her shoulders. This intentional length accentuates her high cheekbones and delicate jawline. Her eyes, vast and round as twin moons, shine with the hue of a clear summer sky. Their cerulean depths both striking and ensnaring.

Despite their innocent, doe-like quality, there is a shrewdness that waltzes behind them. A sharp glint that hints at a cunning mind. She wields her lashes like a weapon, fluttering them with expert precision to charm and manipulate with effortless finesse.

Clad in a gown of sun's own gold, the cheerful yellow beams against her bronzed complexion. The fabric rests lightly on her shoulders, flowing in gentle folds that hint at the softness beneath. The neckline, modest yet flattering, teases, revealing just enough to intrigue without crossing into excess.

A snug brown corset cinches her midsection, emphasizing the dramatic flare of her hips. A yellow bow nestled within her tresses is a merry and youthful token that lightens her otherwise stately appearance.

The golden cross and small pendant around her neck sways gently. The fine chain resting just above the curve of her cleavage. The pendant glimmers faintly, an emblem of her devotion to Saint Silvia, patroness of pregnant women.

Every detail about her, from the proud tilt of her chin to the assured grace of her stride, bespeaks a quiet dominion, a presence of unshaken command. Her modesty belies the strength that lurks beneath, a prowling elegance that enthralls any soul bold enough to stare too long.

My jaw tightens, as a smoldering loathing takes root at the mere sight of her.

That nauseating, two-faced harpy.

Every discourse with her has been a battle of thinly veiled barbs and subtle power plays. Her facade of poise and grace hides a viper's tongue. And I know, without a shadow of a doubt, that her disdain for me is just as strong.

As the two vile love doves step further into the room, tittering ripples around them. A strain winds tight within my chest, like a serpent coiled and waiting to strike. She leans closer to Fino, fingers brushing his sleeve, and it takes everything in me to keep my composure. To bridle the inferno coursing through my veins, lest they devour me where I stand.

I bare no baseless hatred for Felicita; every drop of animosity I feel towards her is well-earned. She's given me no shortage of cause to have these emotions, and each one is more infuriating than the last. Felicita embodies the very essence of a spiteful wench. Cloaked in a veneer of piety and righteousness that only serves to mask her true nature. She despises me for what *she* deems my "blasphemous" ways. Particularly my willingness to partake in and embrace my sexuality. If ever there were a soul fashioned for virtue's pedestal, it is Felicita—faultless, blameless, and insufferably so.

A virgin by choice, she clings to her religious convictions with an iron grip, wielding her purity like a weapon of righteousness. She's too grand to walk among common feet, haughty of mien, and utterly convinced her life choices make her morally superior. Verily, a vexing and venomous dame, through and through.

She's staunchly against anyone engaging in any form of intimate entanglement before marriage. In her meticulously crafted world, that means no kissing, no affectionate touches, and certainly no fornication. She holds these beliefs not just as personal precepts but as universal decrees that she feels *compelled* to enforce upon others.

Anyone who dares to deviate from her strict moral code is met with thinly veiled disparagement. She labels them *harlots* without a second thought. Her judgment is swift and unforgiving. Felicita is convinced that anyone, *and I mean anyone*, who engages in such behaviors is doomed to eternal damnation.

Most irksome of all is her unbending certainty that her way alone is right, while all others are misguided.

She carries herself with an air of smug superiority. Her every word crowded with condescension, as though she floats above the rest of us, mere sinners.

And yet, for all her sanctimonious preachings, I can see the cracks in her facade. Her eyes linger a little too long when she thinks no one's watching, and her cheeks flush just a bit too quickly when specific topics arise. She hates that the same chains she's willingly placed upon herself do not shackle me. In my spirit, I know she is secretly jealous of the freedom I possess, the freedom to live authentically without being shackled by rigid dogma.

Nay, I don't loathe Felicita without unjust cause. She's given me every warrant. Every sneer, every judgmental glance, every holier-than-thou comment. She's a walking contradiction: a woman who preaches purity but is poisoned by envy. A saint in her mind but a serpent in everyone else's.

And in sooth? She deserves the full measure of my detestation. But alas for me, wretched fate bestows the esteemed honor of attending to them.

"Greetings," I dreadfully let slip from my lips, "May I fetch you all a dish of tidbits, or a goblet of wine?" I glance around the table trying to hide my falsehood.

Fino won't even acknowledge me, his gaze is cast elsewhere as if I were but a mere shadow to him, unworthy of his notice. It's not uncommon for him to act even more like a swell-headed bastard when she is around.

"Just some wine for the table," one of the friends squeaks out to break the tension. I give a slight

53

acknowledgment and make my way to fetch their drinks.

I return to the table, with a set of goblets. Carefully, I pour the rich red liquid from its ceramic vessel, noting how each glass fills with a rich and velvety shade. Having filled the glasses precisely to the brim, I set the jug down in the middle of the table. A false simper tugs at my lips before I turn to head back to the serving ledge.

Felicita's sneering voice slices through the air. "Might you hasten a touch more next time?" Her snarky remark ignites a surge of frustration within me.

I spin around, my pulse quickens, and force a nod, replying, "Of course my apologies for the delay"

I resolve to leave, determined to put the encounter behind me. However, as I take two steps away, I hear Felicita's voice again, sharply addressing the table behind me. "That churl[9] must have cripple legs. Taking her sweet time with our drinks."

Now I am enraged. I abruptly face the wicked hag, and reply, "Who are you calling a churl you cox-comb[10], skamelar[11] ronyon[12]!" The words spill from me, and not a trace of remorse follows.

Felicita's mouth hangs agape, her eyes wide as saucers in disbelief. Her eyes narrow, glinting with barely concealed fury as she straightens her posture,

---

[9] Low class, a peasant or a surly ill-bred person"
[10] A vain, narcissistic person
[11] A scrounge or parasite.
[12] An old, mangy, scabby woman

leaning forward as if to assert dominance, and says, "At least I am not a cursed puterelle[13] like you..."

She pauses, glancing around the room, knowing she holds everyone's attention. "Tell me, how many knaves have had their way with you, huh? How many have seized what they desired and left you like the meritless bawdy maid you are? A hundredfold?" She eyes around the room once more. "Two hundredfold?"

Her words become more biting, each syllable sharper than the last as her face flushes with her anger. "Have you lost count? With such ways, no husband will ever take you. And if some unfortunate fool ever does take pity on you, may God grant him mercy. For he'll be wed to the remnants of every man in the village."

Her voice harshly echoes, each word crafted to wound. Her bitterness pours out like a dam broken beyond repair. The table bursts into laughter, and tears swell in my eyes. I steal a glance at Fino, who offers me a gentle, melancholy expression, before allowing himself to join in the scornful mockery with Felicita and their friends.

I rush back to the scullery, as emotions spill over. Endless tears stream down my cheeks. My heart palpitates, mirroring the turbulent opinions within. The cruel utterances she hurled at me repeat on a relentless loop. They pierce my thoughts like daggers.

I gasp for breath, struggling to calm myself, yet the tears fall, nonetheless. A tumult of incredulity and

---

[13] A woman of ill-repute

wrath stirs within me. I cannot fathom how I let her spew such vile nonsense.

How could one so steeped in venom possess such sway over my very soul?

Her scornful words wound me, laced with a barbarity that leaves me feeling exposed and vulnerable. It was as if she had been waiting for the perfect moment to deliver her devastating blow, and I am now left reeling in the aftermath, desperately trying to piece myself back together.

I know the truth about Felicita. Her bitterness and cruelty reflect her insecurities, not a measure of my worth. They don't define me. I am certain of my own being, and in that certainty, I remain steadfast. My strength lies in my ability to live authentically, love unapologetically, and thrive despite the negativity that surrounds me. I'm confident and unfaltering, and I love myself for it. There is nothing she can ever do that will make me change the way I think about myself.

I love me.

Taking a long inhale, I secure my mind, whispering words of resolve, offering a brief, silent, rallying cry to myself. With my thoughts firm, I gather a stack of rags, their rough texture fitting snugly in my grip, and pour a generous amount of wine into a jug. Head held high, I stride back to the main room, the weight of the world no longer upon me.

As the hours crawl by, the night unfolds, and time seems to slip through my fingers like grains of sand. The end of my shift nears, and I find my mind wandering through the chaotic rhythm of the evening. With the last of the patrons filtering out the front doors, I bid them a gentle farewell.

Surveying the main room for any messes, my eyes fall upon the wreckage of a disorderly table from earlier. Their heated argument over trivial matters had led to an unfortunate accident, but now, there's nothing left to do but clean up the mess.

I begin sweeping away the residue of the evening, taking care as I gather the scattered shards of glass. The only sounds are the broom head and broken pieces scraping on the wooden floor.

Lost in this rhythm, I am startled by the sound of the front door creaking open. With my back to the door, I head over to the counter to finish tidying. I call out over my shoulder, "Forgive me, but we are soon to close. You are welcome to enter and take a drink, but please make haste!" And start to gather the few remaining goblets scattered across the polished wine-plank.

A deep, hearty chuckle, rumbling like distant thunder, reaches my ears, accompanied by a genuinely apologetic voice. Spinning around, I gasp as a mountain of a man emerges from the shadows. His presence fills the lantern-lit room.

My lungs catch, my heart hammers, and in my stunned gaze, my grip fails as two wine goblets slip from my grasp. They hit the floor with a resounding crash, fracturing into countless glittering pieces.

The man standing before me is, without question, one of the most striking figures I have ever laid eyes upon. No fear grips me; instead, I am held fast by a fascination I cannot explain.

He stands well over six feet, sporting a burly physique that exudes strength and masculinity. His prominent pecs and powerful arms bear the strength of one who could lift eight full wine barrels with ease. While his legs are thick and sturdy, like a strong standing ancient oak. His shaggy dark brown hair falls just above his shoulders. His complexion is a shade lighter than my rich walnut colored skin.

Mesmerized, and practically drooling, I realize I'm staring. I give my head a swift shake, begging my thoughts to settle. Only to realize that, in my bewilderment, I have scattered yet more shards upon the floor. The large man strides over to assist me, offering another round of apologies for startling me.

As he leans closer, I get an even better glimpse at his friendly features. A jawline hewn as if by divine hands, chiseled to perfection, and beneath it, lips full and succulent, the kind that tempts fate. As we tend to the mess, our fingers brush against each other, the chill leather of his gloves touches my fingertips ever so lightly.

My gaze trails along his enormous fingers, leading to exceedingly large palms. I can't help but notice how small mine appear in comparison. One of his fingers is almost the width of three of mine. It's astounding to think that this man, this statuesque giant, easily steals me to the ground with but a touch.

Together we rise to our feet, pausing for a moment. He stands towering above me, as his lips bend into a gentle, beckoning smile that radiates sincerity. The scent that wafts from him is intoxicating—earthy notes of cedar, fragrant thyme, cloves, and a hint of peppermint musk fill the air. Weaving an irresistible spell that pulls me ever closer.

My gaze lifts from his inviting expression, only to be captured by his eyes. One eye is a striking, piercing blue, vast and endless as the ocean, while the other flares with the sunny glow of honey amber, like the sun's final kiss upon the water at dusk. In tandem, they cast their sultry spell, stealing the very breath from my lips.

"Ciao," he greets, his voice rolls through the air like the slow burn of smoldering embers. The kindness in his tone wraps around me, melting my resolve like butter left to soften under the sun. His gaze holds mine, intense yet bewitching, as if he's sharing a secret only I can hear. All else slips into oblivion, and I am inescapably helpless to the pull of his presence.

"Umm, ciao," I manage to squeak out, my heart hammering in my chest as I struggle to mask the overwhelming attraction that surges through me.

My palms are clammy, and a flicker of nerves take flight in my belly, quick and restless as a hummingbird's wings. Sweat beads on my forehead; despite my attempts at composure, the stifling heat of the moment consumes me, leaving only his intense eyes in focus.

"I'm Adrastus Ovicula, but you may call me Adra." He utters, his name rolling off his tongue with an effortless authority.

The sunken, coarse inflection of his voice wraps around each syllable, resonating in the air like an enchanting melody. It's as if the very sound of his name was designed to draw people in, leaving a savoriness that remains steadfast long after it leaves his lips.

His name sounds like an eternal haven, and a flush of heat rises to my cheeks. "I'm Rosannah Vanali. Rosannah is just fine with me." I reply, trying to be subtle about my flirtation.

"Rosannah." He mimics back and this time my thighs tingle.

Fuck he is stunning.

I glide back to the tavern board, smooth in my step, while he drags a tall wooden seat from the counter's edge.

Adra is clad in a comprehensive leather ensemble that envelops him almost entirely. His outfit features a fitted dark grey long sleeve shirt that hugs his torso, expertly crafted from supple leather that allows for both durability and flexibility. The matching leather bottoms are equally form-fitting, tailored to provide comfort and a sleek silhouette while also offering protection against the elements. His clothing hugs him in *all* the right areas.

Attached to his waist is a unique belt bag, a hybrid of cloth and leather, intricately stitched and brimming with various tools and intriguing items. Draped from his waist down is a half butcher's apron, stained and

60

speckled with muck. Adorning the strap of the belt bag, a carefully curated collection of herbs—garlic, thyme, and other fragrant botanicals—hangs gracefully, cascading down over the front of the apron.

I arch a brow and tease, "Are you some manner of undertaker... physician... apothecary?" My gaze drifts, tracing the sharp lines of his ensemble.

"Something of the sort." Adra replies.

I open my mouth to press further, but he stops me with a subtle tilt of his head. "Pour me a goblet of your finest wine."

I comply, exaggerating a sense of false sophistication as I reach for the jug. His presence has a way of making me want to appear more poised, more refined.

Adra's massive palm wraps around the goblet, the motion is deliberate and hypnotic as he swirls the rich crimson liquid. His eyes lock onto mine, as if they're stripping me bare.

My pulse quickens, and molten heat pools between my thighs. He lifts the glass to his lips, the slow, sensual sip drawing my attention to the curve of his mouth.

My imagination runs wild, unraveling him in my mind- each piece of leather peeled away to reveal hard lines and raw power. My breathing falters, desire curls through, and I wonder if he knows the chaos he's causing with just a look.

CONWAY TITTY

Chapter 5

Adrastus

Her body is poetry in motion, every gentle curve drawing my gaze like a lodestone.[14] The way her hips sway as she moves behind the publican's board is hypnotic, a silent invitation that sets my pulse racing. Her almond-shaped eyes bear a quiet allure, their corners crinkling as she smiles—a smile that seems to light up the room.

Those hazel irises, flecked with specks of gold, glimmer like sunlight filtering through sap. I cannot help but wonder how those eyes might sear into mine with unbridled intensity, or how they might soften when they are veiled in the vehemence of pleasure.

Her skin, smooth and supple, with a hue as rich as a polished walnut, begs to be touched, kissed, and explored. My eyes trace her form. The way the fabric of

---

[14] A naturally magnetic stone

her dress clings to her—highlighting every dip, every rise, every promise is enticing. My thoughts betray me and begin to wander. Her skin would feel soft and pliant under my hands. Her body heating beneath my touch.

My gaze drops lower as she sways. Her posterior, perfectly shaped and teasingly close, moves with a rhythm that makes it impossible to look away. And those breasts—full, plush, and absolutely entrancing. The way they press subtly against the neckline of her dress, causes my mouth to crave a suckle. I imagine how they'd feel under my lips, the weight of them in my palms, the taste of her skin on my tongue.

Her hair, a deluge of thick, luscious spirals, frames her face like a crown. A thought of tangling my fingers in it, pulling her closer, hearing her breath hitch, swarms me. It is a most tempting thought, and enough to weaken my very will.

If I had my way, there'd be no hesitation. I'd step forward, close the space between us, and claim her in a heartbeat. My hands would find her waist, pulling her flush against me as I hoist her onto this very counter.

The thin fabric of her dress would bunch around her hips as my fingers mark her thighs, seeking the warmness I know she's hiding. I'd savor the moment I discover just how drenched she is for me. Her body in accord with her desire as I press her closer, harder, stealing the very air from her chest.

My lips would travel over her skin like a worshiper at an altar, tasting her, teasing her. Each kiss would be a vow, each bite a possession. I'd bury my face in the

64

curve of her neck, inhaling her scent, letting it spellbind me. My teeth would graze her delicate skin, drawing out moans that I'd quickly swallow with my mouth on hers. The idea of her surrendering completely to me fuels a hunger so primeval I can hardly stand still.

When our eyes meet, the spark between us ignites into a raging fire. My cock throbs, straining against the confines of my pants, desperate for her touch. She has no idea what kind of chaos she's unleashing in me, how her beauty, her presence, her very existence consumes my every thought. She's not just beautiful; she's devastating, a maddening temptation that I'm aching to ruin in the most delicious ways.

I can't stop imagining her dress pushed high, my hands everywhere, her legs trembling as I bring her to the brink over and over again. She's not just a craving; she's a feast, and I want to devour her until there's nothing left but her whimpers and the marks of my devotion on her skin. I don't want to wait another second. Let me take her right here, right now, and leave her trembling, gasping, and utterly mine.

"So... adventurer," she teases. Her hazel eyes idle on mine, a mischievous spark dances in their depths. "And what pray tell, does bring you to Messina? Does one seek solace, or are you seeking some rare treasure, or perchance, a sweeter indulgence?"

Rosannah's words pull me from my wandering visions, but the smirk that tugs at my lips betrays my darker desires.

I lean casually against the counter, letting my eyes deliberately stare into hers before trailing, just for a moment, down to her lips. "I'm here for work." I reply, my voice thick with the double meaning she may or may not catch. "I've got a contract to fulfill."

She arches a brow, folding her arms across her chest, unintentionally pushing her breasts higher beneath the fabric. It takes every ounce of restraint not to let my gaze drop.

"A contract, aye?" She muses, tilting her head playfully. "Sounds serious."

"Tis but my duty," I reply, matching her tone. "And is not all labor to be met with earnest purpose?"

She leans forward, a sly grin tugging at her lips. "A fair point, but even fools must earn their keep. A jester must know when to jest and when to bow, wouldn't you say?"

I let out a small chuckle. "Ah, but one could argue being the king's jester is the most serious duty of all." I counter, raising my glass to my lips for another sip. "After all, keeping one's head is no laughing matter."

Rosannah's laugh is bright, the sound prances between us as she chirps, "Touché."

I gaze upon her once more, her freckles, scattered across her face like a celestial map, each one a delicate mark of perfection. Her smile radiates life, wonder and something inexplicably enthralling. She isn't just the most attractive creature I have ever laid eyes upon; she's mesmerizing like a perfectly crafted piece of art.

I've never been so enticed by a mere mortal before. There's just something about her, something I can't quite put my finger on... though, if things go my way, I'll be putting my finger *in* her soon enough.

Trying to break the almost suffocating tension, I foolishly ask Rosannah about the weather and this little town I've found myself in. The question seems hollow even as I say it, but I chalk it up to gathering information, trying to justify my distraction. After all, I was sent here for a reason—a reason that's still concealed in secret. Yet, as her sweet voice begins to fill the space between us, describing the ocean and how the stars reflect on its surface, I realize I'm not listening at all.

Her spirit dominates my senses. My eyes follow the delicate curve of her neck, the way her lips move as she speaks, the gentle rise and fall of her chest. It's as if she's cast a spell on me, one I have no hope—or desire—of breaking.

She pauses, her lashes flutter as she stares at me blankly, waiting. I realize too late she's expecting a response.

Hastily, I lift my glass, buying a moment to recover. "Seems like you must show me the lay of this place when next we meet." Trying to give the illusion that I heard every word she said. "I am sure a certain maiden of your beauty must harbor many secrets, ones well worth unveiling."

Her cheeks flush a deep shade of pink; she averts her gaze just slightly.

Without a word, she sets a platter of meats and cheeses in front of me. My fingers reach out instinctively, plucking a piece of food as my gaze never leaves hers. The taste of the food is irrelevant—pointless, even. I don't need this human sustenance, but

67

how could I refuse something brought to me by her. No, it's not this food I crave.

Rosannah's blush deepens as she notices my persistent gaze. She fidgets with the edge of her covering. She glances away for a moment before meeting my eyes again. "I would be honored to serve as your guide. The Kingdom of Sicily is quite vast, but I could show you a few of my favorite places... if you should desire?"

"I would be most pleased by that." My words spill out without a second thought. My tone is perhaps just a little too eager, but I can't bring myself to care. I find myself having an obsession to understand this human more, intellectually, emotionally, and, let's be honest, horizontally.

This desire isn't normal for me. Sure, I've indulged before—an occasional tryst with a succubus, a fleeting encounter with a nymph, or any number of other worldly creatures whose sole purpose is to satiate hunger. But that's all it ever was, a release. A temporary satisfaction for a need as primal as living. Mortals? They've never even crossed my mind as anything more than a passing curiosity. Why would they?

They're ants, scurrying around, building their fragile little lives, only to have them stomped out in the blink of an eye. It's laughable, really. They're born, they toil, they die, and then the next batch repeats the cycle like clockwork. Disposable, insignificant, endlessly replaceable. Their existence is a grain of sand on the infinite shore of eternity.

Yet here I am, with this... this *need* clawing at me, burning through my veins like enchanted fire. It doesn't make sense. I've faced infernal beings and defied gods without hesitation, yet the mere sight of her—this mortal—has me undone. Her life is a flicker, a speck in the cosmos. There's no logic to it, no reason for this pull. Mortals are fleeting, fragile, and bound to the mundane. But something about *her* defies all that, and it perplexes me.

I finish the last of the finger foods, pushing my chair back from the counter. My actions are deliberate but unhurried. Gathering my belongings, I rise, only to turn and bump directly into Rosannah. She's reaching for my plate, her delicate fingers poised mid-air, and suddenly we're face to face.

Our bodies touch, the faintest brush sparking something far more intense. Her scent wraps around me instantly, a blend of roses and lilies, like a bloom in the moonlit gardens of an enchanted realm. I inhale profoundly, unable to stop myself, as if her very essence is a laudanum I'm already addicted to. The world around us blurs. The hum of the tavern fades into silence, leaving only her and the rising tension between us.

She's so short compared to me. Her frame is a stark contrast to my towering stature. Yet, there's a hidden strength in her, a quiet power that makes her all the more captivating. Still, the thought crosses my mind, how easily I could shield her from any harm; how effortlessly I could pull her close and make her mine, if only she'd let me.

The tension swirls around us, as though the very air is woven with sorcery. Time seems to stretch; we stand frozen, locked in each other's stare, for what feels infinite. Her hazel eyes kissed by the light, glitter like a starry night. Their depths pulling me further into a spell I can't—and don't want to—escape. Her breathing matches mine now, shallow and immediate, as though we're both bracing for something inevitable.

She takes a slow inhalation, and the motion causes a single strand of her dark hair to slip free. It falls across her face like a silken thread. My hand moves on instinct, my fingers brushing her skin as I tuck the stray lock behind her ear.

The moment our skin touches, a jolt of energy surges between us, as though the universe itself is conspiring to push us together. The spark ignites something untamed within me. My chest thumps as her lips part, her cheeks flush, the faint pink blooming against her skin like a sunrise.

Realizing a strange, and unfamiliar sensation bubbles inside me, I stumble over a cough, forcing out a clumsy apology. My voice is foreign, rough, and strained as if trying to push through the knot tightening in my throat. I don't wait for her reaction—I can't.

Turning abruptly, I make for the exit, my boots echoing against the wooden floor louder than I intended.

Behind me, her voice calls, "Buona sera!"[15] but it's distant, like a whisper carried on the breeze.

I shove the heavy wooden doors open with a force that startles me. Their creaks groaning in protest as I step into the night. The streets are empty, silent but for the muffled crash of waves in the distance. The smell of salt and ocean rushes over me, erasing the scent of her roses and lilies that still clings faintly to my clothes. But it doesn't help. It only sharpens the storm brewing inside me.

My body burns with an aching undeniable need, but it's not the true source of the storm brewing inside me. That would be a relief, something customary— something I could control. This... this is something else. It claws at my chest, wrapping tightly around my ribs like an unseen tether pulling me back to her, and I hate it. I hate it because I can't name it, can't fight it. It's not lust, not desire, though those stay at the edges. No, this is stronger, serious, and far more dangerous.

My boots crunch against loose gravel as I try to balance myself. My fists tremble at my sides, clenching and unclenching, desperate for something to ground me. But nothing works. Nothing quiets the unfamiliar pounding in my chest or the way my mind keeps returning to her. To her sweet laugh, her rosy blush, the way her eyes stayed on mine like she saw through the carefully constructed mask I wear.

Why can't I stop thinking about her?

---

[15] "Goodbye, good evening" in Italian

I barely know her, yet every detail is etched into me, every memory of her amplified, impossible to ignore. My chest tightens further, the feeling growing heavier, until it's unbearable. It's as though some unseen force has taken hold of me, refusing to let go, refusing to let me escape her pull.

All I know is that her face resides in my mind, her voice echoes in my ears, and I think I'm falling into something I can't climb out of. And for the first time in my existence, I'm truly afraid.

Chapter 6

Rosannah

My chest heaves as I struggle to control my lungs. My heart races so fast like it might tear free from my chest. He left so swiftly, like a shadow slipping through my fingers, and I couldn't even manage to give him a proper goodbye. The ache in my chest is searing, as though the very essence of the moment mourns his absence. I don't know when, or even if our paths will cross again, and the thought makes weak in the knees.

The way he towered over me, a force of nature barely restrained, with those piercing eyes that held the balance of frost and amber. When he stared at me, it was as though he could see straight into my soul, stripping me bare without a single touch.

And fuck, if he had fully touched me...

If he had leaned in even a fraction, I would have given myself to him without hesitation. I would have let him consume me, body and soul, until there was nothing left but us. I can still feel the ghost of his presence, the pull of him like an irresistible force, drawing me in and leaving me breathless. I would have surrendered to him completely, let him explore me, claim me.

I let my mind wander further into those depraved thoughts. His hands on me — immovable, tracing every inch of my body like he was searching for something only I could give him. My clothes would have been no match for his hunger, torn away in a frenzy as animalistic sounds filled the room. His growls & grunts, full of possessiveness, mixing with my gasps and cries. His lips would have left trails of smoldering intensity across my skin, igniting me in ways I didn't know were possible.

Even now, with him gone, it's like he's still here, like the aftermath of a storm that hasn't fully passed. My skin still frissons where his eyes tarried, and my whole body stirs with this severe need for him. I close my eyes, biting my lip, striving to quell the tidal wave he has left in his wake.

I tidy up the last remnants of his presence from the bar top. All I desire is to return home, throw myself onto my bed, and do something—*anything*—to release this flourishing tension between my thighs.

Locking the front doors behind me, a chill breeze caresses my neck, and for a fleeting moment, I imagine it's his lips grazing my skin. A tremor overtakes my body at the mere thought. Desire clouds me, and I find myself lost in its throes. Without a moment's hesitation,

74

I hasten towards my dwelling, driven by an urgent wish for release.

I climb the steps to my door, heart pounding so loudly it drowns out every other sound. The moment I step inside, I don't bother putting my things away. My fingers are already tugging at my clothes, peeling them off piece by piece as I stumble toward the bed.

By the time I reach it, I'm completely bare, my skin tingling as the cool draft of the room brushes against me. I let myself fall back onto the bed, sinking into the sheets as I sprawl out, squeezing and kneading as I imagine his hands replacing mine. My fingers tease my nipples, rolling and pinching until moans slip past my lips. The ache between my thighs is torturous, and I trail one hand down my body. My fingertips graze my stomach, my hips, until they finally find my lower lips.

I'm drenched. The evidence of my desire is inexorable, slicking my fingers as I slide them through the wetness. A delicate shudder weaves its way down my spine, as his image invades my mind. The way his hands might touch me, while his lips follow their path.

I press a finger inside, then another, mimicking the way I want him to touch me, the way I imagine he would. My other hand moves to my clit, circling it with increasing pressure. My body writhes under the building sensation.

My breath quickens, as my fingers thrust faster, deeper. My hips rise to meet the rhythm, chasing the pleasure that grows more intense as time slips away, movement by movement. The tension inside me spirals higher, until I might break apart completely. I let my mind focus on only him—his mismatched eyes, his voice, his touch — allowing it to stoke the furnace inside me. Allowing it to grow hotter and impetuous with every craving.

Faster, harder, my movements grow desperate, chasing the release of my orgasm. My body trembles, as the tension winds tighter, magic sparking just beneath my skin, until it finally unleashes its power.

I let go, my body seizes, my hips lift off the bed as my gasps convert into a cry. The pleasure courses through me like an unstoppable incantation. It leaves me shaking, winded, and utterly undone, as though the universe itself conspired in my surrender.

In this moment of bliss, as the twitches of pleasure ripple through me, my mind stays focused on Adra. I see his smile, the way it curves, simple and yet so devastatingly confident, like he knows exactly the effect he has on me.

I wonder how it would feel to be in his arms right now, to have his genuine embrace wrapped around me, anchoring me as my body trembles in the aftermath of my orgasm.

Would his hands trace my skin, soothing the need still coursing through me? Would his breath tickle my neck as he murmured something affectionately tender?

This thought, this new emotion, a longing so great it's as though my heart might break from the ache of wanting him here, holding me, imbedding me in the quiet intimacy.

This moment wraps around me like a velvety haze, soft and soothing. My body melts further into the bed, as every muscle surrenders to the pull of rest as the world begins to blur at the edges. My eyes grow heavy, fluttering closed as the thought of him glissades through my mind like a prominent promise. Sleep pulls at me, gentle and unhurried, like the lull of waves drawing me toward a dream.

My mind slips effortlessly into the shadowed realm where he waits—the man in the bird mask. His presence is a constant in my dreams, haunting and enigmatic, but tonight is different. Tonight, the unfulfilled desire from my waking world seeps in, twisting this dreamscape into something darker, more visceral.

The surrounding void is oppressive, endless, a black expanse that seems to swallow all light. And then, he is there. His form looms above me, the pale mask of a bird's visage glowing faintly against the darkness. The cold gleam of his leather gloved hands meets my skin, and a shiver runs through me, not of fear but of anticipation. A current of energy courses through, as if the afterlife is calling to me.

He moves with deliberate intensity, every motion calculated, as though he knows my every hidden desire. His weight pins me down, and his cold leather presses against the bare expanse of my body. The texture is unyielding, the chill almost painful. His touch is both a punishment and a gift. And I crave more.

One gloved hand slides to my throat, firm and commanding, the pressure perfect. It's just enough to remind me that I am his to control in this moment. His other hand grips my hip as he penetrates me with agonizing intention. Every movement is purposeful, as though he's orchestrating a symphony of pleasure and pain, one that only he knows how to play.

The air, or lack thereof, is suffocating in its silence. The only sounds are my own gasps and the rhythmic echoes of his breath behind the mask. The surrounding void seems alive, pulsing with the energy of the dream, dark flashes of light erupting and fading like the heartbeat of this shadowy plane.

His every action is like a waltz along the edge of ecstasy and torment. My body responds to his touch as if it were a spell cast to control me. My hands grip at the surrounding nothingness, desperate for something to anchor me, but there is only him. This masked, faceless figure who knows me better than I know myself. And then, without warning, he stops. His grip releases, his weight lifts, and his cold absence sends panic through me. I search for him, but the void swallows his form. He fades into the abyss, leaving only the faint glow of his bird mask.

Suddenly, I'm jolted awake. My body lurches as I'm torn from the dream's grasp. My chest rises and falls rapidly, the echoes of his touch still pulsing through me as reality forces its way back in.

My eyes blink rapidly, chasing away the remnants of sleep and the haunting void I've just escaped. The room comes into focus, as the shadows of my dream fade. My eyes blink at a figure leaning over my bed, blurry at first but quickly coming into focus. It's Gia.

CONWAY TITTY

Chapter 7

Adrastus

The air within this hidden chamber is a ghostly breath thick with humidity. It carries the faint scent of aged stone and incense long since burned away. It is a secluded space beneath the church, tucked far into its bowels, far from the echoing footsteps of priests and parishioners.

The walls are constructed of uneven stone blocks, worn smooth by centuries of time. Their surfaces mottled with patches of moss and streaks of moisture. A single lantern hangs from a rusted iron hook in the corner. Its weak flame casts flickering shadows that dance along the cramped ceiling. The light barely illuminates the room, leaving much of it blanketed in darkness, a fitting sanctuary for secrets best kept hidden.

The furniture is sparse and utilitarian, as one would expect in a space not meant to be seen. A sturdy wooden

81

table occupies the center of the room, its surface scarred with knife marks, ink stains, and the scratches of tools. On it rests the components of my attire: the bird mask, its pale surface ominous in the lantern light; the wide-brimmed leather hat; and the gloves, neatly folded beside them like a surgeon's instruments awaiting use.

Shelves line the far wall, crudely built but functional, crammed with vials of dried herbs, glass jars of dark liquid, and tattered tomes with cracked leather spines. A pestle and mortar sit on one shelf, dusted with the residue of recent use. Nearby, a basin of water reflects the lantern's flame. Its surface ripples as droplets from the ceiling occasionally fall into it.

The floor is rough stone, uneven in places and scattered with small shards of broken pottery. In one corner, the faint outline of a narrow door is etched into the wall, invisible to the untrained eye. The edges blend seamlessly with the stone, concealed by clever craftsmanship and the natural shadows of the room. It is the only way in or out of this clandestine space. A hidden passage that opens with a precise push on one of the loose stones. Beyond it lies a dark, narrow corridor leading upward, winding its way to a concealed exit within the main church above. The door itself is a secret known only to me. This room is a sanctuary of shadows, its very existence an enigma. It is here that I prepare, away from prying eyes and the noise of mortal lives.

I stand before the mirror. The mask stares back at me, a sharp, haunting visage of a bird's beak, its surface cracked from time and use. It is both a shield and a statement, a deliberate construct to obscure who I am and what lies beneath. Mortals would find it unsettling, perhaps even terrifying. Good. That is the intent.

I lift the mask carefully, its leather straps soft and worn from years of use. The interior smells faintly of herbs—lavender, thyme, and rosemary—tucked into small compartments to block the stench of mortality that often accompanies my work. As I fasten it into place, the world becomes muffled, filtered through the narrow slits of the mask's eyes. It feels more natural than my own skin now, a second face that protects me from their scrutiny.

The rest of the ensemble is just as deliberate. I pull on the dark headscarf, wrapping it securely around my neck. It conceals the space between mask and body, leaving no inch of flesh exposed. The fabric is sturdy, its dark grey hue blending seamlessly into the rest of my attire.

Next comes the long leather coat, its weight reassuring as it falls over my shoulders. It is thick, protective, and devoid of ornamentation, save for the subtle stitching along the seams. The long sleeves brush against my hands as I adjust the cuffs, ensuring there are no gaps, no weaknesses. The shirt beneath is a dark, ashen grey, with its high collar and fitted design serving both form and function. It clings to my frame, an extra layer of security, while the matching trousers provide freedom of movement. Every piece has been selected with purpose—to shield, to conceal, to blend.

I reach for the gloves next, their leather preserving. The fingers fit snugly, every seam perfectly aligned.

These hands aren't meant to heal, to mend, to touch, but only a way for me to leave no evidence of who I am. They are tools, nothing more.

The boots come last, heavy and sturdy. Their soles are thick enough to withstand the uneven streets of the town and the hidden paths I walk when no one is watching. I grab the wide-brimmed hat resting on the table beside me. Its dark leather is shaped to shield both face and form. I place it carefully atop the mask, the brim tilting forward just enough to cast shadows.

I adjust the hat ever so slightly; the mirror reflects the figure I've become. The bird mask slants, its empty gaze meeting mine, revealing nothing and everything all at once. I am a paradox, a shadow cloaked in purpose. The outfit hides my identity, yes, but it also hides what they are not ready to see. Whatever they may call me, I am something more, something they cannot comprehend. The mask ensures their questions will go unanswered; their curiosity diverted by fear.

Tonight, I walk among them, blending into the revelry of their festival as easily as shadows blend into night. They will not see me for who I am, but I will see them. Every movement, every secret, every fleeting moment of their fragile lives will be mine to observe, to understand, to judge.

As I step out from the sanctuary of shadows, the sunlight strikes me like a blade, piercing through the safety of the darkened chamber I left behind. The vibrant hum of the festival reaches me even here, a cacophony of laughter, music, and voices spilling into the narrow streets. It is jarring, this juxtaposition of life's noise against the silence of what I am—and what I am here to do.

My boots echo against the cobblestones as I make my way toward the growing swell of the town square. The air is thick with the smells of roasting meat and spiced wine, an addictive inveiglement for the mortals who will feast and carouse as if tomorrow is guaranteed. They don't know the truth. None of them ever do.

As I walk, my views stray, Rosannah's image threading itself through my every musing. Her face resides like a facsimile haunting yet soothing in a way I cannot explain. This fluttering sensation, this strange emotion that claws at the edges of my reason, baffles me. It is unwelcoming and yet irrefutable.

The festival grows louder as I near the center, but my thoughts are abruptly interrupted when I collide with another figure. Instinctively, I take a step back, only to realize who stands before me. *Erevan.*

His attire mirrors mine; a long, dark coat and the familiar bird mask, but his presence is shriller, more obstinate. The pale beak tilts toward me as he falls into step at my side. "Have you discerned the purpose of our presence here?"

I shake my head; the unease I've been trying to ignore creeping further into my thoughts. "No, and I do begin to wonder if we are ever meant to know."

His silence is heavy, almost accusing, as we walk together through the crowd. The townsmen take no heed of us. Their laughter and chatter oblivious to the darkness that walks among them. The scent of life is

85

everywhere—sweat, wine, food—but beneath it, there is a sourness. There is a faint residue of something rotten that only we can sense.

"Too many of our kind gather here," Erevan says finally, his tone saddled with concern. "This is not the custom."

"Tis not." I agree.

My eyes scan the faces of the mortals as we pass, their joy and carelessness grating against the gnawing tension in my chest.

"If Master summoned this many of us in a single place, for a single contract..." I pause, my words hanging in the air like a noose. "Never is it good."

Erevan nods, his gloved fists flexing at his sides. "Mass gatherings like this, celebrations, they always reek of vulnerability. But this... this feels different."

He doesn't need to elaborate. I feel it too. There is something wrong. A heaviness presses against me despite the sun-drenched vibrancy of the festival. These mortals, laughing and dancing, have no idea how thin the veil between life and death has grown today.

"We'll know soon enough," I mutter, my words meant as much for myself as for him.

As we approach the edge of the square, the shadows of the crowd shift and ripple in ways that should not be possible, like unseen forces brushing against the light.

Erevan and I exchange a glance, though his expression is hidden behind the mask. His unease matches my own. Something is coming. And whatever it is, it will not be kind.

86

Chapter 8

Rosannah

Gia gently nudges my shoulder, her voice timid but teasing. "Ros, come on, you've slept half the day! I brought you some food."

I blink away the remnants of sleep, and groan as I stretch my arms over my head.

Gia grins at me, holding up a plate like it's a prize. "Two eggs, an apple and mozzarella, and a little piece of bread. Buon appetito!" She jokes, wiggling the plate for emphasis.

"You're a saint." I mumble, still half-asleep, as I sit up in bed and let out a long yawn. The words barely make it out coherently, but Gia laughs anyway, clearly pleased with herself.

"I figured since you didn't stop by this morning that you probably had a long night at work." She continues, setting the plate down on my lap.

"So, as your dearest companion, I thought I'd save you from starvation. You're welcome."

I stare at her with as much gratitude as my tired face can muster. "You're too good to me." I pick up the fork and dive into the food. The flavors hit immediately, simple but so satisfying.

I finish off the last bite and set the plate aside. "Grazie, really. You outshine them all." She waves it off, but her cheeks give way to a blush.

Her eyes widen with an almost manic glee, and she practically bounces as she exclaims, "Do you even *remember* what today is?"

I groan, dragging a palm over my face, still trying to shake off the fog of exhaustion. "Uh... Does it grant me the boon of more slumber?" I mumble.

Honestly, after last night's chaos and the restless sex dream that left me in a lustful state, sleep is the only thing I can think about.

"*Ros!*" She huffs, somewhere between scandalized and amused. "How could you possibly forget? Today is *Sagra Delle Castagne!*" Her tone is both jubilant and teeming with disbelief, as if I'd just forgotten my own name.

I blink slowly at her, trying to process the words. "Wait... the chestnut festival? The one where people fight over roasted nuts and drink themselves silly on mulled wine?"

"Aye!" She practically shouts, throwing her arms in the air like she's heralding the arrival of a god. "The *Chestnut Festival!* Ros, it's the best day of the year!

Pastries, *wine,* and—oh my gods—don't forget *the parade!*"

Her energy is infectious, and I can't help but chuckle despite my fatigue. "Very well, very well," I say, holding my hands up in mock surrender. "Mi dispiace![16] I forgot the sacred nut day. Please, I beg of thee, forgive my offense, oh wise festival queen."

She narrows her eyes playfully. "Thou are forgiven... but only for that I shall drag you from the bed and haul you there myself. You have no say in it. Now rise!"

Gia practically skips over to the corner of the room, her enthusiasm spilling over like an overfilled goblet. "Wait until you see what I've been working on!" She calls over her shoulder.

Gia holds up two elaborate costumes. The sunlight streaming through the small window catches on the rich fabrics, making them shine like something out of a noblewoman's wardrobe.

My jaw drops as I step closer to examine the artful details. "Gia... these are *incredible!*"

"I know!" She replies, her face alight with pride.

She holds up the first gown, an opulent crimson dress made of wool with velvet accents. The fitted bodice is adorned with gold embroidery in swirling patterns that remind me of vines climbing a trellis. The sleeves are long and flowing, ending in elegant points, and the neckline is modest yet beautifully framed with a row of tiny pearls.

---

[16] Italian for "I am sorry"

"This one's for me!" She says, practically thrusting it into my arms. "Do you have any idea how long it took to tame that gold thread? And as for those pearls, a true torment!"

"You have truly outdone yourself..."

"Wait, you haven't even seen yours yet!" Gia exclaims, spinning around to grab the second gown.

She holds it up triumphantly, and my breath is taken. The dress is a stunning forest-green, reminiscent of the lush, rolling hills outside town after a spring rain. The fabric, a light but sturdy linen, flows effortlessly as she holds it. The light catches the golden embroidery making it shimmer like sunlight through leaves.

The neckline is adorned with finely wrought floral patterns. Tiny golden roses surrounded by delicate vines that seem to climb naturally along the edge. The long sleeves are laced with narrow gold ribbons. Each cuff mirrors the neckline, but with clusters of tiny blooms, some in golden thread and others in a subtle sage green. It gives the illusion of a garden blooming on the wrists. The dress also has a fitted bodice, but Gia has added a charming touch; larger blooms near the top that taper into delicate, scattered petals as they reach the waist.

"Oh, and look!" She says, rotating the dress to reveal the back. There, between the shoulder blades, is an elegant, embroidered sparrow. Its wings outstretched as if in flight. Its feathers are picked out in polished golds and greens.

"Does it please your soul?" She eagerly awaits my response.

"Truly, wondrous! It's like wearing an enchanted garden. It's perfect." I say with a grin. "The sparrow is such a beautiful touch."

"Isn't it? I had to redo it *twice* because the first one turned out more like a chicken," she says with a laugh, shaking her head, "but it was worth it. Now hurry up and put it on, I don't want to miss the parade!"

Gia claps her hands together, bouncing with excitement as she hands the green gown to me. I hold up the dress, and admire the details, knowing that it is heavy with the tonnage of her effort and care. I am in awe once again at her craftmanship and even more at her creative process.

I pull the dress over my head, the fabric sliding into place. The fitted bodice hugs my torso perfectly, and the weight of the flowing skirt is surprisingly comfortable. The long, pointed sleeves drape elegantly, brushing against my fingers as I fasten the ties at the back.

Standing in front of my mirror I love what I see. I am beautiful. However, a part of me thinks this may be too extravagant for a simple festival, but Gia's wide grin as she stares at me tells me this is exactly what she intended.

"Gia you can't be serious, is this some jest? It fits perfectly; it is beyond belief!" I say as I twirl in the mirror.

She spins around, halfway through tying the pearl embossed ribbons at her waist. She is in awe as she takes me in. "Ros, you look like you just stepped out of a ballad. Nay, an *epic* tale of valor and sweet romance! I think I've set a new standard for myself."

"Of course, most assuredly!" I reply with a wink.

Gia finishes tying her ribbons and adjusts the cuffs of her gown. She steps back, striking a dramatic pose with her hands on her hips. "And what about me? Does this scream 'Queen of the Sagra Delle Castagne' or what?"

I take in all her essence. She is radiant, like she belongs in a meadow under a canopy of trees, dancing in the dappled sunlight. "It beckons *Goddess of the Chestnut Festival!*" I say, grinning. "You're beautiful."

"Well, *obviously*," she says, throwing her hair over her shoulder with exaggerated flair.

We laugh as we help each other with the finishing touches, tying a loose ribbon here, adjusting an embroidered cuff there. Once the tedious task is finally done, I make my way over to the bed, grabbing the pillows and tossing them onto the floor.

I settle down on top of the makeshift cushion pile, crossing my legs comfortably, and wave Gia over. I lean back against the edge of the bed, clutching a pillow to my chest, feeling my cheeks heat up as the memory of last night plays again in my mind.

Gia sits cross-legged on the floor, a half-eaten fig tart in one hand, her other gesturing for me to hurry up and talk. "Come now, Rosannah," she says, "you've been smiling like a lovesick maid all morning, and I know that face well. Out with it... what happened last night, and who is he?"

I groan, burying my face into the pillow to stifle the laugh bubbling in my throat. "I don't even know where to begin," I mumble, my voice muffled by the fabric.

Gia tosses the tart onto a small wooden plate nearby, leaning forward with the air of one who could pry secrets from the very heavens. "Begin with the first of it," she says, "and tell me this... was he handsome, or is this another of those 'his soul is beautiful' that you're so fond of?"

I lift my head, tossing the pillow aside with a dramatic sigh. "Oh, Gia, he's not just handsome. He's... glorious.... grand.... irresistible!"

I sit up straighter, letting the words flow like poetry. "He's tall. Taller than most men I've seen. His shoulders are so broad he could probably block out the sun. And his hair, dark as freshly plowed earth, untamed in a way, as though he's too noble to fuss over it."

Gia's grin grows sly. "And his face? Or are we swooning over his shoulders and hair alone?"

I laugh, brushing a strand of hair behind my ear. "His face... eternal cosmos above, his face... absolutely divine! He has eyes that could stop your heart. One is the color of ice, and the other like honey. And when he stares at you, it's impossible to breathe."

Gia lets out a theatrical gasp, fanning herself. "Saints above, where did you find this man?"

I blush furiously, my laughter spilling over my words. "Oh, stop! I met him at the tavern last night. He said he's here for work, but... there's something about him. He's so confident, but not in an arrogant way. There's this... I don't know, *darkness* about him, it's... it's compelling."

Gia tilts her head, her lips curling into a mischievous smile. "Dark, brooding, *and* mysterious? Ros, you're ensnared already."

"I am not!" I protest, though the heat in my cheeks surely betrays me. "He's simply... intriguing. And perhaps a little too attractive for his own good."

"Too attractive?" Gia repeats. "And what's your plan, pray tell? Will you see him again?"

"I don't even know," I admit, worry covers my bottom lip, "but if I do..."

"You'd best not let him slip away," Gia interrupts teasingly. "If he's half as captivating as you claim, some other maiden will snatch him up faster than a free flagon of ale at market day!"

I burst into laughter, grabbing the pillow and hurling it at her. She catches the pillow easily, laughing along with me.

"I'm only speaking the truth, dear friend. But mark my words... find him again. A man like that doesn't wander into every tavern. If he's truly all you've said, he may just be the adventure your spirit has been waiting for."

Even as the laughter fades, Gia's words stay in my mind, and a spark of hope takes root. If fate will it, I will see Adra again. And this time, I wouldn't let him remain a mystery.

As we rise from our makeshift pillow seats, ready to head for the door, Gia lets out a gasp so loud and dramatic that I nearly jump out of my skin.

"What? What happened?" I spin around, suddenly on alert.

She grabs my arm, her face a mix of panic and determination. "We forgot the *hairpieces!* How could I forget the most important part?!"

I blink at her, confused. "Hairpieces? Gia, the dresses are more than enough."

"No, no, no, no," she mutters, darting back toward the table and rummaging through a small basket I hadn't noticed before. She pulls out two delicate floral wreaths, each adorned with small silk flowers in shades of gold, crimson, and green to match our gowns. Tiny ribbons dangle from the back. "These! They *complete* the outfits," she insists, holding them up triumphantly.

She adjusts the wreath until it sits perfectly in place, the ribbons brushing against my back. "There. Now you are a queen *and* a woodland nymph." She quickly slips the second wreath onto her own head, the crimson and pearl accents complementing her gown perfectly. "And I... well I am like your fabulous fairy companion."

I grin at her, giving a mock curtsey. "Well, then, my fabulous fairy companion, shall we?"

The town comes into view as we crest the hill, and it's like stepping into a dream. Banners in brilliant reds, greens, and golds stretch across the streets, fluttering in the gentle breeze. The streets are lined with garlands of ivy and flowers, their fresh scent fusing with the tantalizing aromas of roasted meats, baked pastries, and spiced wine. There's color, sound, and life everywhere.

The festival is in full swing. The streets are thronging with people dressed in their finest, some in plain linen tunics, others in lavish gowns and cloaks that rival even ours. Merchants have set up wooden stalls draped with vibrant fabrics. Their wares spill out in a dazzling array. One table is piled high with hand-sewn shoes, another with leather bags tooled with carefully crafted designs.

A nearby merchant holds up an iridescent bolt of silk, the sunlight catching the fabric as he gestures animatedly to a group of curious onlookers.

"Even from here I can already taste the feast!" Gia says, her voice dying of hunger, as she grips my arm, practically dragging me forward.

Vendors call out to the crowd, their voices weaving together in a cacophony of tempting offers.

"Fresh bread!" One cries, holding up a golden loaf.

"Fine jewelry from Florence, perfect for a lady of your grace!" Another says, winking at Gia as we pass.

Weaving our way through the crowd, the joyous hum of the festival envelopes us. Musicians are stationed at every corner. Some are playing lively tunes on lutes and flutes, others bang out energetic rhythms on drums. A group of children frolic in a circle, their laughter ringing out above the music.

Further down, a juggler tosses flaming torches into the air, drawing gasps and cheers from the gathering crowd.

"Ros! Over there!" Gia exclaims, pointing to a stall surrounded by the delicious scent of sizzling meat. A vendor is cooking skewers over an open flame. The juices drip onto the coals and send up wisps of mouthwatering smoke.

We hurry over, our dresses swishing around our ankles as we dodge through the crowd. The vendor, a brawny man with a jovial smile and a streak of soot across his cheek, greets us kindly. "Ah, two lovely ladies seeking a bite? You've come to the right place. These are the finest kebabs in all the kingdom!"

Gia doesn't hesitate. "We'll take two each," she says, giving over a few coins before I can protest.

The vendor wraps the skewers in small cloths to keep our hands clean. The moment I take a bite, I'm in The High Realm above, where angels sing and righteous rests. I don't believe in it, but this bite takes me there. The meat is tender and perfectly seasoned, a smokey flavor with just a hint of garlic.

Gia moans dramatically, clutching her chest as she takes her first bite. "I'm never eating anything else again. This is it. This is the pinnacle of food."

I laugh, my mouth too full to respond. We stand there in the middle of the bustling street, stuffing our faces like we haven't eaten in days.

"Aye," Gia states between bites. "We're finding the mulled wine next. Meat and wine, this is the manner life ought to be savored, no finer way to pass our days."

I grin at her, wiping my mouth with the edge of the cloth. "Agreed, we're of one mind. But once that's done, I will not rest 'til I've devoured one of those plum tarts. Did you see them? I shall perish if I do not get to indulge in the deliciously laden pastry!"

"Approved!" Gia says, holding out her skewer like a toast. "To feasts, festivals, and being the grandest maidens here!"

"Cin, Cin!" I reply, tapping my skewer against hers.

The sounds of music, laughter, and sizzling food fill the air around us as we marry back into our environment. I take another bite of the delicious, smokey meat, savoring the way it melts on my tongue, but my attention falters. Something, *or someone,* across the bustling square catches my eye. My hand freezes mid-air as a sudden chill seizes my very bones.

It can't be...

No way....

There, just beyond the crowd, stands the figure that's been haunting my dreams, the man in the bird mask. Unlike the foggy specter from my restless nights, he appears solid, *real.* Too real. My pulse quickens as I try to make sense of what I'm seeing. My heart thumps in my ears.

The mask is the same, an elegant yet eerie visage of a bird's face, pale, and striking against the chaos of the festival. His dark vestments fall in sharp lines over his body. His posture radiates an otherworldly calm that makes him stand out amidst the jovial crowd. I can't break my gape. My eyes roam over him, searching for something...anything...that might explain this impossibility. Then I notice his hands.

The gloves.

My stomach drops, and the skewer nearly slips from my fingers. I know those gloves. The smooth leather, the precise stitching, the faint scuff marks on the fingers. They're seared into my memory, both from the realms of man and my slumbers' whispers. The realization rings through me like a strike of divine wrath. It leaves my breath caught in my throat and my knees threatening to give way.

I grip the edge of the vendor's stall; my mind caught in a whirlpool.

"Ros? Are you okay?" Gia's voice scratches through the haze, concerned but distant, like she's speaking from another realm.

I can't answer. My focus is locked on him. He stands there, still as a statue, but I can identify his stare through the mask. The festival swirls around us, vendors shouting, children laughing, music playing, but it all fades into the background. It's just him and me now, as though the rest of the world has been muted.

He tilts his head, the subtle movement somehow sharper, more deliberate. It's a gesture that is both familiar and utterly uncharted. My spirit, torn between fear, fascination, and something far more untamed.

"By the universe's wounds," I whisper, barely clear over the din of the festival. "It's Adra."

CONWAY TITTY

Chapter 9

Adrastus

Humans and their festivals, a spectacle of excess and futility. I stand at the edges of the crowd, cloaked and unnoticed, watching the chaotic rhythm of their celebrations. How peculiar that they gather to revel in their fleeting existence, clinging to every fragile thread of joy before it inevitably unravels.

Their laughter echoes through the narrow streets, blending with the discordant music of lutes and tambourines. Merchants shout over one another, hawking wares that hold no meaning beyond this moment. Trinkets, baubles, bolts of silk, things they do not need but purchase with feverish delight as if ownership might anchor them to something eternal. It won't. Their lives will end, and these things will remain behind, passed to another pair of mortal hands, and then another, in an endless, pointless cycle.

I shift my gaze to a food vendor, the surrounding air thick with the scent of roasted meat and spiced wine. Mortals huddle there, clutching greasy skewers and earthen mugs, devouring their feast as though it might stave off the inevitable. How amusing, this obsession with consumption, this feasting on borrowed time. Do they not see the irony in it? Their bodies will one day feed the earth, just as they feed now on the spoils of its soil.

A child darts past me, laughing, clutching a crude wooden toy. A cheap, poorly carved thing that will splinter and break before the day is done. Yet the joy on his face is unmatched, pure and untainted by the weight of mortality. I wonder what it must be like to feel so alive, so unburdened by the knowledge of an inevitable end.

Further down the street, a group of young, betrothed pairs, gambol in a clearing. Their movements clumsy and earnest. Their arms entwine, their laughter flowing with the music as though they have forgotten everything but this moment. Perhaps that is the secret to their celebration, *forgetting*. Ignorance of the cruel hands of time that creep ever forward. Mortals live as if each festival might be their last because, for some of them, it will be.

I study their faces, these creatures of flesh and folly, trying to understand what drives them. Why cling so desperately to a joy that is so fleeting, so fragile? Do they truly believe these moments of celebration are enough to outweigh the pain, the struggle, the inevitable decay? But perhaps that is their strength.

In the face of an indifferent universe, they choose to laugh, to dance, to live. It is both admirable and pathetic. I, of course, am the wrong entity to comprehend such desires. My existence stretches far beyond theirs, a span of time too vast for their comprehension. Yet here I stand, an outsider cloaked in shadows, blending into their crowd, observing their peculiar need to squeeze meaning from the meaningless.

I weave through the herd, my dark attire drawing no more attention than a merchant's apron or a farmer's boots. To these mortals, I am simply another figure among the masses. My uniform is indistinguishable from any other worker's garb.

The mask, with its pale beak and hollow eyes, elicits a few curious glances, but nothing persists. They see only the surface, a tradesman or perhaps it's just a costume. And I am content to let their imaginations fill in the gaps. They don't question what they don't understand, not when life's pleasures beckon so loudly.

But then, my steps falter...

There, just beyond the throng, is a figure so striking, so achingly familiar, that the festival seems to blur around her.

Rosannah.

Her presence draws me in like a beacon, and for a moment, I forget my purpose. Her gown, a lush forest-green adorned with glorious golden embroidery, glimmers in the fading sunlight. She moves with purpose; her eyes are focused on me. Her face is full of confusion and curiosity.

"Adra?" She calls, her voice cutting through the noise, unsure but filled with recognition.

My heart, if that is what this strange sensation can be called, stirs, fluttering in a way that leaves me unmoored. It's a feeling I cannot name, one I should not be capable of, but it touches me, nonetheless. I force myself to remain still as she approaches, her rapid steps making the details of her face sharper with every inch.

"Rosannah." I greet cordially, inclining my head just slightly. My voice is stable despite the unfamiliar tumult within me.

Her gaze darts across me in amazement. "I thought it might be you," she says, her words spilling out quickly. "I recognized your gloves..."

I glance at my gloves and nod, acknowledging her observation.

Her confusion gives way to a bright smile as her eyes sweep over the rest of my attire. "But this... this costume! It's wondrous, Adra. You are like a figure from some forgotten fable, straight from a stage."

My lips twitch beneath the mask. "Tis not a simple guise." I admit. "It's a necessity of my duties. My master has... specific desires."

Her laughter rings out, happy and genuine. "Your lord sounds like quite the figure. Does he seek to fright or to inspire?"

"Both in equal share." I reply, tilting my head thoughtfully. "They do have a flair for the dramatic, but

I've learned not to question their decisions. They always have their reasons."

Rosannah's eyes inspect my mask, her curiosity undimmed. I know I must tread carefully. My answers must balance to keep my truth hidden. She cannot know what I am, or why I am here.

But as I speak, my gaze travels shamelessly over her, taking in every curve the gown struggles to contain. The fabric clings to her waist, accentuating the gentle flare of her hips, but my eyes are drawn upward, irresistibly, to the way the gown's neckline cradles her very full breasts. They seem to strain against the delicate fabric, as if begging for touch, for release. The thought stirs something tenacious within me.

My palms ache with the desire to cup their softness, to worship them as reverently as the embroidered golden flowers that frame them so perfectly. My mind drifts further, imagining the press of my lips against her skin, the taste of her, the way she might respond under my touch. Each breath she takes, the gentle rise and fall of her chest, squishes them together. A motion so mesmerizing it borders on hypnotic.

The way the fabric barely contains her, leaves little to the imagination, and my thoughts wander where they shouldn't. I imagine the gown slipping from her shoulders, baring the sweet, supple skin beneath, her curves fully exposed to me. This need stirring within me is maddening, foreign, and yet I find myself sinking further into it, helpless to resist.

She cannot see my eyes, cannot know the heat of my gaze or the way I'm stripping her bare in my mind.

The mask shields me, my silent accomplice in this wicked indulgence. And thanks to the shadow's grace for it, if she could see the desire simmering in my expression, she might never look at me the same again.

Rosannah's sweet, sing-song voice cuts through my darker musings, yanking me from the thoughts I shouldn't be having. "Wait right here!" She chirps, as she spins on her heel and hurries off into the crowd. I am left standing there, wondering what in the abyss she's up to.

Moments later, she returns, towing another figure behind her, a tallish woman with short brown wavy curls that splay wildly above her shoulders. Her big brown doll eyes flick to me with open curiosity, and a puckish smirk tugs at her lips. She's dressed in a gown of velvet crimson hues, with a corseted waist and pearl details.

"This is Gia." Rosannah announces, her tone brimming with pride as she beams at her friend. "My dearest companion."

I incline my head politely toward the spirited woman. "Gia." I say, keeping my tone measured, though polite enough to convey respect.

Before I can say more, Rosannah nudges Gia, her smirk taking on an almost conspiratorial edge. "This is the man I was telling you about!"

My brow arches beneath my mask. I shift my eyes to Rosannah, who suddenly finds an unusual amount of interest in adjusting the sleeves of her gown. A slow smile pulls at my lips as I decide to seize the moment.

"You've already spoken of me to your closest friend? I must have left quite the impression."

Rosannah's cheeks flush the most delightful shade of pink, and she stammers, "Well...uh..." clearly caught off guard. Gia lets out a sharp laugh, crossing her arms as her gaze flits between us.

"Oh, you did indeed. She's scarcely stopped talking about you. It is most entertaining."

Rosannah's blush deepens as she swats Gia lightly on the arm. "Don't make it sound so dramatic!"

"I don't know," I say leaning in, my voice dropping just enough to tease. "I think I'd like to hear more of this... 'entertaining' account."

Rosannah groans, burying her face in her palms before daring to peek at me between her fingers. "You're impossible." She mutters, though that smile betrays her.

"And you're utterly charming when flustered." The sight of her reaction is proving far more delightful than I care to admit.

Gia, clearly amused, studies us with a grin. She clasps her hands together, as she glances toward a nearby vendor. "I'll leave you two for a moment," she announces, "That stall has the most gorgeous ribbons. I must see if they've got anything to match my gown."

Before either of us can protest, she's off, her chocolate curls bouncing as she weaves through the crowd. The sudden silence between Rosannah and I is heavier than the lively noise of the festival around us.

She shifts, brushing a strand of hair behind her ear, and then offers me an uncertain, yet utterly disarming smile. "Well..." she says lightly, glancing at the bustling stalls around us, "shall we walk? No sense in just standing here waiting."

"By all means." I reply, gesturing for her to continue.

The crowd parts for her almost instinctively, and I follow, grateful for the chance to speak with her uninterrupted. We stroll through the winding streets, the hum of the festival surrounding us.

Rosannah motions toward a vendor selling colorful glass trinkets, the sunset making them glitter like jewels. "Look at those. Aren't they lovely? Though I can't imagine they're terribly practical."

"Practicality isn't always the goal." I say, my eyes fixed more on her than the trinkets. "Sometimes beauty is reason enough."

She glances at me before quickly redirecting her focus. "Aye, I suppose. Still, I'd likely drop one the moment I brought it home."

As we continue, she points out another stall where a merchant is loudly advertising carved wooden figurines.

"Those are skillfully wrought. My father used to make things like that when I was little. Not for selling, though, just for fun. He made me a whole set of tiny animals once. They were perfect, even if the legs were a little uneven." The tenderness in her voice fades, and I notice the sadness in her expression.

"Did he teach you, his craft?" I ask gently.

She shakes her head; her simper drops bittersweet. "No. He died in the war when I was still a babe. I never

108

got the chance to learn from him. I don't have his skill. I'm hopeless with tools. Gia's the one with the clever techniques. She's made dresses, hats, even shoes once. I'm better at... well, talking, I suppose."

She huffs a small laugh, as we approach a stall piled high with pastries. "Oh, wow!" She says, her pitch brightening. "They smell lovely."

"They do." I say, though my attention remains on her. "But I'm still certain the company I have is sweeter."

Her cheeks flush a precious rose color, and her steps falter again as she stammers, "You're terrible!"

"Terrible? I'd argue I'm simply attentive."

I fall back into step beside her, a small smile plays on my lips as she fills the silence with light conversation about the vendors. She talks quickly, nervously, her hands occasionally gesture as if to distract herself from the tension between us.

And though I don't press further, I savor every moment of her flustered state. The way her abashed blush stays, the way her voice wavers when she risks glancing at me. It's a tension I don't entirely understand, but I know one thing for certain, *I don't want it to end.*

The sun has disappeared and the distant sounds of the festival fade as we step onto the weathered planks of the boardwalk. The ocean stretches out before us, an endless, inky expanse. Its surface shimmers faintly under the silver glow of the moon. The air carries a touch of salt and mystery, marrying with the faint remnants of spices and smoke from the festivities.

Above us, the stars blaze with an otherworldly brilliance, strewn across the velvet expanse of the heavens like fragments of a shattered diamond. Each piece catching the light of eternity and casting it back in a silent, eternal dance.

Rosannah stops by the railing, tilting her face to the sky, as her eyes reflect the celestial light. For a moment, she is still, her silhouette framed against the backdrop of the restless sea and infinite stars.

"The stars are breathtaking tonight," she says carrying a reverence that echoes in the stillness. "It's as if they've gathered just for us."

I glance upward briefly, but my gaze inevitably returns to her. The moonlight catches in her hair, casting her features in a gentle glow that makes her seem almost candescent.

"Not as ethereal as you." I murmur, my words hardly perceptible above the lapping of the waves.

She veers to me, her lips revealing a smile, accompanied by the faint dimples in her cheeks. "You've a poet's tongue, Adra." She says, her tone playful, though the blush on her cheeks betrays her.

"Merely an observer of beauty." I lean against the railing.

She laughs, a lilting sound that joins the rhythm of the waves. Her gaze returns to the dark glittery realm above. "Do you ever wonder what's beyond all this?"

She gestures toward the stars. "The sky, the ocean, it so vast, like there's more to it than we could ever imagine."

Her words touch something hidden within me. "Most don't often speak of such things," I say, "Most seem content to focus on the fleeting moments before them."

"Aye, I have never quite fit amongst the common sorts." She says with a small shrug. "I do not find myself drawn to the sermons of the church or its strict doctrines. I would not call myself devout, but perhaps... spiritual, in a way. Does that make sense?"

She intrigues me, fostering a complexity that few mortals possess. "It's uncommon," I reply, "but perhaps that's what makes it interesting."

She rests her elbows on the railing, staring out at the vast expanse of water. The faint breeze plays with her hair, and for a moment, the world holds its breath.

"I wonder about it often. What fate awaits us when we depart from this realm?" Her voice is serene yet filled with something profoundly vulnerable.

Rosannah's fingers draw absent patterns on the railing, as her thoughts seem to take her far away. "Do we simply... vanish? Is there nothing but silence and darkness?" She pauses, her head dipping for a moment before lifting back to the shimmering water. "Or is there something waiting for us? Something beyond what we can see or imagine?"

Her voice relaxes, and a shiver seems to run through her, though whether it's from the breeze or her own musings, I cannot tell. "Do our souls wander, becoming something new? Or do they remain... unchanged, eternal, or perhaps simply... end?"

The candor in her voice is unsettling and yet a strange welcome. "Does the thought frighten you?" I ask, "Death?"

She tilts her head, her expression contemplative. "No," she says after a moment. "Not frightened. Curious, maybe. I wonder what it feels like, what becomes of us. Is it like falling asleep, or something entirely beyond comprehension? I suppose I've always thought of it as a transition rather than an end."

Her answers strike me like an arrow, threading through centuries of experience. Mortals fear death with every fiber of their being; it's the one truth that unites them all. Yet here she is, speaking of it as if it were a companion to be embraced rather than a shadow to be avoided.

"You see it as a journey." I say, more to myself than to her. "A step into the unknown, rather than the fiery hellscape or heavenly light most imagine."

She nods, her stare meeting mine before returning to the stars. "We all end up there, don't we?" She says innocently. "Pretending it's not coming... that seems like the real tragedy. Why not wonder about it? Why not embrace the mystery?"

Her contemplations settle between us, expansive and luminous, much like the stars above. For centuries, I have walked among mortals, watching them cling desperately to life, denying the inevitable, fearing the end with every step. Yet here stands Rosannah, her voice steady, her spirit calm, treating the unknown with reverence rather than dread. And for the first time in eternity, I feel a connection—not the deserted one I forged through duty, but something greater, something I cannot name.

She speaks of what I embody without realizing it, weaving wonder into the fabric of mortality. As the stars continue their silent vigil above us, I can't help but marvel at how, she, a fleeting spark in this endless world, makes the vast unknown seem... *beautiful.*

My eyes drift from the horizon to Rosannah. Her delicate features illuminated by the silver glow of the night. She focuses out at the sea, lost in thought.

"I was hoping to see you again tonight." I say quietly, my voice breaking the silence but not the calm.

Her head turns towards me. Her expression is inquisitive yet sincere.

"I'm starting to enjoy your company more than I anticipated." I continue.

Her lips loosen into a smirk, subtle and genuine at first, then extend into a breathtaking smile, as a sunny chuckle escapes her. "I'm enjoying yours too... And, if I'm being truthful... I couldn't stop thinking about you."

She catches me off guard, sending a strange, unknown affection coursing through me. Before I can retort, she reaches out, and her hand finds mine. Her touch is soothing. My gaze shifts to her fingers resting against mine, a simple act that feels far greater than it should.

We face each other fully, the ocean and stars forgotten as our eyes meet. The world seems to slow, the consistent rhythm of her breath syncs with my own.

The space between us charged with something I refuse to break. Her cheeks flush, and I realize I am holding my breath, waiting for her next words.

"The hour grows late..." Her voice is a near-whisper that carries all the courage she can muster. Her eyes search mine for something, before continuing. "The mirth of the festival seems to have run its course... Might I trouble you to see me safely to my home?"

The bravery in her words ignites something hidden within me, an exhilarating, maddening fire that surges through me. The way she stares at me, unguarded and full of quiet longing, leaves me utterly captivated.

I take her hand. "It would be my pleasure."

Her smile is radiant, but a knowing glimmer sparks in her eyes, a new passion blooming. A hint of something bolder, something that matches the wild pulse of my own emotions.

Her palm remains in mine, as we walk the path leading back to the center of the town. Her fingers are delicate but firm as her warmth seeps into me like sunlight breaking through the coldest shadow. I tighten my grip, unable to resist the pull of her touch, and she glances at me with a shy, fleeting twinkle that sends my resolve spiraling.

The air, thick with the tension between us, remains as we walk, fraught with an unspoken desire that grows with each step. The mild rustle of her gown, the gentle sway of her hair in the moonlight, and the light brush of her thumb against my gloved hand are all maddeningly potent.

This moment isn't just about the festival, the stars, or even the quiet streets we tread upon. It's her. The way her presence fills the spaces I didn't realize were empty. The way every glance, every touch, makes the world around us blur until there's only her.

The festival may have fallen quiet, but this irresistible connection might be the start of something entirely new. Something infinitely more dangerous and undeniably invigorating. And as the town center draws closer, I can't shake the growing, inescapable thought: *I don't want this night to end.*

CONWAY TITTY

Chapter 10

Rosannah

A s the festival concludes, the lanterns flicker and dull, their light fading into the darkness like the final notes of a song.

While merchants quickly pack, their excited chatter is replaced by the rustling of fabrics and the thud of boxes as they call out their farewells Adra's velvety voice breaks the quiet hum of the evening, "Should we find Gia? Where did she wander off to?"

I let out a giggle, shaking my head. "Fear not, for Gia lies far from my worry. She's probably down by the quay testing the structural integrity of a sailor's lips." I pause to wink at Adra. "She has a gift for drawing wayfaring souls, the sort who've spent long months at sea and crave diversion more than bread. The kind eager for earthly comforts."

Adra tilts his head, the eerie beak of his mask catching the moonlight. "Does she, now?" He says, the tenor of his voice hinting at a smile I can't see.

"Verily, without a doubt!" I reply, grinning as I picture her antics. "Gia dreams of distant shores and bustling cities. Like a moth to flame, she is drawn to any soul who bears a tale worth telling or a whisper of mystery upon their brow."

Adra lets out an amusing chuckle.

"She might seem timid and quiet most of the time," I continue, "but give her a goblet of wine, a plate of roasted duck, and even mention anything about art. Suddenly, she's the loudest soul in the chamber. She'll prattle on about brushstrokes and symmetry til your ears ache and you beg for mercy."

I let out a sigh of admiration. "Truly good for her. She has earned her share of merriment. Let her weave her enchantments upon the sailors and live her days to the fullest."

Adra snickers. "She sounds like a woman of great intrigue." He says, but his gaze remains on me. His attention makes my pulse hasten.

I nod, but the conversation drifts away as we continue our walk toward my dwelling. The streets are quieter now. The post glow of the festival fades into the distance, leaving only the rustle of the night air and the faint sound of our steps on the stones beneath.

My hand rests on Adra's arm, while my fingers brush the thick fabric of his coat. Even through the layers, I can touch the solid strength beneath. Every inch of muscle taut and brimming with power.

My fingers tighten instinctively, and my breath hitches as the realization of his sheer physicality sinks in. His bicep shifts beneath my touch, a subtle flex as he adjusts his stride to match mine, and the nuanced movement sends a rush of heat pooling through me.

My mind betrays me, imagining being swept into those arms, held close against his chest. My frame fitting effortlessly into his overwhelming physique. That alone makes my heart pound wildly with a desire I cannot quell.

The thought brings a flush to my cheeks, and I steal a glance at him from the corner of my eye. He towers over me, his broad shoulders and formidable frame emitting a mighty figure even in this dim light. I am incredibly short next to him. But concurrently being at his side, I feel safe in a way I've never known. It's as if the world itself could crumble and he would still stand firm. His power isn't just in the solid frame of his body; it radiates from him. An incontestable confidence that promises nothing could touch me while I'm near him.

I swallow hard, my thoughts spiral as my fingers grip onto his arm. It's impossible to imagine how those muscles would feel under my bare touch. My thighs send more signals of need; my clit begins to pulse gently. Eager to have him touch me, touch me anywhere. I bite my lip, desperately trying to hold back my desires and focus on the pathway ahead.

The silence between us is full of vim and vigor. Every step brings me closer to a moment I can only dream of. My thoughts betray me once more. I ponder, what it would be like if he turned to me now, his hands sliding to my waist, his lips brushing against mine, claiming me in a way that would steal every coherent thought. I force myself to shake the lustful fantasy away, though my heart pounds harder in my chest. As much as I try to collect myself, the tension between us is ungovernable, and I can't help but wonder if he feels it too.

The stroll back to my abode has gone by far too quickly, and a small pang of disappointment stirs in my chest. I don't want the night to end. I don't want to let go of this strange, enthralling energy between us. As we reach my steps, I steal a glance at Adra, the pearlescent beak of his mask catching the moonlight as he shifts his gaze from the building back to me.

My thoughts stray, slipping into dangerous territory once again. I imagine that mask hovering over me. The cool leather grazing my skin as he holds me firmly, while his strength presses me into a heady surrender. The feeling of his bulging cock rubbing up against my body, knowing how badly he wants me, how badly he *needs* me.

It is impossible to hide the soaked desire forming between my thighs. My chest tightens and my body starts to tingle as these unrestrained fantasies start to tug at the corners of my sanity.

"Rosannah." His voice halts my feral cravings in an instant, sending a jolt that thumps along my nerves. My attention scurries back to him, and I realize I've been caught staring. My cheeks are on fire, and there's no hiding it.

His head slopes, the motion deliberate, almost as though he's trying to read me. And in that stable nature, he asks, "Are you alright?"

A laugh escapes me, and I let myself lean into the moment, my voice taking on a daring edge. "Oh, I'm more than alright." I say, meeting his stare, or at least where I imagine his eyes are behind the mask.

Standing in front of my steps, the world around us dissolves into nothingness. The tension between now beset with a carnal need and desires deemed unholy. The quickening rhythm of my breath drowns out the sounds, each inhale syncing with my heart's relentless pounding. My mind is daring me... no, *begging* me, to say what has been simmering in the depths all evening.

The pressure crackles in the silence, begging to be broken. My fingers brush the edge of my gown as I step closer. "Would you like to come inside... for a cup of tea?" The words come out a shy whisper, but I know he hears the intent in every syllable.

A moment of stillness descends as I eagerly await his reaction. His expression is hidden behind the menacing mask, but the subtle change in his stance speaks volumes. I can sense the excitement emanating from him in waves. It is barely contained by the slight flexing of a fist at his side.

With a final burst of restraint, he finally speaks, his voice balancing on this dangerous edge. "I would be delighted."

His answer falls over me, sending another surge of tingles that expel through my body like stars exploding, blinding, and all-consuming.

CONWAY TITTY

Chapter 11

Rosannah

The brief walk to my front door seems so ideal, it must be a figment of my imagination. The closer we get, the more the tension blisters.

As we reach the wooden steps leading up to my modest quarters, the door looms ahead. I ascend the steps, fumbling with the iron key, as the wood moans and creaks beneath us. His tall, broad frame casts a shadow on the entrance. The key turns with a *click*, and I push the door open, stepping inside and gesturing for him to follow.

As soon as he crosses the threshold, I hurry to the hearth, gathering wood and kindling to coax some flames to life. My small chamber is dimly lit by the moon peeking through my window. The faint scent of roses and lilies fills the air.

I kneel by the hearth, striking flint to spark the fire. It catches quickly, as the flames cast a golden glow that stretches across the rough walls. The heat spreads quickly, and I sit back on my heels, catching a glance at Adra over my shoulder. He's standing just inside the room. His grand frame even larger in the small space. The firelight flickers over his haunting beak mask, making him appear almost supernatural. He steps forward slowly, his movements curious as his gaze roams the room.

The faint crackle of the fire echoes. I rise to my feet, brushing my hands against my gown. "It's not much." I say though I'm suddenly hyper-aware of every little detail. "But it's home."

Adra doesn't answer immediately, as he paces casually, taking in every corner. The floor creaks beneath his boots as he steps. I redirect myself back to the hearth, setting a kettle on the iron grate with tottery hands. His imposing presence, and the quiet tension between us hums like a hive in spring, waiting for a raid.

I light a candle that sits on my desk, to brighten the room even more. The glow reveals shelves displaying trinkets and mementos, a woven yarn basket for repairs, dried flowers hanging by the window, and a small, tidy stack of books on my desk. The room is modest but cozy, every corner filled with pieces of my life.

He moves like a shadow, his dark attire enveloping the light. His gloved fingers brush across the edge of my belongings. His attention settles on a shawl hanging near the bed, its ornate floral embroidery glowing faintly.

He reaches out and handles the fabric. "Did Gia make this for you?"

"No, that was my Nona's work. She made it for me when I was a child."

His fingers graze at the edge of the shawl

"She raised me after my mother died in childbirth. And as I mentioned earlier, my father was taken by the war not long after. So it was just me and my Nona.... until she passed."

Adra is silent for a moment, his eyes unreadable behind the mask. When he speaks, his voice is softer. "That's a great deal of loss to carry, even for one as strong as you. Is that why the afterlife intrigues you so deeply?"

I shrug, the corners of my lips tilting upward in a bittersweet expression. "Perhaps, when you are raised surrounded by death, you can't help but ponder what lies beyond it."

The kettle begins to hiss, and I move to grab two earthen mugs from a shelf. The faint *clonk* of ceramic breaks the silence as I begin preparing the tea, mixing leaves and herbs into each cup with practiced ease. Behind me, I hear the faint sound of rustling, and when I glance over my shoulder, I see Adra thumbing through a stack of books on the desk.

His gloved hand pauses on one in particular. He holds it up, the title catching the firelight. "Dante's Inferno? Have you read this?"

"I have." I say as I continue preparing the tea. "'Tis a most curious read, is it not?" I glance over at Adra. "It's as though one has stepped into an entirely different realm. I know it is bound by the doctrines of faith, yet it does make one wonder. What if this is no mere tale? What if it truly is the way of it?" I pause the *clink* of the spoon against the ceramic echoes. "Do you know much about it? *Inferno,* I mean. Dante's vision of hell, a story so finely wrought.... Almost like he'd been there himself."

"I know a great deal about it." He says. "Dante's depiction is... poetic. Creative, certainly. Though it's a human interpretation, colored by his beliefs and fears."

The way he speaks makes something tighten in my chest. There's an edge to his words that presents certainty.

I lean against the table. "You sound like you're speaking from experience. Pray, tell me, you are not some scholar of death in secret?"

His chuckle is low. "A deathly scholar? Nay, but the subject matter is... familiar to me. Let's just say I've spent many a night pondering on such matters."

My brow furrows as I study him, his cryptic tone gnaws at my curiosity. "You are most mysterious, I must say."

His gloved fingers tighten on the book. "Everyone has their secrets, Rosannah. Some are just darker than others."

The way he says my name makes my breath halt; I could float away with exhilaration, higher than any bird. I force a laugh, shaking off the chill that creeps

126

along my spine. "Well, whatever your secrets may be, you make Dante seem naught but mild in comparison."

He doesn't reply right away, his focus remains on the book. "Perhaps, or perhaps Dante understood more than you think." He sets the book down.

I blink, the words sinking in as something unspoken inhabits the silence. When I glance back at him, my breathing stops. His mask and gloves now rest on the chair in the corner. His face reveals that perfectly sharp jawline, roasted pecan skin, and mismatched eyes that seem to pierce straight through me.

I barely have time to process this empyreal sight before he moves. His presence takes up the space between us. I freeze, the tea forgotten, as the intensity of his mystic eyes keeps me in place.

His gloveless hand lifts slowly, as though giving me time to pull back, but I don't. His fingers find my chin, tilting my face upwards. My heart thuds in my chest, every beat loud and insistent, as though it might escape entirely. His thumb brushes lightly against my skin, and his touch lights a fire that smolders zealously between my thighs.

I can't look away, even though I'm standing on the edge of something vast and unknown. The tension between us thickens, the surrounding air alive and crackling with something neither of us dares to name.

My chest rises and falls in shallow, uneven movements as his existence overwhelms me. My mouth parts, as my sighs puff out it. He leans in, achingly slow. His face hovers just close enough that I can feel the faintest caress of his breath. His lips press against mine, gentle at first, as if testing the waters, but the softness doesn't last.

The kiss intensifies, his touch becomes firmer, more insistent, pulling me into him like a wave that refuses to break. His other hand moves to my waist, steadying me, anchoring me against the force of him. I melt into him. My body responds instinctively, as though it had been waiting for this moment longer than I'd realized.

His lips, the way they move with a possessive kind of reverence, makes my body float. My hands find his chest, gripping the fabric of his coat as if I might fall without it. The room blurs around us, the glow of the fire turns into a haze of warmth and shadows. I lose myself in this kiss. The way his tongue feels dancing around mine, makes my clit begin to pulse. I can only imagine what that tongue feels like licking away in my pleasure.

The shrill whistle of the tea kettle breaks through the passionate steam, pulling us from the kiss. I chuckle, my cheeks flushed, and hurry to move the kettle off the grate. My hands shake as I set it aside. The room is impossibly hot, though I know it has little to do with the fire.

"I've been waiting all night to kiss you." He says.

A smile spreads across my lips, small and shy at first, but the way he gawks at me, like I'm the only thing in the room, makes it bloom. His mismatched eyes seem to hold me in place, and when he steps closer, I can't help but lean into him.

"You're beautiful." He murmurs, as though the words are meant only for me.

Before I can respond, I close the distance, pressing my lips to his once more. This kiss is different, deeper, hungrier. His hands find my waist, large and firm, and the way they hold my body makes me small in the best way possible. His touch is purposeful, trailing over my curves with a determination that leaves me breathless.

But then, he pulls back. His hands stilling on my waist. The air in the room shifts. Slowly, purposefully, he steps back, his fingers moving to the buttons of his coat. I can't tear my eyes away as he begins to undress.

The coat slips from his expansive shoulders, falling to the floor in a quiet heap. It reveals an even more impressive bulk to his frame. His chest, still hidden beneath the fabric of his undershirt, is ample and sturdy. The outline of his pecs prominent, as each inhale he takes makes the fabric stretch and shift. Every movement commanding as though he knows exactly how to hold my attention.

And he does.

My mouth falls open as he pulls the shirt over his head and casts it aside. My gaze drinks every ounce of him in. My pulse quickens as my eyes trail over his beastly, burly form.

His muscles are not lean, but strong and solid. The body of a man built for prowess and protection. His arms are thick, the muscles flexing as he moves. His chest is dusted with dark hair that trails downward in a tantalizing line that disappears beneath the waistband of his undergarments. The dark trail

129

beckons my gaze lower. His legs are equally impressive. They bore the girth and might of ancient timber rooted in the ground like he could take on the world and remain unshaken.

He's everything I never knew I wanted; raw, masculine strength paired with a quiet, assertive presence. The firelight dances over his skin, highlighting every shadow, every ridge, every ripple of muscle with even the smallest movement. He is utterly captivating, and I realize that this appetizing man before me is all I have ever yearned for.

My breath comes in flat gasps as my eyes flick back up to meet his mismatched stare. There's a small, knowing smirk tugging at the corner of his lips, as though he's fully aware of the effect he's having on me.

My knees are weak, and my hands tremble at my sides as I stand there, still fully clothed, entirely vulnerable yet completely entranced by the sight of him. I'm stuck to this spot. My heart pounds so hard I can hear it in my ears. My hands are clammy, as I try to process the sheer proportions of him. Excitement and nervousness swirl together in my chest, leaving me both elated and completely out of my depth.

"Your turn." He says, a command not a request.

I swallow hard. My fingers are flimsy as they move to the laces of my dress. I fumble, but can't bring myself to look away from him as I begin to loosen the ties. The anticipation is staggering, a fever of expectancy takes hold, longing grows wild, nearly uncontrollable.

Every inch of me is alive with the awareness of him. The way his predacious eyes swallow me with such severity, sets my skin aflame. His stare doesn't just hold me; it leaves me trapped under its influence. I'm nervous, yes, but it's overshadowed by the aching cravings that cloud my every thought. Nothing else exists but him.

"Rosannah," he says, "get on your knees."

Before I can think, I obey, sinking gracefully onto the floor before him. The order slips from his full lips, making me want to climb his face and grind myself to completion. For fuck's sake I love when a man takes control, and it seems like Adra has no problem doing so.

I stare at his delicious body as I ponder what could be underneath those undergarments. I can't make out the imprint of where his cock would be, it is just a little too dark in here.

Adra steps closer, his gloveless hand strokes through my hair, gentle but firm, and tugs my head back. Bliss floods me, unlike anything I have ever experienced before.

"You're so eager to please aren't you?" He muses, his voice holding an edge of affection. His eyes lock onto mine, and their energy is almost too much to bear.

"My dear mourning star, such a perfect being you are. Stay there, and don't move." He hisses.

Fuck, fuck, fuck, fuck, FUCK!

There is absolutely nothing that I can do at this moment except give in to those dark depraved desires that have broken down the door that leads to my reality. The words repeat over and over as I stare into his menacing eyes. He has me exactly how he wants me, and I am not complaining. This is where I want to be.

131

I want to be his. And I am completely at his mercy.

"Give me your hand," he instructs.

My fingers move instinctively, offering themselves to him without hesitation. He guides my hand slowly until it rests against the unmistakable hardness beneath his pants. It is a lot bigger than I expected. Honestly it is a lot bigger than I could have even pictured. My fantasy always thinks of a massive cock, but...

Holy Fuck! This is a MASSIVE COCK.

My palm presses firmly on his bulge. Feeling the thickness, the ridges of the veins that are trying to peek through the fabric, and the pulse of restrained power beneath. I gasp, my cheeks flush as my thumb traces the prominent outline. My touch explores every inch. And I do mean *every inch.*

"You're curious, aren't you?" He asks, as his lips bow into a knowing smile. His hand remains in my hair, stroking it with quiet affection as though calming a storm that he knows is far beyond control.

"Yes..." I whisper, barely able to find my voice. "May I... may I take it out?"

His mismatched eyes hold mine, his expression unreadable for a moment before he gives the faintest nod.

"Ah, such manners. Asking just right... you may."

With wobbly fingers, I reach up, gradually undoing the ties at his waist. My pulse strikes as I peel back the fabric, revealing him at last. I blink, certain I must be dreaming.

"Fuck!" I yell a little too excitedly.

Adra strokes my hair some more and confidently lets out a moan. His fleshy rock-hard member stands proud. The girth alone deserves awards. This is the biggest cock I have ever seen, ever dreamed, and probably that has ever existed.

My mouth falls open further in a stunned awe. My eyes are beaming with desire, as I glance up into him. My fingers hover over his welcoming arousal. Adra watches me closely.

"Go on," he murmurs, "show me just how perfect you can be."

CONWAY TITTY

Chapter 12

Adrastus

Shadows stretch and twist along the walls, mimicking the motion of my own form, a dark and shapeless void suspended in the dim light.

I do not truly *'stand'* in the way mortals conceive of it. My shadow-self moves as it wants. A formless, black silhouette that absorbs the light rather than reflects it. My edges bleed into the surrounding darkness like smoke. No eyes, no mouth, no face. Only the vaguest impression of a humanoid figure, elongated and endless, exists more as an absence than a presence. I am nothing and everything. Just a mere reflection of their fears, their longings, their mortality.

I do not see myself like she does. She cannot perceive the shadow form I am now. I am but an endless void that watches her, drinks in her every motion, every whispered sigh. My mortal guise is for her benefit, a form I've constructed from the stolen dreams and fantasies of her kind. I am whatever a woman might wish for most profoundly, though she will never know this truth.

Rosannah kneels before me, I am drawn to the mortal beauty that unfurls in front of me like a flower. Her skin glows with a golden walnut hue, and her freckles scatter across her round face like stars spilled from a careless hand. Two dimples deepen in her cheeks, even as her expression remains one of patient submission. She does not tremble, though I can sense the longing radiating from her. A cocktail of desire and fear that perfumes the air and sings directly to my nature.

Her almond-shaped eyes are half-lidded, dark lashes framing hazel irises flecked with gold that shimmer in the firelight, like molten metal caught mid-cast. They smolder with a quiet seduction. An intention that promises as much as it teases. Those eyes have felled kings, and yet here they are, fixed on me with reverence that borders on worship.

Her body is an exquisite symphony of curves, lush and unapologetic. Thick thighs press against the cold wood floor, their suppleness stark against the harsh rigidity of her surroundings. Her naked chest is full, tender, and hanging heavy as they await my hands to lift them with godlike praise. Her breasts gently sway as her breath rises and falls. Her nipples stand out, firm and eager, yearning for my touch, for my mouth to suckle upon them.

She shifts slightly, and her doughy soft belly brushes against her thighs. As she moves, I see a peek of her thigh crease that sits just in between her hip & leg.

Fuck that's my favorite part of her; I want to hold on to it and never let go.

Rosannah's hair falls in long luscious curls that lay towards her mid back, framing her in a halo of dark silk. By the shadow's grace she is a profound masterpiece of beauty. She's an earthly pleasure that feels too luxurious for me to indulge in, yet I am curious to experience it.

Mortals have always seemed pointless to engage with sexually, but one gaze upon her exposed flesh has me crumbling like a cathedral under the weight of sin.

She obeys me so quickly, this beautiful creature, her every motion imbued with tacit promise. Her need is tangible, a taste in the air, an ache that hums between us. The pulse of her desire is like a drumbeat creating a rhythm of unalloyed passion. I am puzzled, not with the fleeting lust of mortal men, for I am no man, but with a hunger far more sinister. It coils within me, black and endless, an abyssal craving to devour her essence, to claim her utterly and irrevocably.

This is no simple desire, it is a yearning as dark as the void itself. I want to bind her, body and soul, into something she could never comprehend. To make her mine in ways that transcend the flesh. To own her in the places where her mortality cannot reach. She would not understand, could never grasp the depth of what I wish to take, of what I wish to make her become.

137

"You are utterly divine like this, Rosannah." I reach down and meet her delicate fingers as they wrap around my cock. I begin stroking myself with Rosannah's hands as my gaze focuses on her juicy lips. Her small hands make me appear even bigger than I am, and frankly, I know I'm larger than any mortal could imagine.

As Rosannah begins to stroke in a rhythm by herself, knowingly finding a pace, my shadow form begins to vibrate. The edges of my void-like essence ripples in response to her movements. I lean my head back, closing my eyes, surrendering to this unfamiliar sensation. It's been too long, far too long, since I've felt anything like this.

The succubi, with their practiced lust and empty hunger, were distractions, mere echoes of pleasure. But this? This is raw, real, *alive*. The excitement of her hand, the delicacy of her skin, the way her touch flutters with admiration and desire, there is nothing like it. Never have I experienced such a singular sensation, one that tingles with unknown delectation. This is uncharted.

"That's it." I manage to growl out. "Just like that, Rosannah. You're perfect."

My words seem to encourage her, and she quickens her pace, drawing another gravelly sound from my throat.

I am surprised as the sudden wet heat of her mouth covers my cock, attempting to take me all in. A sharp gasp escapes me, and my eyes snap downward. And there she is, her gorgeous hazel eyes fixed on me, shiny with submission.

Her mouth stretches out as she tries to swallow me. Poor thing is only managing to get me a quarter of the way. I don't blame her though, hells, it's a lot for any interdimensional creature, much less a mortal. But this sight that beholds me, is truly an unparalleled vision of eroticism.

I watch as she takes me out of her mouth. A spit string connects us together as she wraps her tongue around the head and begins sucking. She pops my cock out of her mouth once more. Her tongue glides along the length of me, licking up and down my shaft, with torturous slowness.

Each lick heightens my pleasure, edging me towards release. Her hand moves to cup my heavy testicles. There is an unmatched contrast that exists between her fragile touch and the sheer weight of them.

Another gruff groan escapes my mouth, as she kneads me gently.

"Do you like it when I touch you like this?"

The question undoes me further. Another groan rumbles from within me, louder this time, as her hand works its magic.

"Yes." I rasp, "More." The command is both a plea and a demand.

Without hesitation, she leans in closer, her lips brushing against the sensitive skin of my testicles, as she licks. Teasing the edges with her wet tongue. Her spit glistens as she coats me in her devotion.

"Put them in your mouth." I order again, knowing she will do as she is told.

She obeys, and so does her mouth as she envelopes me in a torrid saturation. I fight to keep my control as she sucks, gathering spit that drips and trails down her chin. Her tongue explores me as if she is savoring every moment, every taste.

She moves back up to the swollen head of my cock, her lips sealing around it as she takes me in her mouth again. This time further than before. She makes a gagging sound as she pulls off, her eyes watery as drool pours out from those pulpy lips.

A delicate string of spit connects the tip of my cock to her, as is begins to fall slowly onto the floor. I hold her soft cheeks as I pet her endearingly. Her spit has moved from her mouth to her neck and now is sliding down her breasts. She looks so proud of the mess she's making.

"Your techniques are leaving me breathless." My voice is dry and raspy. "I could not ask for better."

She pauses; an airy chuckle escapes her as she strokes me firmly. Her hazel eyes flash with playful mischief as she responds, "I've had some practice."

Fuck, she is dangerous in the best of ways.

Her words though, set ablaze possessiveness within me. Practice or not, she belongs to me now. I can't resist the urge any longer. My fingers tangle in her hair, and I tighten my grip just enough to remind her of who controls this moment. I guide her head, setting a rhythm that matches the beat of my need. Her lips sealing perfectly around my cock as she takes me further down her throat with every motion.

She never breaks eye contact. Those mesmerizing eyes stare up at me, full of determination and a wicked kind of challenge. My shadow form ripples and shifts, barely able to contain the pleasure building within me. My grip tightens as I push her a little further, the sensation bordering on overwhelming as her throat struggles to take more of me.

I'm on the edge of climax, teetering, and begging my body not to hurl me off too soon. An ache unlike any I've felt in centuries, the intensity unravels my every thread.

And then, she stops.

Rosannah pulls back suddenly, her lips releasing me with a wet pop as she gasps for air, her chest heaves. Wiping the corner of her mouth with her thumb, she stares at me with a bewitching twinkle.

"Have I done rightly in your eyes? Do I please you?" She purrs.

"Perfection, my dear mourning star, absolute perfection." I moan as I stroke her hair tenderly.
She beams as she receives recognition for her efforts.

"Now get up! It's my turn to play..." It's sharper than anticipated and I catch a glimpse of rapturous horror in her eyes as she realizes this has only just begun.

Rosannah obeys, rising gracefully to her feet. Her curves glow in the firelight, every inch of her full form emits a tempting vixen that hides within.

I grip her waist and whip her around, pulling her flush against me so she can feel just how much I want her. My cock presses hard against her lower back, and she groans, a sound so needy, so desperate, that alone makes me want to coat her in my cum.

I lower my head, my lips brush against the sensitive spot just behind her ear. Her skin is warm, plush, and I take my time dragging my mouth down the column of her neck. I suck at her pulse point, tasting her, branding her, my teeth grazing her skin just enough to leave a faint mark. She shivers under me, her body arching instinctively, begging for more. I let my lips trail further onto the curvature of her shoulder, my tongue savoring the salty sweetness of her flesh.

A breathy moan escapes me as I pull back, turning her to face me. I need to see her, all of her. My hands hold on to her thick hips as I step back. My eyes rake over her body. Her curves inviting me to hold her, grab her, dominate her. She is perfection. Utterly exposed and unashamed.

"Look at you." My voice demanding I fulfill this hunger. "A flawless embodiment of temptation. Every bend, every freckle, every inch of you crafted as if to torment me. You are meant to be worshiped, to be claimed... to be mine."

My eyes stay with hers, and I can see the need mirrored in her hazel gaze, those golden flecks smoldering like embers.

"Do you know what you do to me, Rosannah? How easily you illuminate the depths of my emptiness? You're a forbidden miracle... an unholy apotheosis... and I intend to take my time with you."

Her lips part. Her shallow breaths a hymn to the malevolent tension crackling between us like the flames of the underworld. I close the distance, the shadows around me twisting as my hands claim her hips, pulling her against me with a possessive force. The night is young, and I have every intention of making her remember exactly who she belongs to.

"Go to the bed." I command, and Rosannah moves instantly, her obedience as enchanting as her beauty.

She displays herself out on the bed. Her curves a feast for my eyes, as her body glows in the candlelight. I follow her calmly, stroking my cock as I approach, savoring the anticipation that thickens the air.

"My dear mourning star, you are a divine creature that demands worship. And lucky for you, I'm here to give praise."

Her body arches as she props herself up on her elbows, watching me with those seductive eyes that seem to slice right through my shadows.

I crawl onto the bed, calculated and slow. My gaze stays fixed on her as she quivers beneath me. I grasp one of her feet, bringing it to my mouth, kissing the soft skin with tenderness and greed. My fingers knead and rub her arches, coaxing gentle sighs from her lips. Her reactions service me, and I let my hands trail up, skimming her calves, her thighs, relishing every touch.

When I reach the top of her legs, I pause, spreading them wide as I settle between them. Her pussy glistens, already eager, already wet for me, and I can't help the moan that escapes my throat. My fingers move to her folds, parting her gently as I stroke and tease her with intentional precision.

Her moans grow louder, sweeter, like a melody meant only for me. My lips find her skin, trailing kisses along her thighs, her stomach, her breasts, every inch of her I can reach.

"Stroke me," I whisper against her ear.

She obeys instantly, her hand wrapping around me as she begins to move in time with the rhythm of my fingers. Her touch drives me further into the depths of desire. Our mouths meet, and the kiss is heavy, frantic. Our tongues exploring, claiming each other.

I press one of my fingers further into her, curling it just right, finding the spot that makes her body quaver, and her moans transform into cries of pleasure. She moans my name, and how delicious it sounds coming out of her.

My movements quicken, persistent, her wetness coating my fingers as I push her closer and closer to the edge. I press another finger into her, filling her as she tightens around them.

"Fuck Adra.... stretch me...please..." She begs in my ear.

Her body begins to arch further beneath me. She grips my shoulders, her nails digging into my skin.

"I'm so close, please..." She begs once more.

"Are you going to cum for me bellezza?"

"Yes...yes..." She manages to gasp out as I move my fingers faster into her now soaked pussy.

"BEG." Every letter adds more emphasis than the last.

144

Gasping and panting Rosannah cries out, "Plleeasseee! Please let me cum!"

My fingers curl inside her, as my anticipation heaves onto her body. Keeping the same tempo, I whisper in her ear, "Cum for me."

Rosannah's body bucks forward, her walls tighten as her orgasm takes over. Her pussy pulsates around my fingers as she releases all that tension. She cries out with harmonious moans and that is music to my ears.

Aftershocks make her body seize as I wiggle my fingers out of her. She's panting and glowing from the aftermath of pleasure I have given her. A devious smile curls my lips knowing I got her to the point of no return.

My fingers slick with her cum. The scent of her arousal fills my nostrils. The sweet musky smell has my cock throbbing, and it is demanding satisfaction.

"Open your mouth." I hold my fingers to her lips and slip them in. "Taste yourself." My voice is heavy with a sinful corruption.

Her tongue flicks over my fingers, obediently cleaning them as her gaze remains fixed on mine. The depraved hunger in her eyes makes my cock jump.

"Good." I praise her, leaning in to capture her lips in a searing kiss.

Our tongues entwine like vines of temptation. I pull back just enough to whisper against her mouth, "You taste of desire and submission, Rosannah, an addiction I'll feed on until you're lost to me completely."

Before she can respond, I guide her onto her back. Her body melts into the bed, soft and pliant beneath me. I hover over her, she's still trembling. Her body is aching in the aftermath of her climax, but her legs part instinctively, inviting me in.

I settle back on my knees, towering above her, absorbing every camber of her. My cock is hard and heavy, throbbing with the need to claim her completely. I run a hand down her thigh, spreading her wider as I position myself between her legs, savoring this moment. My cock rests against her delicious folds.

"Do you feel that Rosannah?" I say, as I begin to mime thrusts knowing she's dying for me to stop teasing her. "That ache, that need. You're going to take every inch, just like the perfect minx you are. You're mine now."

Chapter 13

Rosannah

I lie back, my body is still vibrating from the intensity of my orgasm. My breaths escape me as I am desperate to catch them. I stare up at Adra, his towering silhouette painted by flickering firelight. My legs are spread wide, every section of my body alive, pleading for his touch, longing for a mere graze from his fingertips.

Give me anything.

I have never wanted, no *needed* someone so bad. I need this man so recklessly that I want the obsession to make me forget myself entirely.

Adra leans forward, his assertive eyes seem like they see right into my soul, like they see every disgusting depraved thought. And you know what, let him. Let him see everything I desire, everything that arouses me. I want Adra to know my needs before I even know them. Then, and only then, he becomes *the* perfect partner. But for now, let him take control and show me exactly what he thinks I lust for.

"Tell me, mourning star, are you ready to receive me?"

His words snap me out of my thoughts of the future. The hair on my body stands up as his voice trails into my ears with caring domination. I stare into his eyes once more; a sinful sparkle pours out of them. "Please," I whisper, my voice begins to shudder, let me feel all of you."

A devious smirk plasters his face, and those simple words grant me access. His cock barely fit in my mouth, I can't imagine what it's going to be like when he stretches my pussy. And I almost fainted from his fingers, and he was only using two of them.

He grips my hips, his strong hands holding me in place as he positions himself at just the right angle, the tip of his cock teasing at my entrance. A sense of frightening delight spreads as I get ready to take him.

I am forcing my body to stay still. I want to raise my hips and shove his cock right in. But I couldn't do that even if I wanted to, as his free arm is pinning me down into the cushion. He is taking his precious time, treasuring this moment and it is breaking me, piece by agonizing piece.

He leans down, his mouth brushing my ear, "Tell me, my dear mourning star, how badly do you want me?"

My fingers dig into his back, desperate to pull him closer, as my hips arch upward to meet him.

"Please," I cry out, my voice louder than intended, "I need to feel you. I can't take this anymore... Adra, please!"

"Such a deprived greedy minx aren't we?"

He chuckles fiendishly, leans down to nibble at my ear, and thrusts himself in. The pressure of his cock inside of me takes my breath away. He stretches me, as my pussy tries to take all of him. A gasping scream leaves my lungs and echoes throughout the room.

"ADRA!" I scream once more.

Pleasure and pain doing their mellifluous ballet upon my flesh. He fills me inch by inch, and it feels like the inches will never stop.

Fuck he is monstrous. I've never had a cock this big.

His girth continues to stretch me all the way around while his length penetrates, causing ecstasy to pool out of me.

His hips press flush against mine, and the pain from him widening me is no match for the uncontainable solace sensation that I am feeling.

"That's my good little minx." He coos while bottoming out. "Fuck you are so tight."

It seems as if his breath is running away from him as well. He lays there for just a moment, while my pussy continues to adjust to his size.

"Mmmm, You take me so well."

He begins kissing my neck and uses his free hand to play with my erect nipples. My inside pulses around his cock, and that signals to him to begin thrusting. They are slow, and hard, making our bodies pound together in a continuous beat. And with each one it is

149

getting harder to keep my composure. I want to cum already.

Fuck he feels so damn good...

"That's it," he pants, "take all of me."

My breasts begin to bounce as our bodies collide. My chin tilts up as my head buries further into the pillow. Words cannot describe the euphoria I feel. Adra's mouth is dangling open, and I know he is feeling the exact same way.

His massive form eclipses everything else in the room. The weight of his body, the sheer power of every thrust, are making me forget my own name. My fingers clutch at his back as he continues to thrust. My nails dig into his flesh as his hips slam into mine. Moans flow freely from our lips. Both of us are completely present in this moment.

"Tell me your mine." He growls, his voice rough and full of possession. "TELL ME!"

"I'm-I'm yours!" His cock penetrates me, making it impossible to speak.

"Louder!" He snarls back.

"I'M YOURS!" I cry out, arching beneath him, my body tightening as I cling to him. "Don't stop Adra, please don't stop!"

His pace quickens, the rhythm of his thrusts becoming harder, greater, as though he is determined to claim every part of me. My legs wrap around his waist, pulling him impossibly closer. The friction hits my clit and destroys my reality as I begin to release.

"Every inch of you is mine, do you hear me? I'll make sure you never forget who you belong to."

I can feel him throbbing inside me. His movements are becoming erratic, and I know he's close.

"Cum with me," he moans.

As soon as I hear his words, I come undone. My body seizes; my vision blurs and I see stars. He follows as a gruff bellow tears from his throat as he fills me. His release floods into me. Time stands still and we are both enveloped in our own little world of euphoric bliss.

He collapses over me, his chest heaving, his breath synching with mine as we lay tangled together in the aftermath. Slowly, he pulls out, and I shiver as his cum leaks down my thighs, warm and sticky.

Before I can process the moment, he's moving. His lips trail down my legs, his tongue following his release as he licks me clean. The sight alone makes me gasp. My body is already stirring again despite the intensity of what we've just shared. I stare as he laps up the mess, we both have created.

When he's finished, he moves back up to me, his eyes diabolically perverse. He cups my face, his thumb brushing over my cheek as he leans in. His lips capture mine in a kiss that's intense, slow, and intimate. I can taste us both on his tongue. The salty, musky blend of our cum. It's messy, raw, and blasphemously obscene.

"You taste cosmically rapturous. I could stay like this forever... savoring you."

I can't help but smile, as my fingers slide into his hair. I pull him closer. "Then don't stop." I whisper back, my voice quaking with the promise of more.

And just like that, I'm lost to him again.

Adra's arms wrap around me, safe and protective, holding me close. The fiery intensity between us ebbs, transforming into a profound passion that wraps around us like a silent oath. My body molds against him. The rhythm of his breathing grounding me, a stark contrast to the chaotic passion we'd just shared. His chest lifts and falls like a tide beneath my cheek, and I can hear the comforting, rumble of his heartbeat.

For the first time, I am consumed by a peace so esoteric it feels foreign, almost fragile. The chaos and burdens of the world beyond this room fade into a dull, forgotten echo, their weight no longer mine to bear.

In this moment, nothing else exists, only the safety of his arms holding me close. Feeling as if time itself has bent to cradle us in this feeble sanctuary, where the rest of the universe cannot reach.

His hand strokes idly along my back. His touch gentle, as he traces slow, soothing patterns over my skin. It lulls me, drawing me further into a dreamlike haze. I let out a contented sigh, as my body relaxes fully against his.

It's rare to be this safe, this wholly cared for. This unfamiliar sensation is almost pervading in its simplicity. My postulations begin to cloud as I fade into the edges of sleep. I let myself sink further into his embrace.

His arms tighten around me, and I swear I hear him whisper something, though it's too soft to catch. It doesn't matter. For now, I let the pull of sleep take me, knowing I'll wake here, still in his arms, still at peace.

Chapter 14

Adrastus

The room is cloaked in silence, save for the rhythmic sounds of Rosannah's breathing. Her body is warm and pliant against mine, perfectly molded to fit me.

The moonlight spills through the window, casting a silvery glow over her form. I take in every detail of this graceful mortal. The way her lashes rest against her cheeks, the freckles that scatter like faint constellations across her skin, the gentle movement of her chest as she dreams. I can't help but run a hand lightly down her arm, feeling the silky texture of her skin under my fingers.

And then she snores. It's barely audible, a faint little puff of air that escapes her lips as she shifts in her sleep. I freeze for a moment, caught off guard by the sound. It's... ridiculous, completely unguarded, and utterly human. A strange sentiment stirs in my chest, an unfamiliar flicker of something close to amusement, no, closer to affection. I find myself smiling, an expression I rarely wear, and reach out to tuck a stray strand of hair behind her ear.

"You're even adorable asleep." The words barely discernible, a secret shared only with the silent room. The sound of her tiny snores, so opposite from the boisterous presence she holds when awake, is strangely endearing. It's another layer of her that I didn't expect to see, another thread in her web that's slowly ensnaring me.

I do not sleep. I never have, and I never will. Sleep is a mortal indulgence, unnecessary for one like me. Yet, as I lay here, still and silent, there's an odd comfort in this moment, an inexplicable peace that I can't ignore. This night has been... *strange*.

I'm not in the habit of remaining after fulfilling such desires. I was sent here for a purpose, to fulfill a contract, nothing more. My work is efficient, detached, a means to an end. And yet, something about this mortal, my Rosannah, makes it difficult to remain so removed. I shouldn't stay. I know that. But the sight of her like this, vulnerable and at peace, makes it hard to move.

I watch her sigh, watch the faint smile that bend her lips even in sleep, and I can't help but wonder...

What would it be like to stay?

To be the one she wakes up to every morning, to hold her like this without the responsibility of my duty pulling me away.

Why is she different? What is this fresh sensation that pulls at the edges of my resolve?

I shouldn't be here, dreaming of what it would be like to remain, to spend more time with her, to weave myself into her days and nights. And yet, the thought waltzes through my mind, impossible to ignore.

The first streaks of dawn begin to creep into the room, the sun brushes against the horizon, and I find myself caught in the rare stillness of the moment. Her tranquil expression, the weight of her body against mine, it's as if for just a brief time, I too, can feel the fragile, fleeting peace that mortals so desperately crave. And I almost let myself believe it could last.

Abruptly, the summoning arrives—a sharp, potent pull that resonates through me like a bell tolling in the void. Master calls, and my duty waits for no one, no matter how much I might wish otherwise.

Carefully, I untangle myself from her, moving slowly so as not to disturb her slumber. She shifts, murmuring something unintelligible before falling still again. Her tiny snores continue unabated. I stand at the edge of the bed, watching her for a moment longer, committing every detail of this scene to memory.

With a reluctant, heavy sigh, I let the facade fall away. My human form dissipates like smoke, as my shadow stretches and warps, until I am once again clad in my true guise. The long, dark coat, and the beaked mask shield me from prying eyes. Here, underneath this masquerade, I am safe, untouched, a specter unseen by the world. The mask is comforting, a buffer against the vulnerability I allowed myself to feel tonight. But this is who I am, a shadow, a collector, a servant of the inevitable.

Before leaving, I manifest a perfectly bloomed white chrysanthemum in my hand. Its petals are pristine and glimmer faintly in the dim morning light. It's a fragile thing, much like the mortal woman who sleeps soundly before me. I place it carefully on the table beside her, the bloom a quiet token of a sentiment I dare not name. Leaning down, I brush my gloved palm lightly over her hair, smoothing it back with a strange tenderness.

My gaze drinks her in one last time as my chest tightens with an ache I can't quite place. Straightening, I step back into the glow of early dawn. The chrysanthemum is a quiet reminder of a moment I'll carry long after I've left. I let the light swallow me, dissolving into the breaking dawn as the world begins to stir awake.

I slip out the door, while some of the world is still half-asleep. The surrounding streets are eerily silent save for the distant calls of gulls near the docks. The summoning pulls at me, an invisible tether dragging me toward the waterfront. This cannot be ignored. Walking on the stone streets, my boots stomping below, the tether grows more tense. The air turns serious as I near the shipyard. The faint stench of death amalgamates with the brine of the sea.

As I approach the docks, the pull of the summoning sharpens, guiding my gaze toward the edge of the shadows. There, just beyond the reach of the dawn light, two figures stand, cloaked in the kind of stillness that only those accustomed to hiding can master.

The subtle glint of leather catches my eye, and I immediately recognize them, fellow collectors: Erevan and Corvus. Like me, they are clad in the unmistakable garb of our kind; long coats, ominous beak masks, and gloves that hide every sign of what might not pass as human.

Erevan's attire is of weathered brown leather, its earthy tones blending with the muted dawn. Corvus, as whetted and striking as his name, is draped in maroon. The rich crimson catches the light like dried blood. Both exude a quiet authority, their presence as grim and foreboding as my own.

A mass of townsfolk gather around the dock's entrance. I remain out of sight, blending into the shadows that cast down from the nearby domiciles. The energy that scatters through the crowd is thick with tension and panic. Whispers ripple through, their voices hushed but frantic.

"It's cursed," one says.

"All who enter will be cursed as well," mutters another.

The king's guards, I presume, stand rigid at the edge of the narrow bridge leading to the largest vessel. Their figures are imposing against the pale dawn light. Each wears a grim expression, their chainmail glinting faintly beneath dark tunics emblazoned with the royal crest. Their spears are crossed in a resolute barrier. The polished tips gleam like steel fangs, ready to bite into any who dares challenge their authority.

I move silently through the shadows until I am near Erevan and Corvus. My presence merges with theirs as the daybreak filters weakly through the fog. My voice drops to a cautious whisper, barely audible over the distant murmurs of the crowd.

"What is the meaning of this summons? And why are so many of us gathered here?"

Erevan doesn't look at me as he speaks, his voice measured and grim. "The master needs us here, and for good reason. You'll see soon enough."

Corvus, ever the harbinger of action, tilts his head toward the looming ship. "Make way. The time has come to fulfill our purpose." His voice carries an unsettling finality. He takes the lead, his maroon coat billowing behind him like a specter as we approach the ship's bridge.

The guards tense as we near, their hands tightening on their weapons, as one shouts, "STATE YOUR BUSINESS OR BE GONE!"

Corvus's voice cuts through the tension, smooth and cold. "We are the undertakers. Here to procure the dead."

The guards hesitate, their fear palpable, but they nod, stepping aside to let us pass. The crowd watches, wide-eyed with discernible gasps that echo throughout, as we cross the bridge onto the ship.

The vessel looms above us, its timbers groaning under the weight of death. The scent of decay is a suffocating miasma that even our masks cannot fully filter. Bodies lie strewn across the deck. Their skin is a sickly, ashen gray, mottled with grotesque black pustules that bulge angrily.

Some are piled haphazardly, their limbs twisted in unnatural angles, as if their last moments were spent in agonizing pain. While others appear as though they simply fell where they stood. They lay sprawled lifelessly, their faces gaunt and vacant, lips cracked and stained with the remnants of bloodied coughs. Their veins darkened and bloated, spider-web across their skin, betraying the disease that ravaged their bodies from within.

The air reeks of decay, a cloying stench of rot and sickness that clings to everything, making it a gruesome sight. This ship, a floating tomb, a final resting place for the forsaken.

We've all seen this before, death in its many forms, the ravages of disease and time, but something about this feels different. My gaze remains on a body near the mast, its eyes still open, clouded and lifeless, the veins blackened beneath the skin.

"Do my eyes deceive, or is that what I deem it to be?" I ask, my voice a shadowed whisper, taut with unease.

Erevan moves towards me, "Aye." His reply is a single word, spoken with the weight of grim certainty.

Corvus tilts his head, his mask captures the light as he studies the scene before us. "Do the mortals know?"

Erevan's stare remains fixed on the carnage. "Nay. They remain blissfully ignorant... for now."

I glare at the piles of the deceased, my mind races. I've seen this before, time and time again over the centuries. The cycle always begins the same way, spreading death like wildfire. The plague doesn't stop, doesn't concede. It consumes everything in its path. *And this... this is where it begins.*

My thoughts drift to Rosannah. Her peaceful face as she lay in my arms just hours ago, a rare touch of warmth in my cold, endless existence. I clench my fists, the leather creaks under the strain. I know what's coming, what must happen. But the thought of her being caught in this, of her essence eclipsed by the darkness to come, is insufferable.

I must protect her. Somehow, I must try. Even if it means defying everything I am, and everything I was created to be.

Chapter 15

Rosannah

Morning sun filters through the window, sweet golden beams paint the walls of my room. I stir lazily, stretching as the kindness of the rays gently nudges me from sleep. My body is sluggish, and sore.

Fuck am I sore...

But it's a pleasant tenderness, a remaining reflection of last night's copious copulating. A simple, cheesy smile animates upon my lips, but it withers as I reach out to where he should be, where his solid, comforting presence had held me through the night. My eyes blink the dreams away as I glance over to where Adra was just laying, the bed now empty and cold.

I squint, the quiet of the room suddenly too loud. My fingers brush the frigid sheets where he'd been, the absence of him settles into me like a hollow ache. He's gone.

For a moment, hurt stabs at my chest.

Did I misread everything? Was it just a fleeting moment for him, a night to be forgotten?

My reflections begin to spiral, and all those dark judgements from relationships past, swallow me. Then I see it. Sitting on the small wooden table beside my bed is a perfectly bloomed white chrysanthemum. Its petals are flawless, and its presence is a quiet reassurance.

I reach for it; my fingers graze the delicate blooms as relief settles over me. This wasn't just a one-night venture. Adra thought to leave something behind like a token, or a promise, perhaps. Whatever his intention, it eases the ache in my chest.

How peculiar that he chose the flower of death. I've only ever seen white chrysanthemums at requiems or offered to those lost in grief. Perhaps he simply picked whatever was nearest at the florist's stall, or maybe he's unaware of the flower's meaning. Either way, it was awfully thoughtful of Adra to leave something behind.

"He probably had something to do," I murmur to myself, clutching the flower as I sit up. "Or maybe he just stepped out." The thought is comforting, and the happiness I started to lose returns, blossoming across my face like the flower in my hand.

I glance around the room, the disheveled state of it drawing a daft laugh from me. Clothes are scattered, pillows are askew, and the scent of last night's passion still fills in the air. I stand and begin to tidy, folding blankets and smoothing sheets. My eyes fall to the pillow he'd laid his head on, and without thinking, I pick it up and press it to my face. It smells like him: a musky aroma, that is comforting and familiar.

The scent brings flashes of the night before storming back to me. His hands, his voice, the way he looked at me like I was the only thing that mattered. I can't help but grin, my cheeks heating as I hug the pillow to my chest. Adra is different. And while I don't know what it is that makes him so unlike anyone else, I know that I don't care. All I know is that when he's near, everything feels right, everything feels safe. Adra is all I've been searching for, the missing piece I've longed to find.

As I rectify the last of the room, I set the chrysanthemum back on the bedside table, its delicate petals a quiet reminder:

Wherever he is, I know he'll return.

The sunshine is lively against my skin, as I step out of my small quarters and into the streets of town. The stones are still damp from the morning dew, and the faint scent of salty air wafts in from the distant docks, as I begin my quick journey to Gia's.

The marketplace is alive with its usual energy, merchants calling out their wares, the hum of conversations cover the occasional clatter of carts. Yet, something is off.

As I pause at the baker's stall, buying a crusty loaf for my morning meal, a prickle of dread rests beneath the surface. Their whispers drift to me.

"Did you hear about the ship?" One merchant says in a hushed tone.

"Full of dead sailors," another replies, shaking his head. "Cursed, they say."

I freeze, the words sinking into my gut like a stone.

A ship of dead sailors?

The words echo in my mind as I pass over a coin for my bread, barely registering the baker's thanks. Holding the loaf tightly, I hasten my pace, weaving through the narrow streets. My heart pulsates faster as I piece together what little I've heard. Whatever this is, I know Gia will have more details. She always knows everything.

When I arrive at Gia's shop, I barely have a chance to knock before the door swings open. Gia grabs my arm, her face pale, her usually calm demeanor replaced by frantic worry.

"Get inside!" She says, pulling me into the shop before locking the door behind us.

"What's going on?" I ask, clutching the bread to my chest.

Gia's hands tremble as she draws the curtains. Her actions are quick and jittery. "It's the ship. It was brought in at first light. Ros, I was there, I saw it with my own eyes."

I step closer, placing a safe hand on her arm. "What did you see?"

She takes a shaky breath; her words tumble out in a rush. "The wharves were full of folk, all murmuring of it. They wouldn't let anyone near, but I stole a glance. The ship..." She pauses, clutching her shawl tightly.

164

"The deck lay strewn with bodies, scores of them, sailors all cold and still as stone. Their skin was blackened... covered in sores that leaked with puss. Ros... It was... *horrific.*"

A chill shoots down my spine as I imagine the scene. "An illness?" I ask, my voice barely above a whisper.

Gia nods quickly. "Aye, so they say, a curse... perhaps... but none seem overly afraid, for the sailors were already lost to death before the ship made shore. I've never seen anything like it before."

I pull her into a hug; she trembles against me. "It's going to be okay." I say gently, trying to reassure her even as my own unease grows. "It perhaps was but some mishap upon the ship. Such things happen when one is long at sea. Be it curse or not, we shall manage well."

She pulls back. "You believe so?"

"I do!" I lie, hoping to ease her nerves. Inside, my mind courses with questions and worry.

What happened on that ship? And why does it feel like this is only the beginning?

I force a smile and give her arm a playful nudge. "Enough about the ship. Pray, tell me, what did your night entail?"

Gia's frightened pale face brightens instantly. Her cheeks flush as a mischievous grin spreads across her lips. "Oh, you wouldn't believe me if I were to tell..." She folds her arms and leans against the counter.

"I dare you to try."

Her sudden shift in demeanor sparks my curiosity. "Welllllll," she begins, dragging out the word, clearly enjoying the buildup. "I spent the evening with not one, but *two* seafarers."

My jaw drops. "TWO?"

"Two!" She repeats, her grin widening. "Both... at the same time!"

I gasp, my palms fly to my mouth, then quickly start laughing, more from shock than anything else. "Gia! You didn't!"

"Oh, I did," she says with a laugh, tossing her short brown hair like it's nothing. "It was thrilling. You know I've *always* had that fantasy."

I shake my head, grinning from ear to ear. "You have spoken of this for years! I can't believe you have truly done it!"

"What can I say?" She shrugs, her expression wicked. "They were handsome, charming, and *very* eager to please."

We both dissolve into giggles, the earlier tension in the room melting away. After a moment, Gia sends me a knowing expression. "Do you know what it is like to have two willing men inside of you at once? I mean to fill you to the fullest?" Her eyes narrow and it's like she is reliving the moment. "All while they are absolutely worshiping every part of your form..."

My heart begins to race as I think of the last night's adventures with Adra. One of him was enough to make me lose connection to this realm. I can't even begin to fathom *two* of him.

"Ros, you must give it a go. It was a marvel unlike any other."

My mouth hangs open as Gia spills more detailed secrets of her night. I am filled with pride for her, for daring to explore experiences, that the world casts aside in sinful shame. And I must admit, it does seem a most pleasurable pursuit.

"Now, enough about me. What about you? Tell me everything about Adra."

My cheeks flush at the mention of his name. "Oh, Gia, where do I even start?" I say, fidgeting with the edge of my dress sleeve.

"Commence from the beginning that way I miss no details." She leans forward eagerly. "Don't leave anything out."

I take a deep breath, trying to organize my thoughts. "So...we spoke by the water's edge for a while. His energy makes me feel as though I am the sole soul in all the world. And then..." I trail off, noticing my face grow even hotter.

Gia's eyes light up. "And then?" She prompts, practically bouncing with excitement.

"And then, we went back to my place, and... the experience was beyond compare. He possesses a skill of knowing just what to do. There is no hesitation in him. *He just knows.*" My heart is thumping out of my chest finally sharing it aloud. "Truly, it was a of a nature I have never known before."

Gia gasps, clutching her chest dramatically. "Rosannah! You sly little vixen! Details now!"

I laugh, trying to push past my exhaustion, and tell her more, about how he made me feel, the way he looked at me, and how gentle yet commanding he was. And of course I must tell her about his monster sized member that hides in his pants.

"I have never came so hard in my life, I am not even kidding.... Gia... his cock.... Its huge... massive... *Godly!*" I say as I hold out my hands to mimic the length and width.

Gia's eyes about dropped out of her head. "Did it fit?!" Her mouth slides open in curiosity.

"You know me, I never stray away from a challenge..." I wink at her, and Gia practically melts onto the floor.

"And then this morning, I woke up, and he was gone. But he left this... a white chrysanthemum by my bedside."

"A chrysanthemum? White?" She glances around. "That's *so dark...* and romantic. Did he say anything about it?"

I shake my head. "Nay, but it felt meaningful. I can only hope the stars align, and our paths cross once more before the night is done. There is something about him that soothes my soul. It's like nothing else matters. I believe he is the very man of which my heart has long dreamed. The very person I have yearned for in the quiet of my thoughts." A serene peace settles upon my spirit as I think of him.

Gia sighs, resting her chin in her hands. "You are truly besotted. Entirely so. And truth be told? I do greatly delight in it for you."

We burst into laughter again, the heaviness of this morning's events now fully replaced with lighthearted chatter.

As we talk, Gia pulls out a bundle of fabrics from behind the counter, spreading them out on the table. "Oh, I almost forgot. These came as part of the latest goods delivered from the ships. Are they not striking to the eyes?"

The fabrics are vibrant, rich with colors and patterns I've never seen before. I run my fingers over them, marveling at the textures. "These are gorgeous beyond reckoning." I say, tracing an unclear pattern on the material. "These hold great promise, you could fashion wonders from them."

"That's the plan." Gia wears a proud smile.

I nod, and the thought of the ship haunts me once more, as a chill expands down my spine. Still, for now I let myself bask in the moment, in the laughter and spirit of my dearest companion. Awaiting the possibility that tonight may bring me closer to Adra once more.

CONWAY TITTY

Chapter 16

Rosannah

This night's labor sits troubled, as though there is a hush upon all things, like a breath drawn and not yet let loose. The Lupo Tavern is busy as usual, but there is a strange nervousness that overshadows the lively chatter of the patrons inside. The clinking of goblets, and the laughter of drunks, can't quite drown out the strained apprehensive murmurs that weave through the room. I try to focus on my work, wiping down the bar's counter, and making sure the platter of meats stay full.

Sixty dead.

Sixty bodies pulled from that cursed ship. No one knows how or why they died, and the mystery is nagging at everyone. The unanswered questions hang over this town, cloaked in requiem cloth. Even those who laugh the loudest and drink the hardest can't mask the nervous glances they exchange when they think no

171

one is watching. Their worried eyes darting like mice beneath a hawk's shadow, betraying their fragile façade of normalcy.

Everyone wonders what is to happen, will the curse spill over and claim more lives, or is the sailors' death penance enough to save us all? Those are the thoughts that spiral through the public's minds tonight. Scared, anxious, and itching to know the truth.

I move between customers, forcing a simper and cracking lighthearted jokes to keep myself distracted.

"Don't let the wine run dry too quickly now," I tease a group of men at the far end of the bar. "I'm not running to the back again tonight unless one of you helps carry the barrels."

They laugh, and for a moment, the knot in my stomach loosens. But then the whispers creep back, pulling my worries back to the ship and the sickness it carried.

As the door yawns wide, a bitter draft follows, curling around me like a ghost's breath. Fino steps inside, his wide frame silhouetted against the dim light of the street. Normally, he would make his way to his usual center table, where Felicita would already be waiting with her fierce tongue and her quick jabs. But tonight is different.

Fino walks to the drink rail and sits down near a pair of merchants buried in conversation. I stroll over with a falsified simper, masking the unease bubbling in my chest.

"Well met in such unfamiliar ground," I say, leaning casually against the counter. "What's the
172

occasion, Fino? Decided the table was too dull without Felicita's prattling tongue?"

He gives me a leer, though it barely cracks the surface. "Needed a change of pace, I guess." He says, running a hand through his hair. "Besides, the table is a bit too quiet tonight. I could use some company.... you know with everything going on."

I snort, raising my eyebrows. "Peace? I scarcely thought you knew nothing of what quiet was with her ever at your side. I'm amazed that she has not come bursting in, making her grand entrance."

Fino huffs a laugh, his shoulders relaxing a fraction. "I'll admit, the peace is nice. For once."

He pauses, glancing toward the merchants beside him, then back at me. "Have you heard anything else about the ship? I was promised my tools would come in today, yet all is held back." He peers over his shoulder before replying. "Seems no one wants to go near the cursed quays."

I nod, lowering my voice. "I've heard whispers here and there. Sixty dead is what they're saying. All sailors. Something ill befell that ship, that much is beyond doubt."

Fino leans closer, his expression grim. "Aye, and yet the greater part of townsfolk carries on as if naught has transpired. As if the matter perished with them." Fino glances over his shoulder once more as if someone, or something is watching him. "But I've seen the way people talk about it when they think no one's watching. There's fear, Rosannah. And it's spreading."

His statement instills a renewed sense of disquiet within me; however, I compel myself to laugh, endeavoring to ameliorate the atmosphere. "Well, let us pray that delays be all that troubles you. I'm certain you'd surely find yourself adrift without nails to drive or swords to shape. A man such as you would be lost without a hammer in hand."

"Aye, truly that would be a calamity, would it not?" He takes a sip of the wine I slide his way.

I glance towards the door, wondering if Felicita will burst in and shatter this surprisingly civil moment. But she doesn't, and for the first time, Fino and I manage to hold a normal conversation without her looming over his shoulder with her shrewd comments. It is a most welcome change.

One of the merchants sitting at the counter asks for another round, and as I go to refill his drink, I realize the barrel is empty. With a groan, I glance toward the back room where the replacement barrels are stored. These drums are massive, easily 300 pounds, probably more; and there's no way I can manage them on my own. The previous bartender, Alessandra, clearly forgot to switch them out before leaving, and now it's my problem to fix.

"Fino," I call, "mind lending me a hand in the back? You too..." I gesture to another man nearby. "The new barrels are way too heavy for me."

Both men agree, and we make our way to the storeroom. Between the three of us, the barrel is moved into place without much trouble. Though my arms ache just from helping guide it into position. The other man heads back to the main chamber of the tavern, leaving me alone in the prep room with Fino.

I begin to fasten the tap into the wine cask. "Thanks for your help," I say over my shoulder, dusting my hands off on my smock. "I'd never have managed that on my own."

When I glance up, Fino is staring at me. It's not the usual glance people give when they're lost in thought. His gaze stays, heavy and intense, sliding over me in a way that makes my skin crawl.

I awkwardly chuckle, trying to dispel the tension. "What's the matter? Something on my face?"

His smirk is gradual, relatively creepy. "Not your face." His eyes drop lower. "Just admiring how you fill out that dress."

Before I can reply, he steps closer and smacks my rear, the sound harsh and fearsome in this small room. I choke, my breath caught in my throat, and for a moment, I can only stand there, paralyzed.

Did Fino truly do such a thing?

Fino? Has my mind deceived me?

My rationale breaks, tangled with confusion and disbelief. This is the same man who's always glued to Felicita, practically fawning over her. He's supposed to be smitten with her, not... whatever he thinks *this* is.

I glance up at him, and the expression on his face makes my stomach churn. A smug, pillaging sneer that sends an avalanche of revulsion through me.

Why is he looking at me like that? Like I'm some trophy he's decided he deserves. Like I'm nothing more than a prize he's entitled to take. It doesn't make sense.

None of this makes sense. This isn't flirtation, it's something else, something suffocating and far more disturbing.

My chest stiffens, and an overwhelming amalgamate of emotions battle inside me: confusion, anger, disgust. I don't know what to say, what to do. I am frozen. All I know is that the man standing in front of me is a stranger, not the Fino I thought I knew.

"Fino," I start, my voice faltering as I force a nervous laugh, "what are you doing?"

He doesn't answer immediately. Instead, he brushes a strand of my hair behind my ear. His touch is uncomfortably intimate. His other hand moves again, this time grabbing a handful of my ass.

My stomach twists as he leans in. "You know I've been watching you, Rosannah. Don't act like you don't feel the same." His voice is low and lawless.

I take a step back, forcing space between us. "What about Felicita?" I ask, trying to bring some sensibility back into the moment. "You're practically betrothed to her!"

He scoffs, dismissing the question with a wave. "Felicita's name is not to be spoken here. Do no stray from the matter at hand."

He leans closer, and I whip my head just in time. His lips scrape my cheek instead of my mouth, and the rejection visibly irritates him.

"Don't be such a tease!" He sinisterly growls. "I know your heart's desire. I see how you stare at me. I know you want this."

176

"Fino, stop!" I say firmly, trying to sound braver than I feel. My heart pounds like a drum as he grabs my wrist, forcing my palm against the front of his pants. The hardness there is unmistakable, but the moment I register it, my gut writhes. It's not just the act itself; it's the stark, almost pathetic reality of what he's pressing against me. The smallness, the inadequacy, transforms the moment from horrifying to grotesque, amplifying my disgust tenfold.

The bile rises in my throat, and my entire body recoils instinctively. His grip toughens as if to keep me captured in place.

This is what he thinks I want?

This is what he's so proud of?

The sheer absurdity of it adds another layer to my revulsion, and all I want is to pull away, to scrub this moment from my skin and my memory forever.

"See what you stir within me?" He says, his voice is syrupy with hubris. "This is what you've been wanting, isn't it?"

I yank my hand away, stumbling back a step, but his expression blackens with irritation. He straightens, puffing out his chest as if to remind me of his supposed stature.

"What grievance do you have with me, eh?" He snaps. "Do you know how many maidens would slay for a chance at this?"

He gestures toward himself, as though he's some divine gift. "By my word, you are lucky to even be in my company. I am the finest prize in this village. *Rosannah.*"

The way he says my name makes me want to curl inside myself and never come out.

"I could grant you every desire you have," he continues, "yet here you are, feigning ignorance of it. Playing coy? Really? With *me*?"

He takes a step closer, looming over me. His presence is suffocating as his self-satisfied smirk creeps back onto his face. "Do you think men such as I spring forth like apples from a tree? Take heed, best you reconsider before denying me." He takes another step closer. I can feel his breath on my face. "A pathetic, insignificant harlot like you? You'd be a fool to think you'd find better." His words are fortified with malicious contempt and unwarranted entitlement. Fino takes his grimy hands and grabs my breasts as pushes in to take another kiss.

I break his grip. "I don't want this, Fino. Just... stop. Please, just stop."

His jaw stiffens, and his frustration converts into something uglier. He grabs my wrist once more, bringing my face closer to his, glaring at me with disdain. "You're nothing more than a bondslave of desire Rosannah. That's all you'll ever be." Spit hits my eye as he grits his repugnant teeth.

"You'll die lonely, a spinster. You've ruined yourself. Marry? You? Ha! You'll be lucky if they don't run the other way. No suitor would consider twice." He throws my arm down and gives my body a shove. *"Worthless."* He snarls at me as my back hits the wall.

The venom in his words sting, but I hold my composure. I will not let this vain filled, abhorrent lecher see me cry. He will not have that power over me. I gather myself, watching as he storms out of the prep room. He reaches in his pants and adjusts himself, his rather *small* self, as he steps back into the main assembly room. He grabs a jug of wine from the counter as he passes and takes a long swig. Without another glance my way, he saunters back to his usual seat, where his friends are now waiting, laughing and oblivious to what just happened.

I slump against the prep counter, my fingers gripping the edge so tightly my knuckles turn white. They won't stop trembling, no matter how hard I try to settle them. My chest heaves with shallow breaths, each one scraping like a shard of glass against my throat. The room gets colder, darker, as if all the light has been extinguished, leaving only the harsh, smothering pressure of the interaction. My mind is a chaotic blur of dismay, disgust, and distress.

Please tell me that wasn't real.... This cannot be so....

The memory of his hands, his smug voice, his entitlement, all floods back, wrenching my stomach into knots. I feel dirty, tainted, like his touch has seeped into my skin, a stain I can't scrub away. My body feels foreign to me now, like it doesn't belong, like it's been claimed against my will.

How could he do that? Why would he do that?

Fino, of all people, the man who fawns over Felicita, who struts around town like he's some kind of hero. And now I see him for what he really is: a predator hiding behind a charming facade and a mountain of ego. My disgust with him is only matched by my disgust with myself for not seeing it sooner. For not realizing what he was capable of.

Tears well in my eyes, hot and stinging, but I blink them away, clenching my jaw. I won't cry over him. He doesn't deserve my tears, my pain, any part of me. But the lump in my throat remains, and the misery in my chest refuses to fade. I feel small, fragile, like a fresco that's been chipped and cracked.

Was it something I did?
The thought creeps in, poisoning my mind.

Was it the way I smiled at him? The way I asked for his help? Did I give him the wrong idea?

No.... *NO.* This isn't my fault. I didn't ask for this. I didn't deserve this. The bile rises in my throat as his words echo in my head, cruel and cutting.

"You're nothing more than a bondslave of desire."

"You'll die lonely."

The humiliation burns, but beneath it, something stronger flickers: hatred.

How dare he? How dare he think he can touch me, use me, belittle me like I'm nothing?

I grip the counter harder, grounding myself in the present. My breaths slow, but the sickening influence in my stomach remains. I glance toward the door, half-expecting him to burst back in with another sneer, but the room remains quiet.

For now, I'm alone with my thoughts, with the anguish, with the fury simmering beneath the surface. I can't stay here. Not like this. Not with his voice still ringing in my ears. I need air, space, anything to escape the strangling walls of this room and the memory of his unwanted touch. But even as I think it, the thought of stepping back out there, of facing anyone, is frightening.

My legs are like lead, my body weighed down by shame and exhaustion. All I can do is lean against the counter, and all I can think about is how much I wish Adra were here. The thought of burying my face in his chest, of his safe arms wrapped around me, is the only thing keeping me upright.

Taking in some deep breaths, I step away from the prep counter, collect the empty jugs and start refilling them with wine. Each motion is methodical, mechanical, as I try to push the memory away. I plaster a small, practiced expression on my face, enough to keep the world from asking questions. Then carry the jugs back into the main chamber of the tavern.

The room full of body heat and noise hit me like a clangorous wave. The immediate buzz of conversation almost drowns out my self-deprecating thoughts. As I set the jugs down behind the bar, I see him...

Adra is sitting at the bar's top, as composed and commanding as ever. His glowing eyes watching me beneath the faint shadow of his brow. His mask rests on the counter beside him. My heart lifts immediately, practically jumping out of my chest, as the putrid afflictions of earlier begins to fade into a warmth I didn't realize I could feel again so soon.

I approach, trying not to seem too eager, though the relief blooming in my chest is uncontrollable. The smile on my lips turns genuine.

"I'm so glad you're here. I was hoping to see you."

His gaze scans my face in that way of his, as if he can see right through me. His existence is firm, but I can see the faint furrow of his brow. He knows something isn't right.

I try to hold his stare, and deflect, but my eyes betray me. Without thinking, I glance toward Fino. He's slouched smugly at his table. His arrogant expression is staining the room. My stomach wrings as I take him in, and the memory of what happened in the back room flashes through my mind. I bear away quickly, but the damage is done. Adra's eyes follow my glance. His expression shifting as his focus lands on Fino.

Adra's jaw flexes, the tension in his posture coiling like a drawn bow. A flicker of something sinister flashes in his eyes. Wrath radiates from him like an unseen force. His fingers drum once against the bar top, as though he's restraining himself.

I swallow hard, waving my hand as if brushing away the very idea of trouble. "Oh, it's nothing..." I say quickly, trying to divert his attention, my voice a little too high. "I've just been busy, that's all. Things have been hectic today."

Adra doesn't sound convinced, but his focus returns to me. There's a tightness in his posture, his behavior suddenly serious.

Before he can press further, I pour two glasses of wine, placing one in front of him as I change the subject.

"Did you hear about the ship? All those bodies?" I shake my head, trying to sound casual. "How tragic. It must have been something awful that happened at sea."

Adra's expression shifts immediately, worry swipes across his face. "Rosannah, you need to leave here. Gather your things and go."

I blink, confused by the urgency in his tone. "What? Adra, no, it shall mend soon. Just some ailment that has taken the sailors. Things such as this happen all the time while one is long at sea. Worry not."

His gaze hardens, and the authority in his voice makes the hairs on the back of my neck stand on end. "This is no ordinary sickness. It's spreading. And you don't need to be here when it does."

Something in his tone makes me hesitate, the edge of fear in his warning cutting through my skepticism. "You jest, surely?"

"I wouldn't tell you if it weren't important. Rosannah, trust me. You need to get somewhere safe."

The severity of his words makes me pause, and I bob, though a part of me still resists the impact of what he's saying.

Hoping to lighten the moment, I set down my glass. "Well, if this be our final drink here, I must thank you for the flower you left me. It was so thoughtful. Though I did ponder if you were trying to slip away before I took notice."

Adra's lips bend teasingly, his earlier tension easing somewhat. "Why would I ever leave without a word," he says, leaning forward, "when someone so appetizing was still naked in bed?"

183

My cheeks heat instantly, and I bite my lip, the tension between us shifting into something sinful. "Appetizing?"

His smirk enhances, his mismatched eyes glinting with a tantalizing blend of amusement and unspoken desire. "Utterly." His voice a velvety caress, each word steeped in unwavering certainty. For a moment, the room fades away, the noise of the tavern dulls as I meet his eyes.

Adra's sensual stare dissolves as he leans closer, "I must be off, but I shall return later to check on you."

A smile takes over me, seeing him now is one thing, but getting to see him after my work ends makes my heart skip.

"I'll be waiting for you." Our lips almost touching, as I admire this titillating hunk of a man in front of me.

He takes my palm in his, his touch firm yet gentle, and presses his lips to my knuckles in a kiss that sends a rush of excitement straight through me. The gesture is simple yet filled with a romantic intimacy that makes my heart flutter once more. His eyes meet mine one last time before he stands. He lifts his glass and with a single, fluid motion, he downs the rest of his wine, setting the empty cup on the counter with deliberate care.

"Until tonight," he says, before leaving and striding out of the tavern.

I let out a shaky breath. My body still tingling from his kiss, his touch, his words. My conscious spirals, and I can't help but wonder what tonight will bring. The vision of last night's sexual escapades, of his hands, the power of his body, the way his voice rumbles in my ear, all floods back in vivid detail, setting my skin alight.

I press my palms to the sticky bar counter and let out a calming sigh. I wish I could just leave with him. How he managed to take such a shitty night and make it disappear with one single kiss. A kiss only to my hand mind you.

I don't know how he does it, but when I am with him, nothing else matters. Dreams of Adra continue to plague my mind, with desire, with happiness.... with.... *love?*

CONWAY TITTY

Chapter 17

Adrastus

The moon hangs abundantly in the night sky, casting an eerie glow over the docks as I make my way back to the ship. The night air is dense and frigid, carrying the stench of rot. Shadows stretch long and dark, swallowing the edges of the world. The faint lap of water against the hulls only serves to magnify the silence. Rosannah's beautiful face takes over my thoughts. Her dimpled smile, permanently seared into my mind. Her memory is as gorgeous as ever.

The whiff of death derails my dreams of her. She has no idea what looms over this town, and the thought of her being caught in it, wrenches my innards.

Erevan and Corvus are waiting by the ship, their dark figures blending seamlessly with the night. The dull light of a lantern swings gently from a pillar nearby, casting fleeting glints off their masks. Erevan stands rigid, his brown leather coat blending into the gloom. While Corvus, in his maroon attire, leans against a stack of crates. His posture is deceptively relaxed. Both exude the quiet authority of creatures who have done this work for centuries, but tonight, there's something substantial in their presence.

"You're late." Erevan says, his voice, a quiet reprimand.

"I had matters to attend to."

The ship towers above us. A hulking shadow against the faint moonlight that shimmers on the water. The deck is littered with bodies, their pale, bloated forms lie against the ship's dark wood. Even in this dull light, the blackened sores and empty stares of the dead are foreboding. The scene is grim, a harbinger of what's coming.

Corvus pushes off the crates with a disquieting calm. His movements are haunting. His voice cuts through the stillness of the death. "Master Mortifer has sent word. The time is now."

The way he says it, stern and certain, like the tolling of a distant bell, a grim herald of death itself.

Erevan unfurls an enchanted parchment, the soft rustle unnaturally loud in the quiet night. His expression is impassive as he reads. "The contract is extensive......Seventy-five million."

The number slams into me like a physical blow, the obligation of it settling hard on my chest.

"That can't be right, it's been centuries since we've seen anything like this."

Corvus nods grimly, his dark hollow eyes of his mask coruscant beneath the brim of his hat. "Not since 541."

The remembrance of those years surge to the surface, a vast expanse of people depleted by inescapable death. The bodies consumed by flames. Their distorted forms feeding the pyres that blot out the sky. The air, choking with ash and the stench of decay, echoes the silent screams of a world in chaos. *The first great plague.* And now the shadow of that mortal nightmare stirs once more, clawing its way back into this world.

Erevan holds up the enchanted parchment as it dissipates into nothing. "Master Mortifer doesn't make mistakes. The numbers are correct."

My eyes drift back to the dead sailors laid out in grotesque stillness. Each lifeless body is a reminder of the fragility of life, of how quickly it can all be extinguished. My conclusions dash to Rosannah. Her silky skin, her bright eyes, the way she studies me like I'm more than what I am. The thought of her lying cold and barren, her vibrance stolen by this plague, is too much to bear.

"Another plague," Corvus says, "and it's moving fast. These mortals will fall before they can comprehend the threat."

My fingers grip the ship's railing, the leather of my gloves creaking under the pressure. "She doesn't deserve this." I mutter, the words slip out before I can stop them.

Erevan's head whips toward me; his line of sight penetrates even through the mask. "She?"

I straighten, forcing the mask of detachment back over me. "It doesn't matter." I say flatly, the feeling of somber betrayal in every word.

Corvus steps closer. "Stay focused, Adra. We have work to do." His manner a warning.

Corvus approaches one of the bodies sprawled on the deck, its crooked limbs and ashen skin frozen in the agony of death. With a measured gesture, he hovers his gloved palm over the corpse's chest. For a moment, nothing happens, the stillness stagnant. Then, like a crack in the fabric of reality, a faint glow begins to emanate from the body.

Tiny motes of shimmering stardust seep from the lifeless flesh, rising like ethereal smoke into the night air. The particles swirl, suspended in Corvus's palm, their luminescence casting ghostly patterns across his mask. The energy is otherworldly, a haunting combination of light and shadow, pulsing with the pieces of a soul tethered to its mortal shell.

Corvus's hand quakes, not with hesitation, but with the raw power of the act, before the collection of stardust begins to dissolve. The particles shimmer one last time, a quiet lament, before vanishing into the void.

Somewhere beyond the veil of this mortal world, Master Mortifer waits, to be absorbed into the unseen realm that lies just beyond perception, where all endings converge.

Corvus lowers his hand, the faint energy drifts in the air like a phantom sigh before fading entirely.

Erevan steps to the center of the deck, his leather coat brushing against the planks with every precise movement. His masked face tilts toward the rows of bodies, as if surveying the work ahead. "We must move quickly." His voice is a calm monotone that barely conceals the importance of their task.

I step beside him as Corvus moves silently to the far end of the ship, where more bodies lie crumpled like discarded relics. I kneel beside a lifeless sailor, his face twisted in a final, silent scream. Hovering my palm above his chest, I summon the pull of the other realm.

A hum fills the air, low and vibrating, as the faint glow of stardust begins to rise from the body. The soul is fractured, fragmented, like a broken shard of glass piecing itself together as it swirls upward. The particles gather in my palm, tender and pulsating with the resonance of its mortal life.

As the soul hovers there, suspended in a moment of transition, the faint remnants of its memory seeps in. Fear, desperation, a glimpse of the sickness that claimed the ship. Then, like a candle snuffed out, the stardust disintegrates. The energy grows palpable with each collection. The hunger of the other side is ravenous.

Nearby, Erevan works in silent rhythm, each motion seamless, practiced, as though this is as natural to him as breathing. Corvus, at the opposite end of the ship is collecting another soul. His actions are more efficient. The faint glow of stardust lights his crimson attire, making him appear like a specter drenched in blood. The three of us work together in synchronization, moving with much haste.

The deck is quiet, save for the faint vibrating of souls being drawn forth and the occasional creak of the ship as the waves roll. I glance at Erevan as he stands up, his mask catching the faint glow of the lantern swaying above.

"How many remain?" I ask, though the question appears redundant. The number is already etched into my mind.

Seventy-five million.

A number so vast it seems impossible, yet the evidence lies all around us.

"Too many," Erevan replies flatly, moving to the next body without pause.

Corvus speaks without diverting from the task. "This is only the beginning. Soon, this plague will be everywhere, and we'll be collecting from every corner of the earth."

Chapter 18

Adrastus

I race toward Rosannah's home. The streets are quiet, only the faint crash of the ocean waves behind me. My thoughts are a whirlwind of fear and urgency, a need to see her, to know she's safe.

The tonnage of tonight's task clings to me. I can't let Rosannah suffer the same fate that is going to happen to countless others. I will do whatever it takes to save her from this horrendous atrocity. She must be protected, no matter the cost.

When I reach her door, I rap firmly before stepping back. Within moments, it opens, and there she is, her face lighting up with a smile so radiant it momentarily cuts through the darkness in my chest. She's practically bouncing with excitement. Her giddy, childlike joy striking a stark contrast to the grim reality pressing down on me.

"Adra!" She leans in, her lips aiming for mine, but my mask is still on.

I gently but firmly pull her back. My hands now rest on her shoulders. "Rosannah..." I say, my tone more somber than I intended.

Her expression falters, her brows knit together in confusion. "What's wrong? Did something happen?"

I exhale, settling my dire thoughts. "Aye, something has happened. And it's serious. You need to pack your things; everything you'll need for a long journey. We need to leave this town as soon as possible."

She blinks, caught off guard. "Leave? What are you talking about? I can't just leave. What about Gia? What about my home? My job?"

"It won't matter. You and Gia must leave. This town is no longer safe. You need to go as far away as you can."

Her laughter fades completely, replaced by a growing panic in her eyes. "What are you saying?" She asks, her voice quivering. "What's going on?"

I relax my tone, sensing her distress. "I can't explain everything right now, but I need you to trust me. Pack what you can. Talk to Gia tomorrow and be ready to leave in two days' time."

Rosannah responds calmly, though I can see the hesitation in her eyes. "Gia and I were planning a trip to Palermo. We already have everything we need for the journey."

Palermo. Far enough, perhaps, to keep her safe for now. I nod, though the urgency in my chest still chars.

"Good. Then be ready. I'll meet you and Gia two mornings from now."

Her hands quake as she wrings them together. The tension in her movements mirrors the worry etched across her face. "I'll speak with her tomorrow. We'll be ready."

"Aye, okay." I say, though the words appear insincere, inadequate for the gravity of what lies ahead. My voice eases, a moment of rare gentleness slips through. "Now, you need to rest. These coming days will be long, and you'll need your strength."

Standing outside her door, I hesitate, my gloved palm rests against the wood. Rosannah studies me, her eyes wide, searching, filled with panic. The impact of everything unsaid hangs heavily between us.

I push the door open, guiding us back inside into the safety of her sanctuary. The room is heated and the floral scent drifts in the air. She glances back at me, her expression giving a small smile as I close the door behind us.

"Come." I say gently, as I place a hand on her lower back, feeling the tension in her body beneath my touch. Carefully, I guide her toward the bed, her movements timid, as though she's unsure if she should resist or surrender to the exhaustion weighing her down.

As she sits on the edge of the bed, I kneel, helping her settle. My hands are secure on her body as I ease her back against the pillows. The glow of the candlelight plays across her face, highlighting the worry. I pull the blankets over her with care, tucking them around her like a protective barrier against the world beyond these walls.

"You'll be there, right?" She whispers. "You'll come with us?"

For a moment, I couldn't answer. Her words hold an immense amount of tonnage she doesn't fully grasp. It's a plea that cuts deeper than I'm prepared for. She doesn't realize what she's truly asking. That she's asking me to choose her over everything I've ever known, everything I've ever been.

And yet, as I see into her eyes, there is no apprehension. "I'll be there." I say, carrying a promise I will not break.

Her lips part, as though she wants to say more, but instead, she exhales softly. The tension in her body is easing. Her eyes flutter shut, as her breathing slows. Though the faint crease of worry remains on her brow, even in sleep.

I remove my mask, and place a kiss upon her forehead. It's gentle, as my lips receive the warmth of her always delicate skin. I inhale the smell of her, and my body begs me to stay. It begs me to crawl into the bed and never leave.

Every passing second away from Rosannah hurts. My heart aches and my thoughts torment me. Especially now, this sense of helplessness is substantial. I know that fear has no place in me, but this is inescapable.

I stand away from her bed, give her blanket one final pull to make sure she is tucked in, and head for the door.

The stars overhead appear distant and indifferent. Each step away from her is taxing. My boots echo against the stone pathways. The contracts are relentless. The pull of my purpose is inflexible. Death follows me everywhere. Souls are always there to collect, no matter where I go. But tonight, the thought of her slipping into that void threatens to break me. I clench my fists, the leather straining, and steel myself against the foreign surge of emotions that proceed to overtake me.

For the first time in my existence, terror coils in my chest. A fear so raw it shakes the foundations of everything I am. The thought of failing her is a terror I've never known. If it means defying Mortifer, if it means shattering the purpose I've served for centuries, so be it. She is more than a contract, more than a fleeting mortal life.

She is my Rosannah.

And I will not let her become another nameless soul lost to the abyss. I will fight against fate itself if I must.

Not her.

Never her.

CONWAY TITTY

Chapter 19

Rosannah

I am restless, tossing and turning all night. The seclusion of my room strangles me. My mind is perplexed by Adra's warnings.

I've been falling in and out of slumber all night. His haunting words cling to me like a second skin. Whenever I try to close my eyes, panic forces them back open. Though I lack specific knowledge of our current situation, I have a strong feeling that something is seriously amiss.

Every sound outside, every creak of the wood is amplified as I fight sleep. I find solace in my calming breaths and fearless fantasies about the adventures I get to have in Palermo with Gia. Focusing solely on this enables my body to unwind and drift back into my dreams. Then it happens.

The sound shatters the quiet. *A scream.* A harrowing spine-chilling sound tears through the air like a barbed blade. My eyes snap open. My heart pounds so loudly in my ears, it muffles the outside sound. The scream is followed by more wails, overlapping, rising, frantic. I am frozen, unsure if this is reality or some distorted dream. But the screams don't stop.

I throw off the covers, and rush to the window. Pulling the shutters open, I'm met with the sight of townsfolk running through the streets. Their faces pale and contorted in fear. Shouts echo off the stone walls, frenzied and unintelligible. The louder they grow, the more my stomach drops.

I don't think I just move. My fingers fumble to pull on my housecoat, shaking so badly I can hardly tie the simple cloth. The frigid morning air hits me as the door swings open. My feet barely touch the ground as I scramble toward the town square.

The streets are riddled with hysteria. Townsfolk all around clutch to one another, shouting prayers and profanities alike. Their voices a chaotic tangle that fills every corner. Shadows shift and lurch in the morning lights, making everything distorted. I stumble closer towards the commotion. My breath catching as I weave through people clutching their loved ones. Their faces are off-color and fraught.

"Stay back!" someone shouts.

"It's the curse!" another cries, but I push forward.

The unease is prominent. A crowd forms a wide circle around a lifeless body sprawled on the cobblestones. Felicita is on her knees beside it. Her bloodcurdling cries splitting the dewy morning with a grief so severe it makes my stomach churn. My nature stops when I see who it is. *Fino.*

His body lies crooked, and unnaturally stiff. His skin is a sickly gray mottled with festering blackened wounds. His lips are cracked as his mouth hangs open. A portrait of pain and panic. The scream death never let finish. His once-lively eyes, half closed, dull and lifeless. He carries the same markings as the sailors from the ship. They cover his body like a grotesque tapestry of ruination. Starved rats eat away at his fingers, gnawing on the bones. The scene is horrific, grisly, and nausea claims my gut, clawing its way upward. I think I'm going to retch.

Felicita's cries cut through the oppressive silence as she clutches at her own face. Tearing at her cheeks as though the pain might somehow wake him. "Why? Why him? God, save him! Save us!"

She collapses into an unstoppable wail, pounding her fists against the cobblestones as she prays desperately. Her words dissolve into incoherent sobs.

The sight is excruciatingly somber, and yet I can't look away. My legs are like iron, melded to the ground as I stare at the lifeless body of the man I just saw last night. The memory coils around my throat like a noose, taut and asphyxiating. His smirk in the stockroom, the way he grabbed me. The entitlement radiating off him like a noxious cloud. Anger flares in my chest, but it's swallowed by something bitter: melancholy.

Fino, full of arrogance and life just hours ago, is now reduced to this. A shell, devoid of the spirit that made him human. Tears sting my eyes, and I take a shaky step back. Felicita's unrelenting cries pull me back in.

She's praying now, her words jumbled and frantic. Her voice breaks with each plea to the heavens.
But then she stops. Her head snaps up. Her red-rimmed eyes sear into mine. Her face contorts with detestable rage, and she points a trembling finger at me.

"YOU!" She screams. "YOU DID THIS! YOU BROUGHT THIS CURSE UPON US! YOU DEVILISH CREATURE! YOU SINFUL WHORE! THIS IS YOUR DOING!"

Her words are a slap. The accusation rings in my ears. The crowd around us stirs. Their whispers grow louder, more intimidating. Eyes focus on me, quick and probing, filled with suspicion. My breath snags in my throat as Felicita collapses back into her prayers. Her voice screaming every word. I take a step back, shaking my head.

"No, I—I didn't..." I stammer, but my voice is drowned out by the growing murmur of the crowd.

Before I can defend myself, another scream erupts from down the street. The crowd surges, rushing toward the sound like a wave of panic. My legs move on their own, carrying me with them, though every instinct screeches to run the other way.

As we rounded the corner, the scene was grimmer than I could have ever imagined. The sight makes my blood run cold. Another body lies in the middle of the street, twisted and marred by the same blackened sores. Rats feast on her face, chewing on her cloudy eyeballs, and once jolly cheeks. A woman stands over it. Her
202

hands covering her mouth as she lets out an earsplitting scream of grief and dismay. Her cries echo through the narrow street, blending seamlessly with the frantic shouts of the crowd. Their anxiety reverberates off the stone walls and settles deep in my bones.

The crowd erupts into chaos. People shove and trip over each other in their desperate rush to flee. The environment is filled with shouts and wails, prayers and obscenities, all blending into a deafening roar. Panic is spreading like wildfire. Doors slam, locks click, and windows are hastily shuttered as the townsfolk barricade against this invisible threat. This very town is being consumed by a despotic, malevolent force.

One thought overpowers me now: *Gia.*

I need to get to her. I need to make sure she's safe. I don't wait. I run.

Ragged gasps escape as I push through the chaos. The streets smear around me. The sound of my heartbeat roars in my ears as I race toward her shop. My mind is preoccupied by the horror I've just witnessed.

An insistent knot of worry strains in my chest as I approach her door. I knock frantically. My fist thumps against the wooden surface.

"Gia! It's me!"

The silence inside makes me queasy and for a moment, I wonder if she's even there. I pound on the door again, louder this time. "Gia! Open up! Please, it's urgent!"

Finally, I hear a lock sliding, then another, before the door creaks open just enough for Gia's face to appear. Her eyes are wide with alarm. Her usually vibrant demeanor replaced by a pale, fragile expression.

The door swings open, and I throw myself into her arms, gripping her tightly. "Thank the moon and stars, I thought — I thought something had happened to you."

Gia hugs me back; her hands rest on my shoulders. "What's going on? I heard the screams."

I lock the door securely behind us as I struggle to catch my breath. The shop's only light is the dim morning rays that seep in. The energy is intimidating but the recognizable scent of dyes and woven threads calms me. The shelves are stacked with vibrant fabrics. Their colors dulled in the subdued light, and the faint rustling of hanging drapes swaying in the draft adds a bizarre stillness to the room.

"It's worse than I thought. Fino... he's dead."

Gia gasps, her palm flies to her mouth. "Dead? How? When?"

"I think this morning," I say, shaking my head as the memory of his corpse flashes in my mind. "I saw him. He had the same markings as the sailors from the ship. The puss filled sores, blackened veins. And Felicita... she was—" My voice catches, and I take a moment to calm myself down. "She was screaming, Gia. She blamed me. Called me a devil. Said I brought this curse."

Gia's expression hardens; a flicker of anger breaks through her fear. "Felicita has always been a dramatic shrew. You know better than to take her words seriously."

"It's not just Fino. There was another body. Another one, just down the street. The sickness from the ship somehow is here, and it's spreading rapidly."

Gia's face pales further, and she sinks onto a stool, clutching the edge of the counter. "What are we going to do?"

I placed a loving hand on her shoulder, trying to calm us both. "We're leaving," I say firmly. "Adra warned me last night. He said we need to get out of this town as soon as possible. Pack your things. We're leaving for Palermo sooner than we thought."

Gia looks up at me, her expression full of disbelief. "Palermo? Now? We're not ready."

"We must be. We already have our supplies. This town isn't safe anymore. We need to go before it's too late."

She hesitates, then nods slowly. "Okay, let's pack."

We move through the shop in silence at first, pulling clothes and supplies into neat bundles. The simple rhythm of preparing for travel feels strangely comforting. A small distraction from the chaos outside.

As the silence stretches on, Gia finally breaks it. "What do you think Palermo will be like?" She asks, her voice tinged with a faint, fragile hope.

I pause, folding one of her dresses. "Big!" I say with a small smile.

"Aye!" She chimes back. "Bigger than anything we've ever seen. The markets, the people... it'll be like stepping into another world."

"I hope so. Maybe we'll pick up some ideas for our shop while we're there."

For a moment, the chaos of the morning lifts as we talk about the food, the new vendors, the adventure that awaits us. But beneath it all, the worry never fully leaves. The thought of leaving everything behind, of not knowing if there will be anything to return to, idles in the back of my mind.

By the time we finish packing Gia's things, the sun hangs low in the sky, casting a golden glow through the fabric shop's small, dust-covered windows. The vibrant bolts of cloth subdued by the encroaching twilight. The unspoken tension is prominent as we stand among the scattered bundles and trunks we've hurriedly packed.

Gia's eyes are rimmed with exhaustion and worry. I pull her into a tight hug, her body tremors as she clings to me. "We'll be okay." She bends against my shoulder, but the silence that follows is occupied with uncertainty.

I step out into the street, the chill of the evening air hits me, carrying with it the acrid smell of smoke from distant chimneys. I walk back to my own place. My steps are slow, each one weighed down by the enormity of what lies ahead.

When I finally reach home, the familiar hospitality of my room does little to comfort me. I sit on the edge of my bed, staring at the small pile of belongings I've started to gather: some clothes, a few trinkets, and a small bundle of food for the journey. It seems insufficient, a weak defense against the uncharted future awaiting us.

That night, sleep evades me. I toss and turn, my mind a storm of emotions. The image of Fino's lifeless body flashes before me. His once arrogant charming face now replaced by the disgusting and frightening call of death. A bitter cocktail of anger and relief roils in my chest.

Good riddance, I think, but the thought leaves a sour taste in my mouth.

He may have been a petty knave, swollen with false grandeur and more manhood in a mouse's shadow than in his codpiece. But honestly? I AM GLAD HE IS DEAD!

He is but the Devil's turd given legs and a tongue. Charmless as a piss-soaked rag yet puffed like he wore the crown. What madness took me that made me squander many moons and suns dreaming about that lecherous toad. Ugh makes my skin writhe like maggots in rot.

It was a cruel death, but you know what? Fuck him! Curse him and his nonexistent lineage for violating me

207

like that. Now that I do ponder it, his end came far too swift. A mercy he did not earn.

Fuck that levereter[17] wandought![18] And while I am at it, fuck Felicita too! That vile harpy cunt! The two of them deserve each other.

Though I warrant she now is weeping over his sorry, cankered corpse. May the stars shine bright, dear Felicita. I won't say I'd pray for the pestilence to find her too, but she did lay hands upon his boil-riddled carcass. Who knows what price that touch shall bring?

My anger changes into sadness swiftly as I am brought back into the truth of the world. The sailors and some of the townsfolk all claimed by the same horrifying sickness.

And what of the others? What's going to happen to this town? To Gia's shop? To the goodly merchants and honest tradespeople who make their fortune by the sea's breath? To my ever-returning folks, who trade coin for forgetfulness and wine for their sins? To the little lambs that gambol with laughter and chase joy through cobbled lanes?

The thought that there might be nothing left to return to grips me with a melancholy I have never felt. And yet, a part of me wonders...

If Palermo proves to be the paradise we seek, shall my heart not root itself there and forget the way back home?

---

[17] Corrupt ("liver eater"
[18] A weak, ineffectual man.

My hopes drift, to Adra. His warnings echo in my mind. I hear the urgency in his voice. Despite everything, the chaos, the uncertainty, he has made me feel safe. Protected. The memory of his touch remains, and for a fleeting moment, the uncertainty eases. It's replaced by butterflies in my stomach. The flutter of their wings becomes a whisper of his name. I picture his face as my eyes grow heavy. His spirit a fleeting comfort in the dark.

Sleep, when it finally comes, is shallow and restless. Filled with fractured images of shadowy figures and lifeless bodies. Nightmares take over my dreams and I am unable to relax. I wake several times through the night. My room bathed in moonlight, the silence pressing against my ears. Each time I close my eyes, and try to will myself back to sleep, the darkness comes alive, full of unspoken threats.

When I wake again, it's to the first light of dawn spilling through my window, golden and simple. For a moment, I lie still, the sincerity of the sun brushes against my skin almost lulling me back into a false sense of calm. Then the harsh, urgent sound of knocking cuts through the stillness, and my heart leaps into my throat.

I sit up abruptly. The anxiety from the day before crashes over me like a tidal wave. I glance toward the door, dread curls in my stomach.

Tugging my blanket tightly around my body, I rise and move cautiously toward the door. My fingers shiver as they rest on the latch. I take a deep inhale before pulling it open, bracing myself for whatever waits on the other side.

Chapter 20

Adrastus

The timid morning sun rays cling to me like a funeral veil as I tread through the fog filled streets. My boots thud hollowly below me as I walk along the stone pathways. They're slick with more dew and muck than usual. The overcast in the sky looms above like the lid of a coffin, giving warning as if to say *death is near.* The foul breath of the grave engulfs the town, carried by a breeze that is the exhale of a dying world.

Echoes bounce off the walls as I walk, wails that sound like spirits too weak to cross into the next realm. Their voices are an unwavering symphony of despair, like a pathway paved with mourning, where hope is distant. The town itself appears more dead than alive. Their dread stifles any joy mortals could have.

I round the corner and abruptly halt. A mother huddles with her two children. Their clothes soiled and

211

torn. Their faces pale as bones. Blood drips from the corners of their mouths as they cough. Their small frames wracked with violent tremors. The mother clutches them both tightly. Her eyes sunken by distress and enervation. They are too weak to move, too far gone to seek help.

I clench my fists, the leather grating as my knuckles flex, a foreign emotion rolls through me, *fear.* Not for them, but for my Rosannah. This plague moves fast, faster than I had anticipated. Every second that I am not by her side feels like an eternity. Every delay, another risk. My torso strains at the thought of arriving too late.

I can't...won't...let her be taken by this.

Quickening my pace, my boots clump loudly against the stone as I head toward her home.

I must see her. I must know she's alive.

I reach her door. My fists pound against the wood, the sound echoing down the surrounding alleys.

"Rosannah!" I call out, "Rosannah! Open the door!"

Nothing. The silence is deafening, each second stretching, as my chest begins to ache. I knock harder this time, "ROSANNAH!", a yell so powerful, the bass in my voice vibrates small pebbles on the ground.

Eventually, the door creaks open, and a bundle of black untamed curls spills into the doorway. Her sleepy face peers out at me, her hand rubs the slumber from her eyes. Relief hits me so hard I nearly topple back. A full-bodied exhale billows out of me.

"Adra?"

I take in every little detail of her. The way her hair falls wildly around her face. The faint crease on her cheek from where she pressed against her pillow. She's alive. By the shadows grace, she's alive.

"We need to go, *now*."

Her brow furrows as she steps back to let me in, confusion fusing with her features. "I thought we weren't leaving until later tonight... We still have to get Gia." I can see the stress radiating from her body.

"Aye everything is happening. This plague, it's spreading faster than I thought. We need to leave. Immediately."

She nods, the urgency in my voice breaking through her grogginess. "Okay, okay... Let me just grab the rest of my things."

As she moves around the room, stuffing the remaining clothes and belongings into her bag, she glances at me over her shoulder. "Fino's dead," she says abruptly, her tone neutral, "I can't say sorrow has found me, more bewilderment. One moment he lives, foul tongue as ever, the next silence."

I can't help the slight smirk that tugs at my lips. "Splendid." I mutter under my breath.

"What was that?" She asks, pausing mid-fold.

"Nothing." I say quickly, though I can't stop the wave of satisfaction as a smile covers my face.

Fino. That pathetic excuse for a man. At least I won't be the one to collect his soul. Erevan or Corvus can have that honor, or better yet, one of the fresh underlings still wet behind the ears. Maybe the newbie, still struggling to harness their power messes with his

213

soul's journey. Maybe he makes it across, maybe he doesn't. It's no more than his due, to be nothing but a mere afterthought in the void.

Rosannah continues packing, shaking her head. "Felicita blamed me." She says, her voice quieter. "She screamed at me in front of everyone. Called me a devilish whore, said I cursed the town."

Her hands tremble as she folds another dress, and I step closer, unable to stop myself. "She's wrong, you are none of those things Rosannah. You're a light in a world consumed by shadows. You're mercy in a place that has forgotten what it means to feel. Don't let her lies poison you."

"You really believe that?"

I step even closer, my fingers brushing against hers. "I do. More than you know."

She holds my gaze for a long moment before nodding. Her lips managing the faintest of smiles. The tension between us waits, as she redirects her focus back to packing. I watch her for a moment longer. My chest contracts with a feeling I can't name.

Rosannah stands in the middle of the room, her bag packed and resting by her feet. Her eyes sweep over the space, dawdling on the little details. The worn wooden table in the corner by her bed. The small cracks in the walls. The way the fading light filters through the window and casts soft patterns across the floor. Her face is calm, but I can see the sadness pooling in her eyes. She exhales slowly, her fingers brushing the edge of the bed as if to anchor herself to the memories held here.

214

I know what she's thinking. I can almost hear the echoes of her laughter in the air, filling the room in moments I wasn't a part of. Her gaze drifts to the spot by the hearth where we first kissed, and then to the bed. The faintest flush of emotion crosses her face as she recalls our first night together.

Her hands are timid as she picks up her bag. She doesn't speak, but her silence is louder than words. I take a step closer, placing a palm gently on her back. She flinches at the touch but doesn't pull away. Her breath stops for a moment before she exhales again.

"It's time." I say quietly, though I can understand her hesitation.

She acknowledges, blinking back the tears that threaten to spill. With one last glance around the room, her lips press into a thin line as if sealing the impact of her emotions within herself. Then, she steps forward, her movements slow as though each step is pulling her away from more than just a home. It's pulling her away from a life that she knows is gone forever.

I guide her to the door. My hand firm but gentle against her back. "You're not leaving it all behind," I say, trying to offer some semblance of comfort. "The memories... they're yours. They'll stay with you."

She doesn't answer, but the exacerbated sigh tells me she heard me. As she crosses the threshold, her head bows, her shoulders carry the weight of what she's leaving behind. I follow her out, closing the door behind us.

Rosannah and I make our way through the streets, her bag slung over her shoulder and mine resting heavily at my side. I offered to carry it for her, but she insisted. The overcast sky casts a gray pallor over the town. The faint sound of coughing drifts from the alleyways, joining the murmurs of the sick and the panicked cries of townsfolk scrambling to make sense of the growing chaos.

Rosannah chatters nervously beside me, trying to lighten the mood. "I can't believe we're finally going! Gia and I have dreamed of this trip to Palermo for so long. It doesn't even seem real."

Her steps quicken, and she lets out a small, giddy laugh, skipping ahead for a moment before glancing back at me. The brightness in her tone like sunlight cutting through storm clouds, beautiful, but fleeting. I don't have the heart to dampen her spirit, even as my own unease festers.

We pass an alleyway, and my nerve halts. There they are; the mother and her two children I saw earlier. Only now, they're no longer huddled together coughing. They're lying still, too still. Their bodies contorted as if their last moments were wracked with agony. A smear of dark, dried blood trails from the mother's mouth, staining the cobblestones beneath her. Rosannah doesn't notice, thank the infernal powers, but I quicken my pace. My hand pushing against her back as I urge her forward.

216

"We should hurry, Gia will be waiting."

Rosannah nods, skipping the last few steps to Gia's shop, her mood lifting again. She stops at the door and knocks, a sing-song cheer in her voice. "Gia! It's me! We're here!"

She waits, rocking back on her heels, but no answer comes. She frowns and knocks again, louder this time. "Gia?" I see her cheerfulness waver. Something shifts in her posture, a tension, a quiet realization.

She glances back at me, her expression uncertain. "Something feels... wrong. She always answers right away."

I step forward, placing a reassuring hand on her shoulder. "Let me try." I say, knocking harder on the maroon wooden door of the boutique. "Gia! It's Adra. Open up!"

Silence.

Rosannah grips my arm. "Adra, I–I think something's happened. She wouldn't just ignore us."

I can see the panic beginning to rise in her eyes. "Stay calm, I'll get us in. Just stand back."

With practiced ease, I kneel and work at the lock. The faint click of the mechanism gives way, and I push the door open, stepping inside first. The shop is dim, the air heavy with the smell of fabric dye and something far less pleasant, something metallic and sour that immediately puts me on edge.

"Gia?" Rosannah calls from behind me, her voice quivering. She takes a step inside, and I instinctively hold out my arm to stop her.

"Wait," I say, but her short self manages to wriggle underneath my arm. I step forward, my eyes scanning the shop. And then I see *her*....

Gia's lifeless body lies sprawled on the floor near a pile of freshly arrived fabrics. The bright colors of the cloth stark against the pallor of her skin. Blood pools beneath her. Her face frozen in an expression of pain and fear. My heart sinks like a stone.

"Rosannah, no!" I reach out to stop her, but it's too late. She's seen.

Her screams pierce the air with anguish. She drops to her knees, crawling toward Gia. Her sobs are wrenching and uncontrollable. "Gia! No, no, no! Gia, wake up!" She wails as she reaches for her friend.

I grab her by the shoulders, pulling her back before she can touch the body. "Rosannah, stop. We must go... NOW!."

She thrashes in my arms, her grief consuming her. "No! I can't leave her like this! Gia! Please!"

Her cries tear at something buried inside me, but I know there's no time for this. "Rosannah... she's gone. There's nothing we can do for her now. *We must leave.*"

She sobs against my chest, her body shudders with the force of her cries. I hold her tightly, giving her a moment to grieve, though every second, a lifetime. "I'm sorry." I whisper. "I'm so sorry."

I pull her to her feet, but not before she breaks free from my grip and rips the gold necklace from Gia's neck, clutching it tightly in her fist. I don't stop her, how could I?

Her legs are weak, she stumbles, and I catch her. I pick her up in my arms and carry her out of the shop. Her cries still echoing through the empty streets.

Once outside, I set her down gently, brushing her hair from her tear-streaked face. "Rosannah..." I say softly, crouching to meet her gaze. "We must go. This town isn't safe."

She bows weakly, clutching the necklace to her chest.

Together, we head for the stables on the outskirts of town. The streets are chaos. Coughing, frantic shouts, wagons being loaded in haste. Those are the sounds of a town unraveling around us.

The wagon creaks under the weight of our belongings as I secure the bundles, tying them down tightly with ropes I salvaged the night before. It's strange, really, how easily the pieces fell into place, almost as if fate itself wanted us to leave.

I had been on the outskirts of town, for a collection, and honestly to clear my head, when I saw it: the wagon. It stood untouched in the yard, the donkey tethered to a post, its reins dangling like an afterthought. I approached cautiously, the smell of death unmistakable even in the open air. Peering inside the house, I found the owner, a frail old man slumped over a table. His skin was pallid. His body unmoving. The markings of the plague were unmistakable.

Once I collected his soul, there was no one left to mourn him. No one to protest my taking what he no longer needed. I whispered a quiet, bitter thanks to the abyss as I untied the donkey and guided it toward the wagon. The beast seemed almost grateful for the movement. I spent the rest of the night preparing, ensuring the wagon was sturdy enough to take us as far as it needed to.

I load the remainder of our things quickly, before lifting Rosannah onto the seat beside mine. She is weightless, limp with exhaustion and grief. Now, as the donkey lumbers forward, the memory of the old man drifts in the back of my mind. His home, his life, reduced to silence and shadows, just like so many others.

The wagon lurches on as we pass over uneven cobblestones, and Rosannah doesn't even flinch. She sits beside me. Her body sagged. Her eyes fixed on the horizon but seeing nothing.

"Hyah!" I call, snapping the reins gently. The donkey responds, its tired gait carrying us away from the chaos that still echoes behind us.

The streets grow quieter, the cries of panic and coughing fade into the distance. The shadowy expanse of the Forest of Mascalia looms ahead. Its dark canopy our only path we have, but it's promising some semblance of escape.

Beside me, Rosannah clutches Gia's necklace so tightly her knuckles are white. Her silence is heavier than the bundles in the wagon, a weight I can't seem to lift. I glance at her, my chest narrowing with the guilt of what I've brought her into and the sorrow of what she's lost.

"I'll protect you." I whisper, the words meant more for myself than for her. "No matter what."

The promise burns in my chest, a flame against the encroaching sickness. As the wagon rolls into the shadows of the forest, I know there's no going back now.

CONWAY TITTY

Chapter 21

Rosannah

Everything around me is a blur, distant and surreal, as the wagon creaks and sways beneath us. My body moves with the rhythm, but my mind is locked in a tormenting haze.

My palm aches from how tightly I clutch Gia's pendant. The gold of Saint Rosalia etched into my palm as if I'm afraid to let go of even this small piece of her. I stare at it, barely registering the delicate engraving, though I know every detail by heart.

Saint Rosalia. The protector. The healer.

Gia used to tell me her story, her eyes lighting up as she spoke about the miracles attributed to the saint. Gia's mother had given her this pendant just before she died, saying it would keep her safe. Gia believed it and wore it every single day. It was one of the reasons she wanted to go to Palermo. To see the city that revered the saint who had brought her comfort in her darkest moments.

The tears come slowly at first, hot and unrelenting. My vision blurs, the shapes of the forest ahead smudging into a watery mosaic. The impact of my grief presses down on me, and I blink, letting the tears spill freely, streaking my cheeks with sorrow I can't contain. Gia's face fills my mind. Her bright smile, the way she'd toss her head back when she laughed, her endless dreams of escaping this place, of finding something bigger... something better.

And now she's gone.

No goodbye. No last words. Just silence and the cold, lifeless shell I left behind on the floor of her shop.

My hands shake as I run my thumb over the pendant, the edges digging into my skin.

It's not fair. None of this is fair. She deserved more. She deserved a life, love, laughter, not this. Not death on a dirty floor surrounded by fabrics she'll never touch again.

Anger rises in me, cutting through the grief like a bilious blade.

How could this happen?

How could she be taken so easily? So suddenly?

My chest constricts further as my tears fall harder, spilling over onto my hands. The pendant now slick beneath my fingertips. I want to scream, to shout at the unfairness of it all, but the words won't come. The pain is too large, crushing my very soul.

Adra shifts beside me, his presence a balanced contrast to my unraveling. His arm wraps around me, loving and firm, a silent reassurance. But instead of comfort, it breaks something inside. The dam bursts, and a sob escapes my lips, as if it's been clawing its way out of me since the moment I saw her body.

The sound surprises me, but once it starts, I can't stop. I cry harder. My shoulders shake as the grief and anger pour out in equal measure. Adra pulls me closer, his arm tightening around me, his hand resting gently on my arm. He doesn't say anything. There's nothing to say, but he lets me cry, lets me press my face against his chest as my sobs wreck my body. His existence is grounding, a fragile anchor in the storm that's tearing me apart.

All I can think about is Gia. Her laughter. Her dreams. Her spark, crushed beneath an unforgiving fate. My tears don't stop. They spill onto Adra's chest, soaking into his clothing, but he doesn't pull away. He just holds me, until the sobs start to subside into quiet, shuddering breaths. My soul aches, immensely raw, but Adra's presence keeps me from completely shattering.

For now, I let myself lean into him, let him bear some of the weight I can't carry alone. The tears keep falling, but I no longer fight them. I just let them come.

The sun dips low on the horizon, painting the sky in hues of fiery orange and dark purple. The brilliance of it seems cruel, as if the world dares to show its beauty when mine has just been splintered. The sounds of the town now completely disappeared behind us, replaced by the rustling of trees as we approach the edge of the forest.

The wagon creaks to a stop, but I barely registered it. The coolness in the air brushes against my skin, but I'm numb. I don't care where we stop, or how far we go. Nothing matters.

Gia was my compass, my counsel, my comrade and my keeper. The only soul I'd trust with my truth. And now... now she has vanished and the world rings hollow.

The ache in my chest is so heavy, so unbearable, that I almost wish it would crush me completely. The city of Palermo, our one and only dream, now feels dull.

What's the meaning of this life, if she not walk beside me? What worth is the world, now barren of her light? Without her, what is my purpose?

Adra climbs down from the wagon, I watch through glazed eyes as he unhitches the donkey and leads it to a tree, spreading fresh hay on the ground. He unhooks the harness, allowing the animal to graze freely. Its ears twitching as it investigates the forest floor. He works quietly, efficiently, while I sit motionless, staring at the darkening treetops. As the affliction of my grief rains down on me, it becomes harder to breathe.

Adra approaches my side of the wagon, his footsteps crunching against the earth. He stops in front of me and holds out his palm. "Come down." His voice is calm and patient.

I blink, shaking myself from this desolating fog just enough to move. Sliding my hand into his, I let him help me down. My legs are weak. My body is disconnected from my mind, but I manage to balance myself. I force the heaviness in my chest aside for a moment and glance at him. "Do you need help with anything?" I ask, my voice flat, lacking any emotion.

He shakes his head. "No. But if you want to help yourself, spend some time with that donkey. Animals have a way of healing when nothing else can."

I hesitate, unsure if anything could soothe the storm raging inside me, but his tone leaves little room for argument. I nod and walk over to the donkey.

The animal glances up as I approach. Its dark eyes calm, its tail swishing lazily at flies. Slowly, I reach out and run my fingers along its neck, feeling the coarse of its fur beneath my palm. The donkey flicks its ears, twitching slightly at my touch, but continues to graze, oblivious to my turmoil.

My fingers trace gentle circles along its back as I take a slow, deep inhale. The sound of its constant breathing fills my ears, grounding me in a way I didn't expect. I lean forward, resting my head against the donkey's shoulder. Its sympathy seeps into me. Its heartbeat is a sturdy, soothing rhythm. I close my eyes and let the sound wash over me, matching my own breaths to its unhurried pace.

For the first time in hours, maybe longer, the tightness in my chest eases. The forest around me comes alive. The chirping of birds settling into their nests. The faint croak of cicadas beginning their nightly song. The rustling of leaves stirred by the cool breeze. The crisp autumn air fills my lungs, clearing some of the heartbreak. For a fleeting moment, I feel still. I feel calm.

Pulling back, I give the donkey a soft pat, my fingers wiggle in its fur. Its calm, unhasty presence like a balm on a wound that hasn't even begun to heal. I see Adra in the clearing, spreading blankets on the ground for our makeshift camp. The light of the setting sun catches on his dark hair, casting his features in a shadow. He's made a place for us to rest, to stop running, at least for tonight.

My heartbeat slows. My mind begins to clear. I take another strong breath in. The night breeze cool against my skin, and silently, I watch as Adra finishes preparing our camp.

There's still a hollowness inside me, a gnawing grief that won't leave, but for now, I let myself focus on the present. The ache will be there tomorrow. Tonight, I'll let it rest.

Chapter 22

Adrastus

T he sun sinks lower. Its final rays bleeding into the horizon and leaving the forest cloaked in a louring gray.

The cold wraps itself around us like an unwelcome guest. I kneel on the ground, laying out the blankets carefully, smoothing the edges as though that simple act might bring Rosannah some comfort. Around us, the forest hums with life, the rustling of unseen creatures, the distant call of an owl, but it's all muffled.

I set the canteen down beside the blankets. My thoughts briefly drifting to the long night ahead. Before I can straighten, she throws her arms around me. Her embrace sudden and tight. She buries her head against my chest. I'm frozen, startled by the intensity of her hug.

Acknowledging her, I wrap my arms around her body. Pulling her close, holding her as though I could shield her from everything. Her grief, her loss, and the chaos we've left behind.

She whispers into my chest, "Thank you."

I tighten my hold on her resting my chin against the top of her head. She is so fragile in my arms, yet there's a quiet strength in the way she clings to me, as though I'm the only solid thing in her crumbling world.

"For what?"

"For helping me when I couldn't help myself."

She pulls back, her hands still resting on my arms. Her eyes connect with mine. They're brimming with unshed tears. "I never would have left if it weren't for you. I'd still be... there. I'd still be falling apart..."

I am unable to find the words to respond. Her vulnerability, her trust, is puzzling. "You don't have to thank me for that." I finally manage. "You didn't need saving, Rosannah. You just needed someone to remind you of your strength."

She blinks as tears fall freely down her cheeks. "And for consoling me, truly, I would have been lost."

I share a small, gracious smile. The kind that I hope conveys what words can't. It's a fleeting expression, but it's enough to make her melt. Allowing her shoulders to relax just a little as the weight she's carrying disperses.

"Take some food from the satchel, eat while you can." I tell her gently. "I'll find some kindling to get this fire started."

She nods, wiping at her eyes as she shuffles toward the bags. Her movements are still a bit slow, but she is finding a purpose now.

As she busies herself, I step toward the edge of the clearing, scanning the ground for branches and twigs. The forest appears vast. Its shadows stretch high and far. My boots crunch against the frost-tipped leaves as I gather what we'll need to keep the night's cold at bay.

Now and then, I glance back toward Rosannah. She's kneeling by the bag, pulling out bits of bread and dried meat. There's a quiet sorrow that clings to her like the chill in the air, but she's moving. She's here.

Night settles around us. The golden hues of the fire flickers and casts dancing shadows against the trees. I sit cross-legged on the blanket, sipping from the water canteen; but my focus isn't on the drink or the night. It's on her.

Rosannah is seated across from me. Her gaze fixed on the fire as she tends to the mutton cooking on the makeshift spit. The light plays on her features, accentuating the softness of her face, the curve of her cheek, the gentle fall of her lashes. Her hair, unruly and full of wild curls, gleams like burnished bronze in the firelight.

She pokes the meat with a small stick, testing it. "It's ready!"

I take the meat she gives me, savoring the simplicity of the meal. I know she needs this sustenance more than I, but I indulge with her anyway. We eat in silence, the crackling of the fire and the symphony of the forest, our only companions. Now and then, I steal a glance at her, catching her doing the same. Her mouth slips into a small smile when our eyes meet, and I can't help the flutter that stirs in my chest.

When we finish, I lean back, patting my stomach dramatically. "I'm stuffed." I declare, letting out a mock groan of satisfaction.

Rosannah giggles, she leans forward and pokes at my stomach. "Stuffed, huh?" She teases. "You look it."

"Heyyy!" I say in mock offense, swatting her hand away, but I'm grinning too much to be convincing.

She laughs, then suddenly sits upright, her excitement radiating off her smile. "Wait! I packed something extra."

She hops up and practically skips to the wagon, rummaging through her bag with a determination that makes me laugh.

When she returns, she plops back down beside me, holding up a jug of wine triumphantly. "It's not a true meal without a drink!" She announces, shoving the jug in my direction.

I raise an eyebrow at her enthusiasm. "And yet you forgot glasses?"

She gasps dramatically, clutching her chest as if I've mortally wounded her. "Ugh, Of course I forgot! How dare I?"

"It's fine. We'll just share. I don't mind." I add a wink for good measure. Her cheeks flush, though she quickly hides it with a playful roll of her eyes.

Taking the jug from her, I pull the cork off with a satisfying *pop.* Lifting it, I pause for a moment before saying, "cin cin," and take a hearty swig.

The wine is sharp, slightly sweet, and warms me as it goes down. I pass the jug back to her. Our fingers brush during the exchange. The contact is brief but charged, a spark that remains long after I've let go.

Rosannah grips the jug with both hands and takes a sip, spilling a small stream of wine that trickles down her chin, neck, and into the curve of her collarbone. My eyes follow the liquid's path. My thoughts immediately darken. *If only...*

I clench my jaw, trying to push those thoughts away, but my body betrays me. My unrelentless cock twitches in my pants.

Now is not the time.

Now is definitely not the time.

She passes the jug back, her fingers graze mine again, and I take it. Her hands are impossibly smooth against the roughness of my mine, and I can't stop myself from imagining them in places far less innocent. I shift, trying to adjust myself inconspicuously, and scoot closer to her under the guise of passing the jug back.

I find myself staring at her again, at the way the firelight kisses her skin, the way her curls fall over her face like they're trying to hide her beauty. My pants always feel tighter when she's around. It's torturous being in her presence sometimes. My body likes to betray me with depraved thoughts at the worst moments.

I must not give in.

Reminding myself that I am on Rosannah's time, not my own. She will signal to me when she is ready to

233

have any sort of intimacy. My sweet mortal has been through so much lately. She just wants comfort, and solace.

Without thinking, I reach out and brush a strand of hair away, tucking it gently behind her ear. She glances at me; her cheeks flushed from the wine and the fire.

A small, closed-mouth smile spreads across her lips. Her dimples deepen. I can't stop the word that escapes me, "Wow."

She giggles, tilting her head. "What?"

"Just you. You're extraordinary. After everything you've endured... you still shine. You're still you. Bright, kind, resilient, and more remarkable than I could ever put into words. You are a marvel Rosannah. A wonder so rare that it can hush the strongest storms and kindle stars in the blackest of nights." I pause as I brush my thumb across her lips. "You have taken hold of me, and I don't know if I'll ever be free from your eyes, nor would I wish it. You have me ensnared by your beauty."

Her eyes soften, the glow of the fire reflected in their depths, and she leans closer. Her movements are unhurried. My breath stills as her face nears mine. Her lips are parted, and I can't hold back any longer.

I close the space between us, and the instant our lips meet, it's like the world falls away. The kiss crackles. It's a collision of passion and desire. A kiss that roars to life, devouring me entirely. Her lips are sweet, impossibly so, moving against mine with a tenderness that carries an undercurrent of vitality. It's like coming home and losing myself all at once.

Her affection seeps into me. The smell of her, irresistibly intoxicating. Her touch securing me in a way I've never known. My hands find her waist, pulling her closer, needing her nearer, as if the space between us is too much to bear.

Every sensation heightens. The faint crackle of the fire, the way her body melts into mine, and the taste of her sweetness mingling with the wine. For a moment, there is nothing else. No shadows of the past, no weight of the future. *Just her.*

Her heartbeat matches mine. Her breath fuses with mine. *Just us....* Lost in the kind of kiss that makes time itself seem irrelevant.

Rosannah pulls away, and she lets out a sigh. Her eyes shine with something I can only describe as admiration. She tilts her head back, looking up at the night sky, as the stars reflect in her gaze.

I follow her line of sight, staring into the vastness above us. The stars seem brighter here. Their twinkle an endless ocean of light against the dark canvas of night. My hand seeks hers, and when our fingers intertwine, her thumb grazing lightly over my knuckles. The touch is so gentle and purposeful it causes my body to vibrate. The simplicity of it. The tenderness feels more intimate than any touch I've ever known.

Rosannah leans into me. Her body is warm against mine, and when I glance down, our noses brush. The closeness is dizzying. Her lips only a whisper away. And then she closes the distance once more, kissing me with such passion. Her hands find my face, while her touch is confident yet gentle, as though she's memorizing every angle, every curve.

She leans further into me. Her weight presses me back until I'm lying on the blankets, as she follows. Her lips never leave mine, as her hands begin to explore. Her fingertips graze my chest and my stomach. The sensation setting fire to my skin. Her fingers move lower, tracing the outline of me. Her touch drives me wild. Rosannah is an expert explorer when it comes to my body.

She rubs her palm against my *(of course)* already hard cock. Applying pressure as she drags her palm up and down my pants. She knows exactly what she is doing to me, and I want whatever she is thinking.

Locked in the kiss, I gasp as she slips her fingers under the band of my undergarments. Her teasing fingers graze the head of my throbbing penis. My body tenses and twitches underneath her touch, and it takes everything in me not to surrender completely to the moment. *I need her.*

Her hand moves up and down my length. Her strokes slow as her tongue moves even slower in my mouth, caressing each other in a saliva embrace. I am on the verge of cumming with every motion. She has me wrapped around her fingers. *Literally.*

She breaks the kiss. Her lips hover just above mine. Her eyes are locked passionately into mine. Her voice carries the weight of everything she feels. "Make love to me, Adra."

Her words make me crumble, and without hesitation I pull her into another kiss. My palms cupping her face as I pour every ounce of desire and adoration into it.

Rolling her gently beneath me, I let my lips trail down her jawline, and over the contour of her neck. Tasting her skin along the way. I could devour her for every meal and still never be satiated. She lets out a sigh as my lips move lower brushing against her collarbone. Her hand still strokes me, driving me to the edge, but I force myself to slow down, to savor this moment. I kiss her shoulder, and down to her breasts. The fabric of her dress is an obstacle that I remove with care.

As I peel it away, inch by inch, her beauty is revealed to me in the flickering firelight. I let out an audible gasp as I kiss her sweet supple skin some more. Leaning back, I let my hands roam free. My fingertips mapping every curve on her body. They trail the mountains that are her breasts, down the valley of ribs, and onto the hills of her belly. Her stomach caressed by my hands and rubbed with affection.

I press my nose into her bountiful breasts and inhale her scent. I could be lost in her forever. Forget the contract let me lay on these flesh pillows for eternity.

Her scent could drive anyone insane, a blend of lavender and need. The night's atmosphere is alive around us with the hum of cicadas and the rustling of the leaves. The background music for tonight's passion.

How lovely the night does sound; all I can focus on is her. The way her body moves when I touch her. The way her breath stops as I brush my lips over her belly button. "My dear mourning star... you are.... everything."

Her hands find my face again, pulling me back to her lips, and I lose myself in her embrace. Every movement is a dance of passion and tenderness as we come together under the canopy of stars.

The firelight casts golden hues over our entwined bodies. Time feels irrelevant, and the horrid world outside fades away, leaving only us. Allowing us to be lost in a moment that feels eternal.

Chapter 23

Rosannah

I can't accept the Universe has granted me the perfect being. I don't understand how luck bestowed itself to me.

How could someone like him even exist?

Adra moves with an innate understanding; every touch, every glance is intentional and passionate. His respirations brush against my skin, permeate my ears, and surround my throat. His hands, generous, loving, and safe, work their way down my body, carefully peeling away the layers of my dress. Every second is a reminder of just how dreamlike he is.

His stubble scrapes along my collarbone. The sensation thistly yet I can appreciate his tenderness. His lips trail lower, leaving a path of kisses in their wake, until the cold night air seizes my bare chest. My nipples harden instantaneously, but the glacial breeze is fleeting as his mouth claims me. His lips close around one with a fervor that makes me arch into him.

I peer down, and there he is, watching me with those unique, smoldering eyes. His gaze binds me in place. His hands knead my breasts as his tongue flicks against my nipples. He is wholly devoted to me, and I can see it in every act.

My moans float in the air, performing a ballet with the crackle of the fire nearby. His modest growl resounds up my neck, as he moves to the other side, sucking and teasing until my body feels weightless from the impression.

My fingers thread through his hair, tugging tenderly, feeling the strands slip between them before trailing down to his broad, firm shoulders. He presses forward. His body grounds me, comforts me, even as he overpowers me. His hands slide lower, catching the hem of my dress. He pulls it down further, exposing me entirely to the arctic clutches of the night. The air bites at my skin for only a moment before he whispers, "Don't worry. You won't be cold for long."

He spreads my legs with a gentle gesture. His torso leans closer, shifting from his hands to his elbows so that every exhale is shared between us.

His lips find my ear. His voice humming with desire. "May I?"

His fingers draw slow patterns along the hypersensitive skin of my inner thighs. "You may." Though my voice shivers with both shyness and anticipation.

Adra's fingers travel higher, the teasing skim of his touch is torturously slow as he skirts just shy of where I need him most. His lips connect with my neck. His kisses are unhurried. They leave trails of yearning that sends my senses spiraling.

"You don't know what you do to me, my dear mourning star." His needy voice pours into my ears. "You afflict me." He stutters as his fingers sweeps right over my lower lips. "I lose myself completely in you." He grabs my inner thigh. "You have awakened parts of me I didn't know existed."

His teeth catch on my neck as he inches up, nibbling on my ear. I swallow hard. My body vibrates beneath him, every nerve alight. His fingers continue their deliberate teasing, skimming just below my clit. They're circling my entrance, already wet and aching for him.

His words pull me from the haze of sensations, "I need to hear you say it, tell me you belong to me." His voice sounds more like a plea than a demand. "Tell me, Rosannah, I want to hear it from your lips."

His fingers trickle the barrier of my opening as the tip of his finger slides in.

Just barley.

I let out a whimper as he slides it right back out.

"Who do you belong to?"

The tension builds, his movements slowing to an agonizing pace. I try to form the words, but they catch in my throat, lost in the fog of my need.

"You." The admission slips past my lips before I even realize it; but the moment the words leave, he rewards me. His fingers slide inside, the pressure and

241

fullness making my body bow instinctively toward him. His lips claim mine at the same moment, and I moan into his mouth.

He kisses me lovingly, earnestly, as his fingers move in rhythm. Stroking places within me that send surges of euphoria through my core. My pussy pulses around his fingers as his tongue capers with mine. We stay together like this, lips moving in perfect harmony. His hands work at a thrilling rhythm. My breaths become ragged. My moans muffled by his kisses as the tension in my body rings tighter.

His fingers bend perfectly inside me. His touch sends me floating higher. Behind my closed eyes, I see a concert of colors: brilliant gold, rich red, pastel blue. It's an explosion of light that mirrors the symphony of sentiments coursing through me. I surrender myself entirely to him, to this moment.

My toes curl with a strange tingle, as my breathing gets hotter and louder in my ears. His fingers paint my body with an orgasm that releases every dreadful, and disastrous event that has taken place over the past two days. It all pales in comparison. None of it holds any importance to me right now. All that matters is this feeling Adra provides me: authentic inconceivable nirvana.

Adra holds me through it. His lips never leave mine. His existence balances my convulsing body, as the aftershocks ripple through me. I clutch at him, burying my face in his neck. I pull him back into a fiery kiss not wanting this to end. I spread my legs wider as I try to use my feet to pull his pants down. We giggle in our kiss as the awkward movement is a lot harder to do lip locked together.

He shimmies out of them, and I can feel his bulging cock pressing against the outer folds of my pussy. He breaks away from our kiss and stares me in the eyes as he begins to cover his cock in my post orgasm wetness.

Adra presses himself into my swollen opening and lets out a mewl of pleasure. His long length slides right in, as my walls grip tight around him. I choke on my own moan as he pushes himself to the hilt.

Adra's body moves against mine. Every thrust in precise rhythm with my moans. The firelight flickers across his face. His fervent eyes are established on mine, and I can hear each individual gasp he takes as if our bodies are meant to be this close. This connected.

Adra's hands grip my hips guiding me to another orgasm. However firm his touch, his gaze is what truly takes me captive. The way he stares at me with such devotion makes me feel like I'm the sole star in his endless sky. I see a reflection of a love so prominent. A feeling so pure, like I'm the center of his universe.

My breaths come quicker, fusing with his, and our movements fall into perfect sync. It's not just passion; it's something greater. Something that feels like it's carving its way into my very soul.

His forehead presses gently against mine. My hands find his face. My fingers outlined his jawline, his cheekbones, desperate to make note of every inch of him. I can feel the subtle scrape of his stubble against my lips, his back muscles flexing as he thrusts into me, as our orgasms wed one another. I know I am close, and he is too, teetering on the edge.

I tilt my head up, caressing my lips against his ear. "Claim me", I pant as he thrusts faster. "Tell me I'm the one you need Adra." My voice is rocky as my pants escape me. "Let these words be ours tonight."

"I'm yours, Rosannah. Completely yours."

His words free me, and in the next moment, we explode. My body bends against his, and cries torrent my lips as ecstasy takes us both. Adra's body shudders as he buries his face in the camber of my neck. His own low strident grunts vibrate against my skin. We are lost, *together*. Tangled in the sheer intensity of it. The connection between us is so robust, it's like nothing could ever shatter it.

As the aftereffects fade, Adra rolls to the side, his arm draped over my waist. We lie there, side by side, staring up at the velarium of stars glittering above us. The forest hums gingerly around, but all I can hear is the erratic pattern of his breathing and the pounding of my own heart.

I close my eyes as the familiar feeling of his safety returns. His hand grabs mine, as my body sinks into a deep relaxation. My eyes become too amiable to open. I take slower lungful trying to get my heart rate to match. The last thing I hear before sleep sweeps me away is the tender, grounding sound of his sigh beside me. It being a gentle reassurance that I am not alone.

Not anymore.

Chapter 24

Rosannah

T he morning greets me with its mellow light. The first rays of dawn paint the sky in hues of gold and pale pink.

My eyes blink open lazily, adjusting to the brightness. The smell of dew fills the air, and I feel it on the ground next to me. The cold droplets kiss my fingers as my surroundings are nothing but the earthy aroma of the forest. Birds chirp their morning melodies. Their calls echo through the trees, and for a moment, all seems peaceful. I'm cocooned in blankets Adra must have tucked around me sometime during the night. They wrap snugly over my body. A smile tugs at my lips as I remember the events of the night before, grateful no nightmare has broken their spell. The recollection brings a sweet flush to my cheeks.

Turning over, I spot him just beyond the wagon. He's dressed. His figure silhouetted against the rising sun as he feeds the donkey a carrot, murmuring something to the animal I can't quite make out. The sight of him, tall and firm, fills me with a sense of security. I hadn't realized how long I had been pleading for this; how long I have been wanting to wake up with someone I so desperately care for. Adra is becoming my favorite thing about mornings, knowing he is always going to be the first thing I see when I wake.

My spirit swells with happiness. "Good morning!" I call out, my speech still interwoven with sleep.

Adra pivots, his cheeks greeting me with a warm smile, "Good morning, bellezza."

He strides toward me, and I sit up, clutching the blankets to my chest, still very aware of my nakedness beneath them. His eyes twinkle with mischief as he leans down, securing my lips in a kiss.

"Sleep well?" He asks, brushing a stray curl from my face.

"Better than I have in weeks." I admit. My cheeks blushing under his wandering gaze.

"Good." He straightens, but just as I start to roll over, he lands a slap on my behind making me squeal in surprise. "Adra!" I exclaim, laughing as I swat at his arm.

He pulls me back into another kiss. His grin is contagious. "Couldn't resist. Now, get dressed before I decide to delay our journey for another hour... or *two.*"

Rolling my eyes but grinning nonetheless, I wrap the blanket around me, shielding myself from the crisp morning air. I try to stretch away my slumber, but the blanket restricts me. There is no better wake up method

246

than embracing the chill. I drop my blanket and lean into a deep stretch. Adra whistles at me as I bend over naked, arms extended wide.

"Get dressed!" He says, as he playfully covers his eyes, peeking between his fingers. "I can't handle you this early in the morning, it's too much!"

I put my garments on as the impact of the past few days' creeps back into my mind. The memory of Gia, of the town, of everything we've left behind. It all hits me like a sneaky blow to the chest. I rattle my head, forcing the thoughts aside. There's no use dwelling on them now. All I can do is move forward, and luckily for me, forward is with Adra.

Once my dress has been sufficiently tied, I help Adra load up the wagon. He glances at me, his brow furrowing as if he can sense my shift in mood, but he doesn't press. Instead, he passes me a bundle of supplies with a gentle, "Here, take this."

I put the final bag on to the wagon and dust my palms off. It is loaded, and all is in place. Adra helps me climb into the front seat, as the wood shifts beneath my weight. Adra gives the clearing one last check to make sure we don't leave anything behind; gives the donkey a friendly pat, then climbs up to join me. We are ready to set off towards the city once again. The creak of the wheels and the continuous plod of the donkey the prelude to the day's adventure.

The dense canopy above begins to break apart as we journey onward, the towering trees that once loomed over us gradually giving way to younger, thinner growth. The air is easier here, less depressing than in the center of the forest. Though the chill of the morning remains, sunlight pierces through the gaps in the branches, casting rich beams that cut through the mist clinging to the forest floor. Each ray creates patterns of light and shadow that waltz across the ground.

The crunch of the wagon wheels over fallen leaves and scattered twigs echoes with the chirping of birds that flit from tree to tree. The earthy scent of moss and damp soil gives way to the faint sweetness of wildflowers hidden amongst the underbrush. A gentle breeze stirs the leaves, sending them swaying. Their movement captures the sunlight and creates a shimmering effect, like the forest bids farewell.

I peek back briefly, the dense woods behind us now seeming like a shadowy wall, an impenetrable barrier to what we've left behind. Ahead, the trees become sparser, their gnarled branches stretching upward as though reaching for the open sky. The blue expanse above grows wider and the first hints of rolling fields peep through the gaps in the thinning forest.

Adra sits beside me, his eyes fixed ahead, and his posture solid as he guides the wagon. The donkey plods along obediently, its hooves sink into the spongy earth, occasionally stirring up a faint puff of dust. I let my views wander; tracing the lines of light that stretch across the path. The way it seems to beckon us forward, toward something new.

As the last of the towering trees falls away, replaced by clusters of shrubs and open glades, a strange merge of relief and sadness fills me.

The forest, for all its foreboding and darkness, had become a cocoon, a shield from the chaos of the world outside. Leaving feels like stepping into the unknown, and yet, there's a sense of hope here too. The sunlight feels hotter, the air fresher, the horizon wide and open before us. We've emerged from the shadows, but the significance of what lies behind us, and what lies ahead, is substantial, intense, and intimidating. Still, with Adra at my side, I can't help but have a flicker of courage in my chest as the forest releases us into the waiting embrace of the open world.

Adra breaks the silence, "Alright, mourning star, let's make this journey a little less dull. I spy... with my little eye... something green."

I glance at him, raising an eyebrow, and giving him a chaotic smirk. "The trees?" I say confidently.

He chuckles, with childlike joy. "Too easy. Your turn."

I tilt my head, scanning the surrounding landscape. "Fine. I spy... with my little eye... something brown."

He squints, his expression exaggeratedly thoughtful. "Hmm. The dirt?"

"Wrong," I say with a teasing lilt, crossing my arms as I wait.

"The wagon?"

"Nope."

He groans, rubbing the back of his neck. "The donkey?"

"You're hopeless. It was the bark on that tree back there."

He glances over his shoulder at the now-distant tree and gives me a mock glare. "That was foul play, it's behind us."

"It's not my fault that you lack the skill of sight."

He grumbles something under his breath, but his expression betrays him. "Very well, your turn again, mayhap this time you can do better than '*something brown*.'"

We continue like this, tossing hints and guesses back and forth. Our laughter rings through the open air. At one point, I spy a bird perched on a low-hanging branch. Its feathers have a brilliant color of blue. When I give him the clue, he spends far too long scanning the trees before I finally point it out, laughing as he mutters about my "unfair tactics."

"You're terrible at this."

"Or maybe you are simply too bent on besting all who breathe."

"Confess it, you are just bad at subtlety." I retort, poking his arm.

He huffs, swaying his head, but his smile is uncontainable. "Fine, I yield. You are the crowned victor. Are you pleased now?"

"Aye, very."

The sincerity of his expression, and the way his laughter lights up his entire face, fills me with fresh joy.

The wagon crests a small rise, and ahead of us, gives way to open fields that stretch toward the horizon. The faint outline of a rural town comes into view. Its small buildings dotting the landscape like scattered tiny stones.

I glance at Adra, trying to keep my thoughts in check, but it's impossible. My soul swells with a feeling so big, so overwhelming, I think it might burst. His profile is fierce against the backdrop of the morning sun. The strong line of his jaw and those unintentional seductive, watchful eyes settled on the path ahead. And that hair, messy but ideal, like he just rolled out of bed looking that annoyingly good.

He's everything I never dared to hope for. His kindness, his wit, the way he makes me believe I am the only thing that matters. It's enough to make me want to scream. Or swoon. Or both. I realize, with a certainty that hits me like a brick to the face.

I'm falling in love with him.

No.... I am in love with him.

Damn it.

Adra must realize I'm staring because he catching me midst my heartfelt unraveling. His eyebrow quirks, "What?"

I whip my head toward the horizon so fast I almost give myself whiplash. "Nothing." I reply, my voice a little too high-pitched to sound convincing.

"Liar." He says, leaning closer, his tone saturated with lighthearted suspicion.

I shrug, biting my lip to keep from laughing, because if I don't laugh, I might blurt out something embarrassing like *I love you, you idiot.*

"Maybe I'm just admiring the scenery." I shoot back, waving vaguely at the horizon.

He chuckles, and the sound sends butterflies into a full riot in my stomach. "Right, I'm sure the trees are fascinating."

I roll my eyes, trying to play off my stirring emotions. "They are actually... very... tree-like."

The silence persists, yet it is not unwelcome. I can sense his eyes dawdling on me, and it takes every ounce of willpower I have not to meet them. Instead, I focus on the road ahead and the sunlight heating my face as I silently yell at myself to get it together.

You're falling for him, Rosannah. No, you've already fallen. And now he knows you're staring at him like a lovesick fool. Great.

But despite my internal chaos, there's something else beneath the panic: hope. A quiet certainty that, with Adra by my side, everything might just be okay. Even if he does have an unfairly perfect face and a knack for making my heart do somersaults.

The sun dips low on the horizon. Its golden glow giving way to shades of early twilight. The gentle clip-clop of the donkey's hooves on the dirt path has become almost hypnotic. However my body is beginning to protest. My legs ache, my back is stiff, and exhaustion creeps in like a guest not called nor wanted.

"We need to stop soon. My body feels like I've been dragged behind a plow."

He glances over, "A plow, you say? What were you doing in the fields while I wasn't watching? Should I be worried?"

I roll my eyes, though I can't help but smile. "You know what I mean. My bones are practically screaming."

"Well, we can't have that. Let's find somewhere to rest for the night."

As the wagon rounds the bend, the faint outline of a small farming village emerges from the haze of twilight. At first glance, it appears picturesque, a cluster of wooden cottages with thatched roofs nestled against the backdrop of rolling hills. But as we draw closer, the illusion crumbles.

The village is unnaturally quiet. The kind of stillness that suggests wrong. The air is serious here, overbearing. The silence presses down making every creak of the wagon unnervingly loud.

The buildings are simple, the timber weathered and gray. The roofs sag as though they're weary from standing for so long. Most of the windows are shuttered, becoming dark voids that seem to watch us pass like empty eyes. A few doors hang ajar, swaying in the breeze, their hinges groan in protest. The once-bustling signs of life, fresh laundry strung out to dry, smoke curling from chimneys, children playing games in the fields; are nowhere to be seen.

Adra slows the wagon as we near a small farmhouse on the edge of the village. The house itself is unremarkable. Its thatched roof uneven, as though it may crumble at any moment. Surrounding it are a few animal pens. Their wooden slats warped and splintered. Inside the enclosures, I see the shapes of pigs lying in the mud. Their bloated bodies are motionless. The acrid stench of decay hangs in the air, paring with the earthy scent of the fields.

My stomach twists at the sight. Death seems to idle here. However it's not loud and catastrophic like the chaos we've fled, but quiet and insidious, as if it's seeped into the very soil.

I swallow hard, as my fingers grip the edge of the wagon seat, while unease coils firmly in my chest. Adra's eyes scan the surroundings. His posture tense but composed.

"We'll stop here for the night." He says quietly, as if unwilling to disturb the silence that hovers over this place.

He pulls the wagon to a halt in front of the farmhouse. The donkey lets out a weary snort. I climb down from the wagon, my legs stiff from the journey, and peek around. The creeping shadows of dusk make this scene even more frightening.

"Charming." I mutter, the attempt at humor doing little to mask the discomfort prickling at the edges of my thoughts.

Adra steps down beside me, his eyes still scanning the area. "Stay here," he says leaving no room for argument, "I'll check the house first."

254

I watch him stride toward the farmhouse, his silhouette towering against the fading light. The creak of the warped wooden steps under his weight makes me flinch. The door swings open with a low groan as he disappears inside, leaving me alone with the eerie quiet.

The faint rustling of the breeze and the distant call of a lone bird are the only sounds. They do little to ease the tension curling in my gut, and I suddenly wish Adra would hurry.

When he emerges a few moments later, his expression is unreadable. "It's empty, no one's here. We might as well use it for the night."

I nod, relief washing over me. "Aye well enough, because I am about to fall where I stand."

"Best I find some firewood, lest we freeze and make statues of ourselves." Adra says, motioning toward the near empty stack by the side of the house. "The hearth lies bare within, and the night will grow ever colder."

"Hasten back! I'd hate to be a statuesque goddess soon."

He chuckles, "Keep me an apple from the supplies, or I must just let the cold be your penance."

I laugh and wave him off as he heads toward the tree line. His tall frame vanishes into the shadows. Heading to the back end of the wagon, I climb up and dig into the supply bag, pulling out a perfectly ripe apple. Its skin is smooth and cool against my palm. I bite into it, and the crisp sweetness spreads across my tongue.

The farmhouse looms behind me. Its presence is both comforting and disturbing. I skim at its weathered facade, wondering about the family who once lived here.

Did they flee, or were they taken by the sickness like so many others?

The thought sends a shiver down my spine. I move my focus to the crunch of the apple and the sounds of the countryside; the chirping of crickets, croaking of frogs, and the rustle of leaves in the breeze.

Chapter 25

Adrastus

As I step inside the farmhouse, the heavy wooden door creaks on its hinges, as the sound reverberates through the small, empty space.

The air inside is frostier than the evening breeze. The kind of chill that seeps into the stones of the walls and refuses to leave. The room is sparse. Its furnishings are as utilitarian as the building itself.

A small, darkened hearth is set into one wall. Its stones blackened with years of soot. The mantle above it holds little but a tarnished metal candlestick tipped with a remnant of wax, and a cracked clay bowl likely used for small offerings or coins. The fireplace is bare, but it promises the possibility of warmth if I can find enough wood to kindle a fire.

A single bed sits against the far wall. Its frame is made of rough planks held together by wooden pegs.

The mattress, a simple sack stuffed with straw, sags in the middle. A testament to its age and frequent use. A faded woolen blanket, patched and frayed at the edges, drape over it. It's not much, but it will be enough for Rosannah. She needs rest, and I can manage on the floor with the blankets we brought.

The floor itself is uneven, cobbled in places with large, flat stones while other sections are packed with dirt. A small wooden table, its surface scarred with knife marks and stains, sits near the hearth, accompanied by two mismatched stools. A bundle of dried herbs hangs from a hook near the window. Their brittle leaves rustling as the door swings shut behind me. The glass in the window is murky, patched with cloth in places, but it allows a dim sliver of twilight to seep into the room.

I take in every detail. My mind cataloging the space. It's not comfortable, not welcoming, but it's shelter. And right now, that's enough. I glance toward the bed again, imagining Rosannah curled up there. Her face soft in sleep. As long as she's safe, as long as she's close, I'll lay on the hard ground without complaint. I've endured far worse.

The faint creak of the boards under my boots pulls me back to the present. My eyes drift to the corners of the room; the shadows appear darker there. The silence too heavy. The stillness too absolute. And though I tell myself it's just an empty farmhouse, the air carries the tax of something unseen. It's just a house. Just stone and wood. Nothing more. I'll make it warm, make it livable, this place, however humble, will serve its purpose.

I step outside; the air fresher but still carries the odor of decay. Around the side of the house, I spot a chopping base with an axe embedded in the wood. Its handle worn smooth from use. However, there's no firewood in sight, not even scraps to burn. I sigh, scanning the area, before deciding to check behind the house.

There's a small barn near the animal pens. The closer I get, the stronger the stench becomes. It's thick, rancid, and a smell I know all too well. *Death*. Not fresh, but not old enough to fade.

The pens nearby are a grim sight. Bloated bodies of swine, their skin marred with blackened pustules. Flies buzz in a maddening symphony, and maggots writhe in the decaying flesh.

I instinctively steel myself as I push open the barn door. The interior is dark, the moonlight barely penetrating the gloom. Near the entrance, a lantern hangs on a nail, and I reach for it. While using the flint and steel left nearby to strike a spark, the flame catches, casting an orange glow that flickers across the barn walls.

My eyes adjust to the light, and I step further inside. The barn is mostly empty, save for a stack of firewood tucked against the far wall. Relief washes over me at the sight.

"Perfect." I mutter to myself, moving toward it. But before I take more than a few steps, my boot catches on something hard. I stumble, the lantern swinging wildly in my hand. I lower it. The light revealing what I tripped over...

259

A boy.

He's slumped against the barn wall. His body stiff and bloated. His face is a mask of death. His eyes half-lidded and glassy, his lips cracked and dry, pustules cover his skin. Their sickly yellow crusts broken and oozing. Flies dart around him in a chaotic frenzy, landing on him as they ready to implant their young into his open wounds.

I see movement under his clothes. I rip open his shirt and see a mob of rats gnawing their way through his innards. The smell hits me full force, a putrid mix of decay and disease. This gruesome scene would threaten to turn even a seasoned mortal's stomach.

For a moment, I simply stand there, staring down at him. He's young, no older than thirteen, maybe younger. A farm boy, by the fashion of his simple tunic and dirt-caked hands. My chest pangs, a painful reminder of the grief I watched Rosannah experience at the loss of Gia.

This boy is just another casualty of the plague. One of countless lives destroyed too soon. And yet, his death feels larger somehow. More personal.

I crouch down, holding the lantern steady as I hover my hand over his chest. Heat radiates beneath my palm; his soul hasn't fully departed yet.

With practiced precision, I reach for it. My fingers caressing against the fragile threads of his essence. His soul rises like smoke, shimmering freely before dissipating into the unseen realm. Another number added to the contract. It should feel routine, but it doesn't. Not tonight.

I rise gradually as my gape remains on the boy for a moment longer before I redirect my focus back toward the firewood. This place is a graveyard, and we can't stay here for long. I gather as much wood as I can carry. My thoughts are serious when a sound cuts through the quiet. Distant at first, then louder. A bloodcurdling scream pierces the stillness of the night.

Rosannah's scream.

The firewood crashes to the ground, forgotten, as my pulse spikes. For the first time in centuries, I feel pure, unwavering panic. The second scream follows, more desperate. My stomach churns as bitter dread resides in me.

I drop the lantern. The clatter echoes in the barn, and I sprint toward the farmhouse. My steps are fatally laggard as though the night itself conspires against me. Every breath burns, every heartbeat pounds like a war drum in my ears.

"Rosannah!" I call out, my voice engulfed in fear. The farmhouse looms ahead. Its shadowy silhouette bathed in the faint glow of the moon. My mind conjures every horror that could befall her.

Is she hurt?

Infected?

Worse?

The silence of the village crowds against me, the empty buildings and lifeless pens boost the growing terror ripping at my chest.

CONWAY TITTY

Chapter 26

Rosannah

Something shifts in the distance. A faint sound catches my attention—a muffled shuffle, the crunch of gravel underfoot. I freeze, all my senses suddenly on edge. My eyes dart toward the shadows beyond the wagon. The flickering remnants of twilight cast strange shapes against the farmhouse and its surrounding pens. And then, *they* appear.

A voice cuts through the stillness, flat and creeping. "Well, well. What's a pretty little thing like you doing out here all alone?"

I whirl around, clutching the apple in one hand as though it could offer me any kind of defense. A man steps out of the shadows, his sneer corrupt and wolfish. He's tall and lanky. His shoulders slouch as if laziness has seeped into his very bones. His clothes ragged, his shirt hanging open to reveal a chest smeared with dirt

263

and grease. His eyes glint in the moonlight, bade and hungry.

Another shadow detaches itself from the darkness, then another, until five men emerge. Their figures are hazy in the backdrop of this full moon. They form a loose circle around me. Their postures relaxed but conspiratorial, each step deliberate, like predators savoring the thrill of cornering their prey.

My heart slams against my ribcage, the rapid thrum echoing in my ears. The surrounding space seems to narrow, the farmhouse, the wagon, even the night itself fades into a stagnant focus on these men.

The stench hits me in waves, a nauseating cocktail of unwashed bodies, sweat-soaked clothes, and the sickly sweet odor of decay wafting from the nearby pig pens. The smell clings to the back of my throat, making it hard to swallow, hard to think.

They stroll leisurely towards me, as though they have all the time in the world to savor this occasion. One of them drags a foot lazily through the dirt, kicking up small puffs of dust that swirl like specters in the luminescence. Another cracks his knuckles loudly, the sound punctures the stale silence making me flinch. The man nearest to me grins. His teeth yellowed and sparce, as his lips curl with vulturous hunger.

"Good sirs..." He drawls, his voice rough like gravel they walk on. "What do we have here?"

His words float in the air, and my pulse quicken as their hollow eyes rake over me like I'm something to be picked apart. One man, his face marked with scars and his greasy hair clinging to his brow, moves closer. His
264

perverse stare idles on my face, then trails slowly, deliberately, down to my chest.

"Looks like she's lost." Another says in mock sympathy. "Poor little thing."

My grip on the apple tightens, my nails digging into its smooth skin as I take a step back. But there's nowhere to go.

The circle tightens, their shadows stretching long across the ground, distorted by the moon. Their debate forces down on me, asphyxiating, invasive.

"Gentlemen," one of them says mockingly, his voice hard with a rural accent, "what a rare surprise, company we did not call for, yet how sweetly this one has arrived."

The circle closes in further, their collective silence more horrifying than anything they've said. The tension of their soulless stares probe into me. My heart feels like it's trying to claw its way out of my chest. Every instinct in me screams to run, to fight, but my body is frozen, paralyzed by the sheer strain of their presence.

The pigs in the pen lie motionless, their bloated bodies a grim reminder of the decay and death that seems to cling to this place like a second skin. I try to swallow the rising panic, but my mouth has gone dry, and the only sound I can make is a shallow gasp.

The men exchange glances, their laughter cheap and cruel, their voices fueled by malice. The fourth man laughs, the sound harsh and grating. "A shame indeed to let such beauty stray so far from watchful eyes. A pity to leave such a fair flower unattended in the dark."

However, as the fifth man steps forward, everything about him sets my teeth on edge.

He's shorter than the others, but still taller than I am. His skin is dark, though the moonlight renders him pale, almost ghostly. His face is angular, while his concave cheeks give him the appearance of a living skeleton. A scab mars his right hand, jagged and angry, and similar marks streak across his face as though a human has clawed him. His bushy eyebrows shadow ruthless, distrustful eyes that seem to miss nothing.

"Ciao, tesoro[19]." He says, smooth-spoken like a courtier in candlelight, but there is rot behind every word. "You look frightened. No need for that. We're not monsters... just laborers of honest toil."

He looks at the surrounding men and winks. "I'm Vincenzo Conti, taker of the dead, digger of graves, and steward of stillness. Where they fall, send word, and I shall see 'em buried proper... or close enough."

He leers, his teeth crooked and yellow, and sweeps into an exaggerated bow, tipping his filthy woolen hat. "And these fine gentlemen, my ever-faithful companions? We're the Becchini.[20]"

He spreads his arms open as if to share the moon with the other wolves. "Rolls off the tongue pleasantly, doesn't it, bella?"

---

[19] "Treasure" in Italian

[20] The Becchini were notorious throughout Europe during the Bubonic Plague. Most cities had similar gangs that would force people to pay for their dead. Whether that be burial or disposal. They would also kill you if you didn't pay. Many died from the illness every hour, that an extortion murder would not even be a dent in the mass casualties.

The others laugh, their voices echoing like jackals. One of them, a man named Marco, steps closer, his broad frame blocking part of the moonlight. His face pockmarked. His nose is crooked from what seems like an old break, and his simper is disturbing. His clothes, like the others, are torn and stained, reeking of filth and old sweat.

"Aye, Vin," Marco says, raspier than the others, "why don't we tell the dolcezza[21] more about our... services?"

Vincenzo's smirk develops, his eyes gleam with something unclean. "Ah, Marco, ever the fountain of brilliance." He says with a curl of lip and a voice like honey turned sour. "Tesoro, you see, the pair who once laid claim to this quaint little home... have come to most grievous ruin."

He swivels towards his men with a sneer. "Alas, fate proves to be most unkind. But..." he pauses, letting the silence stretch, "fortunate for you we happened along. And of course, we are seasoned hands in the quiet settling of troublesome things. Truly, this is a grim business. And by fortune's grace, our hands are free. Though, as with all fine labors... a modest coin is due."

He tilts his head, his gaze pinning me in place, and the way he says *modest coin* sends a chill mounting up my spine. It's not an offer. It's a threat wrapped in silken words. I swallow hard, the apple in my palm is ridiculously useless.

---

[21] "Sweetheart" or "Honey" in Italian

My mind contests, searching for anything to say, anything to defuse the tension, but my voice escapes fiercer than I intend. "Those folk are strangers to me. I hold no ties to their name nor their fates. I am but a mere passerby."

Vincenzo's grin falters, but only for a moment. His expression hardens, while the joking facade slips to reveal an icier masquerade. His eyes are locked upon me like a hunter's pin against a twitching moth.

"Nay, tesoro, let us not begin this bond with falsehood, lest all that follows rot at the root. No stranger settles in so comfortably. And you?" He gestures to me with a casual flick of his wrist. "You look downright at home."

My knees threaten to give out, but I summon the words, fear teetering on the edge of anger. "I told you, I know them not, nor have I ever broken bread in their company!" My voice trembles despite my best efforts to sound defiant. "I owe you naught."

The surrounding men exchange glances; chuckles rumble from their throats. Vincenzo tilts his head, studying me like one might a caged animal, something small and vulnerable but entertaining to torment.

He takes a step closer, and I instinctively step back, the rough lumber of the wagon digging into my shoulder blades.

He notices, of course, his grin returning. "You don't understand how this works, bella..." He continues, his tone syrupy and mocking. "We're doing you a kindness here, a service. We've seen to a most troublesome affair on your behalf. And all we ask is but a touch of... gratitude."

The words trickle from his tongue like venom, and the men around him laugh again, louder this time, the sound echoing in the merciless silence.

"I have no need of your aid," I spit, "and I'm not giving you anything."

Vincenzo's face falls still. "Lying to me, bella? That's a sin against God. And sins require penance."

He steps even closer, the cloying smell of sweat, damp earth, and rotting breath spews over me. "Tesoro," he whispers, "mayhap you have not truly heard me. Payment isn't optional. You either pay in coin..."

His voice trails off as his eyes drop pointedly down my body and then back up. "Or we find other ways to claim what's owed... and I've no doubt a maiden like you might come to relish that bargain."

My voice snags in my throat, and my grip falters on the apple. Behind him, one man—a hulking brute with wild, greasy hair—chimes in, his voice a growl. "Let us cast aside the pleasantries, Vin, time ill favors delay. Aye, she seems the sort to claw and bite."

The group bursts into that jackal laughter once again. Vincenzo raises a hand, silencing them. His cruel smile returns. "Bella," he says pityingly, "don't make this harder than it need be."

I can do nothing but panic. My chest thrashes, my pulse hammers in my ears as they close in. Their shadows stretch long across the ground, merging with the darkness surrounding us.

Vincenzo and the other men attack. Their disgusting, grimy hands grab me. Too many limbs to focus on. I'm being pulled in so many directions as they grab onto my dress, my hair, my face. Too fast for me to even think, they took what they thought was rightfully theirs.

"Wait!" I say, my words tumbling out in a rush. "Please. I'll give you whatever you want. There's no need for this." This is a plea I do not wish to be giving, but what choice do I have?

Vincenzo lifts a finger, signaling the others to stop, though the leering hunger in their eyes doesn't waver. They step back reluctantly, like wolves waiting for their taste of prey that their alpha has claimed.

My dress is torn, hanging precariously off my shoulders, leaving my bare breast exposed and the rest of me humiliated. Tears sting my eyes, but I refuse to let them fall. Not yet.

"Hold her." Vincenzo commands, his voice calm, almost casual, like he's ordering a meal.

Two of the men grab me, their hands coarse as they grip my arms. Panic floods my veins, and I thrash against them, kicking and twisting, but their hold is unrelenting. Vincenzo steps closer, his eyes raking over me with satisfaction.

He reaches out; his scraggy hand grips my chin, forcing me to look at him. "That's better, tesoro." He breathes. "See? A little cooperation goes a long way."

His hand trails down my neck and onto my bare breasts. He twists my nipples; the pain makes me wince. He grabs my breasts and lifts them. Fondling them with

270

his scratchy, soiled hands. Vincenzo opens his mouth and runs his grotty tongue across the cleavage, leaving a putrid spit trail in his wake.

His fingers trace along my face. I clench my jaw, trying to steel myself, trying not to let him see the fear that's tearing me apart inside. His rotting, hot breath fans across my cheek as he leans closer. His lips barely brush mine as I grimace and try to pull away.

"There's fire in you, no doubt," he murmurs with admiration, "but flame is fleeting. And once spent... naught remains but ash." His fingers slide to the torn fabric of my dress, tugging at it, before taking his finger and twirling it back around my nipple. "Fight if you must, but resistance be but folly."

I scan the shadowy surroundings desperately. My mind screaming for Adra.

Please, please come back. I can't do this alone.

But there's no sign of him, only the jeering laughter of the bordering men.

Vincenzo steps back, his grin widening as he addresses his men. "A fine thing to behold, is she not?" He says, sweeping a hand toward me as though unveiling a treasure at market. "Such beauty deserves an audience!"

The men let loose a great roar, their voices rising like thunder.

"Worry not, lads. Each of you shall have a turn. But not before I've seen to her myself."

My legs tremble beneath me. I am trapped, my mind scrambling to hold on to something, *anything*, that could give me strength.

Vincenzo strides back towards me, inches away from my face once more. The stench of his breath makes my stomach churn. He raises a fist, brushing his knuckles along my cheek. The gesture is a threat more than a touch. "So soft," he purrs, "so willing." He grabs onto my hair and takes a lungful. "A ripe, sweet cunt she must have; let's give her a taste of what a real man feels like." He laughs at the rest of the becchini.

"*On... your... KNEES!*" He commands. His rotten breath covers my face, and I gag.

I shake my head. "No..." I hesitate, my body stiff with panic. I will not let this happen—I *can't* let this happen—but what can I do? My eyes dart around again, hoping, praying for Adra, for anyone.

"NOW BELLA!" He screams.

My hands curl into fists at my sides. My nails dig into my palms as I am pushed to kneel. Desperation claws at my chest. "Adra, please." I whisper under my breath.

Vincenzo's soulless eyes sharpen. "Still clinging to the hope of a savior? That's sweet," he sneers, "but no one's coming, tesoro. You're mine now."

The men hoot and holler behind Vincenzo with impatient depravity. Vincenzo towers above me, petting my hair. "Bella, you are so right down there." He croons at me.

He bends down & grabs my chin to make me look at him. My instinct may get me killed, but I'm not going down without a fight. Without hesitation, I spit in his face.

Vincenzo slowly wipes my saliva from his eyes and slaps me hard across the face. My body jolts awake, and all that's left is residual pain.

"Now tesoro, I didn't know you liked it rough, why don't I give you exactly what you desire." He sneers as another slap collides with the other side of my face. "I would keep going, but my cock is intervening here, and I got to listen to him."

He grabs onto the front of his pants and strokes himself. "I haven't had a whore so eager as you. A perfect hole you'll make."

My body unmoving, as demoralizing memories of past partners and unwanted advances come flooding in.

I can't do this again.

I try to pull away, but the two men holding me down have a powerful grip. They don't even budge. Tears swell in my eyes as Vincenzo pulls his cock out. The repugnant fleshy intrusion stares me directly in the face. The tears stream down as I am wrapped in shame. Every part of me feels violated, and I have nowhere to flee. I close my eyes as the tears fall. I *must* do what they say.

I am not the praying type, but at this moment, I am silently pleading with the universe to intervene, *to do something, anything.*

Despair crushes me, and I can't shake the thought that I am betraying the only person I've ever truly cared about. Adra's face flashes in my mind and the shame cuts deeper. I'm unraveling, every thread of who I am is being stripped away. Only guilt and the hollow ache of helplessness is left behind.

Please forgive me, Adra. I'm so sorry. If you can hear me, if there's any part of you that senses my pain, please... save me. Save me from what is about to happen. Universe, please let him know this wasn't my choice. Let him know how much I love him. How much he means to me. I love him more than life itself, more than the air in my lungs, more than anything I've ever known. Adra, I'm yours forever, for eternity, ... Please.... Someone.... Anyone.... Help me.

Vincenzo grabs a handful of my hair and pulls me towards him. My eyes squeeze tighter as his hard, fleshy nub touch my lips. My mouth tries to disappear into itself.

"Open up, bella." Vincenzo says sweetly.

I shut my mouth tauter and try to pull my head away.

He grabs my hair more punishing this time and leads me back to his cock. "OPEN WHORE OR WE ALL TAKE OUR TURNS.... *TOGETHER...*"

My body ceases to function; every muscle locks in place as a dismal, desolate, dread pools through me. All the warmth, all the life, all the color drains from my veins; leaving only a vacant, trembling shell.

My mouth falls open, a desperate attempt to keep the nausea at bay, though the bile rises all the same. I swallow it down, fighting the urge to retch. Every scream, every sob, every ounce of fear I want to release is trapped inside my chest, smothering me. But I force it all down, burying the rising tide of terror, even as it claws at the edges of my sanity. The hard fleshy nub enters my mouth, spreading my jaw wider as my teeth graze the head of his penis.

CONWAY TITTY

Chapter 27

Rosannah

A deafening, unmistakable crack splits the air, and the pressure against my lips vanishes. I gasp, choking as my body collapses into itself, trembling uncontrollably. I open my eyes to the sight of Vincenzo's head twisted at an impossible angle. His lifeless body crumples to the ground like a puppet with its strings cut.

Standing over him, bathed in the moonlight like a vengeful monster, is Adra. His eyes blaze with fury. His entire form radiates a paramount of unrelenting rage that seems to darken the very night around us.

"Rosannah!" His voice shakes with barely contained violence. He catches my gaze for the briefest moment, his expression shifting—just enough to tell me he sees me, that he knows I'm alive. Then, he heads toward the others.

The Becchini scatter like rats, but Adra is faster. His hand shoots out, clamping around the nearest man's head like a vice. The man screams. His voice infiltrated with unstoppable terror, but it's cut short as Adra's thumbs press against his eyes. The sickening sound of bone cracking and flesh tearing fills my ears as Adra's thumbs plunge further. The resistance of the man's eye sockets gives way with a wet, grotesque *squelch*. Blood and viscous fluid spills from the man's ruined eyes, streaming down his face in two glistening gore rivers.

His screams transform into guttural, animalistic wails. His fingers claw at Adra's arms in a desperate but futile attempt to free himself. The man's body thrashes violently. His legs kick up dirt, but Adra doesn't relent.

His grip tightens, his knuckles whiten with the sheer force of his hold, and his thumbs dig deeper. The tips grind against the fragile skull. The man's shrieks grow weaker, dissolving into choking gasps as blood fills his mouth, bubbling and frothing with each ragged breath.

Adra pulls back for a moment, his expression cold and unreadable, before slamming the man's head downward with alarming strength. The impact is thunderous. The sound of skull meeting earth reverberates through the still night. The man's head caves in on one side, while the brittle bones shatter under Adra's force.

Blood and brain matter splatter across the dirt, painting the ground in a grotesque mosaic of carnage. The man's body spasms once, a final, pitiful jolt, before

278

going limp. Adra releases his grip, letting the lifeless form slump to the ground in a heap. What remains of the man's face is a ruin of crushed bone and mangled flesh, unrecognizable as anything human. Ichor pools beneath the corpse, thick and dark, seeping into the dirt like a macabre offering to the night.

The next man bolts, his panic driving him to stumble over his own feet as he sprints into the open field. His heavy boots crunch against the dirt, the sound frantic and uneven. Adra's vengeful gaze locks onto him, and then, spies the axe lodged in the chopping block nearby.

Without breaking pace, Adra strides over, his hand closing around the worn wooden handle. The axe comes free with a solid *crack*. Adra doesn't falter. With an effortless, almost casual motion, he hurls the weapon through the air. The axe spins, end over end, the sharp edge shines in the full moon before it strikes with a sickening *thunk* into the man's back. The force of the impact sends him sprawling forward. His chest hitting the ground cuts his cries of pain short.

He writhes, flailing desperately at the handle sticking out from between his shoulder blades. Crimson stains his torn shirt as his fingers slip against the spreading blood. The man gasps and chokes, his body convulses as he tries to crawl forward. Each movement is weaker than the last. Adra approaches with measured steps, his shadow looming over the dying man. The man shifts his head weakly. His eyes wide with terror. His lips form silent pleas as ruby bubbles spill out of his mouth. Adra doesn't stop, doesn't flinch.

Reaching down, he grips the handle of the axe and yanks it free with a gruesome *squelch*; the motion sends a barbaric spray of scarlet across the ground. The man lets out a final strangled gasp. His body twitches violently, but Adra doesn't give him a moment of reprieve.

With both hands gripping the axe, he raises it high above his head. In one brutal, decisive motion, he brings it down with a sickening *thwack*. The blade cleaves clean through the man's neck, while the sound of splintering bone and tearing flesh follows.

The severed head rolls a few feet away, its lifeless eyes stare blankly into oblivion. Adra stands over the body, his chest rising and falling, the axe dripping with carmine. The metallic tang of death thickens the air, but his expression doesn't pause. There's no uncertainty, no remorse—only the sedulous wrath of a man who has nothing left to lose and everything to protect.

The remaining two men stand paralyzed in shock. Their faces pale and dripping with sweat. Their crazed eyes dart between the carnage and each other. The consequence of inevitable death bears down on their trembling forms.

One of them stumbles backward, his feet barely find purchase on the blood-soaked dirt. His mouth opens and closes soundlessly, like a fish hauled from water, before he manages to choke out, "P-please... we didn't mean—"

The plea is cut off as Adra moves with incomprehensible speed, closing the distance between them in a blur. He grabs the man by the front of his ragged shirt, hauling him off the ground with ease. The man flails, his hands pull weakly at Adra's iron grip. His words dissolve into incoherent sputters. Adra's eyes are merciless.

Silently, he whirls the man through the air. His body arching like a rag-doll. The sickly gleam of the iron rod that once held a lantern, catches my eyes as Adra drives the man downward skewering him like a kebab.

The rod pierces through the man's abdomen with a wet, meaty *crunch*. The impact sends a spray of gore that fountains through the air. His body jerks violently. His legs kick out in a grotesque parody of life. A grating scream tears from his throat, but it lasts only a moment.

His struggles weaken. His head lolls to the side as blood pours from his mouth in thick, frothy streams. The iron rod holds firm, as the impaled man's lifeless body dips forward like a butcher's offering. Clotted crimson drips steadily at the base of the rod and soaks into the dirt below. Adra steps back, his chest heaving as he surveys his handiwork. The man's glassy, lifeless eyes stare down at him. His mouth frozen in a silent scream.

Only Marco remains now, the last thread of defiance in this blood-soaked tapestry. His fist trembles as he raises a knife. His stance wobbles under the crushing impact of shock, yet he forces out a roar. "Come on, you bastard!" He shouts, though his bravado is paper thin.

Adra doesn't delay Marco's death any longer. His response is a sound that seems to erupt from the depths of the abyss itself. It is a sound not of rage alone, but of something ancient. Blood drips from his hands, trailing down his fingers like dye staining a predator's claws. His shirt, torn and saturated with gore, clings to his broad frame. While his face is splattered with the remnants of his wrath. Adra is a vision of pure vengeance.

Adra lunges forward, faster than Marco can react. His bloodied hand snaps out, seizing Marco's wrist before the blade can find its mark. Marco's eyes enlarge, his breath hitches as he struggles, but Adra's strength is beyond human. Adra grabs Marco's wrist as it audibly snaps under his force. He bends the wrist and maneuvers the knife towards Marco. The blade flashes momentarily in the dim moonlight as Adra drives it into Marco's throat with sadistic precision.

The steel plunges deep, and Marco's scream gurgles in his throat, cut short by the blood that erupts from the wound. Adra pulls the blade free and stabs again. The motion swift and unsparing. Once. Twice. Over and over. Each thrust is deliberate and fueled by a diabolic rage. The sound of tearing flesh and crunching bone blends with Marco's wet, choking gasps.

Marco's hands nudge weakly at Adra's arms. His nails scrap against blood-slick skin as his strength ebbs away. Marco's eyes roll back, his body convulses with the last vestiges of life, but Adra doesn't stop. The blade rises and falls, again and again, blood spraying in bright red arcs that paint the ground and stain the already-darkened dirt.

Finally, Marco collapses, as his body crumples like a broken marionette. The knife stays buried in his neck. Blood pools around him in a macabre halo. The dark liquid spreads like ink spilled on parchment. Adra stands over him, chest heaving as his gaze shifts downward, sealing the lifeless body of his final adversary.

The silence that follows is absolute, broken only by Adra's labored breathing and the faint, wet murmur of something behind us.

Vincenzo.

I whip around to see him, somehow still alive. His twisted body writhing weakly in the dirt. His eyes roll toward Adra, and a creaking sound escapes his throat: a pathetic, inhuman groan. Adra's shoulders tense, and he stalks toward him, like a predator savoring the kill.

"Adra!" My voice cracks desperately. "Adra, stop!"

He freezes mid-step, his back to me, his shoulders overcrowded with the power of his rage. For a moment, he doesn't move, the tension in the air is thick enough to choke on. Then, slowly, he turns towards me.

I stand, trembling but resolute, as my torn dress hangs from my shoulders, streaked with dirt and blood. I smooth the fabric down as best I can, though it does nothing to mask the madness burning inside me. My fingers shake as I dust off the grime clinging to me, but my steps are firm as I move toward Marco's lifeless body. The knife still lodged in his throat.

I reach down and grip the hilt, my knuckles white, as I yank it free with a slimy, nauseating *squelch*. A fresh gush of blood follows, spraying across my hands, but I don't flinch. The blade is heavy, but not unwieldy, as I turn to face Vincenzo.

He is lying in the dirt. His body is broken. His breaths come in wet, ragged gasps. His eyes, wide with fear, dart toward me as I approach. His lips quiver, blood begins to bubble at the corners of his mouth as he tries to form words.

"P-please..." He croaks, his voice choked and desperate. I stop just above him, staring down at the pathetic creature who had so gleefully wielded his power over me. His once-mocking smirk is gone, replaced by sheer panic. The sight sends a dark satisfaction rippling through me, a surge of purposeful resolve.

"You want mercy?" I say quaking with rage. "After what you tried to do?"

Vincenzo's hand twitches, weakly reaching toward me as if begging for some shred of compassion. I step closer, my shadow falling over his mangled body like death itself.

"Mercy?" I hiss as my grip tightens around the handle of the bloodied knife.

A cruel, deranged chuckle escapes my lips. It echoes in the still, blood-soaked night, as though the shadows themselves are laughing with me. I crouch beside Vincenzo's broken, paralyzed body. His pathetic frame tics weakly against the dirt. His eyes swell in hysteria as I lean closer. The bloodied knife glinting in my fist.

"You should have fucked off when you had the chance, *tesoro*." I whisper, my voice venomous as mockery twists every syllable.

My smile spreads into something malicious, as I tilt my head, watching the realization of his fate dawn in his eyes. His lips tremble, trying to form words, a scream, but all that comes out is a faint, choking gasp. His chest heaves. His breaths shallow and frayed, as though he's drowning in his own fear. I can smell it on him—the stench of death mixing with his panic. The once-cocky sneer he wore like armor is gone, replaced by the raw, naked truth of his cowardice.

"What's wrong tesoro?" I trail the knife lightly down his cheek. "You were so *bold* before."
The knife continues to trail down his chest until the blade reaches his exposed limp dick.

"No clever insults? No hollow threats?" I taunt.

He flinches, and his breath hitches as the blade presses in, a thin line of blood blooms where it kisses his skin. My laugh is blackened now. It's not just rage anymore, it's power.

"You thought you could take everything from me?" My voice is a vindictive purr as I lean closer. "But look at you now... broken, pathetic, lying in the dirt where you belong."

I tilt my head, feigning curiosity as I drag the knife lightly across the head of his penis. "Tell me, wandought[22]," I continue conversational, "did it ever cross your mind that you'd end up here? At my feet? Begging for your miserable little life?"

His lips quake, but no sound escapes them.

---

[22] A weak, ineffectual man

I snicker, the sound humorless amongst the murderous night. "You must've thought you were invincible," I say mockingly, "untouchable... but here's the thing, *tesoro*... everyone bleeds... even rats like you."

I grip the blade tightly, the handle slick with the blood of the others. With deliberate, agonizing slowness, I begin to slice his penis off.

The steel cuts through his flesh. The resistance, a sickening reminder of the life still pulsing through him. Blood wells up immediately, spilling down in rivulets onto the dirt beneath his immobile body.

His muffled screams tear through the night, the sound of pure, unadulterated anguish. I drag the knife further, the skin peeling back as I work, exposing muscles and sinew. The metallic stench of blood fills the air, blending with the rancid odor of sweat and filth. Vincenzo's eyes roll back, tears stream down his face as his body jerks weakly against the dirt. His suffering is painted across his face. Every muscle contorted, while his eyes reflects the hell he's being dragged through.

Blood sprays outward, flecking my hands. His hushed screams change into choking, rasping gasps, as his body quakes while the life drains from him, inch by agonizing inch. The detached, bloodied penis drips gore onto the dirt as I lift it, the weight lighter than it appears. The mangled flesh glistens under the moonlight, a macabre token of justice served.

I focus my gaze on Vincenzo. His face pale and greasy with sweat. His chest heaving in weak, desperate breaths. A devilish grin spreads across my face as I take a slow, deliberate step closer, letting the blood from the severed piece drip audibly onto the ground between us.

The sound is sickening, each drop hitting the earth like a hammer driving nails into his coffin. His lips quiver, as I crouch down, my shadow enveloping him like an angel of death.

"Open up, *bella*." I mock.

I hold the mangled cock trophy mere inches from his face, watching as his expression contorts into sheer horror. Vincenzo gags before I've even moved. His eyes manically moving side to side in futile protest. But his body is broken. His strength is gone, and he's nothing more than a pathetic, twitching husk.

With unflinching resolve, I grab his jaw, forcing it open with a nasty *crack* as his teeth grind under the pressure of my grip. His feeble whimper transforms into a muffled gurgle as I shove the bloody, mutilated flesh into his mouth. The dismembered piece fills his throat. His eyes bulge as he chokes on the revolting intrusion.

Blood spills from the corners of his mouth, mixing with saliva and falling down his neck as his body jerks in a desperate attempt to expel it. His gag reflex triggers, but there's nowhere for it to go. His mutilated penis is fortunately lodged deep, blocking his airway. I push it in further.

Despite the slickness of blood, my hand forces him to take more as he convulses beneath me. His gurgles grow louder, wetter, more frantic, and his fingers pitifully claw in the dirt. His nails break as he attempts to scrabble to survive. His chest expands; his body spasms as the last flickers of life drain from his eyes.

Finally, with a long, rattling exhale, Vincenzo's struggles cease. His body goes limp, his head lolls to the side. Blood and bile oozing from his mouth. I release his jaw, letting it hang slack, and rise to my feet, wiping the blood from my hands onto his tattered shirt. My breath comes in controlled bursts, as I step back to survey the scene.

The magnitude of everything collapses down on me all at once, and the world seems like it's closing in. My breath catches in my throat as the adrenaline drains from my body, replaced by a tidal wave of misery. My hands begin to shudder uncontrollably. The gruesome scene before me blurs as tears well up in my eyes, spilling over in hot streams down my cheeks.

I turn to Adra, his figure secure and strong amidst the chaos, and the dam breaks. A booming scream tears from my throat as I throw myself into his arms, clinging to him like he's the only thing anchoring me to this world.

"Where were you?" I sob. *"Where were you?!"*

My fists pound weakly against his chest. My strength fails me as the hysterical cries pour out. The tears flow faster. My screams devolve into broken, gasping sobs. The fight, the fear, the rage, all crumbles, leaving nothing but devastating sadness and the ache of what I've just endured.

Adra's arms wrap around me, pulling me close. His embrace is firm but tender. His sympathy seeps into my trembling body as he holds me tightly.

288

"I'm here." Though I can sense the tension in his frame, the weight of his guilt. "I'm here now."

I bury my face in his chest, my cries muffled against the blood-streaked fabric of his shirt. His scent, familiar and grounding, fills my senses, and I clutch at him desperately, as if letting go would mean losing myself completely. The sobs wrack my body, as he strokes my hair with a tenderness that only makes the ache in my chest grow heavier.

The words spill out of me, torrent, and incoherent. "I was so scared, Adra. I—I thought I was going to die. I thought—" My voice breaks, and the rest dissolves into unintelligible cries.

Adra doesn't say anything, but his grip tightens. His chin rests lightly on the top of my head. His silence is heavy, filled with an unspoken sorrow that mirrors my own.

Minutes pass, maybe hours—I can't tell—but eventually, the storm inside me begins to subside, leaving only an emptiness in its wake. My sobs quiet into soft, broken whimpers, and my body, exhausted from the outburst, slumps against his. I feel his touch on my back, reassuring, and I cling to that small comfort like it's the only thing keeping me together.

"I'm so sorry. I should've been here."

I shake my head weakly, unable to respond, my throat sore from crying. All I can do is hold on to him. My tears soaking into his shirt as the influence of everything crowds me, stifling and inescapable.

Chapter 28

Adrastus

I hold her tightly, feeling every tremor of her body as it shakes with sobs that seem to come from the very depths of her soul. She's falling apart in my arms, and I can do nothing but cradle her like a snowflake before it melts.

Her fingers clutch desperately at my shirt. The grip so tight she fears I might drift away if she lets go. Each broken cry tears through my spirit like a sword, grievous and more cavernous than any wound I've ever endured. I press my cheek against the top of her head, breathing in the faint scent of her amidst the blood and dirt, holding myself against her fragility.

I've faced centuries of death, watched lives end in agony, seen entire families destroyed—but this is different. This pain is personal. Her pain now belongs to me, a shared burden I never anticipated but don't want to escape.

Her sobs ring in my ears, each one a reminder of how powerless I am in this moment. I want to take it all from her, to erase every moment of dread, every ounce of despair she's endured. But I can't. All I can do is hold her, whispering words that appear woefully inadequate.

I'm here. You're safe now.

I'll never let them hurt you again.

I repeat it like a mantra, not just for her but for myself, as if saying it will make it true, will rewrite the horrors of the night. My grip tightens around her, as if by sheer force I can keep the world's cruelty at bay. The unnerving sound of her somber sobs against my chest lances me. Each one a wave threatening to drown us both. But I won't let it. I can't let it.

How did this happen? How did I let her get so close to danger?

The question grapples at me, a never-ending ruthless gnaw at my mind. I was supposed to protect her, to shield her from this brutality, and yet here we are, broken and bloodied. Clinging to each other like survivors of a shipwreck. The stark sting of guilt ravages my thoughts.

I let this happen. I should never have left her alone.

I rock her gently, as if the motion could calm the chaos in both of us. Her cries begin to abate, though her grip on me doesn't loosen. She shifts, her head tilting upward. Her tear-streaked face meets mine, her eyes red and swollen, and yet they hold something that takes my breath away. Trust. Vulnerability.

I see everything in those eyes, the pain, the fear, the hope she's clinging to like a threadbare cord, worn thin by sorrow. Never again shall she bear such woes, not while she breathes. Not in this lifetime, nor the next. I will right what's been wronged.

Before I can stop myself, I lean down and capture her lips in a kiss. It's tender at first, a desperate attempt to convey what words cannot. But as her lips respond, the kiss intensifies, luminating a light between us that pushes the darkness away. It's not just a kiss; it's a lifeline, pulling both of us from the edge of desolation.

When we part, her face remains close, her breath uniting with mine. And then, with a voice that quavers but doesn't stutter, she says the words that shatter the only world I've ever known.

"I love you."

The words fall upon me like spring rain on parched Earth. A gentle, holy, and long-awaited deliverance. *Love.* It's a concept I've witnessed countless times in mortals, their sacrifices, their devotion, their joy, their agony. I've seen it inspire bravery and spark destruction. But I've never *felt* it. I never believed I could. Until now.

Those three simple words wrap around my heart like silk, and for a moment, I am no longer made of flesh or shadow, but of light. The stars in her eyes fell to her lips and whispered the ode of paramours. Their warmth spreads through my chest, my veins, and down to my very core. It's petrifying and dazzling. A sentiment so vast and all-encompassing that it's as though love itself has reached inside of me. For the first time in centuries, I feel *alive.*

I don't know how to respond. Saying any words seems meaningless, inadequate. Instead, I lean in again, brushing her hair back and meeting her eyes with as much intensity as I can muster.

"My mourning star." I whisper with such devotion. And then I kiss her again. This time, it's tender and slower. I fill this moment with every ounce of adoration, passion, and care I have. I express an unrelenting, aching need to be closer to her.

Her arms wrap around me, pulling me into her spirit, and for a moment, everything else fades. The atrocities of the night, the weight of my existence, even the fear of this strange, new emotion—all of it melts away into the softness of her touch, and the starlight of her lips.

When we finally part, I sweep her into my arms. Her head rests against my chest, and her breathing slows as exhaustion takes over. By the time I set her upon the humble bed within the abandoned farmhouse, she is half-lost to slumber. Her features ease and arrive at peace for the first time since this cursed nightmare began.

I sit beside her. My gaze fixed solely on her face. The words she spoke reprises in my mind: I love you.

It echoes like a worshiper's melody, interspersing into the elements of who I am. I've spent ages bound to death, to contracts, to an existence devoid of meaning beyond the inevitable. But here she is, this mortal, this

294

fragile, beautiful being, turning everything I thought I knew upside down. Her love terrifies me. It's too infinite, too consuming, too perfect. And yet, it fills me with a quiet joy I can't explain.

As the night stretches, I remain awake, my thoughts absorbed by her. Every memory of her smile, her laughter, her touch plays in my mind, each one sparking a new reaction.

And then those words again: I love you.

I know not the shape of love, nor if my heart was ever fashioned for such grace. Yet for her sake I shall try. I shall try until my strength is spent and nothing of me remains but the will to love her still.

The idyllic impressions cease as I stand at the entrance of the house. I am being pulled towards the forest, another summoning. I transform into my rightful vestments and close the front door quietly behind me as to not wake my precious Rosannah.

The moon is just about to head off for its sleep, as I can see dawn approaching. I follow the pull towards the tree line. My chest pounds, not with dismay, but with apprehension. I know why I'm here. I know who's coming. And then, like a shadow peeling itself from the darkness, Erevan steps into view. His figure is cloaked, his beak-like mask catching the faint glow of the fading moonlight.

"Adra," he begins, "you've been requested. Master Mortifer is... most displeased."

The way he says it, the deliberate pause, is worse than an outright threat. My fists clench at my sides, the tension coiling in my chest like a serpent.

"I know." I reply, keeping my voice calm despite the conflicting squall inside me. "But hear me—"

Erevan raises a gloved palm, silencing me with a single, imperious gesture. The movement is unhurried, intentional, as to remind me of my place. "*Don't.*" He hisses. "Do *not* insult me—or the Master—with your foolhardy pitiful excuses."

I grit my teeth, the words dying in my throat. Erevan steps closer, his shadow elongating, painting the ground black between us. "You laid claim to souls that answer not to you." He continues, his voice a pernicious calm. "You defied the natural order, disregarded the contract. Have you the faintest notion of what you have wrought?"

His mask tilts slightly, the hollowness where his eyes should be boring into me like twin voids. The memory of Vincenzo and his men flashes in my mind— their terror, their screams, their blood staining the earth.

"I did what had to be done. They deserved it."

Erevan lets out a low, sardonic chuckle, the sound ringing like the echo of a death knell. "Deserved?" He repeats, mockingly. "You think *warrant* matters? You think Master Mortifier gives a fuck about your mortal sense of merit? You know the law that binds us, Adra. You know the *oath.* And yet, you chose to defy it."

He steps closer. "Do you understand the consequences of your actions? Master Mortifer can end you, Adra. Not merely kill you—end you. Erase you from every plane of existence... and not just *you*."

At this, he pauses, letting the words hang in the air like a noose tightening around my neck. "Your dear mortal... Rosannah is it?" He draws out her name, twisting it like a dagger. "Her soul could be forfeited. Her essence could be scattered into the endless void... eradicated as if she never existed."

A surge of anger swells inside me. "She's done nothing!" I growl. "This has nothing to do with her."

Erevan tilts his head again, his amusement evident even through the lifeless mask. "Aye, but it does... you think the Master doesn't, see? Doesn't *know*? Every action you take, every disobedience, every choice—it's all tied to her now. Your foolishness has sealed her fate as well as your own."

My fists clench, the leather of my gloves groaning with the pressure. Erevan steps closer, until the cold, deathly aura emanating from him nudges mine.

"Don't waste your eternity on a mere mortal. You know your purpose. Your duty. We control the dead, the souls, the afterlife. You are *not* a savior, Adra. Don't let this illusion of humanity cloud your judgment." His voice lowers, a whisper that cuts deeper than any shout. "Master Mortifier's patience is not infinite. And when he decides to act... there is no realm, no power, no plea that will save you, or her."

Erevan takes a step back, his form beginning to blend into the shadows of the forest. "Be smart, Adra. You are playing a game you cannot win. We have work to do. Don't let her be your undoing."

And then, the darkness swallows him, Erevan is gone. The forest's touch is icier, the trees loom larger, their branches like skeletal fingers reaching for the sky.

Rosannah's face floods my mind. I hear her voice, full of trust, and the thought of her being reduced to nothingness makes me want to deal my own final blow, knowing I could be the cause of her demise.

The first light of dawn stretches across the sky, its golden hues creeping through the cracks of the abandoned farmhouse. The air is now burdened by the impact of Erevan's warning. My chest constricts as I approach the house. The small structure offers little solace against the danger that looms.

I push open the door quietly, the familiar creak of the hinges pierces the stillness. Inside, Rosannah stirs, her body shifting beneath the threadbare blanket. Her curls are wild from sleep, and the sight of her, fragile yet so full of life, sends a wave of both relief and dread through me.

She blinks awake, her hazel eyes catching the morning light as they focus on me. "Adra?" She whispers, her voice still thick with sleep, but hints at her panic.

I'm at her side in an instant, dropping to my knees beside the bed. I cradle her face in my hands, brushing her hair away as her attachment grounds me. "I'm here. I'm here. I'll never leave your side again. I swear it."

Her hand reaches up to cover mine. "I'm never leaving yours, Adra. I'm yours—for eternity."

The words lull me like a ship in a gentle storm, filling every corner of my being with an emotion I still don't fully understand but can no longer deny. My spirit swells, the tension of Erevan's threat momentarily replaced by quiet joy. I lean down and kiss her, passionately, pouring everything I can't say into this single moment. When I pull back, her sleepy smile remains, and for a fleeting moment, the world feels bearable again.

I climb into the bed beside her. Our bodies curling around one another like vines seeking sun. Holding her feels like holding the entire universe, fragile yet infinite. Something I would destroy all the realms to protect.

Her curls brush against my chin, and her contented breaths are a balm to my frayed nerves. Her voice breaks the silence, light but curious. "You seem troubled. What's wrong?"

I hesitate, sweeping my fingers along the curve of her shoulder. I don't want to burden her, but she deserves the truth—at least some of it. "We need to keep moving. It's not safe here anymore. We must head to Catania as soon as possible."

"Is it far?"

"Far enough. Palermo is still a four-day journey. Catania is the next closest city, but it's the best chance we have."

She studies me for a moment; her gracious eyes filled with worry. "You're afraid." She says quietly, a statement rather than a question.

I nod, unable to hide it from her. "Not for me. For you. For us."

Her hand finds mine, our fingers intertwining. "Then we'll go, together. Whatever comes, we'll face it."

Her courage is a much-needed light in this endless darkness. I kiss her forehead, staying for a moment before forcing myself to move. "Let's get ready." I stand and offer her a hand.

We work in silence, the quiet punctuated by the rustle of supplies and the occasional chirp of waking birds outside. The sun climbs higher, casting long shadows amongst us as we load the wagon. Rosannah hums quietly under her breath, a tune that is both haunting and hopeful, as she places the last of the bundles into the cart.

As we climb onto the wagon, I peek at her one last time, her profile illuminated by the morning light. Her strength, her grace—it leaves me in awe.

With a snap of the reins, we set off toward Catania, the unknown awaiting us both. But as long as she's by my side, I have hope that we can survive whatever lies ahead.

I won't let Mortifer lay a single finger on her soul. Not her light, it's not his to take.

I've seen the power of Mortifer, the ruin he can summon with the mere flick of his will. To defy him is to invite annihilation, to walk willingly into the abyss.

But I can't...won't... let it happen. Not to her. Not to us.

Even as doubt claws at the edges of my resolve, the burn of something stronger persists: *love.* She's more than mortal flesh, more than another name on the list. She's mine, and I will stand against the shadows themselves to protect her. Even if it means I am swallowed whole. Let all the realms in all universes bear witness... *I will not let him take her.*

CONWAY TITTY

Chapter 29

Rosannah

With a continuous groaning rhythm, the wagon rolls along the uneven road beneath us. The morning sun filters through the thin veil of mist drifting over the countryside,

My eyes survey the amber poured horizon, but my mind is miles away, stuck reliving the horrors of yestereve. I keep enduring it—the fear, the humiliation, the rage. Vincenzo's leering face, the way his filthy hands grabbed at me. The way the other men circled me like deranged wolves.

My stomach churns as bile rises in my throat. I close my eyes to steady my breathing, to give my mind something else to think about. I've felt this way before—used, powerless, discarded.

But then, arrived Adra. He came for me and tore those useless bastards apart. He shielded me, held me,

303

aided me in my desperate hour of need. He will never be like them. None can compare. None ever will. And he belongs to me.

My fingers tighten on the edge of the wagon seat as I think of Vincenzo's last moments, the way I took *my* revenge. I should feel sorrow or some kind of remorse, but I don't. I feel pride, despite what those vultures tried to take from me.

The memory of shoving that knave's own dick down his throat is both horrifying and oddly satisfying. That pig-fucker deserved to suffer. Every last second of his disgusting existence, I hope was pure pain.

Dead men don't rape.

A small chuckle bubbles from my chest before I can stop it. The absurdity of it hits me, and my chuckle develops into manic laughter.

Gia would have howled, snorted, and horse laughed.

My cackle transitions to tears as I think about her. The weight of her absence is unmeasurable. Gia, my best friend, my sister in every way but blood. Her smile, her eyes...her dreams... they're all gone now, swallowed by the same sickness that chases us relentlessly. A flash of her lifeless body alters my tears into a sob. Having to leave her in that cursed town has been unbearable to process.

There is a gentle squeeze on my hand, pulling me from my grievous thoughts. I see Adra watching me, his eyes glowing with empathy. He doesn't speak, doesn't try to offer empty reassurances. He simply holds my hand, letting me know I am not alone.

Needing to distract myself, I clear my throat and ask, "Adra... will you share more of your story with me? Pray tell your life and the toils that shape it."

His expression shifts ever so lightly, a flicker of discomfort passing over his features. He hesitates, his stare drifting back to the road ahead. "There's not much to tell. It's just... life."

I raise an eyebrow, sensing his evasion. "Nay! Out with it, everyone has a story." I nudge him. "You descend upon me like some avenging angel, tearing men apart to protect me, and you expect me to believe there's nothing of worth or wonder?"

A smile pulls at his lips, but it doesn't quite reach his eyes. "It's not that simple, Rosannah."

I press further, curiosity melding with the desire to know the man who's become my safeguard. "Why is it so hard for you to talk about yourself? What are you afraid of?"

Adra exhales sharply, the tension in his shoulders growing. "I'm not afraid, it's just... complicated."

Understanding the walls he's building, I decide to let it go—for now. Trying to change the subject, I glance towards the horizon. "This sickness," I begin cautiously, "have you seen it before? Have you seen... this much death?"

His expression stiffens, and his fists tighten on the reins. "Aye, it happens more often than you think. When it comes, all one can do is flee. Get ahead of it. Find the places it hasn't touched yet. But it's relentless. It's death, and it always catches up, eventually."

His words icing my bones from the inside out. There is a moment of silence, as if the surrounding flora and fauna hush with Adra's omen.

"How much further until we reach Catania?"

I pause.

Silence.

"Do you think we'll be safe there?"

Adra peers at me, "It's safer than staying where we were. The plague hasn't reached Catania yet—or so I've heard."

His words don't ease the knot of worry in my chest. "But what if it does? What if we get there and it's no different?"

Adra's grip on the reins tightens further, the leather creaking under the strain. "Then we move again." He says firmly. "We keep moving until we're ahead of it."

I nod, though the thought of never stopping, of constantly running, fills me with a quiet dread. "Do you think we'll ever... stop running?"

He studies me for a moment, I see determination in his gape. "I'll make sure you're safe," he says, "no matter what it takes."

I want to believe him. I want to believe that we'll reach Catania and find a way to escape this nightmare. But the shadow of doubt persists, a quiet whisper in the back of my mind. The city feels so far away.

"How far do you think we are from that promise?" I ask, attempting to lighten the worry of my thoughts, though my voice carries a bitterness I hadn't intended.

"Closer than you think, and when we get there, we'll figure out what's next. Together."

The word *together* bounces around in my mind. It is a fragile comfort against the growing uncertainty. I shift in the wagon seat, leaning into him just enough to feel his body. The road before us stretches on, long and ominous, but I can't help but have the frailest ray of hope.

The night creeps in, blanketing the road in shadows, but the distant flicker of lanterns on the horizon pulls my attention forward. The faint glow outlines what can only be the city of Catania. Relief washes over me, my body sagging with exhaustion.

"We draw near, just a while longer." Adra says, though I can understand the weariness in it as well. He flicks the reins, urging the donkey onward, and I nod silently, my eyes fixed on the lights growing brighter with each passing moment.

When we finally reach the outskirts of the city, something feels... off. The streets are eerily quiet, devoid of the bustling activity I expected from a place like Catania. The houses lining the road are murky, save for a few scattered lanterns glowing faintly through windows.

"It seems everyone must have moved to the city center." The unease settling in my chest strengthens as I glance around, searching for any sign of life. The density of abandonment dominates like an unspoken warning.

We stop in front of a well-lit house, its glow spilling onto the cobblestones. The house itself is grand, far more luxurious than anything I've ever seen. The wooden door is framed with intricate carvings of vines and leaves, though the fine craftsmanship is dulled by a fine layer of dust. Lanterns hang on either side of the entrance, casting a golden glow, and illuminating the complex grooves of the aged wood.

I climb out of the wagon and walk slowly up to the entrance. I peek back at Adra, his towering frame obscured by the dull light, before firmly knocking on the door.

"Hello?" I call out.

There's no answer, only the faint creak of wood settling in the cool night air.

I knock again, louder this time. "Is anyone there?"

The door swings open under the weight of my palm, its hinges groaning in protest. I grab the hanging lantern and step over the threshold.

Inside, the house is still, but not lifeless. The scent of perfume and wood polish survives freely in the air. The lantern casts long shadows across the walls. I step further inside; I'm struck by the chaos.

Books are scattered across the floor, their pages crumpled and torn. Fine garments spill out of open trunks, their silks and velvets crumpled as if thrown in haste. Cabinets stand with doors ajar, their shelves stripped bare.

"Adra?" I call over my shoulder, but I hear nothing.

My pulse quickens as I take cautious steps further inside. The carved wooden beams above my head, the embroidered tapestries lining the walls, the polished silver utensils abandoned on the dining table—all of it speaks of wealth I can hardly fathom. Whoever lived here wasn't just well-off; they were important. And yet, they left it all behind in a frenzy.

I make my way to the staircase, the lantern swaying in my hand as I ascend. Each wooden step creaks beneath me, and I grip the banister tightly. Upstairs, the bedrooms tell the same story. The beds are massive; their canopies lined with rich fabrics that have been torn and displaced. Wardrobes stand open, their contents spilling out onto the floor.

My fingers brush against the cold brass of a doorknob as I push open another door, stepping into what must have been the master bedroom. The sight takes my breath away. A massive copper bathtub sits in the center of the room, its surface gleaming in the lantern's light. The opulence of it is staggering. Beside the tub sits a low table covered in golden trinkets—a hairbrush, a comb, and a hand mirror. The bed is vast, draped in lush green silks that shimmer even in the dull light.

I step toward the tub, running my fingers along its smooth, cold surface. The chill of the metal sends a shiver up my spine, but it doesn't deter the thought forming in my mind. *A hot bath.*

309

A chance to feel clean, to let the grime of the road and the terror of the last few days slip away.

"Adra?" I call, my voice carrying down the staircase. "I want to take a bath. Could you start a fire and find a well, please?"

The sound of heavy footsteps echoes up the stairs, and moments later, Adra's broad frame fills the doorway. He takes in the scene before him—the disarray of the room, the gleaming tub, and me standing in the midst of it all.

His eyes glow as they meet mine. "A hot bath sounds lovely. May I join you?" He sends a wink my way and I about fall over in a swoon.

The need rises in my body, and I bite back a grin. "Only if you behave." I tease, trying to hide how much I want him close.

Adra chuckles, the hearty sound filling the room and easing some of the tension that idles in my mind. "I'll do my best." He replies, stepping forward to press a kiss to my forehead before turning to leave. "I'll get the fire started and find that water for you." He peers back over his shoulder and sends another mischievous wink. "I mean, for us."

As he disappears down the stairs, I glance back at the tub, my fingers trailing along its edge once more. For the first time in days, I allow myself to imagine a moment of normalcy. But even as I let the thought take root, the stillness of the house is oppressive, as though the very walls hold its breath, waiting. Something isn't right, but I shove the thought aside.

Tonight, for a moment, I just want to be common again.

I smirk to myself as I lay back on the surprisingly comfortable bedding. My body sinks into the luxurious fabrics. My muscles ache with exhaustion, a deep, bone-weary fatigue that I've been ignoring for far too long. I hear Adra's heavy steps fading as he descends, likely heading to the well he mentioned. Just the thought of heated water against my skin, of the dirt and sweat of the road melting away, makes me sigh in anticipation.

I glance down at my hands, noting how filthy they are. Dirt clings to my nails, a reminder of how much we've endured. My whole body feels the same—caked in grime, blood, and stiff from too many nights on the road. They scream for relief.

I reluctantly rise from the bed and walk back over to the magnificent copper tub. The golden mirror on the small table catches my eye, and I pick it up, holding it to my face. The sight staring back at me is almost unrecognizable. My curls are wild and tangled, framing a face that is worn and tired. Smudges of dirt streak my cheeks, and my lips are dry and cracked from the endless travel. I run my fingers through my hair, wincing as they catch on knots. *This bath can't come soon enough,* I think, setting the mirror back down.

My stare drifts to the golden brush beside it. I'll use it after, when my hair is clean again. The thought of being restored, of being whole, fills me with a strange, guilty excitement.

I map my fingers along the edge of the tub, imagining the heat that will soon embrace me, while

311

my thoughts drift to Adra. Even after all the tragedy, all the fear, I can't deny the way my body hums whenever he's nearby.

My fingers tighten on the edge of the tub as an image forms in my mind—Adra, naked, stepping into the bath with me, the feeling of his skin against mine, the water lapping at us as his hands roam my body.

A flush creeps up my neck, spreading to my cheeks. My breath quickens as I imagine his touch, the way his rough fingers know every inch of me. The way he moves with both hunger and care. I crave him, every part of him—his strength, his tenderness, the thick length of him that fills me so completely it makes me lose myself. My thighs press together instinctively, the ache of need blooming within me.

I sit on the edge of the tub, my fingers idly tracing the smooth, cool surface of the copper rim. The chill of the metal bites against my skin once more. I prop my foot up, letting my toes brush the edge, and the sensation sends a faint shiver up my leg. It's strange how something so simple—a contrast of temperatures— grounds me. My thoughts wander, as they always seem to when I'm left alone.

I close my eyes, and immediately, I see him – my beloved Adra. The sharpness of his gaze, the way his eyes seem to see through every layer of me. His strong bare body, presenting himself to me. His erect cock ready for the taking. My lips curl into a small smile as I let my head tilt back, my hair brushing over my shoulders.

The memory of his touch is unshakable. His hands...so large, so deliberate. They make me feel safe yet beg for more at all once. My fingers brush lightly along my collarbone, retracing where his touch had been not so long ago. It's a ghost of a sensation, but it's enough to send a pulse to the place between my thighs.

My gaze drifts to the mirror on the nearby vanity, and I catch a glimpse of myself. I am different—tired, yes, but there's something else in my reflection. Something brighter, something alive. Maybe it's him. Maybe it's the way he sees me, the way he makes me feel more than just the pieces of myself I've had to scrape together.

I let out a slow breath, my fingers now brushing along the top of my thigh. The cool air of the room prickles against my skin. My mind drifts further. I imagine his hands instead of my own. I run my fingertips up my thigh as I gather my dress. Brushing them lightly over my mound and trailing them down in between my folds right to my clit. A moan comes unexpectedly from my mouth, as I rub my spot with intention now.

Leaning further onto the edge of the tub, I let my bare foot rise to rest against the cool copper rim. My toes instinctively curl, then stretch, as if testing the temperatures.

A faint shiver ripples through me, the cold seeping into my skin and fusing with the residual heat from my body. It's an intoxicating swell of unexpected awareness.

I tighten my grip on the edge of the tub with one hand. My other steadies me as I press my foot down against the metal, the icy chill anchoring me in place. The balance is precarious, and the tension in my muscles strain as I continue the search for pleasure.

My fingers trail down slowly again. The slick I find between my thighs makes my body vibrate. My breath catches as I press my finger a little further inside, feeling just how soaked I've become. All these wicked, depraved thoughts about Adra swirl in my head like a storm, leaving me dizzy.

How does he do this to me without even being here? Without even touching me?

One specific thought ravages my mind. I imagine him kneeling before me, his powerful frame lowered, his intense gaze fixed on me like I'm the only thing that matters. His voice, low and gravelly, murmuring words of desperation—*begging* to taste me. To be inside me.

I can almost feel his breath against my skin, and the way his hands would grip my thighs, holding me open for him as if I were some divine offering he couldn't resist. The fantasy grasps me tightly, making my head spin. My heart pounds in my chest, the rhythm almost too loud in my ears. My fingers move with more purpose, chasing the pleasure that coils tightly in my core.

He would do anything for me.

My lips part as a soft gasp escapes.

Anything, just to touch me.

Goosebumps ripple across my skin at the thought of his willingness. His complete, utter devotion to my pleasure. The image of him, so powerful and untouchable to the rest of the world, brought to his knees...just for me.

My breathing grows ragged, my body throbs with the tension building inside. I bite my lip, closing my eyes as the fantasy evolves. The thought of him ruining every inch of me.

Adra, Adra, Adra.

His name is a silent mantra in my head.

A plea.

A prayer.

I keep rubbing my clit. My fingers move in a perfect rhythm as the orgasm takes control. My breath shifts into a pant. My chest rises and falls rapidly, and my body begins to tingle. I am so close. I don't want to wait. I don't want to hold back. I want to let go. To finish. To drown in a sea of my own pleasure.

But I don't. I slow down, deliberately pulling myself back from the edge. My body quivers with frustration. My thighs clench as I force myself to wait, to savor this just a little longer. The ache between my legs grows unbearable, but there's something deliciously intoxicating about holding myself here. Teetering on the brink.

My fingers falter for a moment before I bring two of them to spread my outer lips. The cold air of the room brushes against my clit, sending an involuntary shudder of pleasure. The sensation makes my eyes roll in ecstasy. I gasp, the sound loud in the quiet room. The sensation of the cool air mixing with the heat of my arousal heightens my every nerve.

Lips held open, I pause feeling the way the anticipation sends another shiver racing down my spine. My heart hammers loudly in my chest as I release my fingers, letting them glide down to my wetness. It coats my fingertips as I slide them up and down, spreading my arousal.

The sensation is addicting as I imagine these aren't my fingers, but Adra's. I close my eyes, while his large rough hands explore me. I press my fingers inside, slowly, intensely, wishing they were his.

My breath catches in my throat as I imagine the pressure, the stretch. I can almost hear his voice, whispering my name like a benediction. My free hand grips the edge of the tub, anchoring me as the pleasure threatens to overthrow everything. My pussy begins to pulse as I penetrate myself with all my desire focused solely on him, and luckily, he's all for me.

Chapter 30

Adrastus

The night binds to me as I make my way back to the house, carrying filled pails of water from the well. The neighborhood is eerily silent, the stillness broken only by the occasional creak of wood or rustle of leaves. The buckets weigh nothing, but my thoughts of Rosannah are hefty. Her inhabitance fills my tenebrous existence with light. She's waiting, likely exhausted from our journey, yet somehow still full of that rare, stubborn fire that draws me to her.

Once inside, I set the pails down by the hearth and get to work building a strong fire. The room gradually warms as flames spark to life. The rhythmic crackle is almost soothing. I pour the water into a large cauldron and set it over the flames to heat. My hands move on habit, but my mind wanders. Rosannah is upstairs, probably already fast asleep, with her curls tangled, and wrapped tightly in the fabric of sheets.

Then I hear it—a sound so unmistakable that it sends an all-knowing twitch straight through me. A breathy moan filters down from above, faint but loud enough for me to catch it.

I approach the stairs. My steps measured with snail-like speed. The worn wood creaks under my feet as I begin my investigative ascent. I pause briefly after the first step, straining to listen, ensuring I don't disrupt the euphonic sounds coming from above.

The staircase is narrow, the wood aged and uneven, making it harder to be quiet with my large stature. My fingers brush lightly against the rail for balance, though I barely make contact, not wanting to risk even the feeblest of sound. The flicker of the lantern upstairs casts shifting shadows along the walls, giving the house a transcendental aura.

As I near the top, her moans grow clearer, and unrestrained. I must stop for a moment to brace myself. My breath reinforces, as my cock hardens at the thought of her. Rosannah's pleasure is deliciously enslaving. I clench my jaw trying to maintain control of my body.

I reach the landing at the top of the stairs. My feet move instinctively now, drawn to the glow spilling from the crack in the door. I am hypersensitive to every noise I make. I pause just enough to lean, and peer through the narrow opening. I choke on my sigh as my eyes land on her.

The sight before me is everything and more. I am nearly undone. Rosannah sits perched on the edge of the copper tub, her dress bunched up around her hips. Her fingers glide between her thighs. Her head tilted back, eyes closed as moans escape her parted lips. The lantern illuminates her ethereal form. Her succulent curves outlined by its swaying flames. Her skin flushed with the color of desire, as the need unfurls through the room.

I remain as stone, not wanting to interrupt her. Though my being screams to burst through the door and take her. My hands rub at my sides as I drink in the sight of her. The way her almost naked body moves. The way the sweat on her forehead glistens, while her fingers delve further, her hips rocking with each motion. I see her tightness clenching around them. The sight is maddening.

My cock throbs painfully against the confines of my pants. I need to release on her—in her.

Fuck, I don't care where as longer as I have her.

I bite down on my knuckle to stifle the groan that threatens to escape me. I can't move; I don't dare. If I step forward, if the door creaks, she might stop.

And I don't want her to stop—not until I say so.

Instead, I lower my fingers to the string of my pants and loosen them, just enough to free my aching bulge. My hand wraps around my length, stroking slowly as I continue to watch her. The friction I create sends ripples of pleasure shooting through me, but nothing compares to the view of her. Those soft gasps and moans spilling from her lips control me. Rosannah sets the pace, and I am only to follow.

She moves faster now. Her fingers thrust harder. Her other hand grips the edge of the tub for support. Her tender foot flexing, trying to help balance. Rosannah's body trembles, as she pants towards an orgasm. I can see she's close—so close.

My jaw stiffens as I struggle to hold back my own noises. My hands mirror the rhythm of her movements. I want to release. My balls are full and heavy, while the vein on my cock pulses. It takes every ounce of willpower to not step into the room and drive myself into her tight pussy.

As her moans grow louder. More desperate. I bite on my knuckles to keep quiet.

Damn, this mere mortal.

My eyes are glued to her every action. She is breathtaking, utterly mesmerizing and I am drunk on the sight of her. Rosannah's hand slows for a moment. Her fingers glisten with her cum. I catch my breath as I watch her lift her fingers to her mouth. Her tongue darting out to taste herself. The satisfied hum that escapes her lips makes me weak in the knees. My grip on my cock tightens, as my strokes becoming more urgent.

Fuck me, I need her.

The way her tongue flicks against her fingers makes my cock throb painfully in my palm. I can't look away. My thoughts melt together—her lips on me, tasting me, teasing me with the same slowness until I cum all over that beautiful face. The image burns in my mind, pushing me closer to unleashing my load all over this door.

Look at that body...every dip and line of her curves wanting to be held by my hands.

I swallow hard. My throat goes dry as I watch her, while my entire body thrums with an eagerness to give her exactly what she wants.

Rosannah gathers a small pool of spit on her fingers and lowers her hand back down. I am hanging by a thread, pleading with my body to stay still, when I realize where she's guiding those lubricated fingers—her asshole, tight and untouched.

Precum is leaking out of the tip of my cock at a rapid rate. I don't think I can hold on much longer, but I keep stroking it as I watch her tease her asshole. She rubs the sensitive rim, her movement slow and experimental. Her moans fill the room. My hand continues to mirror her movements, imagining how impossibly tight she'd feel around me. How her body would squeeze me in ways that would destroy every shred of control I have.

"Fuck." I mutter under my breath, the word slipping out without permission, as my strokes quicken. My palm is covered with my precum.

Look at you, my mourning star.

So fucking perfect.

I am lightheaded. My gaze glued to her shaking body. Her back arches as her fingers push just a little further. She's exquisite. A vision of depravity and beauty, and I'm an utter, hopeless addict.

I lean forward, my fingers gripping the doorframe for balance as I stroke myself harder. The way she moves, the way she sounds, it's too much. Every inch of me aches to step forward, to take over, to claim her as mine in every way possible. But I hold back, savoring the torment, the sight of her falling apart in her own pleasure. And yet, the thought persists, perverted and insistent:

Soon, Rosannah. Soon, you'll be mine... in ways you can't even imagine.

My hand moves faster over my cock, my breath coming out in short, gruff exhales as I lean against the wall. Precum drips steadily from my tip, a glistening testament to the effect she has on me. I can't take it anymore. *I need to touch her.*

Without any other concern, I push the door open, the creak of the hinges startles her. She jumps. Her wide, flushed eyes find mine. Before she can speak, I let out a grainy sarcastic, "Starting without me?"

Her body blushes, a delicious shade of pink spreading from her chest to her cheeks, almost matching the inside of her soaked pussy. She freezes, but her fingers don't stop. If anything, they move faster, pushing further, as if to taunt me. The sound of her wet motions and her escalating moans makes my cock spring. I step into the room, stroking myself as I approach her. Staring directly into her seductress eyes.

"Look at what you're making me do." I say, the words slipping out like an imperative decree. "You've got me leaking with anticipation, my selfish little minx." My words bite at her. "Were you really

322

going to make yourself cum without even letting me watch?"

Her lips part, as a short gasp escapes. Her moans grow louder. Her body arching against her own touch. She doesn't stop, doesn't pull away. Instead, her eyes pierce into mine, and she pushes her fingers faster, harder, as if to taunt me. Her confidence, her audacity.

Fuck she's ruining me.

"You're such a tease." I mutter, stepping closer, my cock aching in my palm. "Do you have any idea how badly I need to cum right now? Watching you like this... hearing you moan for me."

I can't stop myself now, the hunger feeds on her every noise. I'm inches from her supple body; pleasure emanates off her. The scent wraps around me. Those eyes daring me to take her, to do something.

She's pushing me, testing me, and fuck, it's working.

My restraint hangs by a thread. I stand before her, stroking myself quicker. My breathing uneven.

"Keep going. Show me how much you want this. Show me what I do to *you*, Rosannah."

"Is this what you want?" Her seductive lips coo at me.

My tongue hangs out of my mouth. Eyes staring at her wet pussy, and asshole being stretched by her fingers. Before I even realize it, I'm on my knees. My cock pulsating in my palm.

"Yes," I murmur, my voice a husky rasp, "I could watch you do this a hundred times over, and I'd still be

323

watching like it was the first... my dear mischievous mourning star."

The words spill out, filled with a perverse craving that I can't hold back. Rosannah moans, and I swear the sound splits me open.

I crawl closer. My hand still strokes myself in time with her. I am completely mesmerized by the way her body responds to her own touch.

"Don't stop." I say, my tone demanding but I am practically begging. "I want to watch you make yourself cum. I want to see your body pour out that sweet flavor just for me."

Her eyes meet mine, blazing with heat and defiance, and she doesn't falter. If anything, she moves her fingers faster. Her moans grow louder, filling the room, wrapping around me, pulling me further under her spell.

"That's it." I groan, unable to look away. "Let me see all of it."

I watch as Rosannah's head falls back. Her curls tumbling over her shoulders like a cascade of temptation. Saliva pools in my mouth as I imagine the taste of her. My tongue tracing every inch of her soaking wet holes. My hand moves faster, and the air between us is to die for.

She pants heavier, and my eyes stretch as I watch her take one finger out of her tight little asshole and slide it immediately into her pussy. "By shadow's grace... look at you. Fucking immaculate. Filling yourself up like the greedy temptress you are."

My groans enhance as her fingers thrust in and out, both of her holes occupied. "You're so close, aren't you?" I say, my voice hides the excitement I am trying to stifle. "I can see it. I can feel it. Don't hold back. Let me see you come undone."

Her body trembles. Her fingers work in a relentless rhythm. And I know she's right there, teetering on the edge. I'm salivating for her, my entire being devouring the sight, the sounds, the scent of her.

My own climax hovers just out of reach, waiting, desperate to follow hers. "That's it. Let yourself feel it all. Deeper for me. Deeper."

My words seem to spur her on. Her fingers plunging further in a rhythm so perfect it's hypnotic. Her whimpers echo through this shameless space we share.

Her moans turn breathy, broken. She stares at me with a wicked glint in her eyes and whispers, "If you want to see me cum, you're going to have to *beg* for it."

Without hesitation, I shout, "Please, my lady, fuck, please! I need to see you finish. Let me see you cum. Please... please let me taste you. My precious mourning star—please!"

The desperation in my voice surprises even me, but I don't care. My cock twitches in my fist. My strokes become frantic as I match her fervor. She bites her lip. Her eyes locked onto mine as she lets out a passionate moan.

"That's it." I groan, shaking with need. "Please. Show me."

Her legs buckle, as her orgasm overtakes her. Her squirt pours out, dripping down her thighs and pooling onto the floor. The sight of her completely wrecked, sends me spiraling. I let out a *yelp*. Falling onto all fours as I crawl closer. My face inches away from her glistening, cum dripped pussy.

My cock bounces violently in my hand, and with one final stroke, I explode. My release spurts onto the floor, blending with her own mess. My body jerks uncontrollably as I stare at the beautiful chaos before me. Her body glows, trembles with the aftershocks of her pleasure.

"I need to...," I plea between ragged breaths. And without waiting for permission, I bury my face into Rosannah's pussy, the mess of her still dripping from her holes. The sweet, salty tang of her orgasm floods my senses, and I groan profoundly against her. The vibration makes her gasp. I don't hold back—there's no holding back. My tongue laps up every drop of her, greedily savoring her essence as though it's the very elixir of life.

My lips move everywhere, kissing, licking, exploring her swollen skin. My tongue thrusts into her, filling the space her fingers had occupied moments before.

Her body jerks and jolts. She screams my name with shock and pleasure as her hands clutch at my hair, desperately trying to hold on to something, anything. But I'm far from done.

With one swift motion, I lift her effortlessly. My hands grip her thighs as I hoist her onto my shoulders. Her body sits flush against my face; her legs draped over me as I stand tall. My tongue doesn't stop, plunging into her, tasting her, devouring her as though she's my last meal. Her cries grow louder, echoing off the walls, and her fingers tangle in my hair, tugging as if she doesn't know whether to push me away or pull me closer.

My cock is solid again, no breaks for this flesh. I know I crave more—no, I urgently *need* more. I need to be inside of her. I need to bury myself in her pussy. I need to feel her tightening and pulsing around me as I take her completely.

I toss her down onto the bed. Her body bouncing lightly on the spongy surface. She lets out a surprised little squeal. She is a deity born of the underworld, glowing with a mystic light, untouchable by mortal hands, and yet irrevocably mine.

Every inch of her, every curve, every tremble, is a possession carved into existence for me alone. It sends a searing pulse of molten torridity through me. Her eyes meet mine, wide and dazed, like a songbird ensnared in a spider's web. This moment binds us in a way that feels both inescapable and forbidden. A possessive growl rumbles in my throat, resonating like a warning bell.

"Roll over." I command, the impact of my words leaving no room for defiance. The authority in my tone makes her jump a little, and she hesitates, caught somewhere between fear and desire. Her indecision fans the fire in me, a creature that roars louder, demanding submission. I step forward, my hands gripping the edge of the bed.

I tower over her. My shadow swallowing her small, quavering frame in its dark embrace. "Now." I demand, my voice harsher this time, fixed with the kind of power that could bend even the strongest of souls. My eyes burn into hers, daring her to resist, knowing she won't—knowing she can't. The tension between us is hellish, thrilling, a robust promise of things to come.

She shudders beneath my gaze. Her body betrays her mind as she slowly turns, offering herself to me. My heart pounds in my chest. The aching need to be inside her surges through me as I position myself behind her, ready to take what's mine.

"You're so inimitable, my dear mourning star, and you're all mine."

I grab her hips and yank her back toward me, lifting her ass high into the air. Her gasps send a pulse of wicked satisfaction coursing through me.

"Stay." I mutter, my voice, destitute and authoritative. "You know what I want, don't you?" My tongue drags a hot, wet line along her folds before plunging into her asshole. She shakes beneath me. Her moans muffled by the pressure of her own surrender.

My grip tightens on her hips, fingers digging into her flesh as I taste her critically, devouring her like a man starved. My tongue explores lower, teasing the tight entrance of her pussy.

I let out a feral laugh, the sound echoing like a sovereign's law in the dimly lit room. "You're my needful tease, aren't you?" I sneer, pulling back just enough to let my breath ghost over her skin. "Want me to fill both these holes like you sought earlier? Shall I show you how it's meant to be done?"

She lets out a shaky whimper, her body vibrating under my touch.

I bury my face into her once more, my tongue relentless as it alternates between teasing and plunging. Her thighs shake, her breaths shallow, and I know she's falling further into the pleasure abyss I've pulled her into.

"Say it." I growl against her skin, my hands spreading her ass wide open. "Say you're mine. Say you want this. Say you'll take everything I give you."

My voice resonates with unyielding authority, challenging her to disobey. The tension in the air crackles like fire, an unholy energy in this twisted, primal dance. Rosannah lets out a breathless, eager moan, her agreement spilling from her lips like a prayer to something far more wicked than divine. "Yes. Do whatever you want." She pants.

And with that, my hand wraps around her delicate throat, my fingers pressing into her skin just enough to remind her who's in control. Her pulse flutters under my grip like a trapped bird, quick and frantic. I pull her body back against mine, her ass fitting perfectly against the throbbing length of my cock.

"You're mine." I bark, a promise and a warning all at once. "Every part of you. Every hole, every hair—it all belongs to me."

She whimpers, her body arches into me, and I feel her complete surrender. My free hand moves with purpose, reaching around her, and I press my fingers against her lips. "Open," I command.

She complies, her tongue meets my fingers, and I shove them into her mouth. Her spit coats them as I push further, her whimpers muffled around the intrusion.

"Good, good." My breath hot against her ear. "Get them nice and wet for me. I want to feel your filthy mouth work."

She sucks obediently. Her tongue swirls around my fingers, sending an unholy gratification straight through me. My cock twitches against her, aching for another release I know she's about to beg for. I pull my fingers from her mouth, a trail of spit connecting them to her lips, and I drag them down her body, leaving no skin untouched as I guide them toward her pussy.

"Let's see how eager you really are." My fingers find her soaked entrance. "Show me, my dear mourning star... show me how much you *need me.*"

The room is heavy with anticipation. My hand tightens increasingly around her throat, keeping her grounded, keeping her mine. I coat my cock with her spit, and stroke. Once. Twice. Letting the anticipation build further. My eyes trail the curve of her ass, plump, round. She's perfect, and mine in every way that matters. Soon, she'll know exactly what that means.

Gripping her hips, I push her down into the mattress with force. Her curves caressing under my palms as if molded for me alone. "Stay still. You're going to take every inch of me, Rosannah. *Every. Fucking. Inch."*

I guide my pulsating cock to her dripping entrance. Her cum glistens, inviting me to plunge into the depths of her. The moment my tip probes her pussy; the pressure holds me. I hiss through clenched teeth. "Fuck." I snarl, gripping her harder. "You're so warm, so tight. Let me stretch you out."

I thrust forward, burying myself deeper inside her. The sensation is overwhelming. Her walls grip me like a vice, pulling me further. She cries out, her fingers clawing at the blanket as I stretch her, fill her, claim her.

I lean over her, my chest pressing against her back as my lips brush against her ear. "That's it, take it. Take all of me. You were made for this—*for me."*

Her gasps of pleasure, fuel the creature inside. My hips move with a brutal rhythm, each thrust stronger, harder, as if I'm carving my name into her very soul. My hands roam over her body. One sliding up to grip her throat, the other pressing her lower back down to keep her exactly where I want her.

"You feel that? That's me, stretching you, owning you. *You're mine,* Rosannah. Every part of you belongs to me now."

The bed creaks beneath us, the sound a sinful symphony of our bodies colliding. Her moans and my growls fill the air like a devilish hymn. Her pussy squeezes around me, and I push her further into the abyss of pleasure and pain, knowing I've already ruined her for anyone else.

Her cries bounce off the walls echoing like prayers in this hellish cathedral of our own making. Rosannah screams, her voice filled with both agony and ecstasy as I drive myself further, inch by inch.

"That's it! Scream for me, my sweet. Let them all hear who you belong to."

Her pussy gives way, stretching to accommodate me. The sensation is unreal. My breath matches the rhythm of our bodies colliding. The sound of flesh meeting flesh fills the room.

"Fuck." I pant, my hands gripping her hips so tightly that bruises will surely blossom there by morning. "Do you feel that? Do you feel how perfectly you fit me?"

She moans louder. Her voice breaking as I push harder, each thrust a claim, a mark, a vow. She leans up and her head tilts back, hair spilling over her shoulders. Her flushed face a vision of depraved beauty.

My fingers snake up her spine, tangling in her hair as I pull her back against me. "Louder!" I demand, my breath hot against her ear. "I want to hear how much you love this. I want to hear you pray for more."

Her response is a series of desperate moans. Her body arches into mine, her hands claw at anything she can reach, as if it can anchor her to reality.

She screams my name, choking on every word. "Please... don't stop!"

I chuckle darkly, leaning over her, my lips brushing against the back of her ear as I whisper, "Stop? Oh, my beloved, we're just getting started."

Chapter 31

Rosannah

My breath is frayed, moans spill from my lips without control, a melody of pure surrender. The sensation of Adra behind me, his weight behind every thrust makes my bones rattle.

"Please... fill me. I need you to fill me." His body shifts and his large hands grip my hips, while the other glides down my back, trailing an inferno of need along my skin.

Suddenly, I feel his fingers press against my asshole, it startles me at first, but it's exactly what I want. He pauses for a moment circling my rim with his fingertips. "You want me to fill all of you?" His breath hot against the back of my neck.

I nod frantically, my words falling off my tongue as I pant, "Yes...Yes...please."

He takes his fingers away from my asshole, then returns them covered in his spit. He pushes three fingers in, stretching me as I cry out in pleasurable pain. My body arches trying to govern the sensations. My pussy is filled with his cock and now my ass is stuffed by three of his beefy fingers. The combination is shattering.

His cock plunges further and his fingers continue to intrude. I can't even get my thoughts straight. Hells, I can't even think. All I can feel is the dominating pressure that I asked for.

"You take me so well. I love feeling you stretch around me."

He releases another long moan as he begins slowly thrusting his fingers inside my ass. I can't even make a noise. I'm choking on my own breath, and the bed is suffocating. Adra fills me in a way that steals every ounce of air from my lungs, leaving me barely able to keep my thoughts together. The intensity of it—the way his cock and his fingers work me in opposite rhythms—is astounding. My fingers clutch at the sheets as my back half is arched in the air, taking everything he wants to give me.

The intensity of his actions, like the way he knows exactly how to push my limits right to the edge. His fingers curl inside my asshole, while his cock thrust inside my pussy. Hitting spots I didn't even know where there.

I close my eyes and stars burst behind my lids. "Adra! I can't... it's too much—"

"Yes, you can," he interrupts, his tone both commanding and tender, "let me take you there. Let me give you everything you have every wanted."

The way he says it makes my body relax. I start to breathe in rhythm with his thrusts, allowing myself to feel the pleasure of both holes being filled. Allowing myself to get out of my head, fight past the pain and *really* feel him. The only sound I can make is a unintelligible grunt.

He thrusts into me harder, his fingers never relenting. "Look at you. You're a vision. So beautiful. So fucking perfect."

I moan loudly as the pressure inside me builds to a breaking point. My head falls back, and my mouth drops open as I gasp for air. My body is on fire, but I feel more alive than ever.

Adra's movements match every sound that manages to escape from my lungs as my orgasm arrives. All I can hear is him, panting above me and the sounds of our skin colliding together.

"I'm...going to..." I whisper, my voice broken and breathless, but he hears it. Without a word, his free hand moves to my throat, his fingers wrapping firmly around it, pulling my chin up towards him.

The moment he applies pressure, cutting off the air, my body reacts instantly. I gasp, or at least I try to, but it's no use—his grip is firm, dominant, leaving me at his mercy.

"You don't need words." He possessively growls, as he squeezes tighter around my neck. My body bows even more to fit with his.

I manage a weak nod, my pants a silent agreement, but it's not enough for him. "Say it!" He demands, his thrusts growing slower. His cock stretching me impossibly wider. "Tell me you're mine."

I choke out a breathless "I'm yours." The words tumbling from my lips with desperation.

He releases my throat just enough for me to suck in a dire breath. "Now, take everything I give you. Don't hold back."

I whine in response. His hand moves from my throat to my jaw, tilting my face up so he can claim my lips in a bruising kiss. His tongue dominates mine, and I pant into his mouth as his rhythm becomes faster. My vision blurs, as the world around me fades into nothing.

The lack of air heightens everything. I am weightless, my arms feel numb, and both of my holes are being stretched by the man I love most. The countless times I've fantasized about this, dreamed of this, touched myself to this—it's all been building to this moment. And yet, it's so much more than I ever imagined.

This is a dream come true.

"You were made for me." He growls. I try to breathe through the haze of pleasure but it's no use. The stretch, the pressure, his thrusts—it's all too much, yet not enough.

I want more. I need more.

My walls flutter and tighten around him with every push. "Feel it all." He grunts.

My legs shake; my eyes roll into the back of my head as the oxygen is cut off from me. I'm so fucking close.

Adra leans down, his lips brushing against my ear, his breath hot and heavy. "Cum for me! Let go, I want you to cum all over my cock."

And that does it, those three simple words: *cum for me.*

My breathing stops, my body seizes, every muscle tensing as my orgasm takes me for a ride. My inner walls strain around his cock. My clit pluses as he slowly pumps into me. It's not just pleasure—it's release. All the tension, all the anger, all the fear and sorrow from the past days are pouring out of me.

Tears prick at the corners of my eyes as I surrender completely. My body grows limp in his hands. The moment Adra releases his grip on my throat, I gasp like a fish out of water. The cool air rushing into my lungs like it's the first breath I've ever taken. I can feel his warm cum filling inside me. The sensation makes me flutter. Knowing that he is claiming me, filling me, branding me, there's nothing more intimate, more perfect.

Our breaths the only noise. His chest presses against my back as he rests against me. The rhythm of our panting syncs, each inhale and exhale as if we're one body, one being. The weight of him on me, the way his heart beats in time with mine, and it's almost too much—too much emotion, too much connection. I can't tell where he ends, and I begin.

Adra shifts, his fingers loosening their grip on my hips and slowly withdraws from my holes. I

337

whimper at the loss, but it's nothing compared to the sensation that follows. The warmth of his cum begins to spill from me, trickling down my thighs and pooling against my sensitive skin. Before I can fully recover, he moves behind me. His hand's part my thighs wider, and then I feel it—his tongue.

A sharp squeal escapes my lips as he laps at the mess we've made. His long tongue sweeping across my pussy, collecting every drop of us. Adra's tongue swipes over my clit, and I jolt from the lick, letting out a loud cry.

Instinctively, I press my hips back into his face, the bridge of his nose brushes against me. "Clean up your mess." I say breathlessly, a smirk tugging at my lips as I glance back at him.

Adra's laughter rumbles against my skin before he responds in an exaggerated sing-song voice, "Yes ma'am."

He grips my thighs tighter, burying himself as his tongue continues its work, savoring every last drop of us. His enthusiasm sends ripples of aftershocks through me.

"You taste better with me inside you."

And with that, I can't help but squeal again as his mouth ravages me, leaving no vestige of our union behind. When he's finally satisfied, I collapse face-first onto the bed, utterly spent. Adra's laughter echoes through the room, hearty and full-bodied, filling the house like the most joyous melody.

I lift my head just enough to glance at him. "What's so funny?" I ask, trying to sound annoyed but failing as a grin spreads across my face.

He leans back on his heels, his eyes sparkling with amusement. "Oh, nothing," he says, waving dismissively, "just you. You're the only one I've ever been submissive to, and it makes me laugh at how quickly I follow *your* commands."

I roll onto my side, propping myself up on one elbow, my curiosity piqued. "You mean you're usually the one in control, not the one being controlled?" I arch a brow, my lips curve into a teasing smirk.

Adra leans closer, his smile growing wider. "Something like that." He replies. His teeth flash as his grin stretches further. "But I'll admit, I quite enjoyed being controlled even it was just for that brief moment. Maybe we might do more of the same, if that would please you?"

I chuckle at his suggestion, the thought of this powerful, commanding man willingly submitting to me sends a delicious thrill through body. "Well, only if you're good will you get rewarded."

Adra lets squeal slip out. "I'll be very good," he says, his excitement barely contained, "but first, my sweet mourning star, you wanted that bath. I promised you a hot bath, and I always keep my promises."

I'm touched by his attentiveness, and nod toward the door. "Yes, you did. Now go fetch that water at once and don't take too long."

Adra stands, pulling his pants back on, and flashes me one last wolfish grin before darting out of the room. "Anything for you, my lady." He says over his shoulder with mock formality as he disappears down the stairs.

Left alone, I sigh deeply, letting my body sink into the bed. My mind replays the last couple hours. I really did enjoy listening to his every command as if his words were law. A small, wicked smile spreads across my lips as I think about his earlier admission.

Maybe controlling Adra would be fun...

His colossal figure, so powerful, yet bending entirely to my will. I close my eyes, letting fantasies swirl in my mind, already imagining what it might be like to have him fully at my mercy. For now, though, the promise of a hot bath beckons.

Chapter 32

Adrastus

The steam rises in tendrils from the copper tub as I pour in the heated water. The hiss of boiling liquid meeting cold metal sounds like a serpent readying a strike.

Rosannah watches me from the bed, her messy curls framing her face like a halo, as her body drapes lazily across the bedding. Her presence alone steadies me, even as my thoughts remain divided between her and my obligations to Mortifer.

"I'll be right back." I tell her, setting the empty pot aside.

"You'd better make haste." She teases, stretching like a lazy cat.

I pick up the water pails, descend the stairs and step outside. The fresh air encapsulates me. The streets are silent except for the whispers of wind through the trees. I walk around the back of the house towards the well. I scan the surrounding area of fields and gardens, spotting a nearby house just on the other side. And then I see them.

The bodies.

They lie scattered across the porch. Too far away for Rosannah to have noticed when we arrived. But I see all.

My jaw clenches as I move toward the well, knowing what I must do. Mortifer's warning pounds in my mind like a brand, and if I neglect these souls for much longer, it won't just be Erevan and Corvus coming after me.

After setting the pails aside, I trek through the field and approach the nearest corpse—a man slumped in the corner—skin gray, eyes white, and blackened pustules cover his face.

My palm hovers above his chest, and I close my eyes, summoning the power I've known for centuries. There's a tug, faint but resolute, as the soul begins to detach from its earthly shell. A faint glimmer emerges, swirling with whispers of a life once lived. The energy of it is dense, and I whisper the ancient words that guide the soul to its destined place.

Another number. Another soul for the contract.

I continue with the rest of what seems to be his family that lie on the porch opposite him. A girl no older than five, and woman that bears the ring as a wife. The burden of their nature remains as I take each soul. Upon completion, the atmosphere is crueler, and I can't help but envision what their life must have been.

342

Did they love each other like I do for my Rosannah? Were they as happy as she makes me? Did they know this was the end?

I take a moment for myself, as the threats of my beloved being taken from me fill me with severe worry. These emotions that have occurred since my path crossed hers are unbearable at times. It has also been some of the easiest most profound joys I never knew were possible for my kind.

I stand and take one last look at this departed family. Souls with no chance, only a brief understanding of what living truly was. I walk back through the field, return to the well, and fill the pails before heading inside the house we occupy.

When I reach the bedroom, Rosannah is already in the bath. Her body half-submerged in the steaming water. The sight of her steals the breath from my lungs. Her head tilts back against the edge of the tub, and her lips part in a sigh of contentment.

My chest swells with a strange, inexplicable pride, knowing I've provided this moment of peace for her. "Is it too hot?" I ask, hurrying to pour in the fresh, cool water.

Rosannah eyes flutter open to meet mine. "It's perfect, I was beginning to worry you'd abandoned me."

"I'd never. I was just enjoying the fresh air after, well...you know, covering the house in our musk." I wink at her, and she laughs, the sound warming me more than the fire downstairs ever could.

I perch on the edge of the tub, watching her with reverence. She is radiant. Her skin glowing in the

343

dim light of the lanterns. Memories of the past hours flood my mind, and my body reacts instantly.

I shift, annoyed at my lack of control, but the sight of her—her relaxed form, her contented sighs—is too much to resist.

"May I rub your feet, my sweet mourning star?" I ask, hoping to focus my hands on something other than my own longing.

Rosannah's eyes gleam with mischief as she retorts, "You may not." I blink, momentarily surprised, before she continues with a sly smile, "I command you to."

I grin; excitement flows through me. "As you wish, my lady."

I reach into the water, taking her leg gently in my hands. The tension in her body is palpable, and I work it away with careful, deliberate strokes. My thumbs press into her sole, making small circles, and her sigh of relief is a melody I could listen to forever.

Her moans spur me on as I work my way down to her toes, massaging each one with care. Unable to resist, I lift her foot to my mouth, pressing my lips to her big toe and suckle gently.

Rosannah's eyes fly open. "Did I say you could do that?" I freeze, unsure if I've overstepped, but her foxily smile tells me otherwise.

"Now you must." She adds with a wink, thrusting her foot back toward me.

Chuckling, I obey, taking her toes into my mouth again, this time with even more devotion.

She sighs with satisfaction, her words floating down to me like a benediction. "My noble one, how good you are."

That phrase makes my cock stand at attention, and I realize just how profoundly she's wrapped herself around my very existence. "I'll do anything to please my mourning star." I whisper against her skin, the words a vow. "Whatever you desire."

And I mean every word.

Rosannah's eyebrows arch, "The other foot now." She lifts her opposite leg from the water and gifts it to me. Her wet calf gleams in the lantern light, droplets sliding down her smooth skin. I set her first leg down gently, as my hands move to cradle the new one. I begin to massage her calf, my thumbs pressing into the tender muscles and working their way down to the tips of her delicate toes. I move calmly, consciously, taking my time.

She deserves this, every ounce of relaxation and care I can give her. Her gaze fixes on me, unwavering, her eyes flicker with mischief. Whatever she is thinking in that filthy and depraved mind of hers I'm sure I'll end up loving.

"Stop." She blurts out. "Stand up."

I follow her commands and place her leg gently back in the water.

"Take off your pants."

The words trigger the most joyous parts of me, of the universe, or perhaps the depths of the void itself. Either way, I can't disobey her. A flush rises to my face as I nod, standing from the edge of the tub. My fingers

345

work quickly to undo the laces of my pants, and they drop to the floor in one fluid motion. My cock springs free, hard and aching, the tip already glistening with precum. It bounces lightly as I rise to my full height, and I catch Rosannah's eyes roaming over me.

"You have the most ravishing cock, Adra." Her is voice sultry, as her eyes idle on me like a caress. "But you must know that..."

I bite back a grin. My chest swelling with both pride and desire. "Thank you, my lady." I try not to laugh, knowing full well that this "form" of mine was crafted for the desires of mortal women. I was built to be exactly this—to be irresistible.

Her smirk expands, and she tilts her head, the water rippling around her as she shifts her weight. "Now, stand there and stroke yourself. Don't stop until I say."

My mouth goes dry, and I swallow hard. The order sends a thrill coursing through me, and I nod again, unable to do anything but obey. "As you wish, my lady."

My hand wraps around my cock. My fingers slick over the head as I begin to stroke myself in slow, measured movements. My eyes never leave hers. She's a vision in the steaming water, her curves just barely visible beneath the ripples. The way her damp curls cling to her face only makes her appear more ethereal— like a goddess came to life. The tension builds within me as I watch her. My strokes quicken, each motion sending sparks of pleasure through me.

My mind swims with thoughts of her—of how she feels, how she tastes, how she sounds when she cries out my name. I see the hunger in her eyes. She's not just watching me; she's enjoying it too.

"You're perfect my lady. Everything about you...you are wild and spellbound... you sing to my ruin and I want nothing more than to lose myself in the madness of you."

She tilts her head, a small, knowing smile playing on her lips. "Don't stop. I'm not done looking at you yet." Rosannah leans back in the tub, her chin resting on the edge as her eyes slide across my skin. "Turn around for me."

I pause mid-stroke, my breath catching in my throat. Her request is simple, but it feels monumental. The thought of her gaze raking over me, of her taking her time to study every part of my form, sends a tepidness coursing through me that has nothing to do with the heat of the bathwater or the steam filling the room.

Slowly, I release my cock and turn away from her, letting her have the view she desires. My back faces her, and I hear the subtle intake of her breath.

The lantern light flicks against the walls, casting shadows that stretch and shift over the room. I can sense her eyes tracing the ridges of my shoulders, the expanse of my back, the curvature of my waist. My form was crafted to be imposing, a symbol of strength and control, but in this moment, under her watchful gaze, *I feel cherished.*

"You're phenomenal," she coos, "each scar, each muscle—it's like the universe poured its finest craftsmanship into you."

I feel pride and vulnerability as her words float into my ears. I've never thought of myself as something to be admired. My human form is simply a tool, a vessel for the work I was created to do. But here she is, seeing me as something more.

Seeing me as a man.

I roll my shoulders, the motion unintentional but my muscles flex. Her soft hum of approval makes me beam despite myself. "Do you like what you see, my lady?"

"I do. You're magnificent my noble one. You are strong... bewitching."

Her words settle over me like a balm, soothing the wounds of doubt that I hadn't realized I carried with me for centuries. I glance over my shoulder, meeting her star filled hazel eyes. "You make me feel things I never thought I could." I admit quietly.

She leans forward, resting her arms on the edge of the tub. "Come closer, I want to touch you."

I obey, stepping backwards until I'm close enough for her fingers to reach me. I kneel with my back facing the tub. She outlines the curve of my shoulder. Her touch is light and delicate as her fingers slide down my back, following the lines of my muscles. I close my eyes at the sensation. It's a grounding reminder that I'm here, with her, at this moment.

"You carry so much." She whispers, her palm pausing over the center of my back. "More than anyone should have to." I hear the water slosh as she shifts in the tub. "Let me ease some of that burden, even if it's just for tonight."

I swivel to face her, taking her hand in mine and bringing it to my lips. "You already do, my mourning star, more than you'll ever know."

Her beautiful eyes engage with mine. "Move to the front of the tub, by my feet." She commands.

I obey instantly, my steps quick as I make my way in front of her. The firelight dances off her damp skin, her hair a cascade of wet curls framing her flushed cheeks. She shifts closer to the edge of the tub. Her feet emerge from the water, glistening and delicate, the droplets rolling down her skin in lazy rivulets. My cock twitches in anticipation, and her eyes flicker down to it.

She leans back, stretching her legs out, her toes brushing against me, featherlight. "Grab my feet," she says, her voice lower, sultrier, "and fuck them."

I blink in surprise, the boldness of her command catching me off guard. "What?" I stammer, my voice betraying what my cock begs for.

She quirks an eyebrow, "You heard me." She says, the playful lilt in her tone makes my knees weak. "*Do it. Now.*"

I swallow hard, my throat dry. "Yes, my lady." I reply, as an eagerness I've never felt follows.

I take her feet in my hands, her soles soft against my palms. My breathing stops as I press them, together, positioning myself between. My cock throbs as the pressure of her feet closes around me and I begin

349

to thrust gently. I can't help but let out a shaky, "thank you," as I stare down at her.

Rosannah leans back in the tub. Her posture relaxed. Her seductive eyes hooked on me with dominating satisfaction. "You are such a good listener."

"Thank you, my lady." The genuine joy in my voice betraying how severely her approval affects me. I'd do anything to hear those words.

I close my eyes and continue penetrating this makeshift hole that she has provided for me. I hear the water splash as her body shifts in the copper tub. "Open your eyes, Adra."

I obey.

Her hands have disappeared beneath the water, and I watch as her fingers work between those thick thighs. Her head tilts back as she rubs her clit. The other hand trails up her body, pinching and teasing her nipple. The faint moan that escapes her lips almost makes me drop to my knees.

"You don't know what you do to me, Adra," she croons, "you make me feel needy. You make me want you. You make me crave you."

Hearing this makes my cock throb harder as I thrust faster between her soles. I'm completely consumed by her—by the sight of her touching herself, by the sound of her voice, by the sheer power she now holds over me.

She slips a finger inside herself, and I groan, the sound guttural and filled with jealousy. I want to be the one touching her.

"Don't you want me, Adra? Don't you want to feel me again?"

"Yes, my lady." I gasp, the words spilling out of me. "Yes, more than anything."

Her gaze sharpens, and her lips curl into a devilish smirk. *"Beg."*

Before I can even think of the words, they are already tumbling from my lips. "Please, my lady." I say hoarse with desperation. "Please, let me be inside you again. Let me worship you. Let me make you feel everything you deserve. I'll do anything—anything—to please you."

Her eyes sparkle with satisfaction. Her movements slow as she studies me. Steam rises around her, curling in the air like a phantasma veil. "Worthy and obedient, luck bestows me. Now, get in the tub."

CONWAY TITTY

Chapter 33

Rosannah

Adra settles into the burnished bath. The water spills out, making a mess onto the floor. I pay it no mind, for all I care about is him and the way he sees me. The rich copper tones of the tub look dull compared to his radiant mismatched eyes. The intensity strips me bare, even though I have already given him everything.

The steam curls around him like smoke from some unearthly forge. I sit up, the water descends my skin, and crawl toward him. The water laps at my thighs as I close the distance between us. The room appears smaller. The air stouter, as if the universe itself is leaning in to watch.

Adra's chest expands as I straddle him. My legs slide over his. The heat of the water is nothing compared to the vitality burning between us.

"My lady." His hands hover as though he's unsure whether to touch me.

I love the way I can make him nervous with just a look. Before he can say more, I press my palm against his mouth, silencing him. His pupils dilate, and a muffled groan escapes between my fingers. I position myself above him, feeling his thick, swollen cock pressing against my pussy. I sink down, letting the entire length of his shaft fill me completely.

A delicious stretch that makes my breath skip and my eyes flutter shut. His muffled groans change into a whimpering sound, and his hands grip my hips instinctively, guiding me as I take him. The water swishes around us.

I open my eyes to find him staring at me. His fingers tremble against my skin. I remove my hand from his mouth, and his pleasure follows. "You... you're going to be the death of me."

I lean in so that my lips are just a whisper away. "My noble one your cock feels incredible, let me take more of you." I roll my hips against him, eliciting another groan from his chest. I press my hand back over his mouth stifling the moans that continue to sneak out. "Stay quiet. I don't want to hear a sound from you."

A shivering sigh escapes my lips as I sink further on him. My stare fixed onto his gorgeous amber and ocean eyes. They reflect every ounce of restraint he's desperately clinging to. I bite my lip to keep from grinning; he is helplessly under my complete control. His need written across every tense line of his face.

I begin to move, lifting myself up and settling back down, feeling his thickness stretch me with each bounce. He lets a moan slip out. I press my palm harder on his mouth. "Not...a... sound..." I say between rides.

Adra acknowledges, as he struggles to obey. His fingers grip the edge of the tub, knuckles white with the effort of staying under control. Knowing just how much he is holding back sends a charge racing to my ego.

I quicken my pace, the water a tidal wave as I ride him harder. My pussy embracing the stretch and girth of him. I let my head fall back, as moans freely come from my lungs. They are shamelessly loud as I relish the way he fills me up. The contrast is delicious. My free, unabashed cries of pleasure against his muffled grunts and trembling restraint. The desperation in his eyes makes my stomach flip with euphoria. "You're struggling, aren't you? It's hard, is it not?" I purr directly into his ear. "Not being able to touch me, not being able to make a sound."

His eyes close, and his body shudders beneath mine. I roll my hips harder, making him feel every bit of me. "But my noble one, you'll do exactly as I say?" I lick the side of his face. "I trust you know how to listen well, aye? Prove to me you can wait."

Adra's head tips back, his throat exposed, the cords of muscle taut with tension. He lets out a whine against my palm.

"Shh!" I press my fingers harder against his mouth, while my other hand grips his shoulder for balance. "I told you—no sounds."

I know he's right on the edge. His control slipping with every second that passes, and it only makes me move faster, harder onto him. I give myself fully to the pleasure. The steam rises around us, the water ripples violently as my orgasm arrives. "Adra..." I pant, "I'm going to cum.... make me cum..."

My body is consumed by the sheer orgasmic bliss. My moans are coarse as I reach the peak of my climax. My fingers grip his luscious hair tightly. My palm still tries to stifle any noises he's so desperate to let out. I let out a yell of ecstasy as my pussy flutters around the girth of his impossibly thick cock.

I let my palm lift from his lips, and he bursts with pleading words. "Please, my lady! Please let me come. You feel so good. Fuck, you feel so good. Can I please have release?"

Never have I seen a man beseech with such fervor. He begs as if the world might fall apart if I turned away. And my depraved self can't get enough.

By the moon and stars, he is so fucking spellbinding. Who's favor have I won to have the fortune to be with such a man? Thank you, universe.

"Not yet." I draw out the words savoring the power that they hold. Adra whimpers, his head tipping with tension as he continues to move inside me. His cock spreading me open as I cling to him in my post cum state.

"Please!" He cries again, his voice cracks with urgency.

I lean closer to his ear. My lips feel the stubble on his jaw. "No...Not yet." Denying his thirsty need to cum.

Slowing my pace, I give us a moment to breathe, to collect ourselves, though the pulsing ache inside me demands more. Adra's chest heaves against mine. His hands grip my hips like they're his lifeline. He's holding on, barely.

I cup his face, forcing his eyes to meet mine, they flicker with frustration. "Now my noble one," I say, "since you've been such a pleasant listener, I'm going to let you decide how to make me cum again. In whatever way that pleases you most. Then—and only then—can you ask again for your release."

His eyes reveal the dangerous glint that flashes across his face. His lips curl into a devilish grin, full of fiendish promises. "You've made a big mistake, my dearest mourning star."

My heart skips at his words. He shifts beneath me, his hands sliding up my thighs and gripping me firmly. "Now, let me show you just how determined I can be."

In one smooth, powerful motion, Adra lifts me from the bathwater. The heat of the moment now replaced by freezing air on my saturated skin. I shriek as the cold brushes against every part of me. I instinctively curl into his arms in search of warmth.

"How dare you!" I squeal, shivering, but he only grins. He says nothing, only schemes.

Being carried effortlessly in his arms, I understand just how safe he makes me feel, and how

357

easily he could ruin me in the best ways possible. His chest is hot, his muscles flexing with every step, and the heat in my body reignites despite the chill in the air.

As we descend the staircase and back into the greater chamber of the house. I survey the room, then my eyes fixate on it. A long wooden trestle stretches before us, its surface covered in the clutter left behind by the previous occupants—silver candlesticks, scattered plates, and remnants of a life abandoned in haste. Hewn from dark, seasoned oak, this massive boardroom table is burnished to a deep, honeyed sheen by age, oil and countless feasts. It is a table not merely for meals, but for declarations, bargains, laughter, and judgment. But now, it's for us.

With a single sweep of his arm, Adra clears the table, sending the items clattering to the floor with a thunderous *crash.* I can't help but giggle at his theatrics. Before I can react further, he lays me down on the smooth, brumal wood.

The moment my back hits the surface, my breasts bounce. He spreads my legs apart, and my body vibrates in anticipation.

"It seems like it's time I take my next meal. I'm famished." He says, as his fingers grip the insides of my thighs, holding me in place. He is holding me open with a reverence that feels almost sacred.

Before I can reply, his mouth descends. His tongue licks a slow, planned path over my clit. My back arches off the table, my hands flying to clutch at the edges as breathless sighs escape my lips.

He enhances his movements. His tongue and lips working in perfect tandem with the fingers he slides inside. His fingers curve just right, hitting a spot that makes me seize forward. My heart batters in my chest, and my head begins to whirl. I glance down at him, as his dark curls still damp from the steam of the bath, focusing entirely on me. Seeing him between my legs, as his tongue lavishes me, makes me want to cum again—but I hold back from ending this too soon. I throw my head back, closing my eyes, letting the waves of paradise wash over me. My fingers digging into the wood.

"Mmmm, you taste scrumptious, my lady."

I can only whimper in response as my mind is too clouded with stimulation to form words. My body moves on its own accord. My hips reach toward his mouth as I chase the sensations he's giving me. Then, Adra's mouth suddenly stops.

"Be right back. Don't move. Keep your eyes closed!" He yells from another room.

I let out a pitiful sigh and the ghost of his mouth is no longer where I need it most. But I take this moment to reflect on what an incredible gift he is.

The most deity like man to ever walk this world and he's fully devoted to me.

Before I can get lost in my thoughts, something shifts. The comforting rhythm of his fingers vanishes, now replaced by something... different. My eyes snap open, and I glance down at him, just in time to see the unmistakable wooden curvature of a rolling pin in his hands.

359

A *rolling pin*?! My mind screams, a mixture of shock and curiosity bubbles up inside me.

Those are for pasta, for bread, for the kitchens—not for... oh my gods....

The rounded wood presses against my entrance, stiff and unfamiliar. "What!" I manage to gasp, however, intrigued.

His lips transform into that wicked grin I've come to know all too well. "What's the matter, mourning star? Too much?"

"This is—this is *huge!*" I stammer; my focus sharpens as he tilts the rolling pin just enough to tease me with its weight.

"Is this okay, my lady?" He asks. "I found it on the counter...in the cookery. It's... well...it's the same shape as me—only bigger—but my imagination got the best of me. I can stop if you want."

"Adra, I..."

"You can handle it."

He always knows how to push me, how to challenge me in ways I never expected. Part of me wants to protest, but a much larger part—the part that craves him, that trusts him with every fiber of my being—wants to let him continue.

He leans in closer, his breath hot against my thigh as he presses gentle kisses there. "Tell me to stop, and I will, but I promise my lady, this will be most enjoyable."

I stare into his eyes, the sincerity in them melting away any hesitation I might have had. And I nod. "Okay, I trust you."

360

His smile swells, and he places another kiss on my skin before redirecting his attention back to his task. Slowly, carefully, he eases the rolling pin against me. Its surface glides with ease. The sensation is unlike anything I've ever felt before. Unfamiliar, yes, but not unwelcoming.

"Oh my gods!" My head falls back against the table as my body adjusts to the intrusion. The rolling pin stretches my pussy even wider than his cock does. The hard wood is firmer than his. My clit pulsates as I stretch around this foreign object.

"That's it." He says, his voice filled with pride. "Just like that. You're doing so well, my lady."

His words of praise makes me relax around this makeshift dildo, and I can't help but let out a spiritual moan. My knuckles are white from gripping the table's edge. "Please don't stop. I just—I wasn't expecting it. I've never used anything like this before... It feels amazing." My cheeks flush as I admit the truth. "Please, keep going."

"As you wish, my lady." He leans down and presses a tender kiss on my belly.

I cannot comprehend what's happening to my body. Adra's energy and creativity seem boundless, and I find myself surrendering to his every whim. The rolling pin stretches me more than I ever thought possible, as Adra works it in and out of me with a continuous rhythm. Every push sends a new level of euphoria coursing through my body. "More, please... more!"

My fingers dig further into the edge of the table as if I need something to anchor me to this earth, but my mind feels like it's floating somewhere far beyond this room.

"Anything for you, my lady."

The sight of him between my legs—his broad shoulders hunched, his mouth worshiping me while his hands control the makeshift dildo with such precision—is picturesque. I now know most would kill to have him in this position. Many fantasize their depraved thoughts, I am living mine.

The pressure is astounding but in the best way, each thrust of the rolling pin coaxes moans from the depths of my belly. Adra's tongue follows the rhythm of his hands, flicking and lapping at my most sensitive spot. Amplifying the sensations until I feel like I might shatter completely. My thighs tremble uncontrollably. My mind spins with the absurdity of the situation, but there's no shame, no hesitation—only pleasure.

A rolling pin? Who would have thought something so ordinary could feel so extraordinary? Leave it to Adra to make even the mundane into a tool of utter ecstasy.

The rolling pin moves faster now, harder. The stretch is delicious, as the pressure builds in my core. My legs start to quake as the familiar crest of an orgasm, but this time it's different—more intense, more consuming.

"Adra!" I pant, my voice trying its best to reach him. "I... I can't—"

"You can!" His words spark a second wave of adrenaline, and I lose control of my sanity.

"I need more, Adra." I lean forward spreading myself wider. "I need you."

Adra slows down his motions.

"Put your cock in my ass! Fill me!" I shout over my moans. He starts to pull out the rolling pin. "NO!" I scream with bliss. "Don't stop! Both! Please!"

I watch as his eyes enlarge with shock, and honestly, he is probably just as excited as I am knowing he gets to fill me in both holes with something other than just his fingers. He smiles the biggest cheesiest smile I have ever seen and says, "At your service my lady."

Adra spits on his thick cock and thrusts it straight into my open asshole, while shifting the rolling pin in the other. I feel the pressure of his cock stretching my ass out once again. His fingers are nothing compared to this dildo and cock combination I'm feeling inside of me.

"HOLY FUCK! ADRA! THAT'S IT! RIGHT THERE! FUCK! FUCK! FUCKKKKK!" I try to cry out between thrusts, but my panting and grunts make it hard to even breathe.

As he moves faster in my ass, the rolling pin moves at an opposite speed inside my pussy. The pleasure is so intense I can't feel my face. My whole body is levitating. I can feel every inch of him and every inch of the makeshift dildo moving in synchronization. The room starts to spin as I am gasping for breaths but can only manage to get out loud shrieks.

This is nothing like his fingers. This feeling is two monster cocks fucking me stupid. I am so close to cumming, but I never want this to stop.

I manage an immense inhale, before taking my hand and immediately start rubbing my pulsating clit. Adra groans louder at the sight of me adding even more pleasure to the already insane situation. "Don't Stop! Whatever you do, don't stop!"

Adra grits his teeth and thrusts on knowing both of us can't hold on much longer. Sweat drips down his face as the shadows from the fire he stoked earlier waltz across in celebration. The tapestries on the walls and the carved wooden beams above illuminate in the firelight. The richness of this place appears almost dreamlike. My body is humming. My walls are tightening. My back arches off the table and I yell, "Cum with me!"

My body bucks and my eyes roll in the back of my head as squirt rushes out of me. Adra yells out my name as his cum fills my asshole. His body convulses as he pushes himself further into my ass, burying himself balls deep. He sits inside for a moment. I can feel the throbbing of his cock letting himself unload within. His delicious grunts fly freely as he jolts with the last pump.

Adra slowly takes his cock out, followed by the rolling pin. I wince as the once fullness now empty. His milky white cum dribbles out of my ass onto the wooden table, that is now also soaked in my juices.

I close my eyes letting my thoughts wander as the aftermath of my orgasm ripples. Flashes of the possible future begin to sprout in my mind like spring blossoms breaking through the frost.

Is this what it's going to be like all the time with him?

A strange blend of excitement and trepidation fill my chest. The thought is as intriguing as it is terrifying—this idea of a life with Adra. Just like the night on the board walk I knew he was the one for me from that moment.

Images play behind my closed lids—him smiling at me across a table, candlelight flickering between us; his calloused fingers braiding my hair in the quiet of a morning; the two of us standing beneath a lemon tree, the wind carrying the scent of ripe fruit and wildflowers. But then, darker visions seep into the edges of my mind. His shadow stretching longer than the rest, whispers of the dangers that cling to him like smoke, and the faint reflections of warnings not yet fully understood.

What have I gotten myself into?

The thought flits through my mind, but it doesn't stay long. Adra's voice is like a tether, pulling me back. "Mourning star are you okay?"

I try to answer, but my chest is tight. My breath is short. My chest bangs from what just transpired, leaving me utterly dazed.

"Rosannah, amore?" He presses, his concern evident as his fingers brush the side of my face. His touch grounds me, and I manage to flutter my eyes open, my vision clearing. There he is, this impossibly beautiful man, hovering over me like some celestial being. His eyes are filled with so much care, so much love. A lump rises in my throat. It's his face I see, etched with devotion and virtue, and for a moment, it feels like nothing in the world could touch us.

I let out a weak, breathy laugh, a grin tugging at the corners of my lips. "Yes," I whisper, still catching my breath. "I — I've never felt like this before. I feel weightless. I feel..." I trail off, unable to find the right words to encapsulate the astounding joy, peace, and connection coursing through me.

Adra's eyes search mine as though he knows exactly what I want to say. "Complete?"

My soul intensifies at his words. "Yes, *complete.*"

The word, an understatement, but it's all I can manage at this moment. Without thinking, I lean up and press my lips to him, pouring every ounce of gratitude, affection, and devotion I have into this kiss. His arms wrap around me, pulling me closer as if he can't bear the thought of any distance between us. The world outside, this rich abandoned home, all fades away, leaving only the two of us in this stolen sanctuary. The opulence of the room seems pale in comparison to the richness of this moment.

As we pull away, our foreheads rest against each other, breaths synching.

"You have no idea what you mean to me." His voice almost breaking. "You've given me something I didn't even know I needed."

Tears prick my eyes, but I smile, cupping his face in my palms. "And you've shown me what it means to truly be seen. To be loved."

CONWAY TITTY

Chapter 34

Adrastus

I take a profound breath, as if the burden of centuries has finally been lifted from my shoulders. As though the chains of duty and death that have bound me for so long have finally shattered.

In this moment, life and death, contracts and obligations; all of it fades into nothingness. All that remains is her, my Rosannah. She is the center of my universe, the axis upon which my very existence spins.

Her soft, messy curls tumble across her face like a frame for a Giotto masterpiece, each strand bouncing as she giggles. Sweat beads on her forehead from the energy of our activities, catching the light of the flames from the hearth and making her shimmer like dew-drenched petals at dawn.

Her smile is radiant. Her dimples carve deep into her cheeks, as though they are marking this

369

moment for eternity. She is glowing, and not just with the post coitus glow. She is truly shining. The light from within her makes her seem celestial.

Looking at her feels as if the very stars have descended to earth, gathering themselves in her eyes. She fills the air with a magical potency, as though she carries within her the secrets of the universe. She is a revelation. A reminder of all the things I never knew I craved... I *needed* until now. She is untouchable, and yet completely mine, a paradox I can hardly fathom. The world could crumble around us, and I wouldn't care, so long as she remained the center of it all.

For the first time in my existence, the shadows I have carried seem distant, pushed back by the spell light of her. Rosannah is my sanctuary. The one thing that makes all this pain and chaos bearable. I am utterly unworthy of her. And yet, here she is, lying beside me on this wooden table in this forgotten home. I don't know what love was supposed to feel like for mortals, but I know this is it. I've seen it from afar. Husbands clutching their dying wives, mothers cradling their sick children, but I never imagined I'd feel it myself.

"Rosannah," I whisper. She studies me, her eyes gorgeous as ever, and I have the courage to say:

"I love you too."

The words feel monumental like the turning of a great wheel that sets the stars in motion. The expression that blossoms across her face is something I will carry with me forever. She wraps her arms around me, hugging me with such a fervor that I feel the fragility and beauty of the human connection in its purest form. I squeeze her, tighter than I thought possible, as though letting go would smash us into millions of pieces. And then, a single tear escapes my eye, trailing down my cheek. I don't bother to wipe it away. This sadness, this realization of how much she means to me and how devastating the thought of losing her would be, is something I embrace.

I sit up, cradling her in my arms, and step off the table. She's so light, so small in my arms, yet here I am carrying my whole world. The fire flickers against the walls as I lay her down on a nest of blankets near the hearth. I settle beside her, propping myself on an elbow so I can take her in fully. The firelight performs its known ballet across us. It's quiet, but the silence isn't empty. We lie there for what seems like a millennium, simply staring at one another, lost in the quiet comfort of each other. The crackling fire providing the only soundtrack to this moment.

Hours pass, and finally, Rosannah sighs break the silence. "You make me forget about the illness, the deaths, the fear." She says, her words wrapping around my heart like a tender caress. "You make me feel safe. Feel loved. Feel important. I love you, greater than I have ever loved anyone or anything. Looking at you reminds me of the possibilities of life, reminds me of the joy that comes. You are the fresh air. You are the sun rays upon my skin. You are love."

I don't deserve her.

371

My fingers brush her cheek as she leans into my touch. "You've given me something I never thought I could have. I never thought I could feel like this, but..." I pause, scanning her face for my next words.

She doesn't know the truth.

She doesn't know anything.

The joy I'd allowed myself to bask in begins to slip away. I can't hold on to it no matter how much I want to. My chest is tearing away at me from the inside as the words I know I have to say begin to grapple their way to the surface. I see her staring at me, with a love so innocent, so pure. It is painful to look at.

"My dearest mourning star," I begin, my voice catches in my throat, "there is something I want to tell you, but..." I hesitate, the words threatening to choke me. "I can't. I can't because it would jeopardize everything."

Her brows knit together as confusion spreads across her beautiful face. "What do you mean?"

I force myself to continue, though each word is like I'm carving a piece out of myself. "I am so carefree with you. You've made me feel things I never thought I could, things I didn't even know I was capable of...*shouldn't* be capable of..."

I know what I am about to say will change everything. I know I will lose her, but I can't hold back any longer. I can't let Mortifier hurt her, and if she is with me, there is no stopping him.

"But this..." I gesture between us, considering the gravity of my own words. "This dies. Just like everything else. *Death* comes for it all."

The instant the words leave my lips; I see the light in her eyes fade. She sits up abruptly, the blanket slipping from her shoulders, exposing the vulnerability in her trembling form. Her tears come quickly, glistening like fragile pearls as they streak down her cheeks. "I don't understand. Why are you saying this? Why now? After everything, after what we've shared... you're just giving up?"

Her pain hits me like a dagger. "Rosannah," I say, reaching for her, but she recoils, and it feels like she's taken my heart with her.

"How can you say these things?" She demands, her voice rising. "You're giving up on us? On me? I thought you were different, Adra. I thought you were the one thing in my life that was real."

I can't argue with her. She's right. I should have walked away long before this. I should have spared her the pain I always knew was coming. But I didn't. I stayed. Because I'm weak. Because I'm selfish. Because the thought of being without her was more unbearable than the thought of breaking every rule, I've ever known.

"I never wanted to hurt you. I thought—" My words stop. My throat tightens.

What could I possibly say to make this better?
To justify what I've done?

"You thought what?" She snaps, her tears now a torrent. "That you could love me for a moment and then throw it all away? That you could use me to feel something and then just... leave?" She presses a palm to her mouth as another sob escapes her.

"Rosannah..." I start again, but she is already standing, gathering the blanket around her like armor.

"Don't! I can't listen to this. I can't do this."

She rushes from the room as her sobs echo up the stairs. The sound of the bedroom door slamming shut rings like a final blow. A definitive end to everything I've dared to hope for. I stand there, frozen, as the silence swallows me whole.

What have I done?

The question loops endlessly in my mind, louder and louder, until it's all I can hear. My knees give out, and I collapse into the chair by the fire. My head falls into my hands. The house seems distant now, emptier. I glance up, and the daunting enchanted parchment appears on the little side table next to me. I stare at it. The inked lettering peer back at me like a curse.

Who am I kidding? It is a curse.

The souls I'm bound to claim. The contracts I've sworn to fulfill. They're all that's left of my purpose. But her face flashes in my mind, her smile, her laughter, the way her hand feels in mine.

She deserves more.

The thought gnaws at me, but the selfish part of me—the part that longs for her, that loves her—can't let go. Even now, as I sit here drowning in my own misery, I know I would do it all over again just to know her love for one more moment.

The warmth of the fire seems to mock me as I sit alone in this darkened room. My hands clench into fists. Rosannah's words echo in my head, over and over, like the toll of a bell marking the end of something precious.

"Why are you saying this? This can't be happening."

Her tears... I could feel the strain of each one, as if they were my own. My thoughts are a whirlwind of guilt, regret, and something far more painful: *love*.

How did I let it come to this? How did I let her in so genuinely that the thought of losing her feels like my very essence is being torn apart? I shouldn't have let it get this far. I should have been stronger. I should have stayed distant. But I didn't. I couldn't. The way she sees me as if I'm not a monster, as if I'm a man worth loving—it's all too much. And yet, it's not enough. It never will be. Because I can't give her what she deserves. I can't give her the truth. I can't give her forever.

I hear the faint creak of the floorboards above me where she's locked herself away. She's up there crying, and I'm the reason why. My fists shake as I stare at the fire, its embers glowing like the remnants of a life I can never have.

"I'm so happy with you... but this dies. Just like everything dies. Death comes for it all."

I mock at myself. The words taste bitter in my mouth even now.

How could I say that to her? How could I crush her like that when all she's done is love me?

But I had to. I must protect her. From me, from what I am, from the truth that would destroy her if she knew.

I glance at the enchanted parchment once more. The intricate script detailing the souls I'm bound to claim. The ink seems to shimmer at me like it's demanding to be selected. The numbers are daunting, millions of lives left; millions of people I must touch, must take.

And for what? For a Master who will obliterate me without a second thought if I fail to fulfill my duties? For a purpose that suddenly feels hollow in the face of what I've found with my Rosannah?

I run my fingers through my hair, tugging at the roots as if the pain might wake me from this torment. I'm angry. I'm angry at Mortifer, at the contract, at myself for daring to believe, even for a moment, that I could have this. That I could have her.

"She doesn't know the truth. She doesn't know anything."

If she did... if she knew the burden I carry, the darkness that follows me, she would run. She should run. And yet, selfishly, I don't want her to. I want her to stay. I want her to love me, even as I know I don't deserve it. Even as I know that every moment I spend with her risks everything.

The fire pops, a sharp crack that startles me from my thoughts. I glance toward the stairs. My spirit is heavy with the knowledge that I've hurt the only person who's ever truly seen me.

Rosannah, my light in this endless shadow. My tether to something real. I've destroyed her trust, and for what? To protect her? Or to protect myself from the pain of losing her?

I lean forward, resting my elbows on my knees as I take a sorrowful breath. My mind drifts to the contract again, to Erevan's warnings, to the cold inevitability of my existence.

"Adra, you know the rules. Don't waste your eternity on a mortal."

But what if she's worth wasting it for? What if she's the reason I've been wandering for centuries, the reason I've endured this cursed half-life?

I hear a faint shuffle from upstairs, and my chest stiffens again. I want to go to her. I want to hold her and tell her everything. But I can't. Not yet. Not until I figure out how to protect her from the truth. From me.

The hours pass slowly, each one dragging me further into my thoughts. When the first light of dawn begins to creep through the windows, there is no relief, only the pressure of another day. Another day to lie to her, to pretend that everything is fine. Another day closer to the inevitable.

I rise from the chair and poke at the fire. The embers glowing faintly in the morning light. My hands shake as I concentrate back on the contract, the names blurring together as my mind battles.

How can I keep doing this? How can I fulfill my duty and still protect the one person who's ever made me feel alive?

I don't have the answers. All I know is that I can't let her go. Not yet. Not ever. Even if it destroys me.

Especially if it destroys me.

Chapter 35

Rosannah

This bedroom is suffocating. The ornate walls that once seemed so luxurious now appear like they're closing in on me. Their details seem to ripple and sway in my tear-blurred vision, transforming this space into a dizzying, oppressive cage.

I sit on the edge of the bed. My hands clutch the blanket. My fingers grip the fabric so tightly that my knuckles ache, but I can't let go. I need something to hold on to...*anything.*

Tears pour down my face in endless, hot streams, leaving salty tracks that sting my raw skin. My chest heaves erratically, each breath a struggle. I try to calm myself, but it's impossible. The sobs burst out of me in violent, guttural cries that echo around the room. My throat burns from the force of my weeping. The muscles in my abdomen ache from the relentless convulsions of my body. It's as though my very soul is being wrung dry, every drop of strength squeezed out until there's nothing left but this unbearable, hollow ache.

I press my palms against my cheeks, trying to muffle the sounds of my own misery, but the sobs claw their way out, regardless. My vision swims with tears, and the room around me dissolves into a haze of colors and shadows.

My nose runs with snot. My lips tremble uncontrollably, and I don't even have the strength to wipe my face. I just let it all spill out, tears, mucus, choking breaths, until I'm left shaking like a leaf in a storm. Every breath is an uphill battle. My lungs strain against the crushing weight on my chest. The blanket beneath my fingers is damp with sweat and tears. My body is weak, fragile, as though a single gust of wind could blow me away.

How could he?

The words play over and over in my mind like a cruel taunt. *"This dies,"* he says. Like we were nothing. Like all the love I poured into him meant nothing. I believed him. I believed every touch, every word, every look.

How could I have been so blind?

I bury my face in my palms. The ache in my chest is too much to bear. My body quakes as the consequences crash down on me all at once. The loss of Gia, the trauma of the past few days, and now this—Adra's cold dismissal. It's as though every piece of my world has been shattered, and I'm left scrambling to hold on to fragments that keep slipping through my fingers.

I rock back and forth, desperate for some kind of comfort, even if it's self-inflicted. But the act only makes me feel smaller, more helpless. My sobs come in waves, sometimes quieter, sometimes so violent that I double over, clutching my stomach as though trying to hold myself together.

My hair sticks to my damp cheeks and neck, and the room is stifling despite the chill of the night air seeping through the cracks in the shutters.

Maybe I should have stayed with Gia.

The thought pierces through me, sharp and bitter. If I had just stayed, we would have faced this plague together. We could have died together. At least then I wouldn't feel this... this gnawing emptiness. At least then, I wouldn't have allowed myself to believe in something as fleeting as love.

The pain is overwhelming, all-consuming. My mind replays Adra's words again, each repetition like a knife twisting deeper into my heart.

"*This dies.*" The phrase echoes in my head, cruel and ruthless, a constant reminder of the love I thought was real, now reduced to ash. It's too much. It's all too much.

I press my face into the blanket, letting it soak up my tears as muffled cries continue to escape my lips. I want to stop. I want to breathe. But the agony has taken hold of me, completely dragging me under like a drowning woman caught in an unrelenting tide. It seems endless, like I'll never come up for air, like I'll never feel whole again.

I glance toward the window, the faint glow of the moon casting silvery light across the room. The sight makes my tears fall even harder.

He said he loved me. He held me like I was the only thing in the world that mattered. How could he say those words, only to push me away moments later?

"I'm a fool." I whisper to the empty room. My voice cracks, and the sound of it only makes me cry harder. I let him in. I let him see every vulnerable piece of me, and now... I'm left with nothing.

I curl up on the bed, clutching the blanket tighter around me as if it could shield me from the pain. I can still see his face, the way his eyes filled with sorrow as he spoke. He was hurting too, I could see it—but why does that make it worse? Why does it hurt more, knowing he pushed me away even though he felt something too?

For a long time, I just lie here, letting the heartbreak settle into my bones. But as the hours stretch on, something begins to stir within me.

Amidst the heartbreak and despair, a faint flicker of determination starts to take root. Gia's face comes to mind—her laughter, her smile, the way she talked about Palermo like it was some sort of paradise. She dreamed of going there, of starting a new life filled with freedom and opportunity. That was *our* dream. And now... it's my dream to carry on.

I glance out the window again, this time seeing the faint promise of dawn beginning to creep over the horizon. My spirit feels bruised, broken even, but I know I can't let it stop me. Not now. Not when I have nothing left to lose. No one to hold me back. Nothing slowing me down.

I'm too drained to keep crying. My body feels like a battlefield, every muscle aching by the sheer exhaustion of the past few days. I shift on the bed, the movement making me wince. My legs are sore from the endless journey, the strain of riding in the wagon, and the... intense intimacy I shared with him. My throat is raw, probably from the screaming, both in ecstasy and despair.

A sad little giggle bubbles out of me as I think about how ridiculous it all seems now. I wipe my tear-streaked face with the edge of the blanket, shaking my head at myself.

My throat is sore, and I can't even decide if it's from crying or from the... other things we did.

But the laughter fades almost as quickly as it comes, replaced by the gnawing pain in my chest. My soul feels like it's been ripped in two, and the edges are bleeding. I close my eyes trying to center myself, to find something solid to cling to in the mess of emotions swirling inside.

A sudden coughing fit shakes me, breaking the stillness. It's sharp and jarring, like my body is rejecting everything—this night, this pain, this entire journey. I reach for the mug of water on the nightstand. My fingers tremble as I bring it to my lips. The cool liquid soothes my throat, but the coughs persist, scraping at me from the inside. I drink more, swallowing greedily, as if the water could somehow wash away everything: my heartache, my exhaustion, my regrets.

Setting the mug down, I lean back against the pillows, clutching the blanket around me. My mind won't stop racing; every thought is a painful reminder of what I've lost. I picture Adra's face, the way his expression softened when he looked at me, the way his touch made me feel safe, desired, loved.

Was it all a lie?

The belief stabs at me, and my chest tightens again.

Did I imagine it, or did he truly feel something for me too? And if he did, why would he say those things? Why would he let this end?

I force myself to calm down. I can't keep doing this. The exhaustion in my body is too much to ignore, my limbs heavy as lead. My eyes sting from crying, and the radiating ache in my head makes it hard to focus on anything other than the pain.

I wipe my tears with the back of my hand, though they're quickly replaced by fresh ones. I must go to Palermo. I can't let this heartbreak define me. I can't let Adra's rejection, stop me from chasing the future I want. Palermo is waiting for me. It's one step closer to freedom. One step closer to the life Gia and I dreamed of. And if I don't keep moving, I'll lose myself.

The dream gives me a small spark of hope. I sit up, brushing my tangled hair from my face. A minor resolve settles in my chest. I'll tell Adra in the morning. I'll tell him that I'm continuing the journey with or without him. If he still wants to come, fine. If not, I'll go alone.

I exhale a shuddering breath and close my eyes, whispering a silent promise to myself.

For Gia. For me. For the dream we both believed in. When morning comes, I'll be ready to face whatever lies ahead. Even if it means doing it with a shattered heart.

CONWAY TITTY

Chapter 36

Adrastus

I've spent the entire night sitting by the dying embers, replaying every moment with Rosannah. I've been up trying to think of alternative solutions, what could work and what can't. But the conclusion is inevitable.

She must go on without me. The work must be done.

The plan sits heavy on my chest, but it's the truth. I can't let my selfishness—my feelings—stand in the way. Not when there's so much at stake.

I move quietly through the cookery, searching the cupboards for anything to alleviate the blow of what I'm about to do. My hand brushes over a small tin of tea leaves. An apology in the form of tea? It's pitiful, really, but what else can I offer her.

I set the kettle on the fire, listening to the quiet hum of the water beginning to heat. My fingers tap

387

against the counter as I wait, each second dragging painfully.

When the kettle finally whistles, it sounds like a scream in the stillness. I pour the water over the leaves, watching as the liquid darkens. Steam curls upward, carrying faint, herbal scent with it.

Will this cushion the words I'm about to say?

No, probably not. Nothing will. But it's the only kindness I can think to give her right now.

Tea in hand, I climb the stairs to the bedroom, each step more substantial than the last. I pause at the threshold and slowly open the door. The sight of her steals the air from my lungs. Rosannah lies there, sweet face in sleep, her curls spilling across the pillow like a dark halo. She seems so peaceful, so innocent, and yet the impact of last night's heartache persists in the slight crease of her brow. Even in sleep, she seems afflicted.

I let out a profound sigh and approach the bed, setting the tea on the nightstand. Gently, I kneel beside the bed and reach out, brushing a stray curl from her face. "Rosannah," I whisper, my voice low and tender, "wake up, bellezza."

She stirs. Her lashes flutter still heavy with sleep. She ponders for a moment, her expression is unreadable. Then, the sadness seeps in, clouding her.

She knows. She feels it already.

It's like a punch to the gut. I offer her a small smile, weak and uncertain. "I made you tea." It sounds insincere, so inadequate.

She pushes herself up slowly, clutching the blanket to her chest as she looks at the steaming cup beside her. "Thank you." Her eyes search mine, and I can see the questions there, the unspoken plea for reassurance, but I have none to give.

I clear my throat, forcing myself to meet those beautiful hazel orbs. "We must get you going soon. It's still a long journey to Palermo, and it's best if you leave as soon as possible."

Her brows knit together, confusion and a panic flash across her face. "You're not coming?"

"I've made the decision, that it's best if I don't go with you." Each word like a stone in my throat,

The silence that follows is deafening. Her lips part as if to protest, but no sound comes out. I can see the hurt, the betrayal, the disbelief crashing over her. And I feel it too.

Fuck me, how can I do this to her?

How can I leave her?

"You're... you're not serious... Adra, you can't mean that."

I find myself wanting to give in, but I can't let myself break.

This is for her own good. This is for her safety.

"I care for you more than anything. That's why I must do this. I can't keep you safe if I stay. My presence... it only puts you in danger. You must understand, this is the only way."

Her tears come suddenly, spilling down her cheeks as she shakes her head. "No... no! You don't get to decide that. You don't get to make that choice for me. I was going to leave here on my own." Her voice shakes. "I told myself last night that I needed to continue on this

389

journey without you... for *myself*... but... I love you, damn it! And I chose you. I can't do this without you."

Her words destroy me. I begin to collapse, but I force myself to stand firm, to hold on to the bitter truth that this is what must be done.

She deserves more than I can give her. She deserves a life free of the darkness that surrounds me.

"I'm sorry, Rosannah, but this is how it has to be."

She sits across from me, her delicate features dimmed by an expression of confusion and trepidation. Unshed tears glisten and threaten to spill over. I can feel her body shuddering even though we aren't touching each other. Her energy quakes like a fragile bird.

"I don't—I don't underst—" she begins, but the words are abruptly cut off by a raspy wet cough that erupts from her chest. She covers her mouth instinctively. Slowly, she pulls her hand away. The sight of crimson streaks her pale fingers. Blood. Thick, dark blood.

The moment stretches endlessly as I kneel beside her, the tea forgotten and cooling on the table. Rosannah's shocked eyes are sealed on her bloodstained fingers.

I know what this means. I've seen it a thousand times before, but never like this. Not with her.

"Adra?" Her voice splits the ominous silence. It carries the grievance of a thousand fears. I lean closer, holding on her every word, though I already know what she's going to ask. I wish I didn't. I wish I could unsee the blood, the faint tremor in her hands, the shadow in her once-bright eyes.

"Am I...?"

I close my eyes, swallowing the lump in my throat. There's no escape from this. No diminishing the truth. I open them and meet hers, forcing myself to say it.

"Yes." I answer, my speech tearing. "My dearest mourning star, you are dying."

The quiet that follows is like a gaping chasm, swallowing both of us whole. Rosannah sits motionless, fixed on her fingers, as if staring at the blood might somehow undo the truth. Her breaths are shallow, interrupted by small, wet coughs that splatter more blood onto her already stained fingers. I feel helpless, entirely powerless in a way I've never known before.

How can I, of all beings, stop this?

I am the collector of souls, the servant of death itself.

This is my domain, and yet... I can't save her.

I stay by her side, my hands gently wrapped around her wrists, as if holding her might secure her to this world just a little longer. Time seems to slow, the only sound her labored breathing. I don't speak, because there's nothing to say that wouldn't crush her further— or destroy me entirely.

She finally moves, lifting the tea to her lips. She drinks slowly. Her face is pale. Her actions are stiff and mechanical. I watch her as she sets the tea down, a fresh streak of blood remains on the rim of the cup.

How did we come to such an end? What folly led me to tangle my heart with one whose fate was ever doomed?

Rosannah hasn't said a word since her question, and the silence is suffocating. Her emotions are chaotic, yet, she is so fragile, so weak.

She was always so full of life, so determined to take on the world, and now... now she's fading.

I'm overcome by a torrent of emotions—grief, guilt, anger, and, disgustingly, relief. Relief because... because this means I can go back to the way things were, back to the work that's always defined me.

No. No, I can't think like that.

I'm a monster for even considering it.

She finally breaks the tension, her voice rasping through the room like a whisper of wind. "Looks like I don't have to go to Palermo by myself." She says with a sad, broken chuckle, coughing again immediately after. Her attempt at humor nearly makes me collapse.

"I suppose not." I force a weak smile, though it stings like a betrayal of everything I am feeling inside.

How can she still smile, still joke, when her body is failing her like this? How can she bear this with such grace while I, an immortal, am falling apart?

She coughs again, and I gently wipe the blood from the corner of her mouth with the edge of a cloth. She doesn't stop me, doesn't pull away. My fingers idle on her cheek for a moment, as if I can somehow memorize every inch of her before she's taken from me.

Because she will be taken.

I can sense the summoning already. The tug in the depths of my being that tells me her soul is nearing its time. It's cruel, this sensation, to know exactly when someone you care for is slipping away and being unable to stop it.

The pull grows stronger, more insistent, and my stomach churns. I've never dreaded a summoning. It's like the universe is mocking me for daring to think I could have something—*someone*—good in my life.

She peers up at me, her expression gentle despite the pain etched into every line of her face.

"I'm so sorry." It's all I can manage; all I can offer her in this moment. It's pitiful, inadequate, but it's the truth.

"Adra..." My heart leaps into my throat, waiting for whatever words she's managed to muster. "What happens next?"

I hesitate to speak. My tongue dry in my mouth.

What am I supposed to say? Lie to her? Tell her it'll be painless, that she'll go peacefully in her sleep? Or tell her the truth—that her soul will be collected, that I'll likely be the one to take it, that I'll have to watch as the light in her eyes fades forever?

"I don't know." I say instead, the power of my own lie crushing me. It's not true, but I can't bear to tell her the reality. Not now. She nods, as if that answer is enough.

She places a quivering hand over mine, her touch lively despite her weakening body. "Just stay with me. Please. Just... be here."

"I'm not going anywhere," I vow even as my spirit splinters. I grip her hand tightly, as if I can hold her here forever.

I don't know how to say goodbye to her.

I don't know if I can.

Death has already claimed her.

Chapter 37

Rosannah

I rest in silence, staring down at the blood staining my hand. The strange crimson, so vibrant against my pale skin, appears like an accusation.

I can't believe it—well, maybe I can. I've watched people collapse, waste away, and disappear into the grip of death these past few days. It's been everywhere. In every cough, every wail of despair from the streets, every shuttered window. But now, it's here. My body betraying me. My death.

Adra's face hovers just inches away. The way he looks at me.... I can't.... Those magnificent, mismatched eyes, glow brighter than I've ever seen them. Like twin flames blazing with all the grief and helplessness he refuses to put into words.

There's agony in my chest, but it's not from the illness. It's from the knowledge that I won't be able to see him like this for much longer. I let my worries drift, grasping at memories to escape the grave strain of this moment.

My Parents. I can see my father's eyes crinkle when he smiles. I have few memories of him, but I can see him perfectly. I think about my mom, never knowing her, never getting to see her face. Maybe now I'll finally get to meet her.

My Nona. Her presence is sharper in my memory, vivid in its sincerity. I see her at the hearth, wrapped in her shawl that smells faintly of lavender and rosemary. Her hands are busy kneading dough or threading a needle. Her stories come back to me in snippets—tales of love and tragedy, of gods and mortals, of women with unshakable spirits who braved the impossible. She'd always finish with the same phrase: "You have that spirit too, mia piccola[23]. You'll do great things." Her voice is so real in my mind that, for a moment, I half expect her to walk into the room, carrying a basket of fresh bread.

Gia. Oh Gia. Her laughter is the loudest of all. I picture her bright smile, her eyes wandering with playfulness. I can hear her teasing me, her words pointed but never cruel. "Stop being so damn dramatic, Ros!" She'd say, her hands on her hips like she was scolding me, though her grin always gave her away. "You've got that inferno

---

[23] dear little thing/my little one
396

flare in you. You're unstoppable when you put your mind to it."

I wonder now if she was ever right. I don't feel like fire. I feel like ashes, spread by the wind, deteriorating further with every breath I take. I wonder if Gia would even recognize me now. Would she still believe in my spark if she saw me like this—broken and fleeting? Or would she laugh, tell me to pull myself together and stop wasting time?

I miss them all so profoundly, it is a wound that will never heal. I want to hold my parents' hands, feel Nona's reassuring touch, hear Gia's laughter fill the room. But they're gone, and soon... soon I'll be gone too.

Where are they now?

Where did they go when they died?

I don't believe in God. I don't believe in a heaven or a paradise waiting for us beyond the veil. But I can't help but wonder....

Will I see them again, wherever it is, we go when we leave this world? Will I float away on the wind, scattered like leaves to shine in the sunlight? Or will it all just... end? Will I dissolve into the void, forgotten, disappearing completely, like footprints on a sandy shore washed away by the relentless tide?

The tears spill over before I can stop them.

This is it. It's over.

My dreams of Palermo, of seeing the world, of becoming someone—gone, slipping away from me like sand through my fingers. I'll never stroll through bustling streets filled with merchants and musicians. I'll never feel the sun on my face as I stand on a balcony overlooking the sea. I'll never have more time with Adra, to see the world through his eyes, to love him.

But then... wonder appears. I'm surprised by it, this strange, quiet curiosity that nestles itself in the corner of my mind.

What happens next? What will it feel like to let go, to surrender to the inevitable?

Will there be peace? Light? Nothing?

A part of me wants to know, to step into that unknown space and finally have answers. And then, finally, acceptance settles. Death comes for everyone. It grips me like vines winding tightly around a tree, constricting and inescapable. It's always been there, waiting.

Why should I be any different?

Perhaps this is my ending, the final chapter of my story, and what better way to end it than to join them? To step out of the pain, the loneliness, the uncertainty of this life, and into... *whatever comes next.*

"It's coming." I whisper, more to myself than to Adra. "And that's okay."

For the first time in days, a strange kind of calm settle over me, like the eye of a storm. Yes, I'm sad. Yes, I'm scared. But there's also a part of me—a small, stubborn part—that feels ready. Ready to face whatever comes next. Ready to let go.

I wipe the tears from my face, glancing toward Adra, wanting to stare at him as long as I can, and...

"WHAT IN THE ACTUAL FUCK?!" The words tear from my throat before I can even register them. I am horrified. My body seizes, and I let out a weak scream. I scramble backward on the bed, weakly trying to get as far from this *thing* as possible.

My heart bludgeons in my chest as I try to make sense of what I'm seeing. Adra stands there—or, rather, something that used to look like Adra stands there—and I scream again. My voice hoarse, as adrenaline floods my body. Fight or flight kicks in, but I can't even decide which one to choose. My legs dangle off the edge of the bed, wobbling as I try to muster the strength to run, but the sight of him—this *thing*—roots me in place.

There is no face. No body. No features. Just a towering void of impenetrable black, an endless, rippling shadow in the vague shape of a man. It's as if all the light in the room recoils from him, unable to touch the space he occupies.

I scream again, slapping my palms over my eyes as if shutting him out will make him disappear.

"Rosannah, it's okay." The shadow calls in a voice that's unmistakably his—but how can it be? How can that voice come from... from this?!

"Who are you?! WHAT ARE YOU?!" I shout, peeking through my fingers. My heart slams so loudly in my ears I can barely hear myself speak.

"Rosannah, amore, it's me." The shadow says. "It's Adra."

My jaw drops, and I stare at him—at *it*—completely dumbfounded. "You jest! That can't be you. That's not... you're... what?!"

Adra—or the shadow claiming to be Adra—raises what looks like a hand, as if to calm me. "I can explain."

He says shyly. "I know it's a lot. Just... give me a moment."

"A moment?!" I screech, standing on weak legs as another surge of adrenaline courses through me. "You're a fucking shadow monster, Adra! *A SHADOW MONSTER!* What the fuck is going on?!"

"I'm not a monster... It's me. I promise. I wanted to tell you earlier, but... I didn't have a reason. And now... well... now you're dying, and it changes things."

My pulse stutters at the mention of my death, but I'm too overwhelmed by the sheer absurdity of the situation to focus on it. "Dying or not, what the hell does that have to do with you being..." I wave my hands vaguely at the void in front of me, "whatever *this* is?!"

He shifts uncomfortably. "Now that you're... transitioning, you can see my true form."

"Transitioning?!" I shriek. "What like I am some creeping worm that has been granted wings?! You mean *dying*, right? Just say it! I'm DYING, and now I get to see my lover's real face, which, surprise, is apparently the abyss?!" My voice yells, and I gesture wildly at the void in front of me. Then it hits...

"You're telling me the man I've been traveling with, the man I've been—oh my Gods, I've had *sex* with this—a walking, talking *void born entity?!*' I throw my hands up, attempting to pace in disbelief.

Adra winces—well, I think he does; it's hard to tell with no face. "Aye," he pauses, "this is what I really am. My true form...is complicated."

"Oh, really? You think?" I blurt back as I finally muster the courage to take a small step closer.
400

"And what, pray tell, does *complicated* 'mean? Are you some kind of demon? A ghost?" I gape at him, struggling to process all of this, "Are you Death?!"

He hesitates, then takes a cautious step closer. His void body ripples like water as he moves. I flinch but hold my ground, too confused and angry to back down.

"I'm not Death," he reports carefully, "not exactly. Death is... my master."

"Your *master*? What are you, his apprentice? His butler? What does that even mean?!"

Adra rubs the back of his...head? If that's even what it is anymore. "Not exactly. I'm a... Grim Reaper, of sorts." He says bluntly, as if that explains everything.

I blink at him. My skull feels like a hive of bees, chaotic and buzzing with no order. "A Grim Reaper? *A GRIM REAPER?* You're telling me you're a fucking Grim Reaper?!"

"Aye." He dips, his tone as flat as his shadowy form. "That's the simplest way to put it. I don't kill anyone, if that's what you're thinking. I just... collect them.... I gather souls and guide them to where they're supposed to go."

I stare at him, dumbfounded. My mind is scrambling for some semblance of logic. "So... what? The undertaker thing? The uniform? The... human form? Was that all a foul deceit? Everything you've told me, a lie?" My breath falls out of rhythm, as panic sets in once more. "That wasn't you?"

He takes another step forward, and I can feel his spirit vibrate even from where I stand. "It was me. Just...

not all of me. It's a form I use to blend in, to make it easier to do my work."

"Your *work*," I repeat cynically, "which is... what, exactly? Lying to people? Seducing them? Making them fall in love with you so you can—what? Harvest their souls?!"

His form seems to shrink, as if recoiling from my words. "No, that's not what this is. What we have is real, Rosannah. You must believe me."

I shake my head, laughing bitterly as I sink back onto the bed. "Real? You think this is real? Adra, I don't even know who—or *what*—you are anymore." I take a difficult breath, trying to calm myself down. I feel dizzy, like I'm going to retch.

All this chaotic information and reveals sends me into another coughing fit. I spit up more dooming signs of my inevitable death. I try to drink some water but choke on my blood. My lungs are weak as I try to calm the coughing. I taste metallic tang of blood marked on my tongue. My trembling hand sets the cup of water back down as I try to focus on him—on whatever he truly is.

"Okay...," I rasp, "you're here to... collect souls?" The words are foreign, absurd and nightmarish all at once.

"Aye, from those that have already passed."

I let the words hover in the air. "And you... you have a human form," I continue, gesturing vaguely toward him, "to blend in with the rest of us? A disguise?" He nods, or what I assume is nodding.

I blink, trying to process everything. "You were sent here by... by your master?" I almost choke on the word.

He nods once more. I try to meet his gaze, but his shadowy form...well...it's blurry.

"Okay...well, how do you know where to go? People die every day. Why are you *here?*"

Adra doesn't flinch. His figure remains tall, but his voice betrays him with hesitation as he answers. "My contract tells me. It gives me numbers, locations. I go where I'm needed. Where the souls are. I was sent here because of the scale. The... the enormity of what's happening."

The blood drains from my face. "You mean the illness...the plague?" I whisper, my lips barely forming the words.

"Aye." Adra's shadow form ripples.

I stare at him. My mind is struggling to keep up with the torrent of revelations. The taste of blood persists on my tongue, a grim reminder that my time is running out, and here he is, telling me he's part of some celestial accounting system for death.

"You knew?" My eyes search his void-like face for something—remorse, guilt, humanity. "You knew this would happen?"

He shifts uncomfortably. His shadowy form soaking up all the sunlight that is coming from the window. "To a degree." He admits. "I knew death would come, aye, in great numbers. But the when, the how, the who...I knew nothing. Only the number was made known to me."

"Numbers?" I echo, the word sour on my tongue. "That's it? We're all just... numbers?"

His shadow nods again, "By the count I am led, where to tread and whose souls to claim. Their names I do not know, nor the tales they bear, not until its time." He pauses and tries to lay a hand upon me, but I turn away. "The day the ships arrived, I saw the bodies piling up... I didn't know what was causing it at first, but when I smelled the sickness in the air... I knew it then, nothing before could compare, nor anything after. Yet, I couldn't grasp the vastness of what lay before me. Not until I saw the final tally."

"What's the number? How many?"

Adra hesitates, his figure stiffening. "I can't tell you that."

"Tell me." I say, my tone sharpening despite the weakness in my body. *"How many?"*

There's a long pause, the silence stretching between us. Finally, he resolves "Seventy-five million."

The number hits me like a slap to the face. A cold sweat breaks out across my skin.

Seventy-five million.

It's a number too large to comprehend, a number that is more like a nightmare than reality.

My vision blurs as tears well up, I shake my head, unable to process what he's telling me. "Seventy-five million? That's... that's everyone. That's the entire world."

"Not the entire world," Adra says quietly, "but enough. Enough to feel like it." He pauses. His form is still as stone. The shadowy edges of him pulse.
404

"Rosannah, never did I dream it would touch you. I swear it."

My stomach churns, bile rises in my throat. "You *knew* people were going to die. You *knew* something catastrophic was coming, and you said nothing?"

"I couldn't tell you." He declares, his voice full of a sorrow I can't ignore. "I am forbidden to intercede. I'm bound by my contract, by my duty. Even had I confessed, the fates would not have faltered. The plague would have came all the same. Death would have came regardless."

"Such words do not lessen the wound." I snap, my anger flaring through my grief. "You knew people—innocent people—were going to die, and you just... stayed silent? You remained by my side, cloaked in falsehood, knowing it all, and still hid the truth?"

His dark figure seems to sag, "I stayed because of you," he says softly, "because I didn't want you to be alone. It's not my place to prevent death, only collect it."

The sensitive emotion in his voice cuts through my anger, leaving me empty and aching. I want to scream at him, to push him away, to demand answers he can't give me. But all I can do is sit there, staring at the man—the creature—who has been my rock, even as everything in my world crumbles around me.

"Not your place?" I cry out. "You've been *with me*, Adra. You've held me, kissed me, loved me... and all this time, you were just waiting for me to die?"

"No...No, Rosannah, that's not why I stayed with you. I didn't... I never foreseen this."

Tears stream down my face. "How am I supposed to believe you? You're telling me you're some kind of... of reaper, sent here to collect the dead. And now I'm one of them."

"Mourning star..." He steps closer.

I hold up a shivering hand to stop him. "Don't!" I whisper with pain. "Don't come near me."

The silence between us is broken only by the sound of my tattered breathing. I fall back onto the bed, and I clutch at the blanket draped over my lap as if it could shield me from the truth.

He steps closer, unsure of how close he can be. "You are not alone."

"I am alone, Adra! I'm dying, and now I'm alone! You—" I choke on my words, my hand flying to my chest as another wave of pain and coughing ruins me.

Adra reaches out instinctively, his hands hovering near me. "Rosannah, please. I didn't want this for you. I didn't want you to become part of the numbers. I didn't want you to be..."

"Dead?" I whisper bitterly, glaring at him through the tears.

Adra moves closer, his presence both comforting and smothering. "Aye my dear mourning star. It means that this illness will claim many lives." He says regretfully. "It means that you... unfortunately are part of that number."

I squeeze the blanket tighter. My mind courses with questions, but none of them have answers I'm ready to face.

Finally, I find my voice again, "Do you... take my soul? Do you... collect me?"

He doesn't answer immediately. Instead, he sits beside me. His spirit is still alarming even though I know it's him. His form darker than the hardest shadows of the room, yet there's a gentleness in the way he reaches for my hand.

It lies in his, but it's not the same. It's not the hand I've come to know. His touch is ice, a cold that pierces through my skin, chilling me to the bone. Gone is the comforting heat of his rough, calloused fingers. Gone is the tenderness I once felt when his hands moved over mine, as if I was something precious. I try to pull away, but his grip, though gentle, holds firm. I stare down at our hands—mine trembling, his, a void of shadowy nothingness.

How did we find ourselves here? How has the world turned so, that this becomes my waking truth?

I think of the way his lips felt on mine. The way his smile used to light up his face. Now there's nothing. No warmth, no light—just an empty, freezing void.

I drown on my tears, searching for those glowing mismatched eyes, though there's no face to read anymore. I ask the hard question again, not wanting the answers, but needing them. "What happens to me? Where do I go?"

Adra's form stills, and he takes a deep breath, though I wonder if he even needs air. "Well, my dear mourning star," he begins, his voice thick with sadness, "you will pass... and I am now here to collect your soul."

His remark smashes through my false reality. Panic takes over, but I force myself to listen.

"After that, I send you to the universe to decide your fate. Whether you go to this... beyond place, where the energy of our soul-being lives on in the infinite... or you are destroyed into the unknown. That is not up to me. There's nothing you or I can do about it."

"I'm dying," I whisper, the finality sinks in.

I look at him, this being who has walked beside me, loved me, deceived me, and yet... I still *need* him. The anger, the betrayal—it all fades, leaving only the indisputable truth: *I am dying, and he will be the one to carry my soul away.*

Chapter 38

Rosannah

I close my eyes, tears fall freely now, tarnishing my cheeks with grief. Every word he says feels true, each syllable a final nail in the coffin of everything I've ever hoped for.

"I must fulfill my duty," he adds, his tone quieter now, filled with something I can only describe as unwavering regret, "and I sure as hell am not letting anyone else take your soul. I'm here, and I'm not going anywhere."

The heaviness in his voice mirrors the weight in my chest, crushing and uncompromising. The silence that follows drags on like an eternity. I sit there, staring at the void that used to be him, trying to make sense of what my life has become.

"So... it was real?" My voice hoarse from crying, coughing, and screaming. My words dangle in the air like a fragile thread, as though the answer could either mend me or destroy me completely. "This wasn't just some cruel trick?"

Adra kneels before me, his shadowy hands reaching for mine. Even though his touch is icy, I don't pull away. There's something in his form that holds me there. His face—or the void where his face used to be—turns toward mine. I can't see his features, but I can feel the pain radiating from him.

"No, my dear mourning star. It was real. *You* are real." His voice trembles with each word. "This was as real as anything I've ever experienced. You are the best part of my existence... the only part that has ever mattered."

Another wave of tears spills over my cheeks. I shake my head, trying to reconcile the man I fell in love with and the being that kneels before me now. "Then why?" I choke out. "Why does it have to end like this? Why did you even let this happen if you knew you'd have to take me in the end?"

He doesn't answer immediately. Instead, his shadowed form quivers, and then he breaks. He sobs—loud, heart-wrenching sobs that tear through the quiet of the room. It's the sound of someone unraveling, someone who's held it together for far too long.

"Because I couldn't stop it," he cries out, "because I didn't want to stop it. I've never taken an interest in mortals. I've watched them for what seems like eternity—watched them love, laugh, cry, grieve. I've taken souls by the millions, Rosannah. And never—not once—did I feel what they felt. I couldn't. I wasn't meant to."

410

His void-like orbs somehow convey more emotion than I thought possible. "But then you..." he whispers, his voice punctures my soul, "you appeared, and everything changed. You showed me what it means to feel, to truly *be*. You breathed life into a being that never knew what life really was. You made me realize how hollow I was, how utterly meaningless my existence had been before you."

He pauses, his shadowy form shaking violently. "You, my dear mourning star... you *plagued* me. Not with illness, not with death, but with love. You infected me with joy, with passion, with something so achingly beautiful that it terrified me. You made me see what I could never have, what I should never have dared to hope for. And now..." His voice gives out entirely, and he collapses back into unconsolable sobs.

When he finally speaks again, it's heartbreaking, as if the words themselves are being torn from him. "Now, it's all being ripped away from me. You're being ripped away from me. And I don't know how to survive this."

He tries to pull himself together, but the tears keep coming. "I've watched mortals grieve their loved ones for centuries, and I never understood it—never cared to. It was just a part of the cycle, a part of my duty. I've never had to grieve before; never had to understand what it means to lose someone you *undeniably* love. But now... now I understand. Rosannah, this is killing me. It's splitting me apart, and I don't know *if* I can survive you never existing again." He falls into a mournful sob.

The room is colder, ominous, as his words sink into the space between us. My soul breaks at the sight of him—this being of shadows and power, crumbling before my eyes. I want to reach out, to comfort him, but I can't even find the strength to move.

"Adra," I whisper, my voice shaking as tears blur my vision. "I—" But the words die on my lips, lost in the overwhelming influence of this moment.

Because what can I say? What words could hold the depth of what we're losing? Of what we've already lost?

He lifts his head, and the way I think he is looking at me — I mean I can feel it, truly feel it. He is looking at me like he's memorizing every inch of me, every breath, every tear and it breaks me all over again.

"I would give anything to save you," he cries out desperately, "*anything*, but I can't. And I hate myself for it. I hate that I found you, that I loved you, only to lose you."

An uncontrollable wail escapes me. "I don't want to go!" My voice is heartsick with the truth. "I don't want to leave you!"

It all crashes down on me, a tidal wave I can no longer hold back. The tears come, and for the first time, I cry for my own death. For everything I'm losing. For everything I'll never have. And for him—*oh, my dearest Adra.* The man who has shown me a love so profound it has changed every fiber of my being. And now, because of me, he will have to bear the pain of losing it.

I peer at him through the blur of my tears, and the sight of him shatters me further. Adra, who always

412

stood so strong, who carried the weight of death like it was nothing, is broken. His sobs shake his entire being. His shadowy form unstable. I've never seen anyone cry like this. It's not just sadness, it's devastation, a separation of the soul.

I reach for him. My arms wrapping around his crestfallen void. His cold form bites against my skin, but I don't care. All I want is to hold him, to remind him that I'm here, that we're here, even if just for a little while longer.

"I'm so sorry." I whisper.

He clings to me like I'm the only thing securing him to this world, his weeping muffled against my shoulder. "Don't apologize. Please, don't. This isn't your fault. None of it is."

But it feels like it is. It feels like I'm leaving him to bear this impossible burden alone, and there's nothing I can do to stop it.

The realization is a lance to my heart. "I didn't think about what this would do to you. I was so focused on seeing my loved ones again, on the idea of reuniting with Gia and my family... I didn't think about what I'd be leaving behind."

His arms tighten around me. "You're not leaving me, Rosannah. I'm the one losing you, and I don't know how to let you go."

We cry together, holding each other as though the strength of our embrace might keep the inevitable at bay. My tears soak into his skin- if it's even skin- and his fingers dig into my back. I focus on the sensation, willing myself to feel every detail. The way he holds

413

me, the sound of his breath hitching in his chest, the way his body seems to wrap around mine.

"I don't want to go." I whisper and begin to sob hysterically.

He pulls back just enough to look at me. His void-like eyes somehow shimmering with an emotion I never thought I'd see there—grief.

"I know, and if I could, I would tear apart the fabric of existence to keep you here. But I can't. And it's going to haunt me for eternity. Every moment without you will never be the same. I will never be the same." He chokes. "You are my entire world. You are my beginning and my end. You are the light in my endlessly dark realm. You are the only love that fills my life."

Adra falls into a core wrenching sob once more, his body falls to the ground, and somber wails pour out of him. He holds onto my legs, as if his cries will make him float away with grief.

I hold his head and beg the universe for some more time. The hopeless words break something inside me, and another sob wracks my body. "I love you! I love you immensely, Adra. For eternity."

"And I love you! More than I ever thought I could. More than I can bear. For eternity."

We collapse into each other again, our tears mixing, our sobs filling the room. We cry for what we've lost, for the fleeting beauty of the love we've found, and for the cruel reality that it's slipping through our fingers. I cry for him, for the pain he'll carry long after I'm gone.

414

And he cries for me, for the life I won't get to live, for the moments we'll never share. The impact of my impending death settles fully over me. But in Adra's arms, as our tears fall together, I feel something else too—an unbreakable love that will remain for lifetimes after I leave this cruel world.

CONWAY TITTY

Chapter 39

Adrastus

My heart aches as I watch Rosannah, her body fragile and her breath shallow. She's so small against the grand bed, dwarfed by the ornate silk sheets and plush pillows that mock in their luxury.

I manage to stifle my tears for her sake, though it feels like I'm barely holding back a flood. "Let's get you comfortable," I say, my voice collapsing despite my best efforts to stay composed. She doesn't protest as I gently lift her, rearranging the pillows behind her back and tucking the blanket around her frail frame. Her body is impossibly light, a stark contrast to the strength I've always seen in her spirit. The thought makes my stomach twist.

Once she's settled, I sit beside her, my hands quiver as they rest on the edge of the mattress. "Is there anything you need? Water? Food? Anything at all?" I barely manage to make words.

Rosannah stares up at me, her eyes glistening with unshed tears, yet there's a calmness in them that stops me in my tracks. She smiles—a thin, tired smile that is like the sunrise after a storm. "Just you." She whispers, her voice so faint.

I can't speak. I can only nod and crawl into the bed beside her. I wrap my arms around her, pulling her as close as I possibly can. Her body feels cold against mine, her pulse weak, but I hold her tighter anyway, desperate to keep her here for just a little longer.

I press my lips to her temple, inhaling the faint scent of lavender that still survives in her hair. "You're so brave. I don't know how you do it. How you stay so radiant, even now."

She chuckles weakly. "Radiant? Adra, I probably look like death itself."

Her attempt at humor makes my spirit crack, and I can't help the sad laugh that escapes me. "No," I say firmly, brushing a strand of hair away from her damp forehead, "you're the most beautiful thing I've ever seen, Rosannah. Even now. Especially now."

Her smile falls, and tears spill from the corners of her eyes. "I'm scared." She whispers.

Her admission fractures me. I swallow hard, my throat burning as I try to find the right words. "I'm here. I'm here, and I'm not leaving. Not now. Not ever."

She nestles closer to me; her hand weakly reaches up to rest against my chest. "You make it easier to let go. To not be afraid."

I can feel my nature breaking in real time. Each thump harder than the last. I press my forehead to hers, closing my eyes as I fight back the tears threatening to spill again.

As the day drags into night, the stillness crowds me, suffocating and monotonous. The air is damp and heavy. There is an oppressive quietness that has settled over the house. The only sound cutting through the silence is the rattle of Rosannah's labored breaths, punctuated by wet coughs. The signs are unmistakable now. Her once vibrant skin has faded to a ghostly white, her cheeks hollow, her lips tinged with blue. Pustules have begun to form along the delicate curve of her neck and the backs of her hands, cruel markers of the sickness that is stealing her away. The sight of her like this—so frail, so far removed from the radiant, fiery woman I fell for—rips at my insides.

I sit beside her on the bed, pleading my mind to remember every single detail of her, making sure I will never forget. Her breath rattles again, a sound so delicate, the very room might break apart from it. My fists clench and unclench in my lap, helpless against the tide of inevitability that is sweeping her away.

I clear my throat, though it feels like sandpaper, and force the words out, "My dearest mourning star, is there anything I can do for you? Anything at all?"

Her eyes flutter open weakly, those dark orbs once so full of life now dulled by pain and exhaustion. For a moment, she doesn't speak, and I think perhaps she didn't hear me. But then, a faint grin tugs at the corners of her pale lips, "A kiss. Please... let me kiss your lips once more."

The request is so easy, yet so painful knowing this might be the last. I comply, swallowing hard as I gather my composure. "Of course, amore."

I close my eyes and let my human form return, pulling it around me like a cloak, though it takes every ounce of strength I have to maintain it. The effort is agonizing now, but for her—for this one last moment—I will endure anything.

When I open my eyes, Rosannah's gorgeous hazel gaze finds mine, and for the first time in hours, a spark of something familiar glimmers in her expression. The stars have returned to her.

Her cracked lips bend into the smallest smile, her hand weakly reaching out to touch my face. "There he is. There is my beloved."

I lean down, cupping her delicate face in my palms. Her skin is icy beneath my touch. Her pulse weak and fluttering, but her eyes—those beautiful, star filled eyes—hold me captive. I muffle my cries just enough to tell her something I hope she never forgets.

"Words cannot form enough sentences to explain how I've felt since our lives connected. That is the moment I knew our souls intertwined. My heart has been wrapped with pure serenity since your hand took mine. I knew you were for me. It's an unexplainable, overwhelming feeling and there was no way I was going to leave it unexplored."

I choke on the words as tears begin rolling down my face. "I took your hand and followed you into the unknown. And today I take your hand into the afterlife and will continue to hold you in mine. On this day, I take your heart and will continue to carry it gently with me for the rest of my existence. Thank you Rosannah for choosing me, loving me. Even though we are just mere stardust, in a vast infinite universe. I am beyond grateful I got to experience a once in a lifetime connection between two souls that are perfectly made for one another."

I wipe my face, but that does nothing for the tears, as they just keep falling. "My soul belongs to you, and this metaphorical heart beats only for you. Thank you for showing me love."

I brush a lonesome curl from her face, tucking it behind her ear. My hands tremble as I cradle her. I smile, though the power of my grief threatens to kill me. I want this to be what she remembers—the depth of my love, not the sorrow of my tears. I press my forehead to hers, for a moment, closing my eyes as a tear slips down my cheek.

Her shaky lips meet mine. In this moment I feel it— my being consumed by the love and despair tangled together in this final kiss.

Our kiss is everything. It holds every moment we've shared and every fleeting dream of what could have been. The taste of her lips brings me back to that first night on the boardwalk, where the ocean air tangled with her laughter, and the world seemed infinite. I can almost feel the salty breeze on my skin, hear the rhythmic crash of the waves against the shore. The sound of seagulls calling overhead and the bright glow of the moon on the water, all comes rushing back, vivid and cruelly comforting. Her laugh had been the music of that night, a melody I'd never forget. Now, it echoes in my mind like a haunting refrain.

As our lips stay together, my mind floods with visions of what was and what will never be. I see us dancing barefoot in sunlit fields, her hair catching the golden rays of the sun as she spins. I imagine the simple moments we'll never have: holding her hand as the years wear on, her face lined with the beauty of age, her eyes still sparkling with that unmistakable star filled joy. I see us sitting together on a quiet evening, her head resting on my shoulder as the world around us changes, but our love remains unshaken.

But these are just dreams—dreams that cut like a blade because I know they will never be. It's cruel how vivid they are, how real they feel, as if the universe is taunting me with what I can't have. The pain is excruciating, yet I hold on to this kiss, this moment, as though it can somehow make everything right.

I try to pour all the love, all the unspoken promises, and all the sorrow into it, hoping she can feel the depth of everything I cannot say. My tears fall on to her. Her body weakens in my arms, her breaths shallow and unstable. Her warmth, the warmth that has become my lifeline, is fading. I want to hold her tighter, as if I can keep her here by sheer will.

But I can't. I know I can't.

Her spirit is slipping away, like sand through my fingers, and I'm powerless to stop it. I pull her closer, my heart breaking into a thousand jagged pieces with every beat. This kiss, this connection, is the last thread tethering her to this world, and I don't want to let it go.

But then, her body weakens against mine. Her chest releases one final exhale that I instinctively draw into my own lungs. Slowly I pull away my trembling hands as they cradle her face. Her expression is peaceful. Her lips curved in the faintest smile, as If she has left this world content. I lean down and press a soft kiss to her forehead. My tears fall onto her still skin. "I love you, and for eternity, I'll continue to love you."

The memories of her laugh, her dreams, her fire flood my mind, each one a pebble being thrown at my already shattered spirit. I lower her body gently onto the bed, supporting her as though she might wake at any moment, though I know she won't. Her head rests against the pillow. Her hair splayed like a dark halo around her face.

My fingers brush against her cheek, trailing to the stray curl that always seemed to fall into her eyes, even when she laughed. I tuck it away one last time. My hand waits as if to remember the warmth of her skin before it fades completely.

My chest tightens as I straighten. My palm shakes as I hover just above her still heart. I close my eyes and draw in the deepest breath I can manage, summoning every ounce of strength I have left to fulfill the task that is impossible.

As my fingers splay over her chest, it begins—a soft shimmer, faint at first, like a ripple on a calm lake catching the first rays of dawn. The ethereal stardust of her soul rises slowly, glowing with a brilliance so delicate it feels sacred. It swirls upward in spirals, each particle shimmering like fragments of captured sunlight. The air is heavy with a reverent silence, broken only by the hum of the energy gathering between us. It dances weightlessly, luminous and heartbreakingly beautiful, like it's her final goodbye.

The radiance bathes the room in an otherworldly glow, reflecting off the golden embellishments of the bedframe and the rich tapestries hanging on the walls. For a fleeting moment, it's as though time itself has stopped honoring her departure. My hand steadies, and the stardust draws toward me, delicate threads of light weaving together as they settle into my palm. The energy of it is startling, as if a piece of her remains alive, even now.

I stare down at the glowing essence in my hand, tears blur my vision. It is both fragile and infinite, as though it contains the entire universe within its shimmering depths.

I speak into the stillness. "You are light, Rosannah. Be free, amore." I send her soul off into the unseen beyond.

My voice falters as I add, "May the universe protect you in its embrace."

I sit beside her for a moment longer, staring at her lifeless body, and for the first time, I am truly empty. The room is silent. Her absence drowns me in sorrow. My hands fall to my sides as the reality of what I've lost crashes over me.

Time passes slowly, I straighten and then stand beside the bed, unable to tear my eyes away from her face, now serene and untouched by pain. The candlelight casts gentle shadows across her features, tracing the curve of her lips that once whispered my name with such love, now silent and still. I use my enchantment to conjure a perfectly bloomed white chrysanthemum and place it delicately into her folded hands. A token of my love I leave to stay with her earthly shell for eternity. The sparrow necklace that rests above her heart shines at me, as if she lets me know to take it. I unclasp the chain and hold the metal in my palm. The one thing I can carry with me that belonged to her. It's the closest thing I can get to feeling her soul.

My feet are stone, as I try to walk away from her, every step a betrayal of the love we shared. The grand artwork and ornate furniture of this wealthy home blur into the background, mere ghosts of opulence in a world that has lost its color. The echoes of our laughter still haunt these walls.

I pause at the doorway. My hand grips the frame as if the wood might fasten me to this moment, might prevent me from walking away from the most beautiful part of my existence. The urge to turn back, to gather her in my arms and will life back into her, is profoundly painful. But even I, a collector of souls, am powerless against the finality of death.

Checking over my shoulder, I drink in the sight of her one last time. She is ethereal, as the gentle light of the melting candle casts a halo around her, like the universe mourns her loss. The bedsheets are tangled around her like the memories of our love—messy, passionate, and ultimately left behind. Her hair, dark as the void I once thought my soul to be, fans out like the wings of a fallen angel.

Tears sting my eyes, as I lift a trembling hand to my lips, pressing a kiss into my palm. I extend it toward her, the simplest of gestures full of every unspoken word, every touch, every shared moment. My throat dries, and my croaky voice emerges as a fractured whisper, splintered by the grief clawing at my core, escapes. "For eternity." The words laden with the promise that not even death can sever.

Slowly, I walk away, each footfall a drumbeat of sorrow, resonating through the empty corridors of this house that once bore witness to our love. The walls seem to lean in, sharing in my mourning as I descend the staircase.

As I reach the front door, I hesitate, the threshold marking the divide between the world we shared and the endless void of what remains. The cold air greets me like a slap, biting into the passion her love once provided. I step into the night, leaving behind not just a room, but the only person that ever felt like a home.

My soul aches, each pulsation is a painful reminder of what was and what will never be. And as I walk away from the life we almost had, the life that was stolen by forces beyond our control, I carry her memory like a cherished wound—an ache that I will bear... For eternity.

CONWAY TITTY

Epilogue

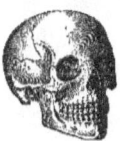

The Bubonic Plague
(1347-1924)

Years have passed since the Bubonic Plague, a curse born on the backs of rats, carried by fleas and whispered in the breath of the sick, first made its grand entrance at the bustling Port of Messina. It arrived silently, invisible, brought in the holds of merchant ships that had once contributed to wealth and prosperity in Italy.

The ships docked, and with them came death, creeping ashore like an uninvited guest. At first, it was only a handful of cases, sailors collapsing on the docks, fevered and delirious. But soon, the sickness spread like wildfire, igniting a chain reaction that no one could stop.

The atmosphere itself seemed different after the plague arrived. The once vibrant streets of Florence and Venice became eerily silent. The laughter and chatter of markets were replaced by the tolling of church bells, announcing yet another soul lost to the pestilence. The stench of decay clung to the air, combining with the faint smell of incense from priests performing last rites. Death had made itself at home, moving from house to house with the swiftness of a shadow.

Adra moved through this desolation, his presence unnoticed by the living, his footsteps silent. The consequence of his task demanded heavily on him, but he bore it with the grim efficiency expected of him. His contract bound him to this work, and there was no room for indecision. Each soul he collected twinkled with the gentlest light, a spark of what had once been life, before it dissolved into his grasp.

The plague spared no one. From the gilded halls of noble estates to the cramped and filthy streets of peasant quarters, it claimed its victims indiscriminately. Entire families were wiped out in days. Children wailed for parents who would never rise again. Streets were littered with bodies, hastily dumped into carts and dragged to mass graves. Priests and gravediggers fell alongside the people they sought to comfort or bury. The rich tried to flee to their countryside estates, only to find that death traveled faster than their horses.

Adra had witnessed countless tragedies over the centuries, but this was different. This wasn't war or famine. This was chaos. Entire towns disappeared, their buildings left standing, but their people erased. In the countryside, fields went untended, the crops wilting under the neglect. In the cities, the dead piled high in the streets, and the living barricaded themselves indoors to escape the invisible killer.

From Italy, the plague traveled relentlessly, its unseen tendrils stretching out across Europe. Ships, once symbols of trade and prosperity, became vessels of doom, carrying the sickness to the shores of England, to the markets of France, to the grand cities of Spain. Death moved hastily.

Adra had lost count of the souls he had collected. Each one a reminder of the countless lives lost, of the joy and love that had been snuffed out like candles in a storm.

His memories of Rosannah haunted him still. Her face appeared to him in quiet moments when he would hold her necklace against his heart. She had been one soul among millions, and yet her loss felt as vast as the devastation that surrounded him. He often thought of her words, of her dreams, of the stars in her eyes even in the face of death. Her memory kept him moving, even as the work threatened to behead him entirely.

Hundreds of years have passed, the plague's penumbra stretching far and wide. Europe fell to its knees, entire towns disappeared from the maps, entire bloodlines erased. In England, churches rang their bells no longer, for the dead were too many to mourn. In France, priests walked among the dying, offering last rites to those who could no longer lift their heads in prayer. In Poland, villages killed off those showing signs hoping to keep the sickness at bay. In Sweden, the frost did little to slow its advance. Russia wept as it buried its people in frozen ground, the cries of mourning mothers echoing across the steppes.

Adra kept moving, a solitary figure in a world drowning in grief. He bore witness to humanity's darkest hour, a silent observer of its resilience and its despair. He saw kindness in unexpected places, a neighbor risking their life to bring bread to the sick, a clergyman offering comfort to the dying, a mother singing gently to her child in their last moments. These fleeting acts of love and compassion were like sparks in the darkness, a reminder that even in the face of unimaginable loss, humanity could still find ways to endure.

But for Adra, the weight of the world was heavier than ever. He walked among the dying; his own sorrow intertwined with theirs. His heart forever marked by the memory of a love that had once given him hope. And as the plague continued its relentless march, he carried on, collecting the souls of the departed, knowing that his task would never truly end. He whispered a silent prayer—not to any god, but to the memory of Rosannah.

"For eternity." The words a promise, a plea, and a lament all at once. And then he continued. The Black Death devastated all, leaving a scar on the earth that would never fully heal.

𝕬𝖈𝖐𝖓𝖔𝖜𝖑𝖊𝖉𝖌𝖊𝖒𝖊𝖓𝖙𝖘

I truly do not think words can even describe the emotions I have felt when writing this book. I poured terror, grief, love and countless others into this story. I wanted this tragic tale of our beloved Rosannah to reach the hearts of many.

If you finished, I thank you with all my being. Thank you for reading my work. Thank you for feeling the emotions with me. I know at times we got feral, horny, angry, but at the end I hope you felt love. I hope you know a love like this is out there. And I hope you know you are worthy of it.

I spent months researching, trying to perfect the atmosphere and toils that would have happened during the 14th century. I wanted it to create a story that could resonate with many. I wanted you to feel like you were there on the day the world changed.

Endless thanks to my dearest Stardusty, who watched me battle these emotions, however intense or tragic. Who listened to my endless rants of "How am I going to do this?" and all the trials that come with challenging myself to write my very first book.

433

Without them, I would not know a love to write about. I would never come close to describing anything so pure. Here I thank them once more, for allowing me to be myself in every way possible. I love you.

I would like to thank the wicked cast of Last Podcast on the Left who inspired me with their hilariously devastating episodes on The Bubonic Plague. And who continues to bring laughs and chaos to this even more chaotic world.

I want to acknowledge the incredible book that I fiercely read multiple times hoping to consume enough knowledge to make this story as historically accurate as possible. Please take the opportunity to read "The Great Mortality" by John Kelly.

I have an immense love and gratitude for my artist Eliza. Thank you for bringing this world to life in the art you have created. Thank you for being so down and easy to work with on this project. Please take time to love and share her with the world. You can learn more about her in the "About the Artist" pages that follow.

I leave this here as a reminder for my future self and as a manifestation for all that is to come:

I wrote my first book. I did it. A challenge I wore now completed. Take the time to celebrate and to honor your emotions along the way. Now for the dream....

I will continue creating and writing incredible books for the readers. I will reach people from all around the world. And hopefully the next ones I write get picked by a publisher, so I don't have to do all the extra work alone. And if I'm lucky and with lots of joy, it becomes a worldwide sensation in all the best ways. I hope my stories touch millions of lives, if not, I tried my best anyway.

CONWAY TITTY

About the Author

Conway Titty is a country-western, Native American creator living in Oklahoma. For the past decade, she has worked as a sex worker and content creator, building a community with a mix of humor, grit, and organic honesty.

A lifelong passion for reading and writing began in childhood and has grown into the dream of publishing novels that resonate with authenticity, something she considers deeply important in both life and art.

Beyond writing, Conway enjoys video games and regularly streams them, using gaming as another way to connect with people. With an eye always on the horizon, she dreams of one day owning a bison ranch, a place that represents freedom, legacy, and a life built on staying true to oneself.

Whether through storytelling, streaming, or chasing prairie dreams, Conway's voice remains unapologetically fearless, sincere, and wild.

Follow Conway on all social media and visit her website at http://authorconway.com

About the Artist

Eliza is a self-taught artist born and raised in Palmdale, California. She has been passionate about drawing since she could hold a pencil, carrying forward a creative legacy passed down through generations. Eliza's work is fueled by her love of anime, fantasy, and all things spooky.

Through her art, she strives to capture imagination and emotion, sharing pieces that reflect her passion and vision. With big dreams and a deep dedication to her craft, she continues to grow as an artist and pursue her creative journey.

Book Cover + Illustrations by Eliza Alejandra Art
@satanssweetcupcake
https://beacons.ai/satancupcake

CONWAY TITTY

www.ingramcontent.com/pod-product-compliance
Lightning Source LLC
Chambersburg PA
CBHW020650110726
47901CB00001B/122